THE SEASON OF
THE HYAENA

THE SEASON OF THE HYAENA

Paul Doherty

headline

First published in Great Britain in 2005 by
HEADLINE BOOK PUBLISHING

10 9 8 7 6 5 4 3 2 1

Cataloguing in Publication Data is available from the British Library

ISBN 0 7553 0339 3 (hardback)
ISBN 0 7553 0340 7 (trade paperback)

Typeset in Trump Mediaeval by Palimpsest Book Production Limited,
Polmont, Stirlingshire

Printed and bound in Great Britain by
Clays Ltd, St Ives plc

Headline's policy is to use papers that are natural, renewable and
recyclable products and made from wood grown in sustainable forests.
The logging and manufacturing processes are expected to conform
to the environmental regulations of the country of origin.

HEADLINE BOOK PUBLISHING
A division of Hodder Headline
338 Euston Road
London NW1 3BH

www.headline.co.uk
www.hodderheadline.com

James Charles Patmore
24th September 1921–8th June 1995

*Beloved husband of Jo, father to Jenny, Andrew and
Melissa*

PRINCIPAL CHARACTERS

PHARAOHS
Sequenre
Ahmose
Tuthmosis III
Hatchesphut: } war-like Pharaohs of the Eighteenth Dynasty (1550–1323 BC) who founded the great empire of Ancient Egypt and cleared the Kingdom of the Two Lands of the Hyksos invaders

THE ROYAL HOUSE (OF AMENHOTEP III)
Amenhotep III,
'The Magnificent': Pharaoh of Egypt for about thirty-nine years during which time the Kingdom of the Two Lands reached its high pinnacle of power

Tiye: Amenhotep III's Great Queen and Great Wife: a native of Egypt, daughter of Thuya and Yuya, from the town of Akhmin

Crown Prince Tuthmosis: heir apparent of Amenhotep III

Prince Amenhotep: the Veiled One (also the Great Heretic; the Grotesque) – known to history as Akenhaten, younger son of Amenhotep and Tiye

Sitamun: daughter of Amenhotep III and Queen Tiye

CHILDREN OF THE KAP (ROYAL NURSERY)
Horemheb: general
Rameses: Horemheb's great friend and fellow general
Huy: leading courtier/envoy of the period
Maya: Treasurer during this period

Meryre:	Principal Priest of the Era, a fervent follower of the Aten cult
Pentju:	Royal Physician, friend of Princess Khiya, guardian, for a while, of the baby Prince Tutankhamun
Sobeck:	leading courtier, confidant of Mahu

THE ROYAL HOUSE (OF AKENHATEN)

Akenhaten/Amenhotep IV:	Pharaoh
Nefertiti:	Akenhaten's Great Queen and Wife, daughter of Ay

Meketaten Meritaten Ankhesenaten/ Ankhesenamun Tutankhaten/ Tutankhamun: }	children of Akenhaten
Khiya:	Mitanni princess, one of Akenhaten's 'junior' wives, mother of Tutankhamun

THE AKHMIN GANG

Ay:	First Minister of Akenhaten, father of Nefertiti, brother of Queen Tiye
Mutnodjmet:	younger daughter of Ay, married to Horemheb
Nakhtimin (Nakhtmin/Minnakht):	half-brother of Ay, commander of palace troops

OTHERS

Djoser Khufu: }	Atenist priests
Rahmose:	Atenist general
Aziru:	Canaanite prince, bitterly opposed to Egypt
Djarka:	confidant, Lieutenant of Mahu

Introduction

The Eighteenth Dynasty (1550–1323 BC) marked the high point, if not the highest point, of the Ancient Egyptian Empire, both at home and abroad; it was a period of grandeur, of gorgeous pageantry and triumphant imperialism. It was also a time of great change and violent events, particularly in the final years of the reign of Amenhotep III and the swift accession of the 'Great Heretic' Akenhaten, when a bitter clash took place between religious ideologies at a time when the brooding menace of the Hittite Empire was making itself felt.

I was very fortunate in being given access to this ancient document which alleges to be, in the words of a more recent age, 'the frank and full confession' of a man who lived at the eye of the storm: Mahu, Chief of Police of Akenhaten and his successors. Mahu emerges as a rather sinister figure responsible for security – a job description which can, and did, cover a multitude of sins. This confession seems to be in full accord with the evidence on Mahu that has been recovered from other archaeological sources – be it the discoveries at El-Amarna, the City of the Aten, or the evidence of his own tomb, which he never occupied. A keen observer of his times, Mahu was a man whose hand, literally, was never far from his sword (see the Historical Note on p.401).

Mahu appears to have written his confession some considerable time after the turbulent years which marked the end of the Eighteenth Dynasty. He kept journals, which he later transcribed, probably during the very short reign of Rameses I (c.1307

ix

BC). Mahu's original document was then translated in the demotic mode some six hundred years later during the seventh century BC, and copied again during the Roman period in a mixture of Latin and the Greek Koine. His confession, which I have decided to publish in a trilogy, reflects these different periods of translation and amendment; for instance, Thebes is the Greek version of 'Waset', and certain other proper names, not to mention hieroglyphs, are given varying interpretations by the different translators and copiers.

In the first part of the trilogy, *An Evil Spirit Out of the West*, Mahu described the rise and fall of Akenhaten: that Pharaoh's mysterious disappearance, the attempt by his Queen Nefertiti to seize power, and her brutal and tragic end. In this second part, Mahu reflects on the mysteries surrounding such dramatic events. He and others of the Kap, now Lords of Egypt but bound by the close ties of childhood, are still haunted by what has happened, and fearful of what is to come . . .

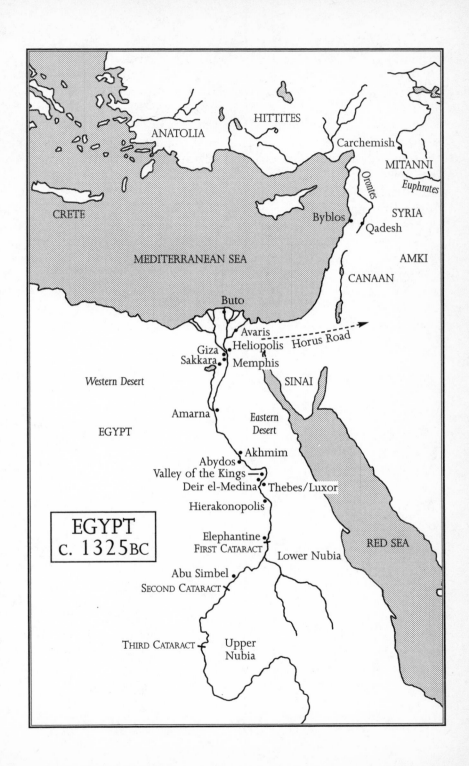

HITTITES

ANATOLIA

Carchemish

MITANNI

Euphrates

CRETE

Orontes

SYRIA

Byblos

Qadesh

MEDITERRANEAN SEA

AMKI

CANAAN

Buto

Avaris

Heliopolis

Horus Road

Giza

Memphis

Sakkara

Western Desert

SINAI

Amarna

*Eastern
Desert*

EGYPT

Akhmim

Abydos

Valley of the Kings

Deir el-Medina

Thebes/Luxor

Hierakonopolis

Elephantine

FIRST CATARACT

RED SEA

EGYPT
c. 1325BC

Lower Nubia

Abu Simbel

SECOND CATARACT

THIRD CATARACT

Upper
Nubia

behhu
(Ancient Egyptian for 'hyaena')

Chapter 1

Death appears before me today like a firebrand glowing in the dark, like stains on the street, blood glistening on the stone. Death appears before me today like the smoke from a fire, like the hot wind from the desert, like pain from an open wound.

The words of the ancient poem are often on my lips and echo through my heart, especially last night, when I was woken by the gruesome roaring from the river bank. I knew what had happened. I went out this morning, the Nubian mercenaries accompanying me down through the gates of the small mansion, a small, elegant palace, but still my prison. We went to the edge of the Nile where the land rises, overlooking the great forest of papyrus green, fresh and supple, nourished by the black silt the new waters had brought.

'We heard the sound too,' the captain of mercenaries murmured.

I did not reply. I do not speak unless I have to. I spend most of my time writing down the truth, or what I think is the truth, about the Dazzling Time, the Shattering Years, the Season of the Hyaena, or so they describe it, when Akenhaten the Heretic Pharaoh promulgated his belief in the one god, the Aten, and built a new city in the hopes of creating a new empire. A time when all of Egypt, the Kingdom of the Two Lands, Tomery, beloved of the Gods, trembled and shook in his presence. Some chroniclers describe those years as a great shadow racing over the land; others talk of a dazzling burst of sunlight. Whatever they say, the Nile still ebbs and flows and the land is soaked in blood. Ah well! I walked along the bank and glimpsed the crimson froth, pieces of flesh floating amongst the reeds. Once again the Nile had tasted blood; crocodiles had ambushed a hippopotamus cow giving birth amongst the reeds, attacking both mother and newborn. They must have feasted well: wine-red bubbles winked and burst on the river's surface, whilst the tang of blood was stronger than the rich odours from the disturbed ooze.

I walked back to the house recalling the words of a holy man who compared life to steps of a pyramid. Each life force, soul or Ka climbed to a different stage: plant, bird, animal or human being. I could well believe it. I have lived amongst crocodiles all my life, hunted with the most savage hyaenas, flown with the heavy-lidded vultures to plunder and peck on the battle-fields of life. I, Mahu, son of Seostris of the Medjay, beloved friend of the Pharaoh, former Chief of Police, 'the Eyes and Ears of the King', the Overseer of the House of Secrets, Keeper of the Secrets of the Heart. I, who have seen . . . well, I shall tell you what I have seen. After all, I have no choice. The Custodian of the Secrets of the Great House of the new Pharaoh, may the Gods bless his name, has demanded that I confess all, that I sit and whisper my secrets like a penitent would to a priest in a Chapel of the Ear. They have shut me up in this mansion with its cool rooms washed in sky blue and its sweet-smelling gardens to finish this task. I sit in my chamber and stare out of the window. The shutters are removed so as to catch the light of day and the cooling breeze from the river. My eye is caught by the glittering water of the artificial pool, or the various greenery of the trees: acacia, terebinth and sycamore. The call of some animal echoes eerily. I start at a flash of colour as a bird wheels against the sky. I always do that, a legacy from the days of battle when the eye is sharp and the heart keen to catch the whirling flurry of an arrow or the shadow of a falling sword, then I relax, I let my body fall slack.

The sun sets, the shadows creep across the gardens. My chamber seems to grow, until it is no longer a writing office with painted walls, their refreshing green borders with dark red bands fade away. It becomes a hall from the Underworld, large and cavernous, filled with shifting shadows. I lift my wine cup and toast the dead as they rise, unsummoned, to greet me. They take their places, smile or glower. Pride of place goes to him, the Great Heretic, the heinous sinner, Akenhaten! They dare not mention his name. They call it cursed, a filthy word, yet to me, the name is like the chord of a harp, the tune of a flute, bringing back bittersweet memories. Akenhaten, the Grotesque, the Ugly One, the Veiled One, with his eerie, misshapen body, hips broad as a woman and pendulous chest; arms, legs, fingers and toes long and spidery thin. 'The Spider', a priest from the Temple of Hours called him, but what does he know? What is he but a worm on the earth, a shaven head, with little between his legs, and nothing between his ears?

Akenhaten enjoyed a majesty all of his own, a splendour and grandeur unknown to many. He comes before me like a statue in a shadowy temple with the sun playing on the red quartzite. I glimpse his high cheekbones, those slanted sloe eyes which seemed to rest on the sides of his face. Yet this is no statue, but a face pulsating with power, whilst the eyes glow with a fever I never truly understood. The lips are not of stone but full, red and pouting. In a temper that long jaw would quiver and the mouth spit out curses like Horus does fire to burn millions. And who comes next? Ay, Akenhaten's father-in-law. A crocodile amongst crocodiles! Commander of the Chariots, Keeper of the Diadem, Fan-Bearer on the Right-Hand Side of the King, God's Father, Chief amongst the Hyaenas. A liar, adulterer, fornicator, assassin, lecher, who slept with his own daughter and his daughter's daughter. Ay, the mongoose man, with the clever, smooth face of a scholar; handsome-eyed and pleasant-mouthed, lean and personable, charming, smiling and utterly untrustworthy, a veritable cobra in human flesh.

Horemheb comes next; square and thickset, dressed in leather armour, bracelets on his wrists and arms, a war club in one hand, a dagger in the other. Horemheb has a heavy face, a drooping mouth and a square chin; his aggressive eyes glare at you. A man of honour who would do the most dishonourable things because ambition roared in his heart like a fire in the furnace. Of course, behind him (yes, I'll speak the truth even though he is the father of kings), lean and sinewy, with pointed face and hawk-like nose, eyes glittering with a malice he nourishes like a mother does her babe, Horemheb's other self: Rameses, sly and crooked, though courageous and fierce in battle, ruthless in enmity. The other Children of the Kap rise to greet me. Oh yes, those I grew up with in the royal nursery after I was placed there by Aunt Isithia, my father's sister, that witch-woman with the soul of midnight and a heart reeking of ancient sin. If Isithia comes I always ignore her!

Who else? Maya – oh soft-faced Maya, his chubby cheeks bulging and heavily painted, round eyes ringed with kohl, full lips painted like those of a temple girl! Maya is dressed in his flounced robes with the embroidered sash; his neck glitters with jewellery. I can even smell his perfume, a mixture of cassia and myrrh. Maya, a woman in a man's body, with a heart as sharp as any woman's. Maya the financier, with his genius for collecting silver and gold, who could shift the sands of the desert and still find a precious nugget. He sits and simpers at me, rubbing his stomach as he did in life, as if, even then, he knew the source of his own death.

Next to him the only person, the only soul Maya ever loved, my friend Sobeck, lean-visaged and hollow-eyed, burnt by the sun in that oasis prison. Sobeck, who had been taught a brutal lesson about the seduction of a Royal Ornament, one of the concubines of the Magnificent One, Akenhaten's father. Sobeck escaped his prison. Shrewd and cunning, he'd found himself back in the slums of Thebes, where he had become a dog killer selling their mummified corpses as offerings for pilgrims. Sobeck, who'd held his own with the Scorpion Men, the sand-dwellers, the desert wanderers, all the filth of the quayside and slums. He fought his way up, like the warrior he was, to become the Lord of Am-duat, the grimy underworld of Waset, Thebes, the City of the Sceptre. In sharp contrast comes Huy: urbane, courtly, diplomatic, with his slender body, wise furrowed face, pointed chin and deep-set eyes. He is dressed like a courtier in his gauffered linen robe and curled wig, fingers and arms tastefully decorated with collars and rings of office. Huy the Splendid One, Overseer of the House of Envoys, the master diplomat, his only concern the greatness of Egypt and making its enemies tremble before it. Meryre the priest also creeps in. He of the holy lips and sneering eyes. A sanctimonious face, round and smooth as a pebble, bland eyes in a bland face, and yet the most dangerous of men! Pentju the physician, troubled and secretive, arrives too. A little man with his hunched shoulders and narrow face, all anxious-eyed with parted lips.

Oh yes, my past is crowded. The walls of the chamber expand, like a long hall of the Hittites. I sip at my wine as my soul travels across the Far Horizon, yet it does not enter the Fields of Yalou, the Meadows of the Blessed, but some hidden time and place which hangs between heaven and earth. I search the caverns of my soul, the chamber of my heart, peopled by those I have loved, fought, betrayed and killed. He also comes, but he is apart from the rest, like the glow of a candle in the dark. I talk of the Divine Child, the Blessed Boy, God's Cherished, the Golden One, Tutankhamun, son of Akenhaten and Khiya, his Mitanni princess, the rival of Nefertiti. Oh yes, so I have mentioned her name! Nefertiti, 'the Beautiful Woman has Arrived'! I always find it strange that the child born to us, the Divine Son given to us, shattered Nefertiti's love and brought the dream world of the Aten crashing to earth like one of those fiery stars which lance through the heavens. Tutankhamun, with his beautiful, child-like face, so composed, so serene; with those innocent questioning eyes, like a young doe fascinated by the hyaenas gathered around him.

I have already mentioned her name, and she comes with the other, Nefertiti and her daughter Ankhesenamun. Both beloved by me, both so different. Nefertiti with her face of pale gold, glittering blue eyes, all framed by that fiery halo of red hair. She comes in many forms like the mischievous minx she could be, teasing and flirting, or all majestic in that blue crown, head tilted imperiously back as she surveys the world from under heavy-lidded eyes. Behind her, Ankhesenamun, treacherous like a marsh covered with the greenest succulent grass, a trap for any man's soul! I am an old man but I recall Ankhesenamun's round sensuous face, those sloe eyes and kissing mouth, her body full and ripe, and I feel the excitement stir. The heart strains. If I could, I'd caress that body and clutch her face between my fingers and kiss that mouth. So, they all are here along with the rest.

I pick up a papyrus pen and wonder where to begin again. How shall I start? The past is like a battlefield, covered in the misty dust of conflict and killing. The war chariots rattle and crash. The horses gallop and charge. The mist shifts; gold, silver and electrum glitter in the sun. I hear the harness snap and stretch, the blast of the war trumpet, the screams of men, the clash and clatter of monstrous feet where the God of battles has sucked up blood. Yes, going into the past is like crossing a battlefield. So, where did it all begin? Perhaps, as all battles do, in the resting time, those days of serenity before the chariots are hitched and the swords are drawn. I shall begin in the last month of the Peret season, when the Nile ran strong and full, washing the black lands with its wet coolness. Yes, that's when it began again, a full year after Nefertiti had taken the poison I had given to her. I'd watched her life-glow fade and felt her beautiful body shudder in my arms . . .

We had left the city of Aten and gone south to Thebes. We were all there, in the Lion Courtyard of the Malkata Palace, the Dazzling House to the south of Thebes. I remember it well. The sun-washed limestone courtyard with crouching lions carved in red quartzite in each corner. Garden banks fringed all four sides, their black soil, especially imported from Canaan, filled with every fragrant herb, plant and flower. I can even recall their smell, especially that of the cornflower with its grey leaves and bright blue flowers. The doors to the inside of the palace were closed and guarded by members of the imperial household troop, hand-picked by Nakhtimin, Chief Military Scribe of the Palace, Ay's secretive, close-faced brother. These warriors stood in the shade, heads protected by blue and gold striped head-dresses, leather kilts fastened around their waists, sandals on their feet, long copper bracelets on their wrists, one hand resting on a ceremonial shield boasting the ram's head of Amun, the other grasping a pinewood spear with a barbed bronze point. They were hand-picked because each of them could cast his spear and pin a butterfly to the wall. They were guarding us, as if we needed guarding!

We lounged under perfume-drenched awnings, slouched on cushions or divans or sat on stools, their panels inlaid with ebony and ivory. We talked and we rested. Before each of us stood a small table of acacia wood bearing gold dishes of sliced melon, pomegranate, apples and cherries. In the centre was Tutankhamun, no more than six summers old, dressed in a simple white robe of the purest linen, his little egg-shaped head all shaven except for the lock of reddish-black hair hanging down his plump right cheek. He sat on scarlet gold-fringed cushions under a purple awning, sucking a piece of melon, smiling beatifically to himself. Beside him Ankhesenamun, now fourteen years old, the girl-woman in her thick braided, perfumed wig bound by a green-gold filet, her face exquisitely painted, jewellery and collars glittering in the strong sunlight. She lounged to face her brother, her future husband, arranging her linen robe to emphasise rather than disguise her beauty. She was teasing him as she would a pet kitten and was rewarded with Tutankhamun's brilliant, innocent smile. Servants holding fragrant pink ostrich feathers ranged behind them, wafting a cooling breeze with their great fans, scenting the air and driving away the marauding flies.

I, as Tutankhamun's official guardian, sat on his right, my lieutenants Sobeck and Djarka behind me. Ay and Nakhtimin sat to the left: Nakhtimin was being promoted more and more into the Royal Circle to offset the military might of Horemheb. The rest ranged either side of us: Horemheb and Rameses, for once out of uniform. Pentju and Huy, Meryre, Tutu, Akenhaten's duplicitous chamberlain, and Rahmose, General of the Troops of the Aten. Some had been fervent in the Great Heretic's cause, others cooler, the rest just self-seeking. They reminded me of a pack of hyaenas lounging in the shade of some rocks. We watched each other, ready to act as a pack, to hunt and tear down any common enemy, or, if circumstances changed, turn on each other. Circumstances were about to change.

On that day, an auspicious day I recall, sacred to the Goddess Hathor, we were watching a stick fight between two of the Nakhtu-aa, strong-arm boys, veterans from the Ptah regiment who had killed three enemies in hand-to-hand combat then taken their hands, penises or noses, whatever trophy had been

9

demanded. These two were the most skilled fighters in their regiment and Rameses had arranged for a display of their prowess. We watched them circle, garbed in loincloths, their oiled bodies coated in dust. They each scored, time and again, until the blood oozed out of sharp cuts and burst welts. They moved like dancers, bare feet slapping the ground, sharp-edged canes raised, seeking the advantage. They were growing tired, wary of each other. I became distracted, my attention diverted by one of those sharp-eared cats much beloved by Ay, a great tabby who had caught a baby hare and was now playing with it in the shadow of a carved lion.

'Again!' one of the fighters shouted.

The warriors drew apart, their sticks clashed. Somewhere in the palace a conch horn wailed, cymbals clashed. I turned and glanced at one of the doors. The guards were already opening it. A messenger came hurrying through, sandalled feet smacking the stone floor. He was drenched in sweat, his tight loincloth grimy and dirty; around his neck was the official collar of an imperial runner. The fighters stopped and drew apart. The messenger flung himself on his knees before Tutankhamun, brow touching the ground. Ay snapped his fingers: the messenger rose, hurried over, whispered in God's Father's ear, then handed him a scroll. Ay rose.

'My lords,' he murmured, 'we must return to the council chamber.' A meeting of the Royal Circle had already been planned for the tenth hour; glancing over my shoulder, I beckoned Djarka and Sobeck forward. For once Sobeck was dressed in the linen robes of a courtier. He was always amused at the double life he led, drifting between the Malkata Palace and the grimy back streets of Thebes. Sobeck had proved invaluable to me in relaying the gossip, the chatter, the doings and goings of the various gangs who, during Pharaoh's absence from Thebes, had grown in power. They'd even launched attacks on the Valley of the Kings in an attempt to rob the royal tombs. In the past few months I had dispensed swift justice. The entrance to the Valley of the Kings was now lined with the corpses of those I had impaled there. Djarka was equally invaluable: olive-skinned and smooth-faced, though his black hair was now greying and he had lost that bubbling merriment. Five years previously he and I had been given no choice but to kill the love of his life and her father, professional assassins sent into the city of Aten to slay the Great Heretic. Both my comrades knew their duty. Djarka carried a heavy Syrian bow and quiver of arrows; Sobeck concealed a long throwing dagger beneath his robes.

'Take their Royal Highnesses inside,' I ordered.

Ankhesenamun had pulled herself up; she was glancing narrow-eyed at her grandfather, Ay. Tutankhamun, however, still sat sucking a piece of melon, smiling across the courtyard as if he could see something we couldn't. As Sobeck and Djarka moved to obey, the mercenaries I had hired from my own people, the Medjay, to the east of Thebes, came out of the shadows of the great carved lions where they had been dozing, enjoying the shade and sharing a wineskin. Sobeck grasped the little prince by the hand and gently pulled him to his feet.

'Soldier!' the boy shouted, gesturing with his piece of melon. 'Soldiers fight!'

Sobeck leaned down and whispered; the little boy laughed, a deep chuckle in his narrow chest.

'Good, good!' he shouted, almost throwing himself into Sobeck's arms.

Ankhesenamun stepped neatly round Djarka, smiled flirtatiously and walked towards me. For a moment she reminded me of her mother, Nefertiti: the same languorous, sensuous yet regal pose, lips parted in a smile, eyes downcast, but when she looked up, I caught her knowing look. She came a little too close. I smelt her fragrance and I could see the line of sweat running down between her breasts. She used the linen shawl to fan herself, turning her head to look at me out of the corner of her eye.

'Mahu.' My name came as a whisper, as if we were lovers or conspirators. 'Mahu, what is the matter?'

'Your Highness will be informed in due course.'

'Your Highness will be informed in due course,' she mimicked, and laughed girlishly, fingers to her face. She snapped open the fan held in her right hand and shook it vigorously before her, those beautiful eyes no longer laughing, but cold and hard. 'I am not a child, Mahu. I am at least fourteen summers

11

old. I have been a Queen and a mother to a child. I shall be a future Queen and the mother of the heir.'

'For the moment, Your Highness, you are what you are and I am what I am. You know as much as I do and, I am sure,' I pushed my face a little closer, 'that when our meeting is over, God's Father Ay, your grandfather, will slide into your quarters to share what we are about to learn.'

Ankhesenamun smiled. It was always the same: parry and thrust like two stick fighters, Ankhesenamun flirting, yet beneath that, menacing, acting the innocent, a woman who had slept with her own father and, if my spies were correct, offered similar favours to her grandfather too. A true temple girl, Ankhesenamun! She'd put the best heset to shame! She was dangerous not just because of her beauty but that air of child-like innocence, which masked a heart and wit as cruel as a mongoose. Oh yes, she was Nefertiti's daughter and Ay's grand-daughter, inheriting every ounce of their cunning.

Ankhesenamun flounced away, fanning herself, shouting out her congratulations to the two stick fighters. She walked so quickly, Djarka almost collided with her, and had to step back, offering profuse apologies. Ankhesenamun just laughed and followed her half-brother through the door. My mercenaries hurried after. They had their orders. Akenhaten's last written instruction was that I was to be the official and trusted guardian of his baby son. This had also been the wish of Tutankhamun's mother Khiya, so I had taken an oath which I regarded as doubly sacred. Tutankhamun was never allowed out of my sight or that of Djarka; even the melon he had been sucking had been care-fully tested and tasted. I stared around the courtyard. The retainers of the other members of the Royal Circle were emerging from the shadows of the corners, chattering amongst themselves, wondering what news had disturbed the Great Ones. I studied these. Each hyaena leader had his own pack, and I wondered how many of them could be trusted: soldiers of different nationalities, mercenaries, people fleeing from the law in other cities. Some had been fanatically loyal to Akenhaten; I did not trust any of them, yet I dared not act. As Chief of Police I was tempted to advise Ay that an imperial edict should be issued disbanding such retainers in the cause of common peace and harmony. Ay would have loved that! He'd have insisted, whether I was Chief of Police or not, that my scouts, as I called them, should also be banned from the palace precincts.

I sighed and followed the rest through the door, walking along the narrow tiled corridor towards the great council chamber. Nakhtimin's guards were already clustered before its copper-plated doors of Lebanese cedar. Many of these men were from the Ra regiment, which had been based near Akhmin, Ay's own town, and they all owed a personal allegiance to what I secretly termed the Akhmin gang: Ay, Nakhtimin and others of their coven. The rest of the Royal Circle were waiting for me. Ay sat on a throne-like camp chair, the ends of its arms carved in the likeness of a lion's head, the legs in the shape of unsheathed claws. Members of the council sat on cushions or small stools. In the middle of the Royal Circle, five scribes from the School of Life squatted ready, trays on their laps, papyrus pens poised.

Once the chamber had been magnificent, but the years of neglect during Akenhaten's stay in his magnificent new city 150 miles to the north had wrought their effect. Plaster peeled from the walls. Frescoes and paintings had lost their vibrancy; the blue and gold pillars were beginning to flake. In one part of the ceiling a cornice had come away, and the dust still littered the floor. The palace had been infested by rats and mice. Ay's response had been to let loose a legion of cats, and the council chamber still reeked of their smell.

I took my seat, wrinkling my nose, even as Meryre, who acted as chaplain and lector priest of the Royal Circle, intoned a prayer to the All-Powerful God. No one dared ask whether he was praying to Amun-Ra, the Silent God of Thebes, or to the Aten, the glorious Sun Disc, symbol of Akenhaten's mysterious Almighty, All-Seeing God. I gazed round the circle. Apart from Meryre and other fanatics of the Aten, the 'devout' as Huy diplomatically called them, I doubted if any, including myself, believed in any God. True, Horemheb was devoted to Horus of Henes, his home town, though he regarded him more as a keepsake, a lucky charm, than a spiritual being. We were the hyaenas, hungry for power, ever watchful of Ay. If he slipped or weakened, the rest, myself included, would tear him to pieces. Yet

13

Ay was cunning as any of us. More importantly, Tutankhamun was his grandson and Ankhesenamun his granddaughter. Although I was the prince's guardian, Ay had assumed all the power of regent, and none dared question him. We all recognised that everyone in the Royal Circle was marked. We had served the Aten. We had been part of the great heresy. Others in Egypt, generals and courtiers, the mayors of powerful towns, particularly Thebes, had grudges and grievances to settle with us. It was that fear of these others which kept us together, and Ay had proved himself to be the most redoubtable leader of the pack.

Once Meryre had finished his gabbling, Ay sat quietly, as if reflecting on the prayer.

'My lords.' He lifted his arms, spreading his hands as if to intone a chant. 'My lords, look around. This chamber represents all of Egypt.'

A few glanced about them; the rest watched Ay.

'We must acknowledge,' Ay continued, 'that the move to the City of Aten proved to be a mistake, but the will of Pharaoh was paramount and we had no choice but to obey.'

A chorus of assent greeted his words. Ay was chanting a hymn we all recognised, every letter, every syllable, so we always joined in the chorus.

'The cities of Egypt have suffered,' Ay continued, 'their temples neglected, their courtyards overgrown, their treasuries empty.' His voice grew stronger. 'Our armies, except for that of Memphis,' he smiled at Horemheb, 'lack supplies, weapons and recruits. Soldiers desert in droves, their officers no longer care, the barracks are empty. Worse still, Egypt's enemies, the People of the Nine Bows, grow more insolent and arrogant.'

Horemheb clapped his hands, nodding fiercely, gazing round, challenging any to contradict Ay's words.

'Outlaws and bandits prowl the Red Lands,' Ay continued. 'Our mines in Sinai are constantly attacked, whilst fresh news comes about unrest in Kush, whose princes forget to pay the tribute due to the Great House of Egypt.'

I sat, eyes half closed, listening to the litany of Egypt's woes. The breakdown in trade, the empty treasuries, low morale amongst the troops, rebellions and revolts in this city or that province, the growing threats from across Sinai where Egypt's client states in the land of Canaan now ignored Pharaoh's writ and fought amongst themselves. To the north of Canaan a great empire was rising. The Hittite princes were becoming more and more absorbed by Egypt's weaknesses, ever ready to encroach on borders, threatening to sweep south and occupy the rich valley lands and sea plain of Canaan. I was tempted to interrupt Ay's speech, but recognised what he was doing. He was reminding us that we were all responsible for Egypt's loss of greatness. At last he finished and sat, hands in his lap, head down.

After some time he looked up. 'What is the greatest danger?'

'Aziru!' Horemheb spat the name out.

'Aziru,' Ay echoed, nodding wisely.

'A prince of Canaan,' Horemheb continued. 'We know he undermines our allies, how he supports the Hittites. Our one great ally there, Rib-Addi, King of Byblos,' he gestured across to Tutu, Akenhaten's fervent chamberlain, 'sent letter after letter begging for help, for just one chariot squadron. Even that letter was never answered, never shown to anyone.'

'Like you,' Tutu leaned forward, face contorted with fury, 'I took my orders from Pharaoh!'

'Didn't you advise him?' Rameses taunted.

'Yes, and so did you,' Tutu retorted. 'But Pharaoh's will was manifest. No troops were to cross Sinai. Our allies were to settle their own problems. Akenhaten planned to go along the Horus Road and bring the word of Aten to his allies.'

'Nonsense,' Horemheb bawled. 'Akenhaten made a vow he would never leave his city.'

The rest of the circle were drawn into the shouting match of accusation and counter-accusation. Ay glanced at me, then looked away: eventually he clapped his hands and kept doing so until all conversation ceased.

'Rib-Addi is dead.' His words were greeted by a low moan. Horemheb would have sprung to his feet but Rameses gently pushed him back on to the cushions. 'The messenger brought the news. Aziru has attacked Byblos, his troops have sacked the city. Rib-Addi was caught, his throat was slashed like a sacrificial goat and he was hung over the main gateway.'

15

'But our ally Tushratta, King of the Mitanni?' Horemheb protested. 'Khiya, mother of the Prince Tutankhamun, was his daughter. He promised us help.'

'The Mitanni dare not move.' Ay shook his head. 'The Hittites have sworn a great oath. If the Mitanni intervene in Canaan so will they.'

'Then we must send troops,' Rameses urged. 'Bring fire and sword to Canaan.'

'Will we?' Ay snapped his fingers and gestured at Maya. 'How much silver and gold do we have, Treasurer?'

'Enough for a twenty-day campaign,' Maya replied, 'and then nothing.'

'Well, General Rameses?' Ay glared at Horemheb's ally. 'How far do you think we'll go on twenty days' gold and silver; which troops shall we send?'

'There's the Horus and Isis regiments at Memphis,' Rameses protested. 'Foot soldiers and chariot squadrons, not to mention the Ra—'

'Ah.' Ay raised his hands in a gesture of surprise. 'So we dispatch across Sinai the only three regiments we can trust, led by the only two senior generals—'

'We can trust.' Huy finished the sentence.

Horemheb and Rameses fell silent.

'If we send the Horus and Isis,' Ay sighed, 'all we will have left are our mercenaries and Nakhtimin's imperial regiment. If we faced revolt or mutiny here,' he shrugged, 'how long would any of us survive?'

'We must wait,' Maya intervened. 'The temples and palaces must be restored, the treasuries filled, the allegiance of every regiment guaranteed. Until then our allies in Canaan must look after themselves.'

'Wait!' Horemheb shouted. 'Wait!' He turned and glared at me. 'Mahu, you are Chief of Police, and Overseer of the House of Secrets. Internal security is your concern.'

'Is it now?'

'You sit there silent,' Rameses taunted. 'As if half asleep. Still dreaming about the glory days, Mahu?'

I held Ay's gaze. I was his ally. He knew that I knew it was not for any liking. We were just men manacled together. We

16

had no choice in the matter. We either stayed together or fell together.

'Mahu the dreamer,' Rameses repeated.

'General Rameses!' I paused.

'We wait with bated breath,' my tormentor murmured.

'General Rameses, you are a dead man. No, don't let your hand near that dagger you've hidden beneath your robes. Don't you realise?' I answered his furious look with my own. 'Every man in this chamber is a dead man! God's Father Ay sings the hymn and we know the chorus. Each of us was a friend of Akenhaten, he whom the priests of Amun-Ra and Thebes now call the Great Heretic. We are blamed for what has happened.' I gestured towards the windows. 'Ask Sobeck. Wander the streets of Thebes, if you dare. There are men who would pay good gold to see your head, and mine, pickled in a barrel! They would love to either impale us alive or bury us in the hot sands of the Red Lands.'

'If we had followed the Aten?' Meryre intervened. 'If we had kept faithful to our master's vision?'

'Shit!' Rameses shouted. 'It's *because* we followed that vision.' His voice faltered.

'That's right, General Rameses,' I agreed. 'Because of that, we are now in crisis. We are so weak, we daren't even let you out of our sight, not to mention your precious regiments. I have reports of unrest from the Delta to beyond the Third Cataract: conspiracies, covens, disaffected officers, treasonable mayors. Did you know certain powerful ones are seriously considering asking the Mitanni or the Hittites to intervene in Egypt?'

'Never!' Maya protested.

'True,' I replied. 'We have no names, yet in every city along the Nile, from the Third Cataract to the Great Green, treason and treachery bubble like water in a pot.'

'So what do you advise?' Horemheb asked quietly. 'That we should be careful?'

I stretched out my arms. 'On the one hand we have those who hate us because we followed the Great Heresy. And on the other,' I glared at Meryre, Tutu and others of their coven sitting across the council chamber, 'there are those who hate us because we deserted the Aten, the Great Heretic's vision. We have no

17

friends, no allies.' I gestured at Anen, Ay's kinsman, who had been installed as High Priest of Amun-Ra in Thebes. 'He is our high priest, yet he dare not even officiate in his own temple. Have you heard of the Shabtis?'

'Shabtis?' Rameses mocked. 'Statues put in a tomb?'

'Statues put in a tomb,' I echoed, 'to represent the servants who will serve their master when he reaches the Fields of the Blessed beyond the Far Horizon.'

'Come to the point,' Horemheb growled.

'I am Chief of Police, and rightly so. All I know is that there is a group, a secret society who call themselves the Shabtis of Akenhaten. Fanatical followers who believe we deserted their master and so should pay for our treachery with our lives.'

The council chamber fell ominously silent.

'You haven't heard of them,' I continued wearily, 'because so far their victims have been minor officials. Priests who served the Aten, scribes educated in its House of Life, merchants and nobles who journeyed to the city of Aten; all are regarded as traitors. At first I noticed no pattern; just another death in Thebes, I thought when I read the reports: a man stabbed here, a boating accident, a fall from a roof, a tainted cup of wine, something in the food which disagreed with them. In the last five months,' I held up my hand, 'there have been at least ten such deaths, and the one thing all the victims had in common was that they once served our Pharaoh in the city of Aten before returning to Thebes.'

'Grudges and grievances,' Rameses scoffed.

'Perhaps, perhaps not, General Rameses. But if I were you, I would keep your bodyguard close and your hand not very far from that knife beneath your robes.'

'So what do you recommend?' Ay's words came like a whisper.

'Swift action, my lord. The Prince Tutankhamun . . .' I paused and smiled. 'See, we've even changed his name, and that of his intended wife. No longer are they pleasing to the Aten, but as Tutankhamun and Ankhesenamun their names now bear that of the God of Thebes.'

'Empty gestures,' Maya grumbled.

'Every gesture is important,' I retorted. 'We must issue decrees saying that the old ways are to be restored. Such decrees should be posted in every city along the Nile.'

'And?' Ay asked.

'The Kushites should be threatened. The silver and gold tribute must be restored. Merchants must be given every help, the Nile patrolled by marines. Bandits and outlaws are to be summarily executed, their bodies impaled along the riverbanks as a warning to others. Desert patrols must be increased, marauding Libyans and sand-dwellers taught a brutal lesson: fire and sword, no prisoners taken.'

Horemheb and Rameses were nodding enthusiastically.

'And here in Thebes?'

I could tell from Ay's face that he agreed, but he was holding something back. The scroll the messenger had handed to him was still grasped in one hand.

'Anyone found guilty of treason should face summary execution. Those we can't trust should be removed from office and dispatched elsewhere. Every one of us here, every official, scribe and officer, must take an oath of allegiance to our new Pharaoh Tutankhamun.'

'But he is not crowned!' Huy intervened.

'He should be, and the sooner the better,' I retorted, 'and his marriage to Princess Ankhesenamum proclaimed the length and breadth of the Two Kingdoms.'

'And Canaan?' Horemheb asked.

'Let the pot bubble for a while.' I wetted my lips. 'Let us dispatch letters to Aziru proclaiming him to be our friend, our ally. Let us send him as much gold and silver as we can, a token of our great favour.'

'And?' Ay asked.

'Invite him to Egypt and blind him. A warning to all traitors in Canaan.'

Horemheb and Rameses were with me. Maya looked disgruntled as, in his mind's eye, he measured out all the gold and silver this would cost. Huy remained impassive; Meryre, Tutu and others of the Aten coven looked sullen as ever. One day we would have to deal with them; as Ay had whispered to me, those who were not with us were against us, yet these men still commanded troops and had friends amongst the imperial general staff.

'Very good, very good,' Horemheb murmured. 'But won't you stir up a hornet's nest?' He laughed sharply. 'Here we are, dyed-in-the-wool Atenists, now demanding the loyalty and allegiance of those who bitterly oppose us, who blame us for Egypt's present ills.'

'Forget the past,' Ay retorted. 'Let us act as if there was no Akenhaten.' He ignored the hiss of disapproval from Meryre and Tutu's hateful glance. 'Let our young prince be proclaimed as Pharaoh, the legitimate heir and successor of his grandfather, Amenhotep III the Magnificent.'

'Like that?' Tutu smacked his hands together. He had risen to a half-crouch. He clapped his hands again. 'Like that, Mahu?' he repeated. 'As if the Great Vision did not exist?'

'A dream,' I replied, 'a nightmare. We were all led astray; now we have returned to the path of truth. We speak with one true voice. We have won the favour of the old gods. Once again Ma'at will rule from the Great Green to beyond the Fourth Cataract.'

'We will still be blamed!' Maya shouted.

'Will we?' Ay declared. 'Give a man a good meal, let him drink deep of the wine, and he'll soon forget his hunger and his thirst.'

'You have decided on this, haven't you?' Meryre shouted. 'You and your . . .' He gestured at me. 'Your Baboon of the South.'

'We have discussed this,' Ay agreed, smiling. 'We see no other path forward. What do you recommend, my lord? That we all troop down to the Nile and take a barge upriver, back to the City of the Aten?'

'I object,' Meryre bellowed.

'We will compromise,' Ay declared soothingly. 'It's best if Tutankhamun, at least for a while, was moved from Thebes. Let him return to the City of the Aten until,' he gestured with his fan, 'Ma'at, truth and harmony are restored. Look, my lords.' Ay turned in his chair to address Meryre and his coven. 'The worship of the Aten will not be proscribed; he is just one God amongst many.' He gestured across the Royal Circle. 'Our proposal has the support of many. Generals Horemheb and Rameses will bring the other regiments down to Memphis and Thebes; their ranks will be purged, incompetent officers, derelict in their duty, asked to retire.'

'You mean those owing allegiance to the Aten?' Meryre asked.

'No capable officer will be dismissed,' Horemheb responded.

'Well, that's our plan.' Ay unrolled the scroll. 'Or at least it was, but I have some news for you which will cast a shadow over all our well-laid schemes.'

'My lord?' Huy asked.

'According to this,' Ay shook his piece of papyrus, 'Pharaoh Akenhaten has returned to Egypt.'

neka
(Ancient Egyptian for 'a serpent fiend')

Chapter 2

For a while the council chamber echoed with cries and shouts. I could only gape at Ay. Horemheb and Rameses sat shocked. Meryre, however, sprang to his feet, screaming at Ay.

'Why didn't you tell us immediately? Why now?' Even then I thought he was overacting!

Ay's gaze shifted to me, a faint smile on his lips. The wily mongoose! He'd kept this information back to shock us but only after he had reminded us that in the eyes of many we were reviled as traitors, the cause of Egypt's downfall, cursed by both factions, those who hated Akenhaten as well as those who supported him. The only reason we hadn't lost our heads or been hung from the Wall of Death was that we still held power, the reins of the chariots firmly gripped in our hands. Whatever happened, we were damned and damned again. If Akenhaten had returned, he'd show little mercy to those he'd once considered his friends, who had betrayed his Great Vision.

'But he's dead! He's dead!' Rameses sprang to his feet, his face contorted with fury, his screams drowning out the rest of the cries and shouts. 'Akenhaten is dead! He has to be dead!'

'Is he?' Meryre yelled back. 'Where's his corpse? Where?'

The question stilled the clamour. Meryre had raised the spectre of all our nightmares. Ay held up his hand for silence.

'Let us,' he announced, 'tell you what we know. An impostor, yes,' he continued stilling the clamour, 'an impostor has emerged out of the deserts of Sinai claiming to be the Pharaoh Akenhaten, proclaiming himself "Beautiful as the Forms of Ra, the Unique One of Ra". He is accompanied by a woman who claims to be Nefertiti. They hold the Imperial Cartouche and are issuing proclamations under those seals. They fly the standards and pennants of the Aten. They first appeared in the Delta supported by Hittite mercenaries.'

'Mercenaries?' Horemheb jibed. 'You mean troops loaned to them by the Hittite king?'

'They have taken Avaris in the Delta,' Ay said baldly.

Now he had our attention. A horrified silence. If this pretender was at Avaris then he could sail down the Nile, his flanks protected by troops, and seize the great cities of Egypt.

'We have troops there,' Rameses murmured.

'The pretenders have been accepted by General Ipumer and the Ptah regiment,' Ay countered. 'The troops were easily suborned by gifts of gold. Elements of the Hekhet and Basta regiments have also gone over to them. According to reports they have reached the Red Mountains.'

'Why didn't we know before?' Huy demanded.

'They moved quickly,' Ay explained. 'They freed the slaves at the Roiau quarry and impaled the royal overseer there; his son escaped to Memphis, that's how we know.'

I gazed across at a wall painting depicting Tuthmosis IV in battle against vile Asiatics; Pharaoh, triumphant, driving his blue and gold chariot pulled by dark, blood red horses over the bodies of the slain against a glorious background of ivory yellow. At the bottom of the picture the artist had depicted one of the enemy caught in a thicket. The man's eyes seemed to stare at me, that horrified surprise of a human being trapped by death. We were caught in a thicket, I reflected. Was this how it would end?

'We must treat with them.' The grizzled General Rahmose, shaking with fever, raised his hand, the first time that afternoon he'd demanded to speak. He sat with Tutu and Meryre and the rest of the Atenists. I wondered idly if they had anything to do with this present mischief; just something about the way they sat . . .

'Treat with them!' Horemheb shouted. 'And what do we offer them? The Kingdom of Lower Egypt? Tribute? Why,' he continued, 'has this usurper been accepted so quickly? Akenhaten's name is reviled.'

'Not in every city,' Rahmose retorted. 'You call him an impostor, a usurper, but what if he is the rightful Pharaoh, the true son of Amenhotep III?' Rahmose let his words hang in the air. He was right. Despised or not, Akenhaten had been rightfully blessed with the double crown of Egypt.

'Mahu.' Ay turned to me.

'General Rahmose speaks the truth.' I chose my words carefully. 'Egypt is now dividing, splitting into factions. Some support the Aten, others Amun-Ra, whilst there are cities and provinces only too eager to shake off the suzerainty of both. What is this usurper offering?'

'He has threatened vengeance against Thebes.' Ay unrolled the piece of papyrus. 'This is an extract from his proclamation: "Woe to the bloody city of Thebes, it is full of lies and idolatry. Soon it will be filled with the clamour of battle: the noise of the whip, of the rattling wheel and prancing horse, of the charging chariot, the flashing sword and glittering spear . . . a great heap of carcasses shall stink under the sun."' He let the papyrus proclamation fall to the floor. 'And so on and so on.'

'I should be sent north,' Horemheb offered. 'Myself and General Rameses. We will gather the Horus and Isis regiments.'

'And if you lose?' Ay declared. 'If your troops mutiny? We are back to what we talked about before. We'd be stripped of both our shield and our sword.'

'Mahu.' Ay pointed at me. 'I ask for your opinion.'

'The Isis and Horus,' I declared, 'should be pulled back to Thebes to defend it as well as to protect us against any uprising. We must play for time, find out who this usurper is and what he intends.'

'And what do you think?' Rameses demanded.

'He *is* a usurper,' I replied more boldly than I felt. 'We all know,' I gazed around, 'how Akenhaten's Queen, Nefertiti, fell sick and died.'

'Poisoned!' Tutu spoke up. 'Nefertiti took poison.'

'Of her own choice,' I lied.

Tutu smiled to himself and glanced away.

'But Akenhaten is different.' Meryre spoke up. 'I asked a question. Where is his corpse?'

27

'How soon will this news be over Thebes?' I demanded, ignoring the High Priest.

'Within a week,' Ay replied.

'Then we must issue proclamations,' I declared, 'depicting this Akenhaten as a usurper, a pretender financed and supported by foreign troops.'

'But he carries seals,' Meryre retorted. 'He flies the standard of the Aten. What if, Mahu, the woman is an impostor but Akenhaten has truly returned?'

I was forced to face the possibility.

'What do we know of Akenhaten's disappearance?' Meryre continued smoothly. 'We know that he rode out into the Red Lands and never returned.'

'And there's more, isn't there?' Ay demanded wearily. 'Isn't there, my Lord Maya?'

The treasurer sat, plump shoulders hunched. He muttered something under his breath. Rameses shouted at him to speak up.

'When Akenhaten disappeared,' Maya said, staring up at the ceiling as if fascinated by its coating of blue paint, its silver and gold stars, 'so did a considerable amount of his treasure.'

'Stolen,' Rameses declared. 'The city of Aten fell into chaos. People were helping themselves.' He glanced round quickly. 'Courtiers, officials, priests.'

'No!' Maya shook his head. 'This was Pharaoh's personal treasure, gold, silver, precious stones, about six large chests full. It could be transported by . . .' He calculated. 'Seven or eight donkeys.'

'And why has this been kept quiet?' Huy demanded.

'Because it takes time,' Maya replied tartly. 'It takes time, my Lord Huy, to go through records to find out what we have and what we don't. I tell you now we don't have much. If the present crisis continues, we will have to start stripping the temples of their gold and silver, melting down sacred vessels. General Rameses,' Maya flung a hand out, 'talks of troops, but only the Gods know how we can provision, arm and pay them.'

I ignored the shouting and yelling. I was distracted by that painting. I also wanted to avoid Ay's gaze as I tried to control the beating of my heart. My mind tumbled like dice in a cup.

How much of this was true? Had Ay had a hand in it? Was he plotting, twisting and turning, spreading out his net? And if so, who was his quarry? I recalled the Shabtis of Akenhaten. I hadn't told my colleagues how beside the body of each victim was found a scarab bearing the crown names of Akenhaten. I often wondered if such secret assassins were Ay's work, a guise, a pretence to remove opponents in the city. He had done it before, so why not now? When I did glance up I caught the fear in his face: a passing glance, a movement of the eyes and lips as if Ay, the great schemer, had, for once in his life, been caught out in the open, his well-laid plans brutally kicked aside. He was looking at me beseechingly, as if uncertain what to say or do next.

Horemheb and Rameses now sat heads together. What were those two panthers plotting? My spies had also brought in reports about their hushed conversations. The Tuthmosid line was protected only by that small boy Tutankhamun. Once he died, why shouldn't some ambitious general seize the war crown of Egypt? The Hedjet of Upper Egypt and the Deshat, the red crown, of Lower Egypt? Did Horemheb nourish dreams all of his own? What was that dark soul Rameses whispering in his ear? I glanced round the Royal Circle. The Atenists were grouped together. Despite their outcries and shouts they looked rather smug, pleased with themselves. Huy and Maya were also exchanging glances. Was this when the hyaena pack broke up? Would we now turn on each other? Rahmose was repeating his request that we treat with this usurper. Meryre kept chorusing like a child repeating a chant that this was a wise move, for how did we know he was a usurper? Pharaoh might be returning to his own. I took the dagger from beneath my robes and began to beat the handle against the tiled floor. The clamour died.

'My lords.' I smiled round in a show of confidence. 'Let us deal with the facts. Queen Nefertiti is dead. She took poison. I know she did. I gave her the cup. I felt her body shudder in my arms; her corpse has been mummified and lies in a tomb in the eastern cliffs above the City of the Aten. A usurper has appeared in the Delta, financed and supported by the Hittites. He has suborned some of our regiments because they are hungry, leaderless and have not been paid in months. It is easy to march

29

across a desert, but the great cities of Egypt will not open their gates so readily. Now, let us turn to this Akenhaten, whoever he is! We know what happened in the City of the Aten. How our Pharaoh quarrelled with his wife Nefertiti and banished her to a palace in the north of the city. He then withdrew himself, taking first his elder daughter and then the Princess Ankhesenamun as his Queens. He had children by both. However, the babies died, as did his elder daughter, Meritaten. What else do we know?'

'We too were banished from his presence,' Huy offered.

'Of course you were.' I smiled. 'And then there was the reconciliation,' I repeated facts they all knew, 'between Akenhaten and Nefertiti: she now reincarnated herself as her husband's co-ruler, adopting the title Semenkhkare-Ankheperure. For a while both reigned together, then Akenhaten disappeared and Nefertiti tried to rule under her new name. She plotted our deaths and had to be removed. A regency council was set up under God's Father, Ay. We decided that Akenhaten's vision was nothing but sand in the wind and moved back to Thebes. We have our Pharaoh, Prince Tutankhamun, to be crowned. So, this usurper is false. He must be dealt with, captured and executed.'

'But what happens if he is the true Pharaoh?' Meryre demanded.

'You go on and on about that!' Anen, the High Priest of Amun, shouted. 'Do you know something, my lord, we don't?'

I stared at Meryre, eyebrows raised. 'A good question, my lord.'

Meryre looked as if he was going to deny everything, but I held his glance.

'Akenhaten,' he declared slowly, 'believed we had all deserted him. He no longer confided in me but in a gaggle of chapel priests, led by two: Khufu and Djoser. At the time of Akenhaten's disappearance, these two and other acolyte priests also vanished. However, before you ask where, you must recall how the pestilence had swept the city. Men died and were given quick burial; others fled.'

'So it is possible,' I persisted, 'that when Akenhaten disappeared, went out into the Red Lands, those precious priests, led by Khufu and Djoser, followed suit, taking his personal treasure with them?'

'That is a possibility,' Meryre conceded.

'And it is also possible,' I demanded, 'that Akenhaten was murdered by these priests, who then took his treasure, including the Royal Seals, and fled along the Horus Road into Canaan and the power of the Hittites?'

Again Meryre agreed. I watched that sanctimonious face and the others grouped around him. Did they really believe Akenhaten had returned? Were they simply guilty of wishful thinking? Or were they part of some far-fetched plot?

'And on your most sacred oath,' I asked quietly, 'you know nothing of this usurper?'

'I object.' Meryre curled his lip.

'I simply asked, my lord. Now I shall give the Royal Circle my advice. We should play for time. Let us send the high priest Meryre as our official envoy. You, my lord, will soon discover if this is our true Pharaoh or some puppet.'

'Why me?' Meryre demanded.

'You are the High Priest of the Aten. You will simply be our messenger. I shall join you.'

Ay gazed in surprise. Rameses was smiling behind his hand. Horemheb was looking at me strangely, as if noticing me for the first time. Huy and Maya were all attention, as were the rest. Ay's head went down to hide his grin. I had done what he wanted: united the council and yet exposed both factions to danger. Meryre would go to prepare the way and I would follow. Tutu was nodding in agreement. Horemheb, Rameses, Huy and Maya also signified their assent.

'Meryre will go first,' I repeated. 'He will simply arrive in peace and ask that this usurper, whatever title we want to give him, is acknowledged by us and that we wish to treat with him. I will be the envoy of the Royal Circle. Meryre and myself will then negotiate.'

'About what?' Rameses barked

'Anything and everything.' I smiled. 'If he wants Thebes, then we will give him it. If he wants to be proclaimed as the God Incarnate, then we shall press our foreheads against the ground.'

'And?' Ay demanded.

'You, my lord, and the rest will be busy gathering troops from every province and city. Thebes should be left under the protection of General Nakhtimin, whilst Generals Horemheb, Rameses and Rahmose collect every soldier they can, every chariot squadron, every bargeload of marines, and sweep north. We shall bring this invader to battle, defeat him and show our enemies, both at home and abroad, that we mean business. No mercy, no quarter, fire and sword, total annihilation.'

'And you, my lord Mahu?' Horemheb asked. 'You will sit at the enemy camp fire with your skin safe and protected?'

'At the appropriate time,' I retorted, 'both my lord Meryre and myself, as well as the small retinue which will accompany us, shall escape.'

'Why?' Huy demanded. 'My lord Mahu, you put yourself in great danger, not to mention my lord Meryre, of course.'

I found it hard to answer that question, but Ay knew my heart. I was truly curious. I wanted to see if the Veiled One had returned. I wanted to plumb this mystery but, of course, I didn't say that. I had other demands to make. Horemheb and Rameses repeated Huy's question.

'In return,' I demanded, 'every member of the Royal Circle shall take an oath, an oath of unequivocal loyalty and obedience to Prince Tutankhamun, who shall be crowned during my departure, whilst his marriage to the Princess Ankhesenamun will be published for all to know.'

Everyone agreed. It would have been treason to refuse.

'Secondly,' I insisted, 'the City of the Aten is crumbling, bats and owls now shelter in the halls, termites eat the wood, the courtyards are overgrown, the sacred pools and lakes are polluted. The tombs in the eastern cliffs . . .' I paused. 'The tombs in the eastern cliffs are protected by my mercenaries; they contain the coffins of those who were our friends and colleagues. They are to be transported back to the Valley of the Kings and given honourable burial.'

Again there was a murmur of agreement. Ay quickly intervened, insisting that Meryre and his entourage of priests leave as quickly as possible, whilst I should follow within the week.

The meeting of the Royal Circle broke up. Ay kept to himself, still seated on his chair, staring down at the rings on his fingers.

Horemheb and Rameses drew Maya and Huy into conversation. Meryre and his group came across. The High Priest was acting anxious, fearful of guarantees about his own safety.

'You are a priest, my lord. The High Priest of the Aten. You will go unarmed, bearing the green boughs of peace. You will be safe.' I grinned. 'Well, as safe as I shall be.'

General Rahmose, face all sweat-soaked, was shaking slightly, so I picked up my striped cloak and handed it to him. I always wore that cloak; it was a gift from Djarka against the cool of the evening, the type worn by his people, the Shemsu: light enough under the heat of the midday sun but sure protection against the freezing cold of the desert night.

Horemheb and Rameses came across and took me aside. Both generals were now elated at the prospect of military action. I idly wondered if I had been too clever. What guarantee did we have, apart from a personal oath, that, once victorious, these two panthers might not turn their troops south and march on Thebes? Ay must have been thinking the same, for he interrupted our conversation, bringing the meeting back to order, proclaiming that we would all take the oath the following morning. In the end that was our best guarantee. Whilst Tutankhamun was alive, the hyaenas who surrounded him would not turn on each other. Already proclamations were reminding the people that the Prince was the grandson of the Magnificent One, Amenhotep III, of the sacred blood and the royal line. Not even Rameses, for all his treachery, would dare raise his hand against Tutankhamun and commit such blasphemy.

The council chamber doors were flung open. We drifted out along the passageway, past Nakhtimin's guards, into the courtyard, where our various retinues were waiting. The sun was now beginning to set, and the breeze was cool. I regretted my magnanimity in giving General Rahmose my cloak. I looked around. He was following Tutu and Meryre into the shadows of the gateway leading out. I glimpsed a white-robed figure abruptly detach itself from a group of priests waiting for their master. At first I thought this man was a messenger bearing important news. He moved swiftly, silently, like a racing shadow, a blur of white. I caught the glint of steel. Rahmose was turning, fearful, still weak with the fever. He could do little to protect himself. The white-garbed figure crashed into him and both men went sprawling. Rahmose's scream rent the air as the knife rose and fell.

The assailant sprang to his feet as if to escape through a door back into the warren of passageways of the palace. Two of Nakhtimin's spearmen followed in pursuit. The man reached the door even as I hurried forward. The door was locked. The man turned and Nakhtimin's spearmen, ignoring my shouts, loosed their shafts. One spear took the man straight in the belly, pinning him to the door behind, whilst the other drove deep into the man's chest. He shook and screamed, arms flailing even as the blood gushed out of the gaping wounds. The spearmen withdrew their shafts and the corpse slid to the ground.

I hurried across with the rest. The courtyard resounded with cries and shouts, the clatter of drawn weapons. Meryre and his group clustered around Rahmose. He lay twisted, one arm going backwards and forwards like the wing of a pinioned bird, heels drumming on the ground. Pentju the physician, who had remained silent throughout the entire council meeting, was crouching beside the fallen man. He could do little. Rahmose's eyes were already glazing over in death, mouth spluttering blood, fingers trying to stem the jagged cuts to his neck, throat and chest. He was a dead man in all but name. I glanced across. The assassin lay slumped in a bloody heap. I went and turned the body over. A young man, smooth-faced, head shaven like that of a priest, but the palms of his hands were coarse and his arms criss-crossed with scars.

'A soldier?' Maya asked. 'Disguised as a priest? He was holding this.' The Treasurer handed over a scarab displaying the throne names of Akenhaten. It was crudely done, the clumsy hiero-glyphs painted white on the hardened black stone. Ay, surrounded by his guards, inspected both corpses and shrugged.

'Mahu,' he demanded, 'find out what happened.'

'I might as well try and get a stone to sing,' I shouted back. I crouched by the corpse of the assassin. The scars on his wrists and arms were superficial, and beneath the blood-soaked robe I could detect no other mark or wound, but on the hardened soles of his feet I glimpsed what I considered to be green dye.

34

'Grass,' I declared, staring at Pentju. 'He was a man used to walking on grass, and those scars on his wrists and arms? I suspect he was a gardener. Meryre!' I shouted.

'My lord?'

'This man was not one of yours?'

The little priest's eyes were hard black buttons, mouth all prim and proper. He looked too composed for a man unused to blood.

'He's not one of mine,' he snapped. 'Though one of our company is missing.'

I immediately ordered a search of the palace grounds. The body of Rahmose was removed to the House of the Embalmers in the Temple of Amun, whilst I ordered the assassin's corpse to be hung in chains by the heels from the Wall of Death, a grim grey stretch of stone, part of an ancient fort which overlooked one of the palace quaysides. The rest of the Royal Circle left as quickly as they could. The courtyard fell silent. Meryre came back.

'That man,' he insisted, 'is not one of mine, but a lector priest is missing.'

'No one knows where he is?' I asked.

Meryre shook his head and waddled off in a show of dignity. I sat in the shade of one of the crouching lions. Pentju came and squatted beside me, staring at the bloodstains on the paving stones. The flies were already gathering in small black clouds.

'You were silent in the Royal Circle,' I said.

'You are very calm,' he replied. 'Rahmose was wearing your robe. Perhaps it was you the assassin was seeking?'

I swallowed hard, rubbing my hands together to hide my own unease. The same thought had occurred to me, but there again, Rahmose was slight, with a balding head, a complete contrast to my own appearance. What did Nefertiti call me? A handsome baboon, with a heavy mouth, snub nose and shock of black hair.

'Redeemed, my dear baboon,' she would say as she pressed a finger against my lips, 'by those large dark eyes.'

'You seem unconcerned.' Pentju broke my reverie. 'I said Rahmose was wearing your robe.'

35

I waved my hand. 'Don't agitate me, Pentju. You are a physician.' I smiled at him. 'Don't they teach in the House of Life not to be misled by the first symptoms?'

Pentju laughed drily, picked up the water skin between his feet, took a slurp, then offered it to me. I refused.

'If you go north,' he put the water skin back, 'our young Prince will be left unprotected.'

'Oh no he won't,' I replied. 'Djarka will guard him, whilst you know that everyone in the Royal Circle needs Tutankhamun's protection. He may be the son of the Heretic Pharaoh, but he is also the grandson of the Magnificent One, the last male heir of the Tuthmosid line. The greatest threat to our young Prince was Nefertiti, and she's gone. Now, tell me, Physician, why were you so silent?'

'That impostor who has appeared in the Delta.' Pentju sucked on his lips. 'It's not Akenhaten. In the last months before his disappearance he often talked to me, Mahu, especially about his son. He entrusted him to me and instructed me that if anything happened to him, you were to be the boy's official guardian. He said you were different from the rest, Mahu, on three points: you had little ambition, you were loyal and you were searching for your soul.'

I glanced away: that was the old Akenhaten, the Veiled One, the Grotesque. I had befriended him when we were both boys, mere strangers in this great palace.

'I tell you,' Pentju continued in a hurried whisper, 'Akenhaten believed that he too had lost his soul. He said he would never find it in the City of the Aten, that he would withdraw into the Red Lands and wait for his God to come.'

'And you think he did that?'

'I know he did.'

'So, do you think he is still alive?'

'He may be.'

'So why shouldn't he emerge to reclaim his throne and once again wear the double crown of Egypt?'

'Akenhaten believed he had found the One True God. People think,' Pentju chose his words carefully, 'that he'd slipped into madness, convinced he was the One God himself, but that's not true. If Akenhaten saw God in anyone, it wasn't really himself,

36

but Nefertiti. He adored her. He loved her. He was infatuated with her. You know that, Mahu. Then the truth about Nefertiti emerged: her arrogance, her pride, the relationship between herself and her father Ay, her persecution of Khiya, Tutankhamun's mother, secretly feeding her potions and powders so she would never conceive. That was the truth which drove him away.' Pentju added bitterly, 'That's what sent Akenhaten out into the Red Lands to find what he had lost.'

'And his treasure?' I asked.

'At the time of his disappearance the City of the Aten was in chaos. The plague was raging like Sekhmet the Destroyer. You saw it, Mahu, streets littered with corpses, the funeral pyres on the cliffs above the city turning the sky black with their smoke. I suspect Akenhaten and a group of his priests, donkeys laden with the treasure they might need, slipped out of the city.'

'Would they go north?' I asked. 'To Canaan?'

'That's possible. Akenhaten's mother, Queen Tiye, and all her kin from Akhmin were once Shemsu. They wandered from Canaan, across Sinai into Egypt. They made Egypt's Gods their own but they never forgot their own God, the God of Canaan, all-seeing, all-powerful, not to be worshipped in idols or statues. They regarded the Sun Disc, the Aten, as His symbol.' Pentju shrugged. 'You know this as well as I do.'

I did, but I was trying to make sense of what we had been told.

'I kept quiet,' Pentju sighed, 'because I know the truth. The creature at Avaris is an impostor, possibly one of the priests.'

'But still a danger to us?'

Pentju clapped me on the shoulder. 'Mahu, it was dangerous as soon as we became Children of the Kap, the Royal Nursery.' He picked up his water skin and walked away. I dozed for a while in the shadow of the crouched lion.

'Sir?'

I woke with a start, hand going to my knife. My captain of mercenaries stretched forward his right hand, caked with blood.

'We found a corpse, my lord, a priest, naked and trussed like a chicken for the pot, throat slashed from ear to ear, his body concealed beneath a bramble bush between a clump of persea trees. One of my lord Meryre's entourage has identified him.

37

The assassin must have lured him there and killed him.' He lifted an eyebrow.

'And taken his robes,' I finished. 'One priest amongst many, eh, Captain?'

'Like flies on a turd, my lord.'

'And the assassin?' I asked.

'A gardener, a rose-tender from the inner garden. My lord, General Rahmose was wearing your cloak, the striped one.'

'I know he was wearing my cloak, Captain, and it is one which is eye-catching, a gift from a friend. But,' I got to my feet and clapped the man on the shoulder, 'we'll have to wait and see if the hunter returns for a second try.'

I wanted to confront Ay, Meryre and the rest, but hot temper is ill suited to the search for the truth, so I went to my own quarters. The young Prince was already in the House of Adoration, a small suite of chambers I had set aside for him. I checked the windows and doors, as I always did, ensuring that, despite the heat, they were shuttered and closed. Every entrance was guarded by at least three mercenaries, with the strictest instructions that they were to allow no one in except myself, Djarka or Sobeck, and that they were never to leave unless two others were on guard. I handed my own dagger to the sentries and went through into the antechamber, which smelt of cassia and frankincense. In the small bedchamber beyond, Tutankhamun was already lying beneath the sheets on his bed. The headrest, a brilliant blue and gold, glinted in the lamplight, the post at each end carved in the shape of Bes the Dwarf God, so beloved of children. Between the posts, at both top and bottom, a line of Uraei, spitting cobras, the protectors of Egypt's rulers. I pushed aside the linen hangings, and the little boy pulled himself up, face crumpled with sleep, his wide dark eyes making him seem like a little owl awakening in its nest.

'Uncle Mahu!'

'I have come to check the oil lamps, Your Highness.'

'I am afraid.' The boy knelt on the bed, hands clasped together.

'You are not afraid.' I sat down beside him and felt his forehead. It was cool. 'You are telling me stories,' I smiled, 'to make me stay.' I picked up the goblet of green faience on the nearby table, sniffed and tasted the pure water. 'Djarka will come and sleep in your chamber,' I murmured. I pointed to the small gong hanging from one of the bedposts. 'What do you do if you are really frightened?'

Again that beautiful smile, and his little hands stole beneath the headrest and pulled out a small hammer, which he shook vigorously.

'I hit it, Uncle Mahu, I hit it hard!'

'Good.' I cupped his cheek in one hand. 'And remember, Your Highness,' I kissed him gently on the forehead, 'I am not your uncle.'

'Yes, Uncle Mahu. Have you come to tell me a story?'

'Not tonight.' I grinned. 'But perhaps in the morning I'll tell you about the brave deeds of Ahmose, your ancestor, who drove the Hyksos from Egypt with fire and sword.'

'I know all his deeds.'

'Do you now? And can you count? Do you remember your numbers? How many are in a shet?'

'One hundred, Uncle Mahu.' The boy clapped his hands.

'And how many shets in a kha?'

'Er . . .' His face was all screwed up. 'A kha is a thousand, so there must be ten.'

'And the God Shu? What is the hieroglyph for him?'

'A man with a plume on his head, or sometimes a man with the head of a lion.'

'Good! Good!' I whispered.

'Do you love me, Uncle Mahu?'

'Of course I do. Why shouldn't I?'

'Ankhes . . .' Tutankhamun always stumbled over his half-sister's name, so he had taken to using the shortened form. 'Ankhes says you love nobody.'

I stared at the little boy dressed in his shift, head slightly to one side, waiting eagerly for my reply. I kissed him on the forehead.

'Sometimes, Your Highness, I find it difficult to love, but you are different.'

'Did you love my father?'

'Of course.'

'And my mother?'

I recalled the small, black-eyed Khiya, the Mitanni princess whom Nefertiti had nicknamed the Monkey.

'A great lady, Your Highness, and one I loved.'

'Ankhes says you do not speak with true voice.'

'That is so of everyone except yourself, Your Highness. Nevertheless, I swear that when I speak to you it will always be with true voice.'

Tutankhamun flung his arms round my neck.

'Ankhes,' he whispered in my ear, 'does say you are the best of all.'

'The best of what, Your Highness?'

'The best amongst the hyaenas!' he whispered.

I felt cold, and slowly withdrew. The little fellow smiled up at me, face eager for my reply. His innocence disturbed me. I stared around. I had done my best to make the chamber comfortable. The walls had been washed and repainted with country scenes: a fowler out with his nets, birds and insects, including a locust of pinkish-yellow hue resting on a light papyrus stem. Above this, birds flew with widespread gorgeous wings against a dark green sky. A dove with bulging throat cooed over a golden nest containing a silver egg. Next to it, a group of pelicans, father, mother and brood of young, advanced unknowing towards the fowler's net. I felt a surge of depression. I had tried to make this chamber pleasant for the boy, with its countless niches for oil lamps in coloured glass which would glow all night. Nevertheless, the sight of those pelicans advancing unsuspecting towards the net held by the fowler, with his unshaven face and red-ochre skin, now seemed sinister. I recalled the assassin.

'Go to sleep, little one,' I whispered. I made the boy lie down and pulled up the sheets.

'Will you tell me a story?' Tutankhamun asked sleepily. 'Ankhes says you are a hunter, the Striped Hyaena.'

A shiver, as if some evil spirit crawled over my shoulder, made me start. I gently pressed his hand.

'Is that what she calls me, Your Highness, the Striped Hyaena?'

'Of course, Uncle Mahu, because of your cloak.'

I recalled Rahmose all a-sweat, the kohl rings round his eyes

running in dark rivulets, my cloak about him, striding across
the courtyard, the assassin streaking like a flame to kill him.
Tutankhamun was asking me more questions, but I gently
chided him and began to hum a song Djarka had taught me, a
lullaby shepherds would sing to their flocks.

I waited until the boy was asleep, then left looking for Djarka
and Sobeck. They were sitting with our men in a nearby courtyard. A Nubian mercenary was entertaining them, dancing to
the eerie sound of the flute and tambourine, arms moving rhythmically, body swaying in fluttering steps. He was dressed in a
loincloth beneath a thin linen robe. In the light from the torches
he too looked threatening, with his cropped head, huge earrings,
necklace and beads, a leopard skin hanging about his arms: a
spirit of the night dancing round the pools of light! The shadows
fluttered as if the ghosts of the dead had come back to mimic
the actions of the dancer. I felt uneasy, and sharply asked Sobeck
and Djarka to accompany me back to the House of Adoration.
My own chamber lay next to the Prince's; its windows were
unshuttered to allow in the fragrance of the gardens, braziers
and oil lamps glowed warmly against the cold night air. Djarka
scrutinised the wine jug and filled three goblets, a sweet-tasting
white wine from the imperial vineyards to the north.

'You have eaten, my lord?' He squatted next to Sobeck. I
leaned back against the cushions.

'My belly is full because my heart aches.'

'Poetry?' Sobeck teased.

'The truth,' I replied. I told them what had happened in the
council chamber; the threats posed by the usurper, now crowing
like a cock on his dunghill at Avaris. As I spoke, I watched
Sobeck. He lived closer to the crocodile pool than I; he was
often the first to pick up rumours and gossip. Yet he too was
surprised. He sat, face tight, eyes narrowed, whistling under his
breath as he shook his head at the news.

'Could it be Akenhaten?' he demanded.

'What do you think?' I turned to Djarka.

Perhaps it was talking to the young Prince, feeling his soft
cheek, yet I noticed that evening how my friend, my servant,
had aged. Furrows marked his mouth, his eyes were tired, there
was an ashy tinge to his night-black hair. Djarka had not

41

forgotten. He had never truly reconciled himself to the death of his beloved a few years earlier.

'Djarka, you are of the Shemsu? Those who wander the desert.'

'As is Ay.' Djarka smiled. 'As was his sister, Great Queen Tiye. All those who come from the town of Akhmin were once wanderers from Canaan.'

'And my question . . .'

'I know your question, master.' Djarka's voice was sardonic. 'Did Akenhaten go out into the desert to meet these people? Did they spirit him away?'

'And the treasure?'

'I certainly remember the priests, Khufu and Djoser.' Djarka sipped at his wine. 'And the other chapel priests. They were fanatics, true servants of Aten. They may have taken the treasure and followed their master.'

'But why?' Sobeck asked. 'Why leave the power and the glory of Egypt for some village in Canaan? It's more likely Akenhaten became a recluse, or his own priests murdered him!'

'And you have heard nothing about this impostor?' I asked.

'I am a Lord of the Darkness,' Sobeck retorted. 'My kingdom is not your kingdom, Mahu. However, I drink your wine – so don't distrust me, Baboon of the South. I stand and fall with you. I knew nothing of this! So, what will happen now?'

I told them what I had suggested. Djarka and Sobeck objected, remonstrating angrily.

'A foolish move,' Djarka snapped. 'If you go north you'll be killed!'

'If we stay here and dither,' I objected, 'the same will happen. We haven't the wealth or troops to fight a war in the north, or against Thebes or against any other enemy which may emerge.'

'No, no.' Djarka lifted his hand. 'I agree you must go north, but go with Meryre. This impostor and his army must be linked to the Atenists. If Meryre goes first, he may well spend the time plotting your death. Insist that you go with him, that you too are protected by the power of the Aten. Stay close to him, as a friend. Act as if he is your ally rather than your enemy. If you go in the company of a high priest, your life too is sacred.'

'Do that,' Sobeck offered, 'and I will go with you. What about the young Prince?'

'He'll be safe,' Djarka declared. 'I'll see to that. If there's one person who keeps the Royal Circle united against all enemies it's Prince Tutankhamun, so the sooner he is crowned the better.' He paused as the captain of my guard came in, knelt and nosed the ground before me.

'The assassin, my lord. We searched his quarters.' He straightened up and stretched out his hand. I took the small yet brilliant ruby glowing like a fire. 'That's all we found.'

I dismissed the captain. Sobeck plucked the ruby from my hand and held it up against the light.

'I have heard of similar stones,' he murmured, 'being on sale in Eastern Thebes.'

'The Shabtis of Akenhaten?' I asked.

'Can I have this?' Sobeck grinned.

'It's yours.'

'I have told you before,' Sobeck continued, 'the narrow streets and alleyways of Eastern Thebes have nothing to do with the dreams of a God. What you must ask yourself, my dear Mahu, is who told the assassin that you were wearing a striped robe?' He turned and grinned. 'Oh, by the way, the door the assassin tried to escape through, unlike many in this palace, was jammed shut by a thick wedge of wood.'

The frieze on my wine cup, a Libyan being chased by Saluki hounds, seemed to come to life in the flickering light of the oil lamps.

'A gardener,' I mused, 'who owns a precious ruby, kills a priest to take his place. How do you think he inveigled that priest away from the rest?'

'Some of the shaven heads have exotic tastes,' Sobeck retorted. 'But whoever bought him – I mean the gardener – was quite prepared to sacrifice him. I suspect,' Sobeck popped the ruby into his leather pouch, 'that given time, the real assassin would have had the gardener disposed of and the ruby taken back. I mean, once the wearer of the striped robe was killed.'

'Who,' Djarka asked, 'is this real assassin?'

'Ankhesenamun calls me the Striped Hyaena,' I whispered.

'Beware of the woman from outside,' Sobeck intoned a maxim

of the scribe Ani, 'who is not known in the city. She is a water deep and boundless.' He wagged a finger in my face. 'Beware of such a woman.'

'Many thanks for the advice. Oh, by the way, Djarka, the painting of the pelicans in the House of Adoration? Have it changed tomorrow; remove the scene of the fowler and his net.'

mesu-hesui
(Ancient Egyptian for 'terror-stricken beings')

Chapter 3

I went along a painted corridor deep into the palace. The windows on either side overlooked the gardens, but these had been ill-tended and the stench of corrupt vegetation blended with the fragrance of the flowers. Nakhtimin's mercenaries stood on guard in alcoves and recesses. From the courtyard below I heard a servant recite the curse against crocodiles; these river beasts sometimes followed the irrigation canals into the palace, where they'd lurk amongst the bushes and shrubbery. The chilling, ominous prayer wafted up:

> *Stop crocodile, son of Seth!*
> *Do not swim with your tail,*
> *Nor move your legs any more,*
> *May the well of water become a well of fire before you*
> *Stop crocodile, son of Seth.*

I crossed a courtyard blazing with light; guards stood aside, copper-plated doors swung open. I entered the women's quarters, at the centre of which lay Ankhesenamun's chambers, with their red and yellow lotus pillars, floors of polished tile and walls decorated with the most vivid paintings. Flunkies, servants and officials lounged about: the Director of Her Highness' Nail-Doers, Chief of the Scented Oils and Perfumes, Holder of the Imperial Sandals, Keeper of the Jewellery, Master of the Cloths, all eunuchs with the bulging belly and breasts of pregnant women. They gossiped and moved around in a swirl of perfume, all officious, pretending to be busy. A cat chased a black and white monkey, which scampered up a pillar screeching in annoyance. A blind harpist, dead-eyed, plucked at strings. Dancing girls and acrobats in beaded, fringed loincloths, bodies coated in perfumed sweat, hair piled high in bound cord, were trying to clear a space to practise their skill, whilst flirting with the burly mercenary officers.

I went through more doorways, their lintels and pillars carved with lacework inscriptions, into a small room which served as a chapel where a group of shaven-headed priests garbed in panther skins lit bowls of incense before a statue of the Pharaoh Tuthmosis. This was once the heart of the Great Palace of Amenhotep the Magnificent, Ankhesenamun's grandfather, who loved to collect pottery and vases of cobalt blue and delighted in covering the walls with the symbol of every deity of Egypt: the goose of Amun, the bull of Ptah, the goat of Osiris, the ram of Khnum. The air was sweet from fat drenched in perfume and the scent of countless flower baskets, as well as the incense smoke from the small thuribles glowing in the corners. A chamberlain stopped me outside the Painted Chamber. He knocked and led me in. I flinched at the heady perfume whilst my bare feet felt the lapis lazuli dust strewn on the floor. Caskets and coffers lay about, lids open. Lamps and candles glowed, glittering on the robes piled in a heap. A pet goose screeched whilst a monkey squatting on a table devoured a plum, its juices dribbling down on to the floor. On either side of the curtain were two black wooden busts of Akenhaten, their eyes of jasper peering sightlessly into the darkness, a reminder of his presence which caused a shift amongst the shadows in my soul. The carved face, in the light of the oil lamps glowing beneath, exuded an eerie life of its own, as if still possessed by the power of that mysterious Pharaoh.

The chamberlain bowed towards the busts, then pulled the curtains aside. Ankhesenamun was sitting on a high stool circled by oil lamps. She was naked except for a loincloth, a see-through veil thrown across her shoulders. She was being anointed on her face and head by her friend and constant companion Amedeta, who served as her principal lady-in-waiting.

In looks, they were almost similar. Amedeta was slightly older, yet she had the same sensuous face, sloe eyes and pretty mouth. She was dressed in a diaphanous robe and floated around Ankhesenamun grasping an unguent jar carved in the shape of two chickens trussed for sacrifice. She moved silently, body swaying beneath the robe, the heavy tresses of her perfumed wig almost shrouding her face, around her throat a silver necklace. She and Ankhesenamun were murmuring to each other. As I approached, they began to recite a love poem aloud, beautiful lilting voices mouthing the words together:

I am your most beloved sister.
I am to you as the field in which I have grown flowers,
All kinds of fragrant herbs flourish there.
Delightful water channels cool me and you,
A lovely place to walk with your hand in mine.
Our voices thrilling, our hearts full of pleasure to be
walking together.
I lived by being close to see you,
To see you again is better to me than meat and drink.

When they had finished the poem, Amedeta continued her anointing whilst Ankhesenamun stared out through the window as if listening to the sounds of the night. I heard the rattle of a chain and glanced to the corner; it was only her trained cheetah stirring in its sleep. I coughed and stepped forward. Ankhesenamun turned. I had to remind myself that she was only a girl between fourteen and fifteen summers, for in the oil lamp she looked a beautiful, sensuous woman with those heavy-lidded eyes, her lips parted.

'Why, Mahu, Baboon of the South! Why are you here so late at night?'

Amedeta had moved so her back was towards me. I could tell she was laughing quietly to herself.

'And how is His Majesty?'

'He sleeps.'

'Why *are* you here, Baboon of the South?'

'I prefer that title, Your Highness, to the Striped Hyaena.'

Ankhesenamun laughed and whispered to Amedeta. The lady-in-waiting turned, smiling seductively over her shoulder at me. She put down the oil jar and slipped from the chamber.

'Well, Mahu, why are you truly here?'

'The Shabtis of Akenhaten.'

'What Shabtis?'

'Do not act the innocent with me. You know what happened.'

'I know Rahmose was killed and his assassin now hangs from the Wall of Death.'

'Rahmose was wearing my cloak.'

'So?'

'I was the intended victim.'

'You don't really believe that?'

Ankhesenamun got off the stool and came towards me. She pulled the gauze-like shawl tighter about her, which served only to emphasise her full breasts, their nipples painted in gold.

'Would you like me to dance for you, Uncle Mahu?' She stretched out her arm, clicking her fingers, and moved rhythmically, languorously, little steps, hips swaying.

'I do not want you to dance for me, Your Highness, but to answer my questions.'

She paused, hands coyly together.

'Mahu, you are so dull.'

'I'm alive. I could have been dead. I want to know how a gardener owned a precious ruby. How a gardener attacked a man wearing a striped cloak. You knew what I was wearing this morning.'

'Oh, Mahu, others know you wear it!'

'How many others give gardeners beautiful rubies?'

'Oh no.' Ankhesenamun flounced down on a high-backed chair. 'I know you wear a striped robe. So according to you I seduced the gardener, gave him a ruby from my casket and told him to kill you. However, he made a mistake and murdered Rahmose instead. He then tried to flee, but the door he tried was wedged fast shut and the guards killed him. He was a gardener in the royal household, so someone here must have hired him.'

'Your Highness is very knowledgeable.'

'I am knowledgeable because you are right. I did arrange it. The gardener,' she pouted, 'well, he was a friend and has done similar tasks before.' She played with a sphinx armlet of gold inlaid with lapis lazuli, cornelian and turquoise, and then, as if bored by that, picked from a nearby table an ebonite fan edged with gold and shook it vigorously to cool her face.

'I am not a child, Mahu. I have been married to my father. I have given birth to one child who died. I am surrounded by enemies and so, like you, I bite before I am bitten. Why not ask me outright and I'll reply?'

She rose and went through the curtains behind me, I heard her pull across the bolts on the door. She walked back, no longer seductive and languorous, but businesslike, pacing up and down, twisting the ring on her finger.

'I heard the news from the Delta about the impostor who has appeared.'

'You are certain he is an impostor?' I asked.

'I am sure. Well,' she shrugged, 'I think so. But leave that for a while.' She turned to face me squarely. 'I had Rahmose killed because I believe those sanctimonious hypocrites Meryre, Tuthmosis and the rest of the devout are much more dangerous than you, or even Grandfather, think. If they are not killed, they'll certainly kill you.'

'You have proof of this?'

'The gardener,' she raised her hand, 'I told him exactly what to do, which door would be left open, but he was becoming too arrogant. I placed the wedge beneath the door. He paid the price for his insolence.'

'But you said you had used him before?'

'Sobeck must have told you how there are other precious rubies for sale in the markets in Eastern Thebes.'

'I am sure there are.'

Ankhesenamun sat down on a chair. 'Mahu, I am thirsty. Pour us each a goblet of Carian wine and come and sit close to me.' She gestured to a footstool. 'We are allies, not enemies. Father trusted you, that's why he made you guardian of his son.'

I filled the goblets, came back and sat on the footstool, staring up. You are Nefertiti's daughter, I thought, if not in looks then certainly in soul. As if she could read my mind, Ankhesenamun tweaked the end of my nose, a favourite gesture of her mother.

'I thought you'd come, Mahu. You've been back in Thebes

only a few months. I could not search you out but had to wait for you to approach me. So, I shall tell you the truth.' She grinned. 'Or at least part of the truth. I am with you and the Prince, not with my grandfather. He nurses ambitions, you know, Mahu.' She chuckled at my look of puzzlement. 'As long as Tutankhamun lives,' she whispered, 'Ay, Horemheb and all the rest of the hyaenas are kept in check. But if my half-brother dies, to whom does the double crown go?'

'You could rule as Queen,' I replied. 'It would not be the first time.'

'But who would support me, Mahu? Grandfather? Horemheb?'

'Hatchesphut ruled alone.'

'History!' Ankhesenamun snapped. 'And she married her half-brother so there was always a male heir. Between me and the darkness, Mahu, there's nothing.'

'So, Ay dreams of becoming Pharaoh?' I laughed. 'It's not inconceivable.'

'But so do others, Mahu! Horemheb claims to be a royal bastard, of the blood of Amenhotep the Magnificent. And why stop there? What about General Rameses? Or even Huy, Maya . . . ?'

'No,' I replied, shaking my head.

'Or even Meryre? That's why they are all united against this usurper. Enough contestants for the crown imperial reside at court without pretenders in the north.'

'Meryre?' I scoffed.

'He sees himself as High Priest of the Aten, the spiritual successor of my father, but he is corrupt and sanctimonious.' She leaned closer, her lips only a few inches from my cheek. 'Did you know our High Priest invites me to his supper banquets? In his cups he admitted he would love to see me and Amedeta couple together on a bed. A vile man, Mahu, of bounding ambition, without the talent to match. This trouble in the Delta, I suspect Meryre has a hand in it, whatever he says! In his cups he is silly and clucks like a chicken. But sober, Meryre is as dangerous and as threatening as the rest. What if, Mahu,' she drew back, 'Meryre and the Atenists use this usurper to sweep the board clean of all of you, Horemheb, Rameses and the other Children of the Kap? How long do you think little

Tutankhamun will survive, or myself?' She smiled thinly. 'Though Meryre has ambitions in that quarter: marriage to me when he proclaims himself Pharaoh of Egypt.'

'No.' I shook my head in disbelief. 'I have spies in Eastern and Western Thebes; Sobeck and Djarka sift the gossip like wheat from chaff.'

'Do you think Meryre is going to tell anyone?' Ankhesenamun laughed. 'Do you know the whereabouts of all my father's treasures?' She rose and walked across the room, keeping her back to me as she took off the shawl and donned a sleeveless shift. Then, rewrapping the shawl, she came back and sipped from her wine cup.

'How do you know all this, Highness?'

'Because Meryre thinks I'm his ally.'

'And why should he think that?'

'Because I told him that the Shabtis of Akenhaten are a sect of assassins controlled by you.'

'What?' I moved so violently the wine in my cup slopped over. The cheetah scrambled to his feet but Ankhesenamun turned and cooed softly in his direction. The great cat stretched, amber eyes glowing at me, before sprawling back on the floor.

'Listen to me, listen to me,' she urged. 'The Shabtis of Akenhaten do not exist. The gardener was seduced by Amedeta, who paid him to kill minor officials, supporters of Meryre's circle, Atenists who appeared to have forsaken the great vision.'

'One man!' I exclaimed.

'And why not?' Ankhesenamun laughed. 'You are Chief of Police, Mahu. There is murder and rapine in Thebes every day, whilst at night the city is as dangerous as a crocodile pool. I decided to strike at Meryre; the gardener was my weapon. At the same time I lulled Meryre's suspicions. He believes I am opposed to my grandfather and the Children of the Kap.'

'And what does he intend?'

'Eventually to seize power himself.'

'But why not confront him? Hand this information to your grandfather? Ay and the rest would tear him to pieces.'

'What proof, Mahu? Apart from hushed conversations. And how would I convince God's Father Ay, not to mention the rest, that I wasn't a part of Meryre's plot?'

'So why did you have Rahmose killed? Meryre will think that I am responsible.'

'Mahu, in his eyes you and the rest are already guilty. Rahmose was dangerous.'

'He was an old soldier suffering from fever.'

'He was dangerous to me, Mahu. God's Father Ay had singled him out.'

Ankhesenamun paused and closed her eyes.

'Rahmose, how can I put it, was beginning to have reservations about Meryre's ambitions.'

'Of course,' I whispered. 'And if he was suborned by Ay, Rahmose might tell God's Father what the Princess Ankhesenamun had been involved in.'

'Did I say just God's Father Ay?' She smiled, opening her eyes. 'Or me? No.' She shook her head. 'Rahmose was also being courted by his former friends Generals Horemheb and Rameses. They, too, have been busy on their own business.'

I put down the wine cup and placed my face in my hands. What Ankhesenamun had told me made sense. The Royal Circle was breaking apart; the only clasp was Tutankhamun. If he died there would be three factions: the generals, led by Horemheb and Rameses; the great nobles and officials, Ay, Huy, Maya and possibly myself; finally the Atenists, led by Meryre. Each would try and suborn the others. Alliances would be fluid as people changed groups or decided to jump from one camp to another. Nothing was distinct. Horemheb and Rameses had the Memphis regiments, but Ay had Nakhtimin's troops and the mercenaries around Thebes. Which way would Huy and Maya go? Not to mention Pentju and Sobeck? The latter controlled the gangs of Thebes and would be useful in any attempted coup.

'So the Shabtis are a figment of your imagination?'

'Yes. I portrayed them as fanatics deeply loyal to my father's memory, acting on their own or controlled by one of the factions in the Royal Circle. I promised Meryre that I would discover if anyone else was involved.' She blinked prettily. 'Apart from you.'

'And what else have you offered?' I demanded.

'That you will eventually surrender the Prince into his care.' Ankhesenamun tapped me on the cheek. 'Don't be foolish,

Mahu, the only thing I have offered is myself. Meryre nearly choked in his excitement.'

'And now the Shabtis will disappear?'

'Naturally. I've caused enough chaos. The gardener served his purpose. Meryre believes I am estranged from God's Father Ay and looking for other allies.'

'Has he mentioned anything about the Usurper in the Delta?'

She shook her head. 'Only hints. Once, in his cups, Meryre mused on what would happen if my father returned, but that's as much as he said. Now, Mahu, you are going to ask why I am telling you this. I have heard the decision of the Royal Circle. You and Meryre are to be sent north to negotiate.'

'Who told you that?'

'Now, Mahu, I only promised to tell you part of the truth. I've shared my little secret so that you will be safe. I'm warning you. Now you know some of what I know, you'll be wary of Meryre. Be vigilant; you must do whatever you have to.'

'Of course,' I whispered. 'If something happens to me, Tutankhamun becomes more vulnerable, and the more vulnerable he becomes . . .'

Ankhesenamun pressed her fingers against my forehead. 'You and I, Mahu, are closely linked to my half-brother. You are the one man my father trusted, even when his brain became fevered and his wits wandered. He entrusted Tutankhamun to you, and in doing so, entrusted me. Of all the hyaenas you are the most loyal. You have no ambition.' She took her hand away and laughed. 'Or at least, I think you don't.'

'How can you be so sure,' I demanded, 'that the Usurper is a liar?'

'I could say I know because I know.' She paused and shivered slightly in the breeze seeping through the window. 'I hate the darkness, Mahu. My father used to sit in the dark; he would glower at me and my sister, Meritaten. He would often challenge us: could he trust us? We'd reply that we were his daughters and his wives, but he'd shake his head. Sometimes he would shout abuse or just sit cradling a wine cup, muttering under his breath. Meritaten was weak, often terrified and deeply disgusted that she was her father's own wife.' She picked up my wine cup and thrust it back into my hands. 'Eventually, I was banished from my father's presence; only Meritaten remained, then Mother came back. After Akenhaten disappeared and Nefertiti had proclaimed herself his co-regent, Meritaten confessed . . . I don't know whether she told the truth . . .' Ankhesenamun's eyes held mine. 'Meritaten confessed,' she whispered, 'that Akenhaten had not disappeared! He was murdered by our mother, and his body still lies concealed in the City of the Aten.'

She clucked under her tongue and the cheetah padded across and crouched by her. Ankhesenamun gently scratched between its ears, and the cat purred deeply in its throat.

'You are surprised, Mahu?'

'Not that Akenhaten was murdered,' I responded, 'but that Nefertiti was responsible.'

'Their love had turned to hate.'

I pulled a face. 'I find that difficult to accept. How did Meritaten know all this?'

'Because Nefertiti told her.'

'But she produced no proof?'

'None at all.'

'And did she say where the body was buried?'

'Nefertiti claimed that those mercenaries, the same ones you destroyed when you ousted her from power, prepared the body and hid it away in a cave under the eastern cliffs.'

I stared at the cat, eyes mere slits, purring with pleasure. During his stay at the City of the Aten, Akenhaten had ordered tombs to be dug in the limestone cliffs which overlooked the city. One such sepulchre had been prepared for him but never finished. Now these caves and caverns held a host of caskets and coffers of those who had died at Akenhaten's court: some by natural causes, others hastily buried when the great pestilence had struck.

'I often asked Meritaten,' Ankhesenamun continued, 'if my mother was lying. Meritaten was easy to frighten; I wonder if my mother was quietly threatening her with a similar fate if she didn't co-operate.'

'But Nefertiti never told you?'

I started as the beaded curtains shifted in the light breeze.

'Never once.' Ankhesenamun rubbed her hands together, and leaning over gently, whispered at the cheetah, caressing the side of its face. The cat yawned, stretched and padded back to its corner. Ankhesenamun rose to her feet clasping her wine cup and moved across to the window.

'So, Mahu, we are united in this!' She glanced over her shoulder. 'It is foolish of you to go north with Meryre, though I know the reason. You must take care. Think carefully before you trust yourself to that treacherous snake and whatever he has plotted.' She turned away, a sign that the meeting was over. I rose, bowed and left.

Amedeta was waiting in the antechamber, sitting on a divan, head resting back against the wall. I wondered how much she knew and how much she could be trusted. She glanced at me from under her eyelids and raised a hand slowly in mock salutation. I responded and returned to my own quarters. Djarka was already in the House of Adoration. Sobeck had returned to the courtyard, where one of the mercenaries was now singing a low mournful song. I retired to my chamber.

For a while I sat in my chair, going over the events of the day. That was how it was in the Malkata Palace at that time. Time would travel smoothly, events would pass, one day into the next, week after week, month after month, like the river flowing between the banks, until something happened to shatter the serenity, to make the hairs on the nape of your neck curl as you realised events were taking a more dangerous twist. So it was then. The Royal Circle, which had remained united in a state of self-preservation after Nefertiti's death, was now breaking up. Ankhesenamun was dabbling and I had to decide whether she was doing it of her own accord or at her grandfather's bidding. The real reason she had confided in me was not because of any trust – at the court of the Malkata Palace trust was as rare as water in the Red Lands – but more because I was the Prince's protector and guardian. As Tutankhamun matured, my importance would grow. I would become his eyes and ears; after all, the bonds fashioned in childhood are often the strongest.

I dozed for a while, regretting slightly that I had given my word to join Meryre's embassy to the north. A servant came in and asked if I wanted something to eat. I replied that I didn't. I heard him clucking under his tongue, muttering about how the laundry woman had left a basket of laundry unpacked. I was so tired I ignored the remark until I abruptly remembered how, earlier that day, before the Royal Circle met, I'd seen two women unload clean linen from their basket.

'Leave it.' I whirled round, but the man was already busy with the linen. He stared up in astonishment.

'My lord, it's—' He stepped back, screaming with pain, dropping the linen on the floor, clutching his arm. I jumped up, grasped the conch horn where it hung from a hook on a post and blew a blast. The man staggered back and collapsed to the ground, still screaming. I moved carefully, and even as I did, the linen cloths on the floor shifted and one, two and then a third snake coiled out, long, slim and black with a yellow dash on their foreheads. I recognised them as the most dangerous of snakes: rock adders. One bite was fatal enough.

Outside echoed the sound of hurrying feet, and my captain of mercenaries appeared in the doorway. Sword drawn, he stared in disbelief. The servant now lay on the floor, feet jerking, body in convulsions. His hideous choking chilled the blood.

'Stand back,' I warned.

The mercenary captain saw the snakes creeping out from beneath the sheets. They posed no real danger, immediately sliding towards the warmth of the braziers. The servant was beyond help. White foam laced his lips; he gave one last convulsive cry and lay still.

'A spear!' I shouted.

The mercenary captain slid one along the floor. I picked it up, edged around the furniture towards him and threw myself out of the door. The mercenary captain followed, and taking off his cloak, stuffed it under the bottom of the door to seal the snakes in.

'My lord, you are well?'

'For a man supposed to be dead,' I wiped the sweat from my face, 'I am passably fine.'

'An accident?'

I gazed into his bloodshot eyes.

'One snake, Captain, perhaps! Three or four in a pile of laundry . . . don't be stupid!' I went and sat on a chair in the antechamber, and gestured towards the door. 'Leave that for a while, at least for an hour. When you open the door you'll find the snakes near the braziers or oil lamps. Used to the sun, they'll seek whatever heat there is. That chamber must be searched from ceiling to floor. I also want you to find out who brought the laundry basket up here.'

I sat waiting for the shaking to stop. Sobeck arrived. I told him what had happened and asked him to check the House of Adoration. He returned.

'All is well.' He pulled a stool towards me and sat down. 'An inauspicious day for you, my lord?'

The captain of the guard returned, and announced that two women had been seen carrying a laundry basket into my chamber.

'Didn't you search it?'

'We did,' the Captain protested. 'But the snakes were probably coiled at the bottom. When you lift a lid off a basket, master, and you see linen sheets, the idea of snakes never occurs to you.'

I bellowed at him not to be sarcastic and ordered him to arrest the two laundry women and bring them before me. Sobeck poured me some wine. A short while later two women, whom I recognised as serving in the royal quarters, were hustled up, their faces creased with sleep, terrified at the accusations levelled against them. The guards had not been gentle; one of the women already had a bloody lip. They nosed the ground before me, their cries and shrieks ringing through the chamber. I pressed a foot against each of their heads.

'Look up,' I ordered, withdrawing my foot.

Both women raised tear-streaked faces.

'The Captain has told you?'

Again shrieks and cries from the older one, but the younger, apparently her daughter, glared fiercely at me.

'We will die,' she protested, 'for something we did not do.'

I told her mother to shut up and turned back to her.

'Why, what *did* you do?'

'We were in the laundry room,' she gabbled. 'We were eating bread and drinking beer, our usual meal, our duties finished. A messenger came in. We thought it was one of the chamberlains. He said laundry had to be taken to your quarters and we were told to do it immediately. The basket was outside the door.'

'But you brought fresh sheets,' I countered, 'earlier today.'

'He said wine had been spilt, that we were to take the basket up immediately. So we did, it was searched by your guard and we left it in the chamber. We were puzzled because we looked at the bed and could not see any stains; it was as we left it earlier. My lord, we are just servants. We do what we are told.'

I studied both women closely and recognised their innocence. I drained the gold-embossed wine cup and thrust it into the young woman's hands.

'In future only take orders from someone you recognise – now go!'

I told the mercenary captain to clear the chamber and sat for a while with Sobeck.

'Before you ask,' he stretched out his legs, 'it could be anyone. That's the real danger here, Mahu. This is not like a battle where you know friend from foe.'

That night I slept in the Prince's chamber and awoke early to prepare for the great oath-taking in the Hall of Appearances. I shaved and washed carefully. I donned my finest robes of pure-white gauffered linen, bound round the middle with a blue and red-gold sash, collars of gold round my neck. I went and greeted the Prince, then walked along cavernous echoing passages and into the central courtyard with its soaring statues of Anubis and Horus. The rest of the Royal Circle with their retinues clustered at the foot of the palace steps. I had walked there alone, determined to show how the events of the night before had not frightened me. Of course, the news had spread. Each one came up to express his horror; to urge that the perpetrator of such an assault should be searched out and executed. I thanked them all grimly.

The High Priest Anen came down the steps, his acolytes, heads all shaven, dressed in their purest robes, almost hidden by the gusts of incense. We lined up in formal procession and climbed the palace steps, past the pillars brilliantly decorated with every known colour depicting inscriptions and paintings of long-dead Pharaohs, through the great bronze-plated doors and into the Hall of Appearances. Here the divine choirs were ready, singing a hymn to the Gods of Egypt. Afterwards we took the sacred oath: to serve our Prince loyally and win the munificence of the Gods for the well-being of Tomery, the Kingdom of the Two Lands.

Once we were in the council chamber, however, the mood changed. The gravity of the situation was brought home to us by Anen, who, instead of the introductory prayer, gave full vent to a litany of lamentations.

> *Wild beasts of the desert drink at the rivers of Egypt,*
> *The land is in mourning and woe,*
> *Things happen now which have never happened before!*
> *Men take up arms to battle because the land is in disorder.*
> *Each kills the other and hate reigns amongst the people of*
> *the towns.*
> *The gods turn away from us men,*
> *The country is in distress and misery.*

He paused and stared around the Royal Circle. My gaze never left Ay, his cunning face all concerned and anxious. I idly speculated whether the dirge was his idea or that of Horemheb and Rameses, who were nodding in agreement at every word. Anen continued:

> *Death is never idle.*
> *Men are growing poor and our women are barren.*
> *The people of the desert take the place of Egyptians.*
> *Our officials are slain.*
> *The food of Egypt has no taste.*
> *The children of the great are thrown into the street.*
> *The House of the King has no more revenues.*
> *We are marching to ruin.*
> *The great are hungry and in distress.*
> *The poor of the land have become rich whilst its owners*
> *have nothing left.*
> *He who once had not a yoke of oxen now owns herds.*
> *He who had not a loaf of bread now owns a barn,*
> *His granaries are filled with the goods of another.*
> *Even a bald man who never used pomade owns jars of*
> *scented oils.*

Anen paused once more. At any other time I would have guffawed with laughter, but Anen's harsh sermon was reminding the members of the Royal Circle that we faced revolution where the first would be last and the last first.

He who went on messages for others now has messengers in his service.
The ladies who rested in their husbands' beds now sleep on the ground.
Slaves are the mistresses and adorn their necks with gold and malachite,
Whilst noble ladies go hungry and prostitute themselves.
Butchers glut themselves on meat which they used to prepare for the ladies.
He who was once too poor to sleep with a woman Has nobles for his mistresses.
Laughter has perished.
Affliction runs through the land mingled with lamentations.

Anen knelt down. The scribes sitting in the middle of the circle had taken down every word, but once Anen had finished, Ay made a sign for them to cease their writing. I noticed how each of these scribes was a high-ranking member of Ay's retinue.

'Things are bad,' Maya drawled in a futile attempt to provoke laughter, 'but not that bad.'

'Aren't they!' Meryre shouted back. 'Yesterday evening General Rahmose was assassinated, and I understand,' he turned his black kohl-ringed eyes towards me, 'that a similar attempt was made on the lord Mahu, Chief of Police, Protector of our Prince.'

'True. We face disorder and revolution,' Ay murmured, 'but these dangers will pass.'

'Will the lord Mahu come with us to the Delta?' Meryre asked with a wave of his hand. 'Lord Mahu, your presence is vital to determine how this – how can I put it – new crisis is resolved.'

'I will accompany you,' I replied.

'Ah, yes.' Meryre plucked at his robes. 'But should I go?'

He let his words hang in the air. Huy clicked his tongue in annoyance.

'The Shabtis of Akenhaten,' Meryre continued, 'have carried out attacks on all those who once served in the City of the Aten. Now they strike higher: General Rahmose, Lord Mahu.'

'What do you want?' Horemheb's voice cut across the room. 'My lord Meryre, you know your presence is needed in the Delta. We all agreed to this yesterday. This usurper would never dream of attacking a high priest, particularly one of the Aten. Nor would they lift their hand,' Horemheb played with the ring on his finger, 'against the official Protector of our Prince. Your persons are sacred and safe. If any of us were sent on such an embassy we would be dealt with as traitors.'

'More to the point,' Rameses intervened, 'General Horemheb and I are needed here to raise whatever troops are necessary to deal with this usurper. The House of Silver requires the attention of Lord Maya, whilst it is essential that Lord Huy maintains rigour in the House of Envoys and tries to discover if this usurper is supported by other princes.'

'Of course,' Meryre intervened with a smirk, 'my lord Ay could accompany us.'

Ay just sat, hands on his thighs, staring across the council chamber.

'My lord,' Horemheb retorted, 'such a remark borders on insolence. Will you go or won't you?'

'On two conditions,' Meryre snapped.

'If you go,' Ay intervened, 'then, my lord, you should be gone within the week. We have spent enough time on this matter. I regret the attacks. General Rahmose's death has caused great grief and heartache. Once you are gone, we shall observe the official days of mourning. As for the assault on Lord Mahu, careful search will be made. So, my lord Meryre, what are the conditions?'

'First, that Prince Tutankhamun be removed from Thebes. The events of yesterday prove this city cannot be trusted. There are many here who hate the Aten and wage war against those who serve the One.'

'And where should he be removed to?' I asked.

'Back to the City of the Aten. He will be safe there.'

'But the city's dying,' Rameses snapped. 'Its houses are crumbling, its palaces deserted.'

'It's still safer,' Meryre insisted. 'Would you not agree, Lord Mahu? It can be approached from the Eastern Desert, but the terrain is difficult and controlled by sentries on the clifftops. The only other approach is by river, and that can easily be guarded.'

A general discussion broke out. I looked to Ay for guidance, but he gazed serenely back. That was God's Father! Ay was determined on confronting this usurper in the Delta; everything else would have to wait. He moved his head, glancing at me out of the corner of his eye, whilst his fingers played with the blue and gold pectoral glittering on his chest. That look was enough. Ay was prepared to co-operate with Meryre and he would probably advise me to do the same. The High Priest had been astute. Thebes *was* dangerous. Whatever Ankhesenamun said, only the Gods knew who the Shabtis of Akenhaten really were. The City of the Aten was easy to protect and Tutankhamun would be safer there.

'Will the Lady Ankhesenamun go with him?' I asked.

'My lord,' Meryre spread his hands, 'who accompanies the Prince is up to you, his official protector. I am simply saying the City of the Aten is safer.'

'And full of your supporters,' Rameses shouted.

Huy and Maya nodded in agreement.

'My supporters?' Meryre retorted. 'Those who support me support you as well, as I am sure those who support you support me. The Prince will be well looked after by Mahu's retinue. What are you implying, Lord Rameses? That some faction will seize the Prince and have him crowned? But Pharaoh can only be crowned either in Memphis, where you have your troops, or Thebes. The coronation regalia will remain here.'

'But the City of the Aten will be full,' Rameses insisted, 'of your supporters, those who follow the cult of the Aten.'

'As Thebes is full of our enemies,' Tutu retorted.

'And now we come to our second demand,' Meryre continued smoothly. 'My lord Tutu,' he gestured round, 'and other supporters of the Aten will remove themselves from Thebes. The assassination of General Rahmose has clearly demonstrated the dangers of staying here. I demand they be given the protection in the great fortress of Buhen.'

64

batiu
(Ancient Egyptian for 'red-haired fiends')

Chapter 4

'Steady, steady, keep on course!'

The pilot and captain of our imperial barge, *The Joy of Isis*, stood in the high prow above the gold carving of the Goddess Isis and carefully took the soundings as they guided us through the sandbanks, heading for mid-stream. The Nile was at the end of its inundation but was still fast and strong, whilst its concealed sandbanks were a danger to the most experienced sailor.

We had left Thebes early that morning, three days after the meeting of the Royal Circle. Ay insisted that speed was the order of the day, so the royal barges and their escort of marines had been quickly prepared. The sky was already scored with red. In the accompanying barge, *The Glory of Seth*, I could hear Meryre and his entourage singing their hymn to the Sun Disc, impervious to the shouts and calls of their own captain and pilot.

Sobeck and Djarka sat outside the cabin which stood amidships, a long, high chamber decorated inside and out with lozenge shapes of gold, blue, green and red. The huge mast soared above us, its red sails reefed. The oarsmen sat ready, but the craft was still in the hands of the captain, his pilot and the two helmsmen manning the great rudders on the jutting prow, which was carved in the snarling face of Sekhmet the Destroyer. I climbed on to the archers' platform and stared at the five great war barges full of marines and imperial guardsmen who would accompany us most of the way. Inside the cabin, Prince

Tutankhamun and Princess Ankhesenamun were resting; the latter had only been allowed to bring the lady Amedeta, whilst I considered it safer if Djarka alone looked after the Prince.

The river mist had now burned off. From behind us rose a cheer as the crews of the other barges realised they were free of the sandbanks. A strong, fine day. On either side of us stretched the rich black soil, and, beyond, the various shifting golds and greens of the ripening rye, oat and wheat fields. The gleaming white of the temples of Luxor and Karnak eventually disappeared. The captain left the pilot shouting at the steersmen to maintain the course set. The leading oarsman intoned a hymn to Hapi, the River God, 'Our delight is in him who guides us . . .'

The refrain was taken up by the men as the oars were lowered. Other hymns rose faintly from the accompanying barges. I climbed down, and Sobeck and Djarka followed me further up into the prow, where we could talk free of Ay's eavesdroppers. Djarka rolled out carpets, of bead matting but still better than the hard wood of the ship, and we ate our morning meal: light beer and yesterday's bread followed a pewter bowl of sliced fruit. Sobeck dipped his finger in the beer and carefully wrote four hieroglyphs, three birds and a sitting man, the word for 'beware'.

'Beware of what?' I teased.

Sobeck gestured at the cabin, then at *The Glory of Seth*.

'Beware of the Princess Ankhesenamun,' he murmured, 'as well as Meryre.'

I had informed him during our hasty preparations about what had happened at the Royal Circle, though we had never discussed it. Meryre's proposals had been finally accepted. We would journey upriver. Djarka would take the Prince and Princess into the City of the Aten, whilst Tutu and other members of Meryre's entourage would withdraw to Buhen, the great fortress which dominated Egypt's route south into the land of Kush. I would proceed, with Meryre, to the Delta.

'I am surprised,' Sobeck sipped from his beer, 'that God's Father Ay agreed to all of it.'

'My lord Ay had no choice, and neither do we,' I replied. 'Thebes is very dangerous, full of discontent. The Shabtis of Akenhaten do pose a threat to anyone linked with the past, though I must admit . . .'

'What?' Djarka demanded.

'I am confused,' I responded. 'Some of it I understand, some of it I don't. Meryre and myself will, I suppose, be protected. The City of the Aten is a secure place for the Prince. I can understand Meryre's entourage wanting somewhere in which they will feel safe whilst at the same time assuring us that there will be no danger to the Prince during his stay at the City of the Aten.'

'What is Meryre plotting?' Djarka demanded.

'Meryre doesn't concern me,' I replied. 'My lord Ay does. What if, let us say,' I dipped a finger into my own beer and drew a circle on the dry wood, 'the Royal Council is the rim of a wheel. The centre is Lord Ay.'

'And the spokes?' Djarka asked.

'The lady Ankhesenamun,' I murmured. 'What if the lady Ankhesenamun, on behalf of her grandfather, Ay, conspires to be the ally and friend of every faction in the Royal Circle?'

'Including Horemheb and Rameses?' Sobeck scoffed. 'Such officers would have little to do with her. She is the daughter of Nefertiti.'

'She's also the daughter of Pharaoh,' I retorted. 'They might not be interested in her but they could be interested in what she can offer. One day she will be Queen of Egypt and, if the Gods have their way, mother of Egypt's heir. I know she has made similar approaches to Meryre whilst at the same time contacting me.'

'So Ay controls his own granddaughter?' Djarka asked.

'Yes,' I agreed. 'Using her to find out what is happening in each camp.'

'But the murders?' Sobeck demanded.

'What if . . .' I paused. 'What if the Shabtis of Akenhaten are just a group of assassins, individuals like that gardener, controlled by Ankhesenamun and her grandfather? They use them to strike at those who, apparently, betrayed Akenhaten. They keep alive and vibrant the sense of danger, of imminent threat . . .'

'So General Rahmose's death was to frighten Meryre and the rest?'

'Possibly.' I clinked my goblet against Sobeck's. 'What if

69

Meryre is truly frightened? Ay draws him into discussion. He agrees that I will accompany him to this usurper's camp but offers him the fortress of Buhen as a place of sanctuary.'

'Well away,' Djarka agreed, 'from both the Delta and the troops of the usurper, and just as far from Thebes and the City of the Aten.'

'Yes, I can follow your reasoning, Baboon of the South,' Sobeck agreed. 'Ay has now neatly divided his enemies. Meryre is sent north, his supporters go south, whilst the Prince is moved out of harm's way. Yes, it possesses a certain twisted logic, though it's a dangerous game to play. If this usurper sweeps south, and Meryre's faction decide to support him, they occupy one of the most powerful fortresses in the kingdom, the gateway to the gold mines of Kush.'

'Ay is a gambler,' I replied. 'He will deal with one danger at a time. He first wants to strengthen his hand in Thebes, use this crisis to get rid of his enemies. Meryre to the north, Tutu to the south, even Generals Horemheb and Rameses are preparing to leave for Memphis.'

'So Ay remains in Thebes building up his power? But why, Mahu, should the Shabtis of Akenhaten – and it must have been them – launch an attack on you?'

'We know it was the Shabtis of the Akenhaten,' I replied. 'When the room was cleared of snakes we found two Aten scarabs lying on the floor – they'd been overlooked in the confusion. That made me reflect about the night of the attack. I was tired, sitting in my own chamber. I didn't ask that servant to come in to see if I needed food or to clear those piles of linen. So I made very careful enquiries. According to a chamberlain, the servant who was bitten by the snake claimed he'd been sent to my chamber; the fellow repeated the same story to my mercenaries who let him through. He actually told them how he had been summoned to clear certain cloths away as well as see if I needed anything to eat or drink.'

'So he was the intended victim?' Sobeck demanded.

'Yes, that attack was to show Meryre that the Shabtis of Akenhaten strike at anybody, not just members of his retinue. A carefully measured ruse to heighten fear, to keep the Royal Circle united, at least for a while, in the face of the common threat, which makes me think that Ay and his wily grand-daughter are behind all this.'

'If you've reached that conclusion,' Djarka murmured, 'then so will others.'

'I suppose they will. It's just a matter of who will move first. Who will succeed? Once this present threat is removed, things will become a little clearer.'

Our journey north continued uneventfully. We passed Denderah, the great turning on the Nile. At first nothing seemed wrong, out of place or amiss. The river traffic was busy with pleasure boats and fishing smacks. On the banks the peasants and farmers, rejoicing at the effects of the inundation, were preparing to sow another harvest. Yet every so often we saw plumes of black smoke, dark against the light blue sky, whilst the smell of burning mixed with the rich stench of Nile mud, fish and rotting vegetation. The marines I sent to investigate brought back reports of desert raiders on the eastern banks, whilst on the west, Libyan war parties had plundered unprotected, isolated communities. Sometimes these marauders were captured and their corpses impaled on stakes, fixed on the high cliffs above the river, black shadows against the sky. On one occasion we passed a sandbank where at least ten river pirates had been impaled by the mayor of the local city. The breakdown of law and order could also be glimpsed in the empty quaysides. Occasionally we'd go ashore, my standard carried before us displaying a leaping gazelle against a gold and blue background and, on the reverse, the white feather of Ma'at. We marched along silent streets into deserted market-places.

Elsewhere the effects of disruption were difficult to detect. The quaysides and docks of the great cities were busy. Barges unloaded aromatic gum, bark, cinnamon, gold, ivory, ebony, as well as precious wood from Canaan. When we returned to the river, we passed numerous barges carrying jars of wine, liquors, fruits, Lebanese cedar, oxen, cattle, and on one occasion even a herd of baby ibex. At Abydos, however, where the great mass of the Temple of Osins stretched above a dark forest of green palm trees, Governor Motep nosed the ground before me in the

71

precincts of the Temple of Min and whined about the growing incursions and lawlessness.

By the time we reached the City of the Aten I had learnt a lot. Egypt's great cities were prosperous, their quaysides and workshops busy as always; the carvers of stone and wood, the goldsmiths and merchants did flourishing trade. Nevertheless, any town which lacked troops or strong fortifications, any farmstead or village vulnerable to attack, lived under a constant danger from sand-dwellers, Libyan raiders or the host of river pirates who skulked in the lonely stretches of the Nile, seeking out the weak and vulnerable. Of course, news from the Delta had not helped matters, heightening the growing sense of panic, of confusion at what was really happening and what fresh dangers were emerging. Perhaps it was this that changed my mind when we reached our destination.

I stood by the taffrail and stared out at the City of the Aten, its white buildings dazzling in the late afternoon sun. The City of the Aten! I had visited this cove stretching up to the eastern cliffs when it was nothing but sand and shale. I had seen all the power of Egypt transform it into Akenhaten's Holy City, the place where God and Man met. I had witnessed all its glory, the power of Pharaoh and the splendour of Nefertiti. I had also mourned its decline, ravaged by plague as well as by murderous conspiracy and bloody intrigue. I stared across at its deserted quayside. The ghosts of all those I'd known, loved and hated came out to greet me. I stood there, ignoring all requests and questions, till the sun set and my body chilled. I stood and reflected on all I had seen and made my decision. We would not land there. I brushed aside Meryre's furious protests. He could land if he wanted to; the Prince and I would continue north to Memphis, the white-walled city.

At Memphis, Horemheb's principal staff officer, Colonel Nebamun, entertained us in the courtyard of his elegant two-storey house overlooking the river. He offered incense to Seth the Announcer of Battles and quickly came to the point, the question which had so infuriated my entourage.

'Why,' he asked, glancing up at the awning snapping under a strong breeze, 'didn't the Royal Circle at Thebes act more swiftly? More importantly, why have you brought

Tutankhamun and Princess Ankhesenamun into Memphis? Didn't the Royal Circle order them to be left in the City of the Aten?'

Sobeck and Djarka, not to mention Meryre, had made similar remonstrations, but on this matter I was adamant. I was wary of the lawlessness and my own darkest premonitions. I told Colonel Nebamun that the Royal Couple would be entrusted to him here in Memphis until the present crisis passed. Meryre sitting beside me clucked his tongue and shook his head, but lacked the authority to oppose me. Colonel Nebamun, resplendent in his gold collars and silver bees of bravery, did not object. I also promised that before I left Memphis I would issue formal letters accepting responsibility for what I had done. Nebamun sipped at his wine and nodded agreement. As for his questions about how the Royal Circle in Thebes had reacted to events in the Delta, I told him it was best if his commanding officer informed him personally when he arrived. Nebamun accepted the hint, quietly remarking that ever since he had heard the news, the city regiments had been put on a war footing and were ready to march.

'And the usurper?' I demanded. 'What strength does he have?'

Nebamun squinted up at the sun. 'We know he has taken the city of Avaris and is camped in the fields beyond. He has about a thousand chariots, two thousand footmen and a host of mercenaries.'

'Mercenaries?' I demanded.

'Libyans and Kushites, some sea people, but mostly Hittites.'

'Do you think the Hittite king is behind this pretender?'

'I have told you what I can, my lord,' Nebamun replied. 'I have used every spy I could. I have questioned merchants, traders, pedlars, but the enemy camp is closely guarded. They have dug a ditch around all sides with a high palisade. Every entrance is guarded and protected. Men who are regarded as spies face summary execution. They say a veritable wall of impaled corpses circle the camp. You can smell their stench before you see them.'

'What is the usurper waiting for?' Meryre demanded.

'More troops,' Nebamun declared. 'We also know he is sending raiding parties back across the Horus Road into Sinai.

73

He is robbing the mines of precious gold and silver, then using the plunder to pay troops and hire more.'

'Haven't you thought of infiltrating the camp?' I asked. 'Surely there are men here who would serve as mercenaries, or pretend to?'

Colonel Nebamun's close-set eyes studied me.

'My lord Mahu, I was a mere stripling when I served under your father, Colonel Seostiris, a cunning officer. I learnt my craft well. I hand-picked six men and dressed them as mercenaries and sent them north. I told them to join the usurper's army and send information back. I have neither seen nor heard from them since. According to a merchant, all recruits are closely interrogated. It's not an impossible task to discover that someone has served alongside the imperial regiments then ask him what he is doing there. I suspect,' he added bitterly, 'my men are dead. I'll send no more.'

He picked up a piece of lamb, richly coated in herb sauce, and chewed on it absent-mindedly.

'These spices,' he remarked, 'were brought by a merchant who also traded with the enemy. He had no choice. He said the usurper was well advised by Hittite officers and strict discipline is maintained in his camp. Any looting is prohibited, martial law has been imposed, merchants and traders go freely about their business, and anyone who breaks these decrees faces summary execution.'

As he stretched out for the wine jug, his hand trembled; Nebamun recognised the danger and so did I. This mysterious usurper was not the chief of some band of robbers or desert marauders. He was leading a highly organised army and was eager to curry favour with the cities and towns of the Delta. He was demonstrating that he was not there to rob and pillage but to claim back what he regarded as his own. Nebamun glanced at me sheepishly.

'Between here and the Delta, my lord, lie other garrisons. My loyalty is known. This city will be defended, the troops have a personal allegiance to General Horemheb.'

'What are you saying, Colonel? That officers in other cities cannot be trusted?'

'It's obvious.' Nebamun shrugged. 'Soon the invader will

74

march south. He'll issue decrees. Troops will be given a choice: either fight or go over.'

I thanked him for his advice and returned to my own quarters. Lady Ankhesenamun was loudly haranguing Djarka; when I arrived, she turned on me. 'I have been confined in a cabin,' she snapped. 'We were supposed to land at my father's city; now we are placed here, surrounded by smelly, sweaty soldiers!' She beat a tattoo on the table, her long nails rapping hard. Beside her crouched Tutankhamun, playing with his toy soldiers. Lady Amedeta turned her back on me as if eager to study the painting of a dancing heset girl, a vivid eye-catching picture.

'My lady, these smelly, sweaty soldiers,' I replied wearily, 'will give their lives for you. I trust Colonel Nebamun; he is a soldier of the old school. You and His Highness,' Prince Tutankhamun smiled up at me, 'will be protected by him as well as by Djarka and my mercenaries. These, too, will give their lives for you.'

She pouted and flounced, but I could tell from the laughter in her eyes that she was only acting. Ankhesenamun never cared where she was; she was probably intrigued to be in a place where General Horemheb and Rameses had their strength. She would exploit every opportunity to ferret out information, question, flirt and suborn, anything to increase her power and that of her grandfather. She sat down in the throne-like chair; Tutankhamun rose to stand beside her. She stroked his head gently, whispering endearments to him.

'And what will happen now?' Her head came up.

'I shall journey further north,' I replied. 'Send messages to the usurper that we wish to negotiate. You will remain here. In a few days Generals Horemheb and Rameses will arrive, bringing more troops from Thebes and the garrisons along the river.'

'And?'

'There will be a battle, my lady. We shall either win or lose.' I bit back my words. Little Tutankhamun was standing, solemn-faced and owl-eyed. 'Of course we will be victorious,' I added hastily and, bowing, left, cursing my own stupidity.

I sent Djarka to the Prince and asked Sobeck to join me on the flat-roofed terrace.

'It will be cooler there.' I smiled. 'And no one can hear.'

I took a wine jug and two cups. Sobeck followed me up the stairs. Nebamun had already erected a canopy; cushions were piled against the protective ledge which ran round the terrace's four sides.

'What are we going to do?' Sobeck demanded. 'What if Meryre is leading us into a trap?'

'I suspect he is. The further I travel north, the more I believe we are part of a great conspiracy. Meryre is behind this nonsense; I fear he is coming north to tell this usurper everything he knows. I am even beginning to wonder,' I slouched down on the cushions, 'whether the Shabtis of Akenhaten are his work.'

'So what do you suggest?' Sobeck dabbed at the sweat on his neck. 'Are we to go north to put our heads on the slaughter block?'

'What other choice do we have? I only wish I knew,' I filled both wine cups, 'what Meryre intends.'

Sobeck and I argued for most of the afternoon, talking too much whilst our drinking matched it. I went down to sleep and woke in the cool of the evening coated in sweat, the wine tasting bitter on my breath. I washed and changed, and went back on to the roof, watching the sun set, recalling those days I had spent with Akenhaten, when such an occasion was sacred and holy. From the courtyard below drifted the sound of sentries, the bark of a dog. Djarka came up to say the Prince was retiring. I crossly replied that I would soon be down.

'My lord, you are frightened?'

Djarka stood at the top of the steps, peering at me through the poor light.

'Do you remember, Djarka,' I came over, 'the night we killed those two assassins then hid their corpses?'

'How can I forget?' His voice caught in his throat. 'One of them was a woman I loved. We killed her and her father and buried their corpses between the walls of their house.' Tears filled his eyes. 'At night, when I am asleep, I have nightmares. I am back in that house, sitting in the cellar, and her ghost comes out, at first all sweet and coy, but,' he put his face in his hands, 'she's a ghost, Lord Mahu, a phantasm of the night. You are frightened now, aren't you, by the terrors of the day?'

'I am very frightened,' I agreed. 'As I was that night: fright-ened of being wrong, frightened of being hurt, wondering what is best to do.'

'And?'

'I don't know why I refused to leave the Prince and his sister at the City of the Aten.' I grasped my stomach. 'A feeling, an unspoken fear, a suspicion . . .'

'About whom?'

'I don't know,' I confessed. 'We have witnessed the devasta-tion along the Nile; a return to the City of the Aten is out of the question. As for going north, what seemed a good idea is, perhaps, not so clever. Sobeck and I could be going to our deaths.'

'But you are with Meryre.'

'I don't trust that self-righteous, mealy-mouthed hypocrite. He seems so eager to go north, he entertains no anxieties about what might happen. He could be quietly supporting this usurper; this mission could be a pretext to meet him so they can plot together.' I got to my feet. 'But if we don't go, we'll never discover the truth, whilst Horemheb and Rameses must be given time.'

The days passed. I turned the problem over and over, one poor night's sleep after another. Nightmares peopled by sinister images and forms crowded my dreams. My Ka seemed to spring out of my body to wander the haunted halls and fiery lakes of the underworld. One morning I woke suddenly in the ghostly light. I thought I heard my name called, yet my chamber was empty. I went to the Prince's apartments but all was well, the guards vigilant, so I decided to go up on to the roof terrace and watch the sunrise. I turned to the east. The sky was changing; already the light was picking up the pyramid tombs in the necropolis of Sakkara. I knelt down, eyes fixed on the sun disc, a golden orb surrounded by a fiery red.

Memories poured back of other sunrises, of crouching down with Akenhaten and Nefertiti to worship the glory of the dawn. Faces of long-dead companions and enemies rose to haunt me. A gentle, lilting song wafted up from the courtyard. I looked over the parapet. A young mercenary was singing a hymn to some unknown God; he sat sprawled with his back to the wall, mending a piece of harness. He should have been on guard, standing on the parapet wall overlooking the broad stretch of grass, trees and bushes which separated the house from the river bank. I was about to shout down when the breeze caught my face. Looking back, I ask again, bearing in mind that voice which seemed to wake me, do the dead come to warn you? As I glanced up, the morning mist shifted, like linen gauze being pulled back, to reveal a truly heart-stopping scene: war barges, black and low in the water, packed with men, were streaking silently towards the quayside. I couldn't make out their armour but caught the glint of their weapons. I counted five or six, all heavily laden.

'Nebamun's men?' I whispered. 'Marines coming to reinforce the house?'

Again the mist shifted. A black standard flew from one of the barges, inscribed with white hieroglyphs depicting 'HATT HANT US', the fiery furnace in the Ninth Hall of the Underworld where spirit souls of the enemies of Ra were burnt, hieroglyphs also used for the Hittites. Another standard was raised bearing the symbols of the Storm God the Hittites worshipped. I stood like a statue. Was I awake? Was I dreaming? I opened my mouth to shout, but the full enormity of what was happening kept me silent. Bargeloads of soldiers were nearing the quayside of Nebamun's house. They had come to kill, plunder and possibly seize or murder the Prince.

Heart in my throat, I raced back into the house. Sobeck heard my clatter on the stairs and burst into my chamber. I pointed to the far window, even as I found the conch horn. I blew hard but my spittle blocked it. I cleared my mouth and blew again, a long, wailing blast. Gasping for breath, I informed Sobeck of what was happening and told him to arouse the Colonel and everyone else. I hastened to the royal quarters. Djarka was already up; something must have alarmed him, for he was already arming himself. I told him to stay where he was and guard the Prince, and if affairs warranted it, to take him and Ankhesenamun and flee. Bleary-eyed mercenaries blundered into the chamber even as another conch horn wailed somewhere in the house and from the small barracks adjoining it. I screamed at the soldiers to arm and gather in the courtyard. Ankhesenamun, a robe about her, hair falling down like a black mist round her face, came in sleepy-eyed asking what was wrong. Amedeta, sensuous and as lovely as her mistress, slipped in behind, almost concealed by Ankhesenamun. I wondered, then, did they share the same bedchamber?

'What is the matter, Mahu?' Ankhesenamun pouted.

'You heard the alarm, my lady.'

'Mahu, are we under attack? I thought you said we would be safe here?'

'We will be,' I snarled, 'if you keep out of the way!'

I hurried down to the central courtyard. Nebamun and his officers were already there. The old colonel proved his worth. Sobeck had wondered if the man had been too often under the sun without his helmet, but Horemheb's trust in him was quickly verified. He shouted and snarled for silence and coolly ordered gates to be reinforced with beams and carts. Postern doors and windows were also to be protected and defended. He turned to his staff, quietly issuing a stream of orders. Archers, ordered by their officers to remain silent, were quickly led up the steps and hid behind the battlemented walls. In the court-yard beneath, further ranks of archers lined up, bows and quivers ready. Behind them file after file of Menfyt, foot soldiers in their red and white striped head-dresses, swords and shields ready, war clubs in their sashes.

'You raised the alarm?' Nebamun asked, as he stripped to his loincloth before putting on a linen gown and fastening over it a bronze and leather war kilt. I told him what I had seen. 'About five or six barges in all,' Nebamun mused, screwing up his eyes. 'About five hundred men,' he added. 'Possibly more. We have less than half of that.' He raised a hand. 'Ah well, my lord Mahu, if we survive we'll ask how they knew as well as how they got here.'

Meryre came into the courtyard huffing and puffing, podgy fingers clutching his robe, eyes lined with black kohl. He was wearing a silver medallion round his neck depicting the Sun Disc. He acted all surprised and agitated, but I wondered how much he knew. I glanced at the other members of his retinue. They, too, were wearing the Aten disc. Was that some sort of sign to the invaders? Were they under orders to spare anyone wearing the Sun Disc?

'What is the matter?' Meryre fanned his fat face.

'We are under attack, my lord,' I replied drily. 'We don't have to search out the usurper; he has come hunting for us!'

'You can stay and fight,' Nebamun offered.

'I am a high priest!'

'Then you had best go find a temple and pray, or you'll become a dead high priest.' Nebamun turned away and grasped my wrist. 'I want you to command the archers on the wall,' he continued, ignoring Meryre's angry splutter. 'My house fronts the river.'

I glanced over my shoulder. Meryre was already waddling away.

'Forget him.' Nebamun's fingers dug deep into my wrist. 'They must have come for the Prince. The sides and back of the house are sheer wall, though they may try and force windows and doors. If they've brought battering rams . . .' He pointed to the far wall. 'Some of that's granite, as is part of the house, but the rest is simply dried mud bricks under a coat of plaster. If they discover a weak spot they won't need to use the gate.' He gazed round even as his officers ordered the files of archers slightly forward, away from the foot soldiers. 'They'll invade here,' Nebamun declared. 'This will become a slaughter yard. I've also put men in the house. Already messengers, the fastest runners we have, have been dispatched to the barracks on the other side of the city. It's only a matter of time.'

Nebamun turned away to confer with his staff officers. Sobeck and I collected our weapons and joined the archers crouching on the parapet. I peered over. The ground between the wall and the river was cut by a pebble-dashed path, then a line of greenery with trees and bushes sloping down to the quayside. The enemy had already landed; their advance party were shadows moving amongst the trees. I crouched back, looking along our line of men. Most of the archers were Nubians, hair cropped and oiled, dressed in white padded loincloths, leather quivers beside them, dark feathered shafts peeking out. Each Nubian carried a bow and a curved sword. They remained silent and watchful. I thanked the Gods that they were veterans, men who would not lose their nerve when the fighting began.

Once again I peered over the wall. It was a stomach-churning sight. The enemy advance guard had already cleared the trees,

80

streaming up through the greenery towards the main gate. Anyone unfortunate enough to be in that area must have been killed silently, immediately. The front ranks of the enemy were Libyan archers, naked except for their leather phallus covers, cloaks of stiffened bull hide or giraffe skin around their shoulders, greasy hair tightly plaited and adorned with feathers or covered with the mask of some animal: panther, fox or leopard. They were a fearful sight, bearded faces daubed with war paint. Even more terrifying were the few Shardana warriors, mercenaries from the Great Green, in their leather tunics, strange horn helmets on their heads. They carried long stabbing swords and round bronze shields. Mitanni and Egyptian mercenaries followed next in striped head-cloths, carrying shield and spear: these were the men who would try and scale the walls once the archers had done their task. The Hittite officers were easily distinguishable, dressed in bronze-scale leather armour which fell beneath their knees, faces and the forepart of their heads shaven. They followed the Hittite fashion of allowing their hair to grow shoulder length. Each of these officers carried a standard, a pole with a disc, and above that a blade on which the severed heads of those they had killed were placed. Some of these were dried and shrivelled, others freshly severed, still dripped blood. The arrogant impunity of their surprise attack was astonishing, and Horemheb's warning came back to haunt me: how, during the seventeen years of Akenhaten's reign, he had not fielded one regiment or squadron of cavalry to defend our interests in Canaan. No wonder Egypt was regarded as weak and lax.

I crouched with the rest. We could hear the muffled noise of the enemy. The tension grew. I whispered to the standard-bearer, in charge of the archers, to prepare his men. I glanced down into the courtyard and the silent ranks of our troops. The foot soldiers were formed into an arc to protect the rear and the flanks; even household servants had been armed. I glanced back over the wall. Libyans carrying logs were approaching the gate. Others trotted behind grasping storming ladders, long poles with rungs on either side. They moved silently, still believing they had the surprise. The officer in charge of the archers glanced at me. I nodded. From the courtyard below came the war cry of

81

Egypt. Nebamun clashed his sword, once again shouting the war cry: 'Horus in the south!' Our archers rose to their feet, arrows notched.

'Loose!' The officer's yell was followed by a whirl of arrows. Our men chose their targets well: those carrying the battering rams and scaling ladders, as well as Hittite officers. The silence was riven by screams and shouts. The range was so close, our archers wreaked terrible damage. Attackers were flung back as shafts caught them in the neck, head and face. The enemy line broke, fleeing back to the sanctuary of the trees. Here they re-organised and under the whip of their officers renewed their attack, waves of men pouring up the grassy embankment, screaming their war cries. They advanced behind a range of shields and a screen of archers who kept up a hail of fire against the parapet wall. Now our men, standing or kneeling, became targets. Brightly coloured shafts found their targets; bodies tumbled from the walls or slid down nursing some hideous wound. The enemy were keen-eyed and skilled; our line of men began to thin.

The attackers now brought their battering rams up against the gates and walls; others placed their assault ladders in position and started to climb. Some of these were pushed away, but the flood of men was too great. The archer next to me fell. A Libyan dressed in a panther skin, face daubed and painted, great tattoos across his chest, scrambled over the wall. He slipped in a pool of blood, and I dashed his brains out with a war club even as our trumpets ordered us to withdraw.

We left the parapet, hurrying down across the courtyard and into the protection of Nebamun's ranks. We were hardly in position when the first line of the enemy troops cleared the wall. Most were brought down in a whirl of arrows, but the gate was being forced and eventually broke. The carts were pushed back, attackers climbing over them. More of the enemy now cleared the parapet. Their own archers were brought into play to protect a group of Canaanites who pulled away the carts and obstacles from the gates for a fresh flood of attackers. Nebamun, protected by his shield-bearer, shouted orders. Our archers loosed volley after volley, trying to stem the flood at the gates, but it was impossible. The courtyard in front of us was filling with the enemy; they used the carts, together with the shields, and even corpses, to shield themselves from our archers, as they edged closer and closer.

A blood-curdling scream echoed from the house. Nebamun gestured at me. I took some archers and a group of Nakhtu-aa and we entered the Hall of Audience. At least seven or eight of the enemy had flanked the house and broken through a window. They'd killed the meagre guard and were now trying to force the stairs. Dark, heavy shapes in their dyed animal skins, carrying sword and shield, they were being held back by Djarka and household servants armed with bows. Even Ankhesenamun was there, beautiful as Sekhmet the Destroyer, bow in hand, a quiver of arrows held by Amedeta. Three of the enemy were already down. We hurried across, even as the black shape raced in front of us. Nebamun's war dog had broken free from its chain. A ferocious mastiff, it tore down one of the attackers, jaws slashing his throat. We closed with the rest, hacking and cutting. I heard a shout and turned. A Libyan had slipped behind me, sword raised, face snarling. An arrow pierced him full in his throat, whilst another smacked into his chest. Djarka, bow in hand, smiled at me, Ankhesenamun behind him. To this day I never really knew who shouted my name or loosed that first arrow.

We cut the throats of the wounded enemy and tried to reboard the windows. Clouds of smoke billowed about; the attackers, eager for pillage, had also invaded the nearby mansion. Screams and yells carried faintly on the breeze, but there was nothing we could do to help. We hurried back. A fierce battle raged in the courtyard. The Egyptian ranks held, but a ferocious hand-to-hand combat had broken out. The Hittite's officers were leading a pointed wedge, desperate to break through to assault Nebamun and his staff and, after that, penetrate the house. The press was so thick that those in the rear ranks could only stand and watch. Now and again archers tried to loose but grew increasingly fearful of hitting their own men. Black plumes of smoke rose from the riverside.

I reached Nebamun just as the Hittite wedge finally broke through. A furious blood-spilling scramble ensued, hacking with knife, sword and club. The ground grew slippery underfoot. The Hittites were so furious, wild-eyed and reckless in their bravery,

I wondered if they had been drinking or were drugged. I did what I could, fearful yet more frightened of being a coward. One of Nebamun's staff officers collapsed beside me, almost dragging me down in his death throes. We began to push the Hittites back even as we heard the shrill trumpet blast and the cheers of our men. The assault slackened. The surviving Hittite soldiers were looking over their shoulders. The lines in front of us gave way. Nebamun shouted that his chariot squadrons had arrived. Of course, the ground outside the gates was too narrow and restricted to deploy them, but the troops they brought now harassed the enemy's rear. More importantly, the chariot squadron had also paused to fire the barges. The enemy's retreat was blocked and a bloody massacre now took place. No quarter was given. The killing was relentless. The courtyard swilled with blood, and in places the corpses were piled two or three high. Some of the enemy escaped across the walls only to be hunted down; a number even broke into the house, but they were caught, dragged out and executed.

At last the enemy threw down their weapons. There must have been about forty or fifty prisoners who were cruelly shoved and pushed into the centre whilst Nakhtu-aa combed the courtyard. The Egyptian casualties were dragged out and taken through the gate, where a makeshift hospital was set up under the trees. The enemy wounded had their throats cut; those still able to stand were hauled to their feet and pushed over to join the rest of the prisoners. Nebamun ordered a part of the courtyard in front of the house to be cleared. The regimental standards of the Horus and Ptah were brought out and placed beside a hastily built altar dedicated to Seth the Destroyer. The line of prisoners, arms bound behind their backs, were hustled up and forced to kneel. Nebamun grabbed each by the hair and, with his own war club, dashed their brains out. The ominous silence of the slaughter yard echoed with the moans of the captives, the exclamations of their escort and that hideous rushing sound as the war club smashed bone and brain.

Two Hittite officers had survived. They were not treated as the rest. Instead, Nebamun took them down into the cavernous cellar of his house. He ordered them to be hung by their wrists from the beams, and a fire lit beneath their bare feet. Sobeck and I and Nebamun's principal officers gathered round. We were joined by the Colonel's chief scribe, who understood the Hittite tongue.

The blood lust was still upon us. We nursed bruises and injuries, whilst the cries of our wounded were pitiful. The Hittites were brave, their strange parrot-like faces laced with bloody sweat. The cavern was lit by the glow from the fires. At first they tried to curb their screams as they jerked in agony. The smell of their burning flesh was sickening. Nebamun's interpreter kept up his questioning. Neither officer would answer, so Nebamun had the older one, who bore the insignia of office around his neck, cut down and blinded. The questioning continued. The Hittite who'd lost his sight, eyes gouged out by one of Nebamun's men, eventually lost consciousness. Nebamun ordered his throat to be cut and turned to the other, whose face was contorted in pain. The scribe kept up his questions like a priest gabbling his prayers. Now and again I would intervene. The Hittite knew a little Egyptian, but still refused to answer. At last Nebamun kicked away the pile of glowing charcoal beneath the prisoner's feet.

'Tell him,' he ordered the scribe, 'that if he answers our questions he will be given an honourable death. He will die like a soldier.'

The scribe repeated this. The Hittite looked as if he was about to refuse. Nebamun held up his dagger, pricking the prisoner's face just beneath his left eye.

'I know the Hittite customs,' he told the scribe. 'If he loses his sight he will never see his Storm God.'

The scribe translated. The Hittite's body fell slack. For a while he just swayed backwards and forwards, then he muttered something. The scribe smiled at Nebamun.

'He will talk,' he declared. 'In return for a goblet of wine and a warrior's death.'

metcha
(Ancient Egyptian for 'to destroy, to slay')

Chapter 5

A deep-bowled goblet of wine was brought for the Hittite. He sat with his back to the cellar wall, facing Nebamun and myself, who were flanked by officers. Behind us stood two Nubian archers, arrows notched to their bows. At first the Hittite sang softly to himself, head going backwards and forwards. I had met Hittites before in the mercenary corps, as well as those Akenhaten had garbed in women's clothes and called his Orchestra of the Sun. The captive was a young man probably not yet twenty years, a blue tattoo on his right cheek. The scribe who writes these memoirs asks me why I recall such things. It's because they are pictures in my mind. I have to call up the smell, the taste, and once I do, everything else comes back. I recall how musty that cellar smelt. The odour of drying blood, of cooling sweat, our bodies still tingling from the frenetic excitement of battle. The Hittite prayed to his strange Weather God, sipping his wine. Nebamun leaned across and tapped him on the wrist with his staff. A litany of questions began, translated by the scribe.

'Where are you from?'

'The land of the Hittites.'

Nebamun smacked him warningly on the wrist.

'Where are you from?'

'Sile, in the Delta.'

'And who sent you?'

'The ruler of the Two Lands – Neferheperure-Waenree, Akenhaten.'

'How do you know it was he?'

'He wore the Peschet, the Two Crowns.'

'What does he look like?'

My heart skipped a beat as the Hittite gave a description which could fit Akenhaten: tall, thin, with misshapen body, wide hips, long face and strange eyes.

'Who were his closest councillors?'

'Two of your priests, Khufu and Djoser. They go everywhere with him.'

'And who else?'

'Hittite colonels. Commanders of the royal hosts.'

'So this usurper does have the support of your king?'

'Hittite commanders,' the prisoner replied.

'And how many men do you have?'

The Hittite sipped at the wine, and his gaze shifted to me, a spark of amusement in his eyes. He must have heard Nebamun use my name. He put down his cup and jabbed his finger at me.

'He asks if you are the lord Mahu,' the scribe turned to me, 'and so wonders why you are not with the true Pharaoh.'

'How many men?' I repeated Nebamun's question.

'About ten thousand in all.' The Hittite grinned as Nebamun whistled under his breath.

'He's lying,' the scribe hissed.

'And who else?' Nebamun insisted. 'Who advises this so-called Pharaoh?'

'Aziru, King of Byblos!'

A collective sigh rose from Nebamun's advisers.

'Nothing we don't already suspect,' Nebamun murmured. 'A usurper assisted by our enemies in Canaan, and of course, the Hittites love to dabble where they shouldn't.'

'Describe the woman,' I asked. 'This Pharaoh's wife-queen.'

The Hittite put his hands to his head, talking excitedly. I caught the word 'Nefertiti'.

'She is so beautiful,' the scribe translated. 'Red hair and eyes so green like those of a cat.'

'Then she is a pretender.' I smiled at the Hittite. 'The Nefertiti I knew had blue eyes.' I tapped the scribe on the wrist. 'Tell him that. Tell him I saw Nefertiti die.'

The scribe translated. The Hittite shrugged and drank greedily from his goblet.

'He is only telling us what he knows,' the scribe declared. I wondered what the Hittite really knew of the Egyptian language. He grinned at me through broken bloody teeth.

'Perhaps we should kill him slowly and cruelly?'

A shift in the Hittite's eyes.

'You know our tongue?' I taunted.

He made a cutting movement across his throat. I caught the words '*Gerh en arit sapt.*'

'What was that?'

'He says that all of us will die on the Night of Judgment. You are right, my lord Mahu, he does know our tongue.'

'Who sent him on this mission?' I asked.

'Heripetchiu, the commander of the mercenaries.'

'What happens,' I leaned across, pointing to my chest, 'if we go as envoys to this usurper?'

The scribe translated.

'*Shemensuion.*' I used the Egyptian word. '*Shemensuion,*' I repeated. 'A royal envoy.'

'*Set saseer, sekht sasa,*' the Hittite replied.

'Nonsense,' I taunted back.

'*Per khet,*' the Hittite spat out. '*Samu sabas ebu, seba sebu.*'

'He's saying, my Lord Mahu . . .' the scribe began.

'I know what he's saying.' I held the Hittite's gaze. 'That if I go, I will enter the Field of Fire, the House of Darkness, where the demons and devourers are waiting for me.'

'*Mahu mahez.*' The Hittite was laughing now, making a pun on my name. '*Mahu mahez.*'

'So I'll be eaten by the fierce-eyed lion? Devoured by the lion-headed serpent?'

The Hittite nodded like an excited child. The scribe returned to his questioning about the attack. This time the Hittite was more forthcoming. We listened attentively as he described how they had sailed untroubled along the river under false standards, pretending to be mercenaries bound for the garrison at Memphis, the White-Walled City. How no one had challenged them, how at night they had sheltered in lonely places along the river.

'He's telling the truth,' Nebamun agreed. 'The lord Horemheb will be concerned. There are war barges on the river, armed men going backwards and forwards. There are stretches of the Nile to the north of this city where you could hide a fleet of barges. Ask him if he knew that Prince Tutankhamun was here?'

The Hittite replied that he did, and that was why they had come: to take back the Pharaoh's true son and heir, together with his sister.

'How did they know?' I asked.

The Hittite shrugged his shoulders and gabbled quickly.

'He says,' the scribe translated, 'that they knew but he does not know how or why.'

'Did they have friends here?' I asked. 'Allies who helped them?'

Again, the shrug.

'He's a junior officer,' Nebamun intervened. 'I suspect they hoped to take the house.' He fell silent; he did not wish to discuss such a matter with his officers present.

The questioning continued. The Hittite lapsed into Egyptian and began taunting us again. At last Nebamun made a cutting movement with his hand.

'He's told us what he can and he's finished the wine.' He raised his hands and snapped his fingers.

Behind us the Nubian archers pulled back their bows. The Hittite stretched up; one arrow took him deep in the chest, the other in the throat. He thrashed back against the wall, legs and arms twitching, head going backwards and forwards, blood spurting between his lips, then he gave a sigh and his head fell to one side.

'Take his body and put it with the rest.' Nebamun got to his feet.

We left the cellar and went back into the courtyard. I glanced up, Ankhesenamun was smiling down at me from a window, Meryre beside her. I stayed for a while, following Nebamun across that slaughter yard, where the enemy dead were being stripped, their right hands cut off, their corpses thrown into a cart. Nebamun had ordered them to be taken down to a nearby crocodile pool. The quartermasters were surveying the pile of bloody weapons. An army scribe was sitting on a camp stool, writing tray across his lap, busily counting the severed hands, coldly, methodically, as if he was making a tally of bushels of wheat or jugs of wine.

'About four hundred in all, my lord.' He raised his head as Nebamun approached. The colonel wafted away the hovering flies.

'Finish the count,' he said. 'Some of the corpses we will never find.' He gestured at the severed limbs. 'These can join the rest.' He raised his voice. 'I want the courtyard cleaned with water and vinegar, baskets of flowers brought out to hide the smell. This is my house, not a slaughter pit.'

I was eager to talk to Nebamun but I could not discuss anything whilst the rest were present, so I excused myself and returned to my own chamber. I stripped and washed in salt water, anointed myself, put on a clean loincloth, robe and soft sandals. I was dazed and confused after the battle. I still felt as if there were blood swilling around my feet.

Djarka was waiting for me in the Prince's quarters. He was kneeling on the floor; Tutankhamun was playing with toy soldiers. On either side sat Ankhesenamun and Amedeta, both garbed in loose white robes.

'All hail the returning hero.' Ankhesenamun smiled. She rose and filled a goblet of wine, and, coming across, pressed it into my hand. Her perfume was fragrant after the stench of slaughter, the tang of blood and the sweaty mustiness of that cellar. 'We prayed for you, my lord Mahu. How did it all happen?'

I sipped at the white wine. Ankhesenamun stepped back and surveyed me from head to toe.

'Your eyes look strange and your cheeks are unshaven,' she murmured, 'but otherwise not a cut or a mark. What would have happened, my lord Mahu, if they had broken through?'

'They would not have found you.' Djarka spoke up. 'I have told you, my lady, what my orders were.'

I glanced round at the Prince, playing with his toy soldiers, unaware of my presence. Usually he would jump to his feet and run towards me. I went and crouched beside him. He was muttering under his breath, pushing one wooden soldier against another, the usual childish game, but now he did it with an intensity I had never seen before.

'My lord, Your Highness.' I stroked his head.

He kept banging the soldiers one against the other.

93

'My lord,' I repeated.

Again, no reply, so I took one soldier from his hand. He turned quickly, holding the other up as if he were about to strike me; his face was pale, his eyes empty.

'My lord?' I took the other soldier from his hand; his fingers were clammy and cold. I sat down and pulled him towards me. He didn't resist, but just sat there whispering as if he was talking to someone I couldn't see. I glared furiously at Djarka.

'He's only frightened.' Ankhesenamun came up. 'The clatter of weapons and screams below were hideous. He's only a child, aren't you, my beloved?'

She knelt beside me. For a moment that word, 'beloved', and the smell of her perfume, the softness of her shoulder and arm, recalled Nefertiti. Tutankhamun jumped from my lap and flung his arms around her. For a while he just stood there, face buried in her neck. Ankhesenamun patted him gently on the back, rocking him gently as if he were a babe. I got to my feet, indicating to Djarka to follow. In the corridor outside I took him to a window enclosure overlooking the courtyard.

'Is that fear?' I asked.

Djarka blew his cheeks out. 'The fighting was ferocious when those men burst in. Amedeta began screaming; so did the Prince. I dismissed his mood as the result of fear; I let him play.'

'Has that happened before?'

'Once, twice, but it's usually a passing mood.'

'Does he become violent?' I insisted.

'On one occasion, yes. He hit me with a toy scabbard; a piece of flint scored my cheek, and he ran away and hid. When I found him he was fine, though he had no recollection of what he had done. He's only a child.' Djarka repeated Ankhesenamun's words. 'He's been snatched from one palace to another, then brought to this place of slaughter. They were guided in, weren't they? We have a traitor in our midst.'

'Possibly.' I stared down at the courtyard, now empty of corpses; the servants were busy swilling it with water mixed with salt and vinegar. All the dead and weapons had been removed; only a splash of blood on the wall gave any indication of what had happened just a short while earlier. I suddenly felt weak, slightly dizzy. I pressed myself against the wall.

'My lord, you are well?'

'You know what it is like,' I sighed. 'I'll eat and I'll drink. Sleep as if I haven't for days. One thing is certain, Djarka.' I smiled at him. 'We are no longer envoys. Keep an eye on the Prince and tell me if that ever happens again.'

I was halfway down the stairs when a servant delivered a message: Colonel Nebamun wished to see me in his private chamber. When I arrived, Sobeck and Meryre were already present, seated around a small table. Nebamun himself was acting as servant, pouring wine, serving freshly baked bread with spiced duck. He too had washed and changed. No longer the warrior, but the veteran soldier in his white robes and gold collars of office. Nevertheless, his face was drawn and lined, his eyes bloodshot. He nursed a savage cut on his forearm which the physician had already bandaged. Sobeck, who had received a similar cut on his thigh, was trying to tighten the bandage.

'Don't do that,' Nebamun warned. 'I don't know why, but the wound will go putrid. Keep the bandage as loose as possible. My lord Mahu.' He gestured at the cushions.

I sat down and Nebamun served me; the duck smelt delicious.

'Go on, eat,' Nebamun urged. 'I have dismissed the servants.' He squatted down himself. 'I am a widower with no sons, though I am happy enough. Two or three of the local ladies see to my wants.' He gestured around the stark chamber, which boasted only a few chests, stools and tables. It was dominated by a great wall painting showing Amenhotep the Magnificent, in the guise of Montu, God of War, in his chariot hurtling across scores of slain.

'He's my hero.' Nebamun smiled. 'I often come in here to say my prayers. When he was Pharaoh, there was no nonsense about the One.' He glanced quickly at Meryre. 'When he was Pharaoh, Hittite mercenaries did not sail along the Nile and attack the White-Walled City. They plundered neighbouring mansions,' he sighed, 'killed a few servants. I have sent troops to hunt along the banks; some may still be hiding.'

Meryre remained silent, staring down at his food. At last he shook himself from his reverie.

'How did they know we were here?' he asked.

'Are you implying that I told them?' Sobeck retorted.

'Of course they knew,' Nebamun intervened. 'It was no great secret. Your flotilla must have been seen by many. You have been here a few days, people knew . . .'

'We should have left the Prince at the City of the Aten,' Meryre insisted.

I shifted so I could look at him directly: that round pious face, eyelids stained with green kohl, the Sun Disc amulet still around his neck. He sat all smug like a poisoned toad, cheeks bulging ready to spit his poison. He had that arrogant look which, when we were Children of the Kap, always provoked me. He was daring me to confront him, to ask if he was the traitor.

'Shall we continue our mission?' he asked, popping a morsel of food into his mouth.

'No!' I replied. 'You know that we cannot. We are going to our deaths.'

'You have broken the orders of the Royal Circle. The decrees of the Taurati.' He invoked the official term for the regency council. 'You have broken them twice. You could be accused of treason.'

'Then arrest me, or try to!'

Meryre dismissed my words with a contemptuous gesture.

'We must continue our mission,' he insisted.

'Nonsense!' I glanced at Nebamun, but he refused to intervene; this was not a matter for him.

'Then *I* shall continue *my* mission.' Meryre pushed away the small table; he got to his feet and waddled towards the door.

'Priest!' I shouted, clambering to my feet. Meryre paused and turned round. I glimpsed the sword, Colonel Nebamun's, lying on a table just near the doorway, and ran across and drew it. Meryre turned back to the door, but I crashed into him. Nebamun and Sobeck sprang to their feet. I tried to grasp Meryre's head, but his wig came off in my hands. He turned, face all flushed, eyes glittering, and glanced at the sword.

'What are you going to do, Mahu, Baboon of the South? Kill a high priest? We are under orders from the Royal Council.' He tried to push me away.

'This morning,' I hissed, 'those same people we are meant to treat with tried to kill me and everyone in this house, though perhaps not you.' I grabbed the Sun Disc amulet and pulled the chain off his neck. He winced in pain.

'Colonel Nebamun,' he protested, 'this is an outrage, it's sacrilege.'

'My lord Mahu,' Nebamun warned.

'I am the Prince's Protector,' I replied, 'his official guardian.' I brought the sword's tip under Meryre's fat chin. 'I do not think I can allow you to go. I am placing you under arrest.'

'How dare you?' Meryre spluttered. He struggled to break free, but I held him firm against the door, the sword point digging beneath his chin.

'Shall I tell you about the law, Colonel Nebamun?' I kept my gaze on that fat, round face, resisting the urge to beat him or press the sword tip a little deeper. 'Pharaoh's law is very clear. An attack upon the Royal Person, or any member of the Royal Family or the Sacred Circle, is high treason, punishable by death.'

Some of the anger drained away from Meryre's face.

'You are not implying,' his fat jowls quivered, 'you are not saying that I am a traitor? I knew nothing about that attack.'

I stepped back. 'I didn't say you did, but Colonel Nebamun witnessed what the Hittite said. They came here to kill me and to abduct the Royal Personages: that's treason! You know, Colonel Nebamun,' I kept my eyes on Meryre, 'that it is against the law for any loyal subject of Pharaoh to negotiate or treat with traitors. So, because of that attack, our mission has ended. You, my lord Meryre, because you threatened to break Pharaoh's law, will be placed under house arrest. I shall take full responsibility for it. Now, my lord, I understand you are leaving.'

I opened the door and bellowed for the guards lounging at the foot of the stairs. They came hurrying up.

'Escort my lord Meryre to his quarters,' I declared. The High Priest looked as if he was going to resist. 'If he objects, bind his hands.'

Meryre puffed himself out, fat fingers plucking at the beaded shawl around his shoulders.

'I shall go to my own quarters,' he said. 'I need no escort.'

He walked down the stairs. The guards looked at me; I nodded and they let him by.

'Follow him,' I ordered. 'As long as he goes where he should and stays where he should, don't interfere!'

I returned to the chamber.

'Do you think Meryre is a traitor?' Sobeck asked.

I sat back on the cushions. 'He could be, but there again, half of Egypt knew about our mission. I do wonder what would have happened if the raiders had been successful.' I picked up some bread and broke it. 'If that had been the case, we would all have been past caring wouldn't we? But to answer your question bluntly, Sobeck, yes, I suspect Meryre is a traitor, though proving it is another matter.'

'Is he part of the conspiracy or the cause of it?'

'I don't know, Sobeck. It's like watching the haze in the desert; it distorts and confuses, a veil which hides the truth whilst deceit clouds our judgement, yet I am sure that an invisible cord binds Meryre to the usurper.'

'So why does he want to go on this embassy?' Nebamun demanded. 'Is it a pretext to make contact? To tell the usurper, this false Pharaoh, everything he knows about what's happening and plotted in Thebes?'

'Both,' I replied. 'I have been invited along as a guarantee, as an act of good faith for the rest of the Royal Circle in Thebes. Of course, once we got there no one knows what might happen. I would not be the first to die of marsh fever in the Delta.' I shook my head. 'I think that's the truth, though there is something else I can't grasp about this attack.'

'But how did they know we were here?' Sobeck sipped from his wine. 'Oh, I know our flotilla could be glimpsed along the Nile, whilst our arrival here would be known to their spies. But the information that the Prince was actually in Colonel Nebamun's house?'

'I kept something back from Meryre.' Nebamun moved a cushion to reveal a small polished coffer. He opened this and pulled out a piece of blood-stained papyrus. 'We took this from one of the Hittite officers, a crude map, look!' Nebamun traced the drawing with his finger. 'The bend in the river, the shallows, the papyrus grove, the city and the small quayside below my house.'

The papyrus was stained and ragged, covered in signs and symbols I couldn't understand.

'It could be the work of Meryre,' Nebamun continued, 'a member of his entourage or indeed any one of their spies. We had spies in the Delta, much good they proved,' he added grimly, 'whilst the usurper must have spies in Memphis, the White-Walled City, the garrison-home of General Horemheb. Ah well,' Nebamun smiled, 'it is not all bad news. A courier arrived late last night.'

'Yes?' I asked expectantly.

'Horemheb and Rameses are on the move. I have been ordered to prepare the Horus and Isis regiments.'

'Did we make a mistake, Mahu?' Sobeck asked. 'Bringing the Prince here? Perhaps we should have not quartered all our mercenaries in the city but kept them down near the riverside?'

'Of course I made mistakes,' I snapped. 'It's like being in the Red Lands. Everything is masked by a haze. What is real? What is a mirage? Who's telling the truth and who is lying? People like Meryre are hoping we will make a mistake. We are praying they will. They certainly made one this morning. They never reached this house in time. Colonel Nebamun, you are a soldier: how many battles are won or lost by luck, mere chance?'

The Colonel merely smiled. 'I'll have your mercenaries brought back,' he promised. 'The barracks will feed and provide for them. They can camp by the riverside.'

'Why don't we drag that priestly little turd from his chamber?' Sobeck exclaimed. 'Put him on trial, take his head and send it to the usurper as a present?'

'Another mistake,' I countered. 'A high priest of Egypt formally executed without a proper trial? The usurper would love that. The Royal Circle would crumble, break up. Even Ay and Horemheb would ask by what authority I carried out such an act! Putting him under house arrest is bad enough. More importantly,' I scratched my head, 'Meryre has powerful supporters, amongst both the priests and certain elements of the army, not to mention those who just love to meddle, to stir the shit for the sake of the stink.'

'So you'll go no further? Nebamun asked. 'You won't journey north?'

'How can we?' I sighed. 'I still don't truly understand what Meryre wants. We are like a boat in a mist, or a traveller in a sand storm, merely blundering about.'

'The Hittite confirmed one thing.' Nebamun pushed away a silver-edged plate and sat cradling his wine cup. 'I have heard stories, tales of cruelty about the rebel camp at Sile. How the invaders are practising the cruelties of the Hyksos invaders, torturing and burning people. I considered them wild rumours, but he mentioned a House of Darkness, a Field of Fire. I suspect the usurper is showing mercy and clemency to all who accept him and utter ruthlessness to those who don't. No wonder our spies have achieved little success. Well.' He made to rise. 'All I can do is wait for fresh orders or the arrival of General Horemheb. What will you do, Lord Mahu?'

'I don't know.'

I rose to my feet, thanked Nebamun for his kindness and returned to my chamber with its cot bed and few chests. A stark chamber, a soldier's room, with little ornamentation, though I found it restful enough. I slept for a while and rose late in the afternoon. I visited the Prince. He was now fast asleep. Djarka was squatting the other side of the bed, weaving a small basket, something he did whenever he was troubled or agitated. I took his writing tray out to the roof. The ground beyond the wall was still being searched by Nebamun's troops, his soldiers dragging aside the undergrowth, looking for corpses or any of the invaders who might have crawled away. I squatted down even as a piercing screech rent the air. Another scream followed. I went to look. The soldiers had found two of the enemy wounded, dispatched them and were now dragging their corpses along the path.

I sat down with my back to the wall. In the script I had learnt in the House of Instruction as a Child of the Kap, I tried to make sense of the problem vexing me. First, the factions of the Royal Council were beginning to show themselves. Four groups in all: Ay and his granddaughter; Horemheb, Rameses and the military; the administrators like Maya and Huy; and the Atenists led by Meryre. And myself? Friend to all, ally to none.

My allegiance was to the Prince. Secondly, a usurper, a false Pharaoh, had invaded the Delta, aided and abetted by the priests Khufu and Djoser. Thirdly, the usurper was supported by Hittite gold and silver, not to mention troops, as well as Egypt's enemies in Canaan. Fourthly, the Royal Circle had been informed of the usurper's invasion. Meryre's offer to negotiate seemed a wise move by all accounts; it gave Horemheb and Rameses time to collect troops. Meryre had demanded my co-operation. Did the High Priest hope from the start that I'd bring the Prince and Ankhesenamun with me? Fifthly, at the same meeting of the Royal Circle, Meryre had protested how the members of the Aten cult were being secretly assassinated by the Shabtis of Akenhaten. Immediately after that meeting General Rahmose, one of Meryre's most ardent supporters, was murdered. Sixthly, Ankhesenamun had implicated herself in Rahmose's death, assuring me that she had forged an alliance with Meryre, probably with the connivance of Ay. So why the attack on me? A murderous assault which was intended to frighten rather than harm? Seventhly, on the day afterwards, Meryre demanded that his people be given shelter and protection at the powerful fortress of Buhen and that the Prince be moved for his own safety from the dangers threatening in Thebes. Eighthly, why didn't the usurper march south? Why did he delay in the Delta? Ninthly, why the attack on Nebamun's house? True, our flotilla had been noticed on the Nile, as had our landing at Memphis. But all this information could have been supplied by spies.

I placed the pen down and dabbed my finger in the black ink. Somewhere here lurked a great lie. Of course, it was all lies. Nevertheless, even lies have a logic all of their own; this did not.

'Lord Mahu?' Nebamun came up the steps and stood catching his breath. 'We have more news. The enemy flotilla, some of them were seen two days ago, south of the White Walls.'

'South?' I exclaimed, placing the writing tray beside me. 'You mean the barges sailed past Memphis, then came back to attack?'

'According to the fishermen who brought the news. Didn't you say your first destination was the City of the Aten?'

'Yes, yes, I did.'

101

Nebamun spread his hands. 'The news of the battle has spread all over the river. Fishermen came to see what had happened. Two of the barges were recognised. The fishermen said they saw them at least two days ago flying false standards and, undoubtedly, armed with forged passes which they destroyed before the attack was launched. An impudent, insolent gesture, but, Lord Mahu, who would dare to stop a bargeload of mercenaries? As I have said before, troops are moving up and down the river. Look at your escort. Some of them are Egyptian, the rest are mercenaries. At other times, in other places, they could have been fighting against us.'

I thanked him and returned to my own problems. Time and time again I went back over the list I had made. Eventually the mist of lies began to dissipate.

'Ankhesenamun, you lying little bitch!' I murmured. 'Logic dictates you don't control this game; others do.'

I went down to the small dining chamber, the most luxurious room in the house, with its high ceiling, gold-crowned columns, airy windows, its walls painted a rich dark blue. A servant had told me the Princess was there. She and Amedeta lounged on the dais at the far end, cushions piled about them, the table in front littered with plates of meat and fruit. They were feeding each other chunks of pomegranate, laughing and talking without a care in the world. Both had drunk deeply, eyes bright in faces flushed and wet with the perfume from their thick oiled wigs. I stopped before the dais and bowed.

'My lady, I wish words with you.'

'Which lady?' Amedeta simpered.

'My lady.' I glared at Ankhesenamun. She pouted and made to protest. 'My lady,' I repeated.

'Oh! If you are going to stand and glare so ferociously!'

Amedeta, giggling behind her fingers, staggered to her feet and left the chamber, swaying tipsily.

'Well?' Ankhesenamun lay back, allowing her robe to fall open, half exposing a painted nipple; her purple-tinted finger nails caressed this, then, dipping her fingers in the wine cup, she flicked drops at me.

'My lady, tell me the truth.'

'What's that?'

'Something you know little about.'

'Baboon, you mock me.'

'Would I dare?'

She leaned across. 'Why, Mahu, why do you do all this? Why do you care?'

'There's nothing else,' I retorted. 'I am part of this. There is no other place for me to go, no other things to do.'

'Is that the truth, baboon? Is it true that you loved my father and my mother? In the dazzling time before the Aatru . . . You know what that is?'

'A fiery, blood-sucking serpent.'

'Before the Aatru . . .' Ankhesenamun, elbows resting on the table, seemed more interested in the fruit. She picked up a slice of melon. 'Before the Aatru gobbled it up,' she added drunkenly, 'and spat it out in a breath of dry dust. Is that why you are really here, Baboon of the South, because you loved them?'

'True, once I loved them both, as I have loved others.'

'Oh, you mean Khiya the Mitanni monkey?'

'Yes, my lady, your half-brother's mother.'

'Yes. Yes, quite.' She moved the oil lamp forward as if to search my face more closely. 'And now it's Tutankhamun, isn't it? My father, despite his drink and opiates, his frenetic madness, in the end entrusted his beloved son to you. Our Prince is a chain, isn't he, which still binds you to my father? That,' she smiled, 'and the fact that Father might still be alive.'

'If your mother didn't murder him: that's what you told me the other night, when Rahmose was murdered. But of course, you were lying, weren't you?'

She straightened up, all signs of drunkenness vanished.

'You said you were friends and allies with Meryre,' I accused. 'That you cultivated him, flattering him with your attentions. That's true, isn't it?'

Ankhesenamun stared unblinking back.

'You told Meryre how the Shabtis of Akenhaten were controlled by me. You told me that you had a hand in Rahmose's murder because he might reveal to Ay your involvement with Meryre.' I leaned down. 'That, my lady, is a lie.'

'How dare you.' Her hand fell to the fruit knife on the table. I seized her wrist.

'Tell me it was a lie. I know it was a lie. My lady,' I squeezed her wrist, 'I nearly died today. I am in no mood for your games.' I gripped her wrist harder. 'I'll break this, then you and I will be enemies. Now tell me the truth: you knew nothing about this attack. You are only a spectator, not the cause.'

Ankhesenamun winced with pain.

'You became friends with Meryre on the orders of your grand-father?'

'Yes!' she gasped.

'But you have learnt very little?'

'Yes.'

'Because Meryre knows that Ay stands behind you?'

'Yes.'

'But neither you nor your grandfather has anything to do with the Shabtis of Akenhaten. You and Ay are as mystified as I am, aren't you?'

Ankhesenamun nodded.

'And the murder of Rahmose? You had nothing to do with that?'

Again the nod.

'So why did you lie? On the orders of Lord Ay?' I released her wrist.

'Because I am not a child,' she hissed. 'I wanted to impress! My grandfather is as puzzled as you. He fears the usurper. He fears Meryre's power with the Atenists. He is frightened of Horemheb, not to mention Huy and Maya. He needs time to consolidate.'

'We need to survive,' I retorted, stepping down from the dais. 'Goodnight, my lady. Do remember,' I added, 'your arrogance misled me and nearly cost us everything.'

'Mahu?' Ankhesenamun was now smiling through her tears, nursing her wrist. 'We are still friends? We should meet again,' she continued. 'I do like to be disciplined by the Baboon of the South.'

'My lady, goodnight.'

I met Sobeck and Djarka in the small antechamber next to the Prince's bedroom; two of my mercenaries guarded the door.

'Listen,' I began, 'I am sure this is the truth, or some of it: we have walked into a trap of Meryre's making. No!' I gestured for silence. 'Horemheb, Rameses, Maya and the rest, including the lord Ay, want the dream of the Aten cult forgotten as quickly as possible. Meryre is different. He has exploited the mystery of Akenhaten's true fate, as well as Egyptian troubles in Canaan and the Hittite dreams of empire. He and this usurper, the false Pharaoh, are close allies, though I have no proof of this, just as I have no evidence that Meryre is responsible for the Shabtis of Akenhaten.'

'Impossible!' Sobeck exclaimed.

'No, they are assassins who act on his orders. I suspect he uses them to remove members of his own party whom he doesn't trust. More importantly, he feeds and fans the flames of fear and disquiet. Somehow he and this usurper share the same dream, the same vision. To put it succinctly, Ankhesenamum had no part in the assassination of Rahmose; that was carried out on Meryre's orders. Perhaps he didn't trust Rahmose. Perhaps the old general was not as ardent in his support as he should have been. More importantly, Meryre wanted a sacrificial victim. The fact that Rahmose was wearing my striped robe is neither here nor there; he was marked down for death. The gardener who carried out the attack was a secret Atenist. If we make careful enquiries we would learn that he worked once in the City of the Aten, probably in the Great Temple there. He was a member of Meryre's faction. He carried out murders for him, for which he was paid in gold, silver or precious stones. On the morning of Rahmose's murder, Meryre and his entourage entered the palace grounds. Meryre dispatched a priest to meet his agent the gardener.'

'And the priest was also sacrificed?'

'Of course. Meryre can then proclaim that no sooner had he entered the palace than one of his retinue was murdered and his place taken by a man bent on a second murder, the destruction of Lord Rahmose. Meryre also ensured that someone in the palace blocked that door so that the assassin couldn't escape. He was meant to be killed. Meryre needed to prove the assassin was not a member of his entourage so he could point the finger of blame elsewhere.'

'And the attack on you?' Sobeck asked.

'Later that day a member of Meryre's coven – and he must

have such in the palace – arranged for the pile of laundry to be taken to my chamber with snakes hidden in the basket. On that same night a servant was dispatched with strict orders to take the laundry out of the basket.' I shrugged. 'You know how the palace servants are. If you give them an order to throw precious goblets into the Nile they will do so. Why should they suspect any danger or treachery? And so the damage is done. Meryre can point out that the city of Thebes, not even the Palace of Malkata, is safe for him or the servants of our Prince.'

'And so he demands the fortress at Buhen.' Djarka smiled. 'And the removal of the Prince to the City of the Aten?'

'He also knows the Royal Circle will agree,' Sobeck added. 'They wanted Meryre to go north. They knew you would travel with him. Meryre's request that the Prince accompany you to the City of the Aten seems logical enough.'

'For a while,' I replied, 'Meryre had his way. He made no mistakes. He didn't mean for the Prince to be killed. The attack this morning wasn't really intended to be carried out here, but at the City of the Aten. Flying false colours, armed with forged letters, those barges would have landed their troops in a half-deserted city.' I pulled a face. 'We would have been killed, but the Prince, Ankhesenamun, Meryre and his entourage would have been abducted.'

Sobeck whistled in disbelief.

'And what then?'

'Meryre would have had the best of both worlds,' I replied. 'He could claim that he was being held captive, whilst the usurper possessed Egypt's legitimate ruler. Once that happened, the usurper would have marched south, collecting troops on the way. They would have been able to display our young Prince as the true head of their forces. Meryre would provoke uprisings in various towns and cities—'

'Whilst my lord Ay,' Sobeck intervened, 'not to mention Horemheb and Rameses, would have been distracted by these uprisings as well as the revolt which would certainly have occurred at Buhen.'

'I agree. Buhen is the gateway to Nubia. The princes of Kush would be only too willing to rise in revolt in return for promises of more rights and privileges: more independence, greater

106

freedom from Thebes. Horemheb is a shrewd general,' I added, 'or thinks he is. Which way would he have turned? To the north, or to Buhen in the south? Not to mention the uprisings in between.'

'We should kill Meryre,' Djarka declared. 'Claim he suffered an accident or fell ill.'

'Leave him for the while,' I disagreed. 'What we need to do is to find out the true strength of the usurper. Tomorrow morning, Djarka, I will leave Memphis. I'll crop my hair.' I grinned. 'I'll ask Sobeck to give me a few bruises and cuts. I'll travel north to Sile and offer my services.'

'You could be recognised.'

'They won't expect me,' I retorted. 'I'll change my appearance. I know what I am looking for. We cannot trust anyone else. We'll tell no one except Colonel Nebamun. You, Djarka, will remain and guard the Prince and the Lady Ankhesenamun, even though she's a lying bitch who tried to claim responsibility for everything.'

'And me?' Sobeck asked.

I clapped him on the shoulder. 'You have a choice, my friend. You can stay here with Djarka or you can come with me! In the meantime I am going to sow a little confusion of my own. Meryre and his retinue will be kept under house arrest. He will wonder where I have gone.'

'Yes?' Djarka asked.

'I'll tell him I'll swim with the surge of the river and, for a proper consideration, I may even change sides.'

Per Sutekh
(Ancient Egyptian name for Avaris)

Chapter 6

Awaken Seth, Lord of Destruction!
Red of hand and red of hair,
Bringer of War!
He who destroys millions by fire and sword
Who feasts on the slain of battle . . .

I murmured the words, more as a good luck charm than a prayer, as Sobeck and I disembarked along one of the many canals which pierced the Delta. In the far distance were the towers, turrets and silver-capped obelisks of ancient Sile, a crumbling city set amongst the fields and palm groves of that most fertile place. The quayside adjoined a small market town, one of those sleepy, tawdry villages dotted along the Nile and its tributaries, now transformed into a place of war. A teeming mass of armed men wandered its streets, mercenaries from every kingdom under the sun. They swarmed like flies on carrion, lounging in the makeshift beer shops along the quayside or clustered at the mouths of needle-thin alleys and streets. Sobeck and I, to all appearances, were just two more sword-sellers, dressed in leather kilts, high-tied boots and linen vests. Our weapons and blankets, panniers and provisions were heaped on the back of the most docile donkey Nebamun's stable could provide, a good travelling companion who'd been no trouble even on the barges as we journeyed north. I had grown quite attached to it, joking with Sobeck that it provided better company than many a man.

We had prepared our stories, a common tale. We dressed

111

and acted like professional mercenaries much given to raucous song and filthy curses. I had shaved my head and wore a collar of copper, with similar bands on wrists and forearms. Sobeck was attired the same, though he aped the language and swagger of the mercenaries better than I. A true enigma, Sobeck! I had reflected on this during the journey from Memphis. I was Chief of Police. It was my job to collect information about enemies of the Royal Circle. Sobeck, however, had come by choice, boasting as usual that he had nothing better to do. Secretly I suspect this disgraced Child of the Kap wished to be accepted by us all, particularly by me, who had grown up with him at the House of Residence in the Malkata Palace. During our river journey, whenever we were given the opportunity, we discussed the past. I asked if his absence as Lord of Am-duat, the underworld of Thebes, would be noted. Sobeck grinned in that sly way he had, not holding my gaze, and replied he would be a poor chief if he were forgotten in a month.

Naturally, as we approached Sile, such conversations ended. One night, when we moored in the shadow of another village, we caught a pedlar eavesdropping on our conversation outside a dingy beer shop. Sobeck followed him into the dark, knife grasped in his hand, and when he returned, reported we were still safe. Spies and informers abounded, so everyone was careful. Fellow travellers would stare, but never question or discuss what was happening. Nevertheless the tension was palpable. A usurper had invaded Tomery, the Kingdom of Two Lands, and a savage war was imminent. Armed men were everywhere. We glimpsed troops moving along the banks, provision carts and the occasional chariot squadron sending up clouds of dust. Smoke often smudged the sky, and after dark, night prowlers from the desert scavenged amongst the corpses along the river banks. One old man, out of his wits, complained how Seth's red shadow covered the Nile; that the Hyksos had returned with all the terrors of the Season of the Hyaena. Others, more sensible, merely complained about raiders and the lack of patrols, or dismissed us as river scum floating north or south to sell our swords to the highest bidder. The countryside was held in a grip of fear whilst the great cities closed their gates and fortified their walls against these hyaenas, as one old lady, chomping on her gums, called us.

As we moved through that market town towards the usurper's camp, I realised that she spoke the truth. The inhabitants appeared to have fled, leaving their homes to the scavengers: Shardana in their horned helmets and leather garments; Libyans and Nubians festooned with feathers and plumes, faces and bodies painted or tattooed, kilts fashioned out of animal skins flapping against their thighs. Soldiers from the islands of the Great Green were there, and even a few fair-skinned warriors from the lands beyond. All were armed and dangerous, displaying weapons of every kind: bows and arrows, clubs, daggers, swords, spears and two-edged axes. The air stank of sweat and strange perfumes which couldn't disguise the reeking odour of the narrow lanes. The camp followers had also arrived: the wizards with their necklaces of bone and grotesque masks; fortune-tellers, wandering priests, leeches and physicians, dancing girls and prostitutes of every age and country. Nevertheless, although the market town was filthy, order was strictly maintained. Hittite officers and their military escorts patrolled the streets or lounged at the mouths of alleyways, ready to quell any trouble. Here and there stood the huge Hittite war chariots with their crew of three, driver, shield-bearer and archer, garbed in striped robes over metal-fringed leather jerkins and war kilts.

A grisly sight, a dire warning to those who broke the law, waited for us in the centre of the village: a row of corpses impaled on stakes driven through the chest, or up through the bowels. Each victim had been doused in resin and burned; their twisted black shapes seemed like demons frozen in the air. On the ground before each stake was a piece of wood proclaiming their crime: *techar*, spy; *nek*, rape; *thai*, thievery. Despite such bloodthirsty spectacles, the town seemed a noisy, gaudy place, dominated by a swirl of colour, cheap perfume and the chatter of at least a dozen tongues. A place where men greeted each other with open camaraderie, but beneath the singing, the laughter and the raucous drinking a sinister, threatening atmosphere lurked, as men of blood gathered for the slaughter.

No one accosted us, though we had to keep a sharp eye on our baggage; eventually we were through the village into a line of trees fringing the plain where the usurper had set up camp. At first my heart failed at the sight. A great makeshift fortress, surrounded by a moat fed by one of the canals, rose up from the plain, protected not only by the moat but by a soaring mound and a lofty, sturdy palisade of sharpened stakes. A bridge crossed the moat and cut through the mound to the huge double gates with wooden turrets on either side. From these, and elsewhere along the fortress, banners and standards fluttered in the breeze. The air was rich with the smell of wood smoke, burning meat, fried fish, incense, sweat and blood. On each side of the fortress a small town had sprung up of huts, bothies and tents. The air rang with the calls of trumpets, shouts, the neigh of horses and the lowing of cattle. I felt as if I was in one of my nightmares, standing in some lonely thicket looking out on to a city of the Underworld.

'Much stronger,' Sobeck whispered. 'Much stronger than we thought, Mahu. What do you reckon?' He gestured at the fortress and the camp. 'What?' he whispered. 'Ten to fifteen thousand fighting men? Not to mention those we saw in the village, as well as those we met on patrol, foraging or hunting.'

A farmer, his cart laden with provisions, whip cracking the air over his oxen, shouted at us to get out of the way. We stepped aside and joined the other travellers making their way up to the camp. Once we'd reached it, we walked as calmly as we could around the fortress precincts, our donkey plodding patiently behind us. The field camp was like any I had seen: beaten paths snaked between tawdry huts and ragged tents. Camp fires burned, farmers, peasants and a legion of road wanderers offered everything for sale. We noticed horse lines and chariot parks and, as in the market town, the ubiquitous Hittite officers and military police. Walls and canals were protected. Latrine pits had been dug well beyond the picket line. Discipline was ruthlessly enforced. We passed a huge cage containing three naked malefactors being prodded and poked with sharp sticks by a horde of camp followers. A drunk who had defecated away from the latrines was being made to stand in his own ordure. Another, guilty of filching from the cooking pot, lay spread-eagled on the ground, the soles of his feet being beaten by two burly Kushites armed with split canes.

No one bothered us except for the traders or the fortune-tellers shaking their magic cups full of tiny bones. Whores and pimps touted for custom. Cooks tried to entice us with platters piled high with spiced meats. We walked slowly, wide-eyed, gaping-mouthed yet learning as much as we could. I noticed that the side gate, similar to the main, was closely guarded by troops placed before it and in the towers at either side. At the rear of the fortress another gate, leading down to the horse meadows and paddocks, was just as closely guarded. We were allowed to pass by but warned not to stop. At the far side of the fortress stretched another camp, screened off by a soaring palisade. Above this I glimpsed the top of a Mastaba, one of those ancient limestone pyramids used to house the dead before the Two Lands came together. The outer case was crumbling but its top jutted above the high palisade like a spear point against the sky; the sickly-sweet odour of spilt blood and the nauseating stench of burnt flesh were very strong. The guards at the entrance to the palisade were all dressed in black leather armour and jackal masks. A group of mercenaries were passing through the gate. As this swung open and closed, I glimpsed stakes, blackened earth, and heard the deep, cough-like roar of a lion.

We returned to the front of the fortress, a sprawling concourse, part travelling fair or market, with its many stalls and booths. We bought jugs of beer and some freshly baked bread, and settled down beneath a palm tree, studying the fortress which soared above us.

'It seems,' Sobeck declared between mouthfuls, 'there are two camps. That's the main one.' He pointed towards the great double-barred gates, the avenue leading to them packed with soldiers, some wearing the striped head-dresses of Egyptian infantry, the rest a motley collection of mercenaries and Hittites. 'And that's formidable enough!'

'What I would like to know,' I gestured to the left, 'is what is behind that palisade? What does the Mastaba contain and why are those mercenaries entering? They looked frightened. I glimpsed scorched earth, a stake, and heard the roar of a lion.'

'I heard the same,' Sobeck agreed. 'And I keep thinking what that Hittite told us about the Place of Darkness and a Field of

Fire. Many summers ago,' he grinned at me, 'when I was young and handsome and a Child of the Kap, I learnt the history of Egypt and the exploits of Ahmose, who drove the Hyksos out. Now, our history is full of tales about Hyksos cruelty, how they used to love to torture their prisoners in the most fiendish manner. I just wonder if that's a place of Hyksos torture. If this usurper instils terror with his own slaughter yard. We have been round this camp, Mahu, through the town, but never once did I glimpse an Egyptian officer. Yet we know the usurper suborned some of our regiments.'

'The officers may have been purged,' I replied. 'Intelligent men, they would soon realise they'd been tricked. Some of them must have seen the true Akenhaten and gazed upon the beauty of Nefertiti.'

Sobeck gazed around to make sure no one was listening, but this was not a royal palace where other people's business was often your own. In a camp of mercenaries, in order to avoid fights and squabbles, people were only too willing to concede space to another.

'Well, Mahu, I have asked you once and I'll ask again. Why are we here? What shall we do?'

'Gather as much information as we can; cause as much chaos as we are able.'

'Chaos?'

'If I am given the chance,' I replied, 'I would burn that fortress and kill the usurper.'

'I do not want to end my days with a pointed stick up my arse!' Sobeck complained. 'How do we know Meryre won't – hasn't – sent messengers here?'

'Because he's too sly and cunning,' I replied. 'I doubt if there is anything in writing which ties him in with this.'

'Did he believe you?' Sobeck asked. 'When you visited him before we left?'

'He's too closely guarded to send messages, whilst I am sure I didn't convince him. However, I made him think. I apologised for my outburst before Colonel Nebamun. I pointed out that I too had been attacked by the Shabtis of Akenhaten, that my allegiance was solely to the Prince and not to the Lord Ay or anyone else.'

'Did he believe you?'

'He accepted my apology and listened. I didn't tell him I was coming here, just that I was leaving Memphis to make other arrangements.'

'Why should he trust you?'

'Sobeck, why shouldn't he? What do I owe Ay, Horemheb, Rameses or Huy? They only tolerate me because, in the end, I was Nefertiti's enemy as much as theirs. They only accord me a privileged position because of my custody of the Prince. As I pointed out to Meryre, hadn't I been Akenhaten's close companion, his bodyguard, his friend? And do you know what he replied?'

Sobeck shook his head.

'He said he always wondered where my true loyalties lay. I also claimed,' I smiled, 'all hurt and quivering, how never once had he approached me or shown me any gesture of friendship. He objected. I replied that I only accepted his offer to accompany him north because I thought it would heal any breach between us. But that after that attack, I was as suspicious of Sile as I was of Thebes.'

Sobeck whistled under his breath. 'Mahu, Baboon of the South, very cunning.' He toasted me with his cup. 'Meryre may be convinced,' he continued. 'You did agree to accompany him. You were attacked by the Shabtis of Akenhaten, and you now blame—'

'I now blame Ay for the attack at Memphis, or so I told Meryre. I left our pompous little High Priest confused, with plenty of food for thought. Perhaps he thinks we are travelling along the same road. If that attack at Memphis had been successful, I may have been spared. I may have been given a choice to either join the usurper or die. After all, I do have some influence with the Prince, as well as Ankhesenamun.'

'Now she,' Sobeck wagged a finger, 'will have to be watched.' He drained his cup. 'That's if we survive here.' He called across to the potboy serving behind the stall. 'We wish to join the army.'

The boy pointed to the tent, on the right of the avenue leading up to the main gates, guarded by mercenaries in striped robes holding rounded shields and spears. We went across and repeated

117

our request. The men looked blankly at us. Sobeck lapsed into the lingua franca of the mercenary corps. A fat-cheeked, sweaty-faced scribe pulled up the tent flap and peered out.

'We have enough riff-raff!' he bawled. 'Be on your way!'

'We are soldiers,' Sobeck retorted. 'We have fought in the eastern and western Red Lands as well as in Kush. We have stood in the battle line and done more fighting in a day than you have done in your long, lazy life!'

'Let us see them!' a voice shouted from deep in the tent.

The scribe glowered at us, jabbered at the sentry to guard the donkey and beckoned us in. The tent was dark and musty and reeked of wine, sweat and fear. Soldiers lounged on either side, obscured by the poor light. Three men squatting on thick rugs faced the entrance; to the right of these was a line of scribes with writing palettes. The three men, officers by their collars and glittering armlets, were dressed in linen or leather vests; each had a club, sword and dagger by his side. Behind them stood six Nubian archers, bows in hand, arrow quivers hanging by their sides, feathered shafts ready to be plucked out.

'Come here!'

The officer in the middle gestured at us to kneel before him. He was Usurek, a soldier from Avaris, a former standard-bearer from the Ptah regiment and, as we discovered later, one of the few to survive the usurper's ruthless purge of the regiment's officers. In many ways he reminded me of Sobeck: narrow-faced, with high cheekbones, sharp eyes and a cruel mouth. Usurek was a born soldier, a killer to the bone. What was that ancient phrase? *Seka er Sekit*, 'a slaughterer from the slaughterhouse'. The other two officers I forget. They remain nameless and face-less. Like Usurek, their bones are now the playthings of jackals whilst vipers nest in their skulls. At that time they had the power of life and death. The tent we had entered, despite its shabby tawdriness, was the Utcha Netu, the Place of Judgement. Our three judges sat sharing a wineskin.

'You look fit,' Usurek began, 'for visitors from Abydos.'

'Who said we were from Abydos?' Sobeck retorted. 'We come from Thebes. My cousin is Mahu. We are of the Medjay, former soldiers in the regiment of Amun Ra.'

'And?'

'We were discharged.'

'And?'

'For thieving.'

'Then what?'

Sobeck shrugged. 'We served here and there: bodyguards for merchants, princes.'

The questions began, Usurek watching us all the time. They asked about where we had served, what weapons we had used. At the end Usurek shook his head and addressed Sobeck.

'I don't know about you, your speech is soft.'

'My cousin and I were trained in the House of Life.'

'Ah yes, the Silent One.' Usurek turned on me. 'You say you are from Thebes? Served in the regiment of Amun Ra? Then tell me, in the Temple of Karnak, what lies to the right of the Precinct of Montu?'

'The Temple of Tuthmosis.' I kept my voice steady and hoped he wouldn't notice the bead of sweat coursing down my cheek.

'And in the Precincts of Amun Ra, what temple stands by itself near the northern gate?'

'The Temple of Ptah.'

'And how do you know that?'

'Because I have stood on guard there.'

'Karnak has its own police.'

'Units of our regiment still stand on guard,' I persisted. 'You know that as well as I do.'

'Do you have service records?'

'We destroyed them. They were more trouble than they were worth.'

'And what Gods do you serve?'

'My right arm and my penis.'

Usurek laughed. 'You say you were in the regiment of Amun Ra.' He leaned forward. 'The regiment had a famous song, a love poem. How does it go?' He squinted up at the roof of the tent. Sobeck's hand slipped down and grazed my thigh, warning me to be careful.

'Ah yes, I remember. "The little sycamore that she has planted with her own hands opens its mouth to sing."' Usurek peered at me. 'I had a friend in the Amun Ra regiment. It was their marching song. Well, have you heard it?'

119

'Yes, I have, but you have it wrong. The line should read, "opens its mouth to speak, singing of its gardens".'

Usurek smiled. 'You may recite your poem, but we still don't need you. We have enough archers and foot men.'

'But not charioteers?' Sobeck retorted.

'What?'

'You have few charioteers. It is a matter of fact. Few mercenary armies do.'

The atmosphere in the tent changed. The soldiers lounging about got to their feet, going for their swords. Behind Usurek the archers notched arrows to their bows.

Sobeck had made his gamble.

'You didn't tell us you were charioteers.' Usurek was no longer smiling. 'Why should charioteers, hired by any army, trek from Thebes to Sile in the Delta?'

'Because we are charioteers,' Sobeck replied outrageously. 'My cousin and I are very good. I am the driver, he is the bowman.'

'You still haven't answered my question. You said you were discharged?'

'We discharged ourselves.'

'For what?'

'For stealing a chariot and two horses from the Royal Stables.'

Usurek laughed.

'We were in trouble anyway,' Sobeck continued blithely. 'The officers were always picking on us, latrine duty here, picket duty there. So we decided to help ourselves. We cannot go back to Thebes.'

Usurek got to his feet. 'In which case, you'd best come with me.'

He took us out of the tent, shouting at the guards to lead the donkey and calling up others as an escort, then marched us through the camp to the rear of the fortress and into the chariot park. Again, more orders; a collection of harnesses was brought, and two fine bay horses together with a chariot of wood with a floor of interlaced thongs. Thankfully it was a regimental chariot, two-wheeled and six-spoked. I checked the gleaming casing. It must have been an officer's, with its gold and blue electrum embossed and ornamented with silver palmettes interlaced with spirals. There was a leather quiver for arrows embroidered with red and silver, whilst the javelin sheath was a resplendent gold and yellow with a charging lion along the outside. The harness was of good leather, polished and strong and studded with bronze clasps. I felt the yoke pins and axle; they were firm.

At last we were ready. Usurek leading the way, we were taken down to the chariot meadow with its range of straw targets fastened to poles at the far end. At first the horses were strange, the chariot clumsy, but we soon got the feel of the animals, the way the chariot would tilt and sway. All the skills we were taught in our years of training at the House of Residence quickly returned. Usurek became impatient and started shouting. Sobeck, ignoring him, wheeled the chariot round and round.

You know the way it is when horses and driver become one, a glorious weapon of war, wheels spinning, chariot bucking, the horses beginning to stretch out, guided by the reins and a touch of the whip. Our circuits became faster, more skilful, until Sobeck at one end of the meadow urged the horses into a full charge. The chariot thundered forward, racing like an arrow from the bow, the horses moving as one, swaying and turning under Sobeck's careful direction. I grasped the bow, arrow notched. We swirled round the men of straw, loosed arrow after arrow into the target and thundered back. We ignored Usurek's orders to halt, but charged again. The wind whipped our faces. I grasped the javelin, bracing my feet, careful to keep my distance from Sobeck. One after another, the javelins hit their mark. The chariot turned, bucking dangerously; the horses faltered. Sobeck, reins grasped round his wrists, gently steadied them before thundering straight towards Usurek and his companions, who were forced to scatter. Sobeck slowed the horses into a canter and gently brought them to a halt. He dropped the reins and, like any good charioteer, jumped down to congratulate the horses, letting them muzzle his hand, speaking to them softly. Usurek, splattered with mud but grinning from ear to ear, came up to congratulate us.

'No wonder they didn't catch you when you stole the horses. You wish to join the army? Then come, take the oath.'

I shall never forget that afternoon. A rain storm, frequent in that area, came sweeping in, low dark clouds splattering rain to soak us to the skin and turn the ground into slippery mud. We were forced to shelter beneath a tree. Usurek, still congratulating us on our chariot skill, asked further questions about our experiences. I was glad that Sobeck and I had agreed to use our proper names. The questions came so thick and fast, a mere slip would have alerted this man's suspicions. Sobeck had made a wise choice. Usurek conceded they had more chariots than men and, when we asked why, turned away, hawked and spat.

At last the rains ceased. Escorted by Shardana, we crossed to the far side of the fortress and that sinister Mastaba hiding behind its palisade. The guards at the gate let us into what truly was the Plain of Horror. The Mastaba, with its pyramid top, stood at the far end. Its processional way, chapel and priest houses had long decayed. The causeway leading up to the ramp of the Mastaba had been repaired, as had its door, now closely guarded. The approach to the pyramid was dominated by a granite statue of Sekhmet the Destroyer, and ugly, obscene carving covered in lichen and spattered with dry blood. A slab of stone before it served as an altar bearing the sacred things, the *Tchesert*, probably looted from some nearby temple: a holy water stoup, incense holder and sprinkling rod. The ground on either side proved to be the true horror: a great expanse of scorched earth with its own hideous crop, row after row of blackened stakes each bearing the remains of an impaled man or woman. It was impossible to tell either sex or race from those gruesome black shapes.

'Traitors and rebels,' Usurek murmured, avoiding my gaze. 'They are impaled and then burned. When more space is needed, new stakes are planted and the old removed.'

Sobeck was used to the cruelties of Eastern Thebes. I could only stare open-mouthed.

'How long?' I whispered.

Usurek, chewing on the corner of his mouth, kept staring up at the Mastaba. 'Two or three months,' he murmured. 'Our masters have struck terror into the local inhabitants. For those troops who wouldn't submit, as well as spies, speculators, traitors, it is either this . . .' he gestured at the stakes, then nodded at the Mastaba, 'or the House of Darkness.'

Never had I experienced such a place of terror, of abomination, a truly unholy pit: silent, sinister and threatening. I knew this usurper was not Akenhaten. Every ruler, my old master included, has a streak of cruelty, but Akenhaten only inflicted death if he had to, secretly, in some hidden place. This sickening sight was not Egyptian. The reek of decay and charred flesh was like some invisible cloak that muffled the mouth and nose and threatened to choke off your life-breath.

'I have seen worse.' Usurek sounded apologetic. 'Out in the Red Lands and in North Canaan.'

'Hittite work?' I asked

He pulled a face. 'You could say that, or Prince Aziru of Byblos. He claims descent from the ancient Hyskos princes who were driven from Sile hundreds of years ago. Such terror works.' He sighed. 'That's why you are to take the oath here. If you falter, if you fail, if it is proved that you are not what you claim to be, this place is where you will die.'

I gazed around. No bird flew over that sacrilegious plot. No blade of green sprouted. Imagine, if you can, row after row of blackened corpses, gruesome shapes impaled above the burnt earth, and brooding over all of it the eerie tomb of a long-dead prince and the gruesome statute of the Destroyer. The Shardana who had escorted us were also uneasy, muttering under their breath, making signs with their fingers and thumbs against the Evil One.

Usurek was about to lead us over to the altar when the gates swung open and the black-masked guards pushed two prisoners through. They were naked except for loincloths, their bodies covered in blood. They were forced to move at a trot, moaning and groaning, hurrying to stay up with their macabre escort, who held their chains, the other end hooked into the lower lip of each prisoner.

'Fraudsters,' Usurek whispered. 'They were tried by a military court yesterday evening.'

This hideous procession of death hurried past by the statue and up the ramp leading to the Mastaba. Guards appeared from the shadows wearing death masks similar to those of the soldiers who guarded the gates. One of the guards moved a stool across and pulled down the top part of the door as if it was a trap door. One prisoner was lifted up and thrown through, followed by

123

the next, and the trap door was quickly replaced; even from where I stood I could hear their screams, followed by the hideous roaring of a lion.

'By all that's dark,' Sobeck whispered. 'What is happening?'

'They were given a choice,' Usurek declared. 'The Field of Fire or the House of Darkness. When our masters came here they discovered that two lions had moved in from the Red Lands, man-eaters, preying on villagers or lonely travellers. Both beasts were caught, and the Mastaba became their cave. Their food? Well . . .' Usurek gave a lop-sided grin.

I tried not to flinch at the heart-chilling screams of terror and the bestial roars which echoed across. All the time Usurek studied us carefully, refusing to move until the screams stopped and the death escort came trooping back down to the gate. The Shardana clustered together; fighting men, they were still terrified by what they had seen and heard. Usurek led us towards the altar.

'I have never seen such good charioteers,' he murmured. He kept us close as if fearful that the very statue could hear his words. 'Our masters gave us a choice to join or to leave. Many of the Egyptian officers, after a while, refused to accept orders from either Aziru or his Hittite colleagues. When Pharaoh arrived,' a shift in his eyes showed that Usurek no more recognised the usurper to be the true Pharaoh than I did, 'the officers tried to leave immediately. They died here. So, continue to be good charioteers,' he whispered, one finger tracing the scar on his cheek. 'Follow orders. Never moan or complain and, as the old proverb says, "we all might live to see pay day".'

We sprinkled the incense, took the oath, beginning with the words: 'All homage to thee . . .' and left that sanctuary of desolation.

So began our days with the usurper. We sold the donkey, bought a tent near the chariot park and tried to become one of the crowd. Usurek sought us out, eager to use our skills to train others, as well as to talk about what might happen. At first I thought he was suspicious of us, until I realised it was our company that he sought. We were often invited to his camp fire to share food and a jug of beer. From him we learned about the advance across the Sinai, how Avaris and Sile had been seized and Akenhaten had re-emerged, issuing decrees and demanding the allegiance of local garrisons. Hittite advisers and Canaanite mercenaries had bolstered his force, and the usurper's presence had expanded like a cloud. One thing we quickly learnt: entrance to the fortress was strictly forbidden without a special pass. Usurek had permission to come and go as he pleased, but the likes of us were told to keep our distance.

Sobeck and I decided to become in all things professional mercenaries, careful in our talk, prudent in our actions, despite Usurek's best efforts to make us drunk. Time and again we proved our skill on the drill ground. Some of the recruits were born charioteers; others could never handle a horse if they lived for a million years. Usurek decided to put us in charge of a squadron, giving us each a silver necklace as a badge of office.

Six weeks after our arrival in the camp, he woke us just before dawn, inviting us out to the meagre camp fire which one of his escort was trying to build up. He had brought some bread and meat; he shared it out and clapped us both on the shoulder.

'You offered to serve for three months and take a percentage of the spoils?'

'We have already agreed to that,' Sobeck replied harshly. I was more cautious, wondering what was behind our rough awakening.

'As squadron leaders,' Usurek continued, 'you will also be paid certain debens of silver from the war chest, but I have done better for you. You have both been raised to the rank of Nesus, bodyguards.' He handed us small tablets of clay. 'You will be allowed to enter the fortress. So come, we might as well begin today!'

We seized our passes, each hung on a copper chain, put these over our heads, grabbed our cloaks and followed Usurek up the causeway. A captain of the guard rigorously checked us, searching for any concealed weapons, taking our names, studying us closely in the pool of torchlight. I grinned and joked with Sobeck to hide my nervousness. The inquisitive captain was a Hittite, perhaps some relation to the one Colonel Nebamun had tortured in the cellars of his house. We were allowed to pass. One gate was pulled slightly open, and we slipped through into that grim fortress. It was like entering a small city. A great avenue ran north to south, another east to west, quartering the camp precisely. Tents and bothies were erected in neat lines. At the centre of the camp stood a second ramp and palisade which housed the pavilions of the usurper, his advisers, altars and standards. Usurek found us a place in the eastern quarter: a tent made out of camel skin with some crude bowls, jugs and a cooking pot. Once he was satisfied, we returned to our old place and collected our baggage.

Our duties were not radically changed. We spent our days drilling the recruits, but at night we were expected to do a tour of duty either along the picket lines outside the gates or on the towers or ramparts. I was eager to catch sight of the usurper, but the Sacred Enclosure was closely guarded. Three days later, however, my wish was satisfied. The False Pharaoh decided to ride in glory through the camp to show his face to his faithful followers, a glorious procession preceded by standard-bearers and surrounded by officers and flunkeys. The usurper wore the blue war crown of Egypt, the sacred nenes cloak about his shoulders and a beautiful war kilt girded around his middle, its jaguar tails hanging behind. He drove a splendid chariot of state of blue gold and silver electrum, pulled by pure white Syrian mares, proceeding along the broad avenues of the camp to receive the cheers and acclamations of the soldiers. One glance proved he was a usurper: a tall, angular man with bony body, sharp face and cruel eyes. Of course I had to nose the ground as his chariot passed. I, who had looked upon the face of Akenhaten, could only seethe in anger at the impudent insolence of this pretender. The woman behind him was no better. She was beautiful in a garish sort of way, dressed in white gauffered robes, a crown upon her head. Just for a few seconds, with the swirl of red hair, you thought you might be looking upon Nefertiti, but she too was as false as her husband. Oh, she was beautiful enough, though rather small, plump, lacking any of the beauty or grace of the woman who had haunted my heart, still did and always would.

More interesting were those who followed in the chariots behind. Aziru, Prince of Byblos, resplendent in his jewellery and collars of silver and gold, was dressed as a priest in his long

126

white robe, a striped red and blue cloak about his shoulders. There was a man who reminded me of the Lord Ay, with his long, narrow face and expressive dark eyes. In the chariot beside him were two men I did recognise, the priests Khufu and Djoser, shaven-headed, of medium height, faces heavily oiled, eyes ringed with black kohl, full lips carmined. I had met them in the City of the Aten and always regarded them as two fat priests eager for a profit. Now their plump beringed fingers clutched the chariot rail as they beamed out across the cheering soldiers like Lords of Creation. The cavalcade proved the true source of the usurper's strength. Apart from the priests, the rest were Canaanites or high-ranking Hittite officers.

Sobeck and I cheered with the rest, and that evening we joined the feasting, filling our cups with spiced wine, our platters heavy with roasted meat. From the Sacred Enclosure drifted the sound of music. Sobeck and I, acting drunkenly, watched as the trays of delicacies – shellfish, fried lotus sprinkled with spices, antelope, hare, partridges, wild calf, as well as bowls of grapes, melons, figs and pomegranates – were taken into the Royal Pavilion where the usurper feasted with his officers.

'What's the occasion?' Sobeck blearily asked Usurek.

'I have told you not to ask questions,' the mercenary replied, waving a finger drunkenly. 'But today is an auspicious day, sacred to the Weather God of the Hittites, and if our master says we feast and celebrate, then we shall feast and celebrate.'

Sobeck and I pretended to be as drunk as the others. We each found a dancing girl and joined in the festivities. Sobeck even agreed to entertain the rest by showing how he could dance on fiery coals without burning his feet. At last the wine had its effect. The music died, the flame torches and fire faded, though even then I noticed that order was strictly maintained. Hittite guards patrolled the camp, sentries were checked, gates reinforced. It must have been in the early hours when Sobeck and I, throwing aside all pretence of drunkenness and gaiety, left our companions in their stupor and found a lonely part of the camp.

'What can we do?' Sobeck asked.

'We can kill the usurper,' I whispered. 'The next time he decides to show his face, a well-placed arrow to the throat?'

127

'And we receive a nice sharp stake through our arse. Mahu, there is nothing we can do. The usurper and his woman are mere puppets. Kill them and they'll find someone else.'

Despite my best efforts, I had drunk a lot of wine. I felt sleepy and heavy-eyed.

'We have to go,' Sobeck whispered. 'There's nothing we can do here. Every day increases the danger. We have the information we need.'

'No, no.' I tried to think clearly. 'The very fact that we are here we can use later. There are two dangers: this army, and Meryre's faction in Egypt. Both must be destroyed.'

I heard a sound in the darkness. Sobeck tensed. We had gathered in a darkened corner of the fortress near a small postern gate where the rubbish was piled to be taken out each morning. We were well away from the festivities.

'Is there someone there?'

Sobeck and I got to our feet just as Usurek came staggering out of the darkness, a beer jug in one hand, a cup in the other.

'Why are you here?' he demanded.

The way he stood, the sharpness of his question and the way he looked at Sobeck and me showed that he too was not as drunk as he pretended to be. He put the beer jug down on the ground.

'Why are you here?' he repeated. 'Why did you leave the dancing girls to come and talk near a pile of rubbish?' He sniffed at the stench. 'I have watched you, you know. When the procession was taking place. You seemed most interested. When you were drinking, I noticed more went on the ground than in your mouths.'

'We have got a busy day tomorrow.' Sobeck walked forward. 'And we have to be ready.'

He moved his hand so fast, Usurek had no time to react. Sobeck plunged his dagger straight into his belly. Usurek tried to stagger back, but Sobeck's hand went behind his neck, pulling him forward, thrusting the dagger deeper into his belly, pulling him on to it. The mercenary captain, eyes staring, mouth trying to speak, dropped to the ground.

'I had no choice,' Sobeck whispered over his shoulder. 'I thought he was as drunk as the rest. Come, quickly.' He withdrew his dagger. We took Usurek's corpse and buried it beneath the rubbish; afterwards, arms round each other's shoulders, we staggered back to our tent. Once inside, we packed our possessions. I was fearful of what would happen. We couldn't flee immediately as the gates were guarded and sealed, the curfew imposed. Sobeck whispered that we would leave as early as we could and try to reach the river. He sounded optimistic, but I was more fearful. Usurek was a good officer, a captain as well as a scribe of troops. He had his own retinue and would soon be missed.

I am not given to prayer. I don't know if the Aten exists, or if Amun-Ra, the Silent One of Thebes, involves himself in the affairs of Man. All that night my soul was haunted by the images of the Field of Fire and the House of Darkness, and I prayed that our lives would not end. For once, perhaps the only time in my life, the Gods seemed to listen. We were roused the next morning by cries and shouts. I thought Usurek's corpse had been discovered, but instead a wide-eyed herald announced the news that Generals Horemheb and Rameses, together with the Horus and Isis regiments, had entered the Delta and were moving rapidly towards us. Within a day the entire camp would be under attack.

Bar
(An ancient Canaanite God of War)

Chapter 7

Horemheb, Chief of Scribes of the Army, Fan Bearer to the Right of the King, Fitting of Forms and Fair of Face, Horus in the South, the Vengeance of Ra, came storming into the Delta like Montu the God of War. Like Sekhmet of the legend he pounced, breathing fire against Egypt's enemies. Cunning as the mongoose in military matters, Horemheb struck slyly and fast, taking even his own commanders by surprise. The enemy had expected Horemheb and Rameses to move slowly north, bringing up troops from Thebes, collecting more on the way and then arriving at Memphis to organise the two crack regiments and lead them into the Delta. No, that was not Horemheb, the Horus Incarnate! He ordered Rameses to bring up the reinforcements as fast as he could. Learning from Nebamun about Meryre, he told General Nakhtimin to keep an eye on Buhen in the south whilst he made his own preparations. The Memphis regiments were ordered not to wait for Horemheb but to advance as quickly as possible to the edge of the Delta, where Horemheb met them at Bubastis, the City of the Cat. The Chief Scribe of the Army, with his own escort, moved rapidly upriver.

By the time the troops assembled at Bubastis, Horemheb was in command of four thousand infantry, crack troops divided into four corps: the Fire of the Horus; the Power of Isis; the Anger of Seth; and the Glory of Amun. He brought with him units of the Nakhtu-aa, the strong-arm boys, who rejoiced in the nickname of the Roaring Bulls of Anubis. In addition, two thousand chariots, led by the elite corps, Mighty as Horus, provided the hard backbone to this army. Any other commander would have followed the Nile and its tributaries north. However, Horemheb had collected the most accurate maps of the Red Lands to the north-east of the White-Walled City of Memphis, as well as the region around Bubastis, and struck east across the desert. Mercenaries, my own company included, were dispatched to seize wells, oases, any sources of water or shade. Horemheb was streaking east, following the narrow canals into the Delta. In the bitter cold dawn of that fateful day, the usurper's camp was stirring, roused by the news, but it was sluggish; officers and men had drunk deeply, and for a while chaos reigned.

Orderlies came looking for Captain Usurek; we claimed that we hadn't seen him. We furtively prayed that no one would search the mounds of refuse and discover his cold, stiffening corpse. Sobeck and myself were more alert than the rest. We were wondering what to do when we heard the screams from outside the Royal Enclosure. We hurried across. Two mercenaries from Horemheb's advance guard had been captured; foragers or scouts, they now hung from a cross piece supported by poles, heaps of burning charcoal placed beneath their feet whilst their bodies and legs were beaten with flayed canes. The Hittite commander in charge of the torture was beside himself with fury. He tried to extract from them details of how many men Horemheb had brought, his position and line of battle. Of course the mercenaries couldn't reply, even if they had wanted to. They were more hunters than soldiers and had blundered into the enemy camp picket line without thinking. Bloody welts criss-crossed their bodies, and even as we listened, we knew they were only telling their captors what they thought they wanted, exaggerated numbers, regiments which didn't exist. The Hittite commander knew this, and silenced their screams by slitting their throats. By now the enemy camp was fully alert. The Hittite commander recognised us.

'Where is Captain Usurek?' he demanded.

Sobeck shrugged.

'You are from his chariot corps, aren't you?'

The Hittite wiped bloody hands on his leather jerkin with its metal scales and pushed back his long black hair, tying it into a queue at the back. He shouted to his three companions.

'Get three chariots harnessed,' he ordered. 'You two,' he pointed at Sobeck and myself, 'shall come with us.'

A short while later, we left the camp, our chariot being pulled by the two bays we'd trained. It was one of those fresh, beautiful mornings, with the water and greenery of the Delta providing some coolness against the growing heat of the day. Behind us we left an enemy who had not yet decided whether they would prepare for defence or advance to meet Horemheb. I put the question to the Hittite captain as we guided our chariots along the narrow, dusty trackways between the trees.

'Will we go out to meet the enemy, sir? Or wait for them to come on?'

'Deploy, of course!' the Hittite sneered. He spoke the lingua franca in a clumsy fashion. He was more concerned with Horemheb's speed and surprise, and grasping the reins of the chariot he lost himself in a litany of abuse. We passed picket lines and hunters coming in, all surprised by the news that the enemy, who hadn't been expected for weeks, was now almost upon them.

Eventually we left the greenery behind. To our right was the water of the Nile and its lush strips of grass, farming land, palm trees, sycamore and terebinth. We went thundering along that hardened strip which separates the harsh Red Lands from the fertile black soil along the Nile. A silent place, already feeling the heat of the sun, but excellent ground for an army to march fast and chariot squadrons to roll forward. At first there was nothing except the occasional vulture, or Pharaoh's Hen, soaring above us. The heat grew more cloying. We paused to allow the horses to drink from water skins and wet their heads, and then continued. The chariots spaced out, ours in the middle, the Hittite commander to our far right, a battle standard of a lion's head with three horsetails on the bar underneath. The ground dipped and rose. When we reached the top of the hill, the Hittite commander reined in. Beneath us stretched the desert plain, broken here and there by a dip in the land or clusters of dusty palm trees fringing small oases.

Sobeck's keen eyes found what we were searching for. 'There!' he shouted.

At first I could see nothing, just the shifting desert haze and billowing clouds of dust. I picked up the water skin and wetted my face and neck. The Hittite commander took off his leather helmet, throwing it to the floor of his chariot.

'You know we can do no more,' Sobeck whispered. 'We'll never be given another chance like this.'

I followed his direction. The Hittite commander was scoffing that Sobeck had seen a mirage, but then I caught it: the glint of sun on weapons, a moving dust cloud, and above it a smudge of black smoke as if a fire had been lit.

'A camp, or are they moving?' I whispered.

Sobeck, not waiting for the Hittite officer, urged our horses forward down the incline. Clicking his tongue and shaking the reins, Sobeck moved our chariot into the shade of the palm trees of a small oasis, a rocky place with hardy bush and grass sprouting around a small pool. He got down and stood under a palm tree, shading his eyes as he stared out across the desert. The Hittites also brought their chariots down; not their clumsy four-wheeled ones, but fast-moving Egyptian war carriages. The captain was furious at Sobeck.

'You should only go forward on my order. What is it you have seen?'

He and his companions clustered around us. There was an argument. Sometimes the Hittites would lapse into their own tongue. The dust cloud was drawing close; the flashes of light could no longer be dismissed as a mirage.

'The Egyptians,' the Hittite declared. 'And it is not an advance patrol. The entire battle line is moving forward.' He squinted up at the sun. 'If they move fast, they'll be at the camp by noon.'

Sobeck turned and looked at me, and I nodded. We could not go back. Usurek's corpse might have been discovered, and when Horemheb reached the enemy fortress, he would annihilate it with fire and sword. The imperial standards would be hoisted. The broad red and gold streamers which hung above the entrance to the Temple of Amun-Ra in Thebes would be displayed, a sign that Horemheb and his troops would show no quarter and take no prisoners. Sobeck and I drifted back towards our chariot. He took our bow, whilst I moved across behind the Hittites to one of their two chariots. I unhitched a bow and quiver of arrows.

The Hittites were still concerned about what was approaching. The commander turned. Sobeck and I loosed our shafts. Two of the Hittites fell immediately. The commander caught Sobeck's arrow full in the face; he collapsed screaming and coughing blood. My shaft pierced his companion's neck. The other two Hittites were quicker drawing their swords; they were too cunning to attack but, using the trees as protection, drew us into a deadly game of cat and mouse. We loosed shaft after shaft. The Hittite commander, despite his terrible wound, the arrow piercing one cheek and going straight through the other, also drew his sword and came staggering towards us, distracting Sobeck from his aim. This time Sobeck finished the task, putting an arrow through the Hittite captain's throat. I loosed a shaft at the other two, but had to retreat as they burst from the clump of trees, racing towards the third chariot. Skilled men, one seized the reins as the other grasped the bow. Sobeck and I raced in pursuit, but the chariot drew away, arrows whipping the air around our faces.

'They cannot escape,' Sobeck gasped. 'They must not return to camp. They will know we are spies, and the usurper mustn't learn how close Horemheb truly is.'

The Hittite chariot wheeled and thundered out of the oasis, going back the way it had come. We followed in pursuit, Sobeck standing beside me, whip lashing the air. It was a deadly chase. The Hittite chariot was faster, the horses stronger, and the gap between us grew. Every so often the Hittite archer would turn; a master bowman, his shafts were directed at our horses, but we wheeled and shifted using the clouds of dust their chariot sent up. Sobeck moved our horses to their blind side so the archer had to lean across the driver to loose his shafts. We cleared the brow of the hill and continued our pursuit to the clatter of wheels and thundering hooves, the hot breeze breathing sand into our faces. The gap between us grew until the Hittites made a common mistake. Egyptian chariots at full charge require a special skill; wheels and horses must act as one while the driver keeps the chariot on a certain line behind the horses. On this occasion they were travelling too fast. The Hittite misjudged the speed. The chariot swayed to the left and its wheels hit a rock, trapping the horses in a tangle of harness, whilst the two Hittites were thrown out, their bodies bouncing along the ground as if they were already corpses. I reined in. One of the Hittites was sprawled in such a fashion we realised his neck was broken. The other, moaning, tried to drag himself to his feet. Sobeck jumped down and, bestriding his body, pulled his head back and slit his throat.

One of the Hittite horses had broken its leg and had to be destroyed, but we unhitched the other and led it back into the oasis. I told Sobeck to guard the horses; if they had broken loose they would have cantered back to the enemy camp. I climbed into our chariot and left the oasis, charging down towards the gleaming mass of weaponry moving ever closer. Of course scouts were sent out to intercept, lighter chariots, their horses small and fast, each chariot with its driver and infantryman. I slowed down, lifting my hand, shouting the words of peace. The scouts ringed me. One of them screamed at me to climb down. I did so and knelt at the back of the chariot. I heard the thunder of heavier war chariots and glimpsed their colours as they swirled about me. One in particular, with its red and gold electrum displaying the personal insignia of Horemheb, stopped before me. The Chief Scribe of the Army, General of Thebes, resplendent in his light blue and gold-scaled armour over a thin linen robe, climbed down, his square pugilist's face gleaming with sweat and oil. Other chariots drew up even as I pulled myself to my feet.

'My lord Mahu.' Horemheb tossed his bow to his driver and clasped my hand. 'One of our scouts was sure he had seen movement in the oasis. Well,' he looked me over from head to foot, 'your arrival proves the old proverb wrong. "Out in the Red Lands you only meet an enemy."'

He shouted for wine and bread to be brought. I joined him in his own chariot. I lifted the wine skin and bit into the bread, then coughed.

'I know,' Horemheb grinned, 'out here everything tastes of sand and dust.'

He then told me of what he had done. As the dust clouds settled, I looked behind and saw the massed might of Egypt, columns of infantry flanked by chariot squadrons, moving out of the desert haze. The pace of the army was determined by the foot; as the first units passed, I recognised their speed and urgency. The men looked exhausted, covered in dust. Officers strode up and down exhorting them on.

'They were singing when we left Abydos,' Horemheb murmured, raising his hand in salute as the first units passed. 'Now they haven't even got the strength to talk.'

The entire imperial army emerged from its dust haze, at least a mile across.

'According to our maps and scouts,' Horemheb took the wine skin from me, 'we have at least three wells between here and the enemy camp. Now, Mahu?'

I didn't tell him about what had happened at the oasis; only that his advance had taken the enemy by surprise. Horemheb lowered the wine skin, eyes rounded with astonishment.

'You mean to say they were feasting last night and still haven't left the fortress?' He climbed down from his chariot, shouting at his trumpeter to summon his staff officers and urging his line commanders to continue their march. 'Infantry gather at the oasis!' he yelled. 'Chariots further to the east. You'll find fresh water there. The line mustn't be broken. It will be the shortest respite.'

The foot soldiers continued, line after line passing us in billows of dust, clouds rising from the chariots on either flank. Horemheb gathered his corps commanders around him, talking bluntly, now and again asking me to describe the layout of the enemy camp. A scribe, coughing and spluttering, squatted and tried to make a rough map. I pointed out the positions – the moat, the mound, the palisade – and the quality of troops inside the fortress and the army of mercenaries outside. Horemheb's suppressed excitement was shared by his commanders, one of whom was Nebamun. He clasped my hand but was unable to converse across Horemheb's stream of questions and demands.

'We have them.' Horemheb was almost jumping from foot to foot. 'My lords, we have them! They are drunk and sluggish. The real danger is the Hittite officer corps and their skilled soldiers. If we are fortunate they'll demand the fortress be left and the entire army come out to meet us where we have little water or shade. They must know we are tired and thirsty.'

'But still ready for battle!' one of his colonels declared.

139

'We must have victory,' Horemheb replied. 'If the enemy meet us out here and defeat us, Abydos and Memphis will be put to the torch. They will commandeer every barge and float down to Thebes, and take the City of the Sceptre.'

'Meryre?' I demanded.

'He's still locked up in Memphis,' Nebamun retorted. 'He's allowed to take the air and nothing else. There've been rumours of unrest in the south.'

'This usurper,' Horemheb demanded, 'this False Pharaoh. You have seen him, my lord Mahu? Him and his woman?'

'They are both impostors,' I replied flatly. 'They no more have the right to rule Egypt,' I gestured to a dung beetle crawling across the papyrus roll of the scribe, 'than that. They are impostors, puppets.' I gave a short description of the Hittite commanders, Prince Aziru and the two priests, Djoser and Khufu. Horemheb was only half listening. As the boy, so the man. In the House of Instruction, where we had been trained and educated together, Horemheb displayed one quality above all others: he would concentrate on a problem and would not be distracted until it had been solved.

'We must move quickly.' He kicked at the scribe to stand. 'I want the army to be in three divisions. In the centre the foot, archers before them. On each flank the chariot squadrons, a thousand apiece. Skirmishers in front, war chariots behind. I intend to bring them to battle before this day is finished: if those Hittites have any sense they'll know that. So, gentlemen,' he climbed back into his chariot, 'we reach that oasis and form a battle line. Mahu, clear your throat. You are going to do a lot of talking.'

Within the hour, Horemheb's army was deploying its flanks on two oases: the left where Sobeck and I had killed the Hittites; the right about two miles distant, lost in the desert haze. Horemheb's scouts had found Sobeck and brought him back. We were attached to Nebamun's corps. The commissary wagons were brought up; the oxen wouldn't move quickly enough, so chariots were used to share out bread and dried meat. At the same time the Neferu, the raw recruits, an entire legion of them, were given water skins and told to make sure that every soldier wetted his face and cleared his throat. Horemheb seemed impervious to the heat and dust, the host of flies brought in by the mounds of animal dung. Heat or shade, he was the same. Peering along his battle line, he issued a stream of orders. Officers were to check that every man had his weapons and his mouthful of meat, bread and water. The precious horses were also tended to, and the wheels, spokes and axles of the chariots carefully checked to ensure the animal grease still protected them against the harsh dust of the desert. Eventually Horemheb could no longer curb his impatience.

He ordered his splendid war chariot to be brought: it was pulled by magnificent black stallions with white star bursts on their foreheads, the standards of Amun-Ra pushed into the niches on either side of the carriage. He advanced slowly along the battle line, preceded by a herald and trumpeter and followed by the chariots of his commanders, strong-arm boys running on either side. Every so often he would pause so I could deliver my message.

'Men of Egypt, soldiers of the Ra! The man you are marching against is a Hittite puppet, an impostor! I swear by all that is holy, by my own Ka, by sky and earth. I have seen him with my own eyes. He is an impostor, a pretender, a usurper, supported by vile Asiatics, rebels and traitors who will soon be slaughtered by your arms and devoured by eternal fire.'

Along the line we travelled. The heralds signalled the trumpeters to give a blast and I would repeat the message. My voice grew so hoarse one of the heralds had to repeat it. Each proclamation was greeted by a thunderous roar.

'Lovely boys!' Horemheb whispered. 'They will march for me until we reach the Great Green. I have promised them all the plunder of the enemy camp, their gold, silver and women. I have told them to follow in the steps of the great Ahmose and their noble ancestors who drove the Hyksos out of Egypt. The one doubt they had was that they were marching against their own king. Yet they know you, Mahu.' Horemheb had sent heralds ahead to proclaim my name and status. Now he grinned, 'Why, they even consider you a hero!'

Eventually the other oasis came into sight. My message was completed. The salutation of the troops thundered to the sky, whilst Horemheb, like the great show-off he was, went charging up the line, horses thundering, chariot gleaming, to be greeted by the ecstatic cries of his troops.

'They are the best,' Horemheb whispered as he reined in, 'and somewhere to the south, Rameses is bringing up more. The Hathor corps and whatever mercenaries we can find.'

For a while there was inaction, that ominous strengthening silence which precedes any battle. Our men rested in the shade of the chariots or sought more water. At last Horemheb was ready. The calls for the general advance brayed, cracking through the silence, sending the birds fluttering from the trees into a swirling arc against the sky. Sobeck and I were given a chariot as well as leather corselets and war kilts. We dressed, sweating under the strengthening sun. The battle line then moved until we reached a clump of greenery. Here a force of mercenaries waited to oppose us, but they were trampled down, pushed aside, sent scattering or transfixed with arrow, spear or sword. Scouts were sent out and came hastening back. The enemy were deploying from the fortress. By the time we reached the plain, the usurper's forces, standards aloft in the centre, were waiting for us, rank after rank of foot, chariot squadrons on each wing. This was Per-I, the Place of Battle, dominated by Heem Hen-T, the Cry of War. Horemheb did not give the enemy time to invoke the Gods. No heralds were sent forward, no proclamation issued, no makeshift altar built and offerings made to Seth the Announcer of Battles. Our opponents were traitors, pirates, bandits and outlaws, to be destroyed like any vermin.

The men of war prepared eagerly for battle under a blazing sun. Our left wing was based on the now deserted market town, our right on a small oasis, one of those dusty pools of green which bordered the coarse, open land fronting the desert. The enemy still manoeuvred before us. They had more infantry than us and stretched their battle front trying to outflank us on each wing. Sobeck and I clustered around the trumpeters and standard-bearers near Horemheb's chariot. The Great General stood perched like a falcon, watching every manoeuvre, rapping out orders to a scribe. 'Well, Mahu?'

I described our days of drilling raw recruits. Horemheb listened intently and ordered the front squadron of chariotry on the left wing to move backwards and forwards, creating a cloud of dust, whilst at the same time detaching squadrons, moving them behind our lines to bolster our right. Weakening our left flank was an unusual manoeuvre, which brought cries of protest from Horemheb's staff, yet he was insistent. Once this stratagem was completed, Horemheb sent forward massed ranks of archers to loose volley after volley, scoring the enemy foot and their chariot squadrons on the left wing. The latter moved forward, eager to respond and engage, anything to stop that black rain of whistling death. As they did so, Horemheb gave the order to Nebamun, commander of our strengthened right flank and leader of an elite corps, to advance with all haste.

We hurried back to our chariots even as the trumpets shrilled and Nebamun's standard-bearer, appraised of what was happening, shouted and called. Again the trumpet rang out. Sobeck and I were hardly ready as Nebamun's chariot moved forward, standards aloft, displaying the God Ptah in human form, a small statute at the end of a gold-plated pole. We followed. Our chariot line rattled forward, drivers slightly crouched, their companions already notching arrow to bow. At first there was confusion, one chariot slamming into another, horses becoming too excited, but the faster we advanced the more our squadron began to break up into line. Order was restored, horses and charioteers grew settled, trumpets sounded. Our world became one of rumbling wheels, wind whipping the dust by our faces. More shouts, further blasts of trumpets, and our horses moved into a trot then a gallop, followed by the most glorious sights, a whole corps, squadron after squadron, line after line of charging chariots, carriages of electrum gleaming in the sun. The plumes between our horses' ears rose and fell to the ominous rattle of the wheels; the embroidered javelin pouches and quivers slapped against the sides to be lost under the thunderous sound of thousands of charging hoofs.

Horemheb's plan was brutal and simple: to shatter the enemy's left flank and roll the remnants up on its centre, drive the enemy forces away from the fortress and trap them against the tributary of the Nile. Old men discuss such tactics. Veterans bore their grandchildren with stories of such a charge. They dab their fingers into their wine or beer and sketch drawings on the table to show how it was or how it should have been. Yet if you were there, you felt the shock of battle, the thrill of the clash, the heart-stopping excitement of the charge. Sometimes I curse Horemheb's name, for we have fought each other, yet one thing I will concede: he was blessed by the genius of the God of War. He had moved so swiftly, so fiercely to trap his enemy that the usurper had been caught unprepared, and whatever the Hittites were thinking, they failed to act. Instead of swinging their right flank to smash into our left, they did nothing except draw chariots and men from elsewhere to bolster that part of their battle line now under attack. Such fumbling lost them the battle: their own chariot squadrons were hardly moving when we smashed into them, sending soldiers, their mounts and chariots crashing over into the dust. Even the huge Hittite carriages tumbled over, their crews spilling out, bodies being ripped apart under hoofs and wheels. Those who were lucky to survive staggered to their feet only to be sent sprawling again with hideous blows from sword, axe, club or feathered shafts loosed at very close range. Sobeck and I were in the front of the advance, yet we broke right through, turning left to charge back into the rear of the enemy foot, who were so disconcerted they did not know which way to turn.

Even I, inexperienced in war, recognised that the usurper faced disaster. No greater force exists than massed Egyptian chariots at loose amongst enemy foot. Horses and wheels alone wreak hideous damage. If a man jumped aside, he would usually fall into the path of another chariot, and even if he escaped, there was the constant rain of javelins and arrows to face!

The enemy foot were paid mercenaries, more used to pillaging villages than battling against the elite corps of Egypt. They fell back, their left wing seeking protection in the centre. Horemheb then committed his whole battle line. The enemy were pushed back, away from the fortress, across the plain into the green shrubbery which divided the market town from the ancient city of Avaris. The noise and screams were blood-curdling. Men staggered around, holding gruesome wounds to head or body. Horemheb had ordered the imperial colours to be clearly displayed, a sign that no prisoners were to be taken. The battle turned into a rout, which slipped into a massacre. Sobeck and I faced no danger. Occasionally a mercenary would try to board our chariot or bring our horses down, only to be easily dispatched by an arrow or, if he came too close, javelin or club. The ground grew streaked with blood, and littered with corpses. We came up against the Hittite corps, professional fighters who, for a while, stopped our advance. Nevertheless, our chariots milled around them whilst our archers and foot danced in between seeking a gap in their line, a chance to hamstring horses or loose arrows at the chariot crew. Eventually they broke, leaping down from their chariots to join the fleeing mercenaries.

By now we were in front of the fortress. All the guards had disappeared. I drew my chariot alongside Nebamun's, screaming my request at him. The heat of the battle had rejuvenated the old colonel. Lines and furrows had disappeared, eyes gleamed bright in his dusty, blood-streaked face. He listened to my request and turned, shouting at a staff officer. We guided our chariot out of the mêlée, followed by a dozen others. Accompanied by archers and a unit of Nakhtu-aa, we thundered towards the main gate of the fortress. We met no opposition. The gates hung half open, and the Nakhtu-aa pulled them aside and charged in. Other units of Horemheb's battle line, realising the battle was over, followed us, eager for plunder. The camp was now given over to pillage and the rape of women left behind.

'What do you want?' Sobeck, weak with exhaustion, reined in his horses.

We'd reached the Royal Enclosure. Its gates were held open by the corpse of a priest whom our foot soldiers had disembowelled. From within I could hear the shrieks of a woman. I jumped down from the chariot and raced into the usurper's pavilion, its beautiful gold-fringed cloths flapping in the breeze. Inside there was chaos. Corpses sprawled about in widening pools of blood. Two Kushite mercenaries had seized a kitchen maid and were holding her down whilst their companions were tipping over chests and pots. A soldier had found a jug of wine and was busy laying out cups, filling them to the brim, screaming at his companions to join him. I found an enemy scribe hiding behind a large couch; pinch-faced and bald-headed, he jabbered for his life. I seized him by his robe and pulled him to his feet.

'Your life will be spared,' I shouted, 'on one condition. Where are the records? Where are the usurper's letters, his proclamations?'

The man's jaw quivered in fright.

'The records?' I repeated.

He pointed to the far corner of the tent, where three or four reed baskets had escaped the attention of the marauders. I went across and emptied the contents out on to the ground. Sobeck, using all his authority, ordered five of the mercenaries to come over and protect us whilst I went through the contents. The records were a mixture of papyrus rolls and clay tablets; all of them bore the cartouche or seal of Akenhaten. I wondered where the usurper had obtained this. Sobeck found me a leather sack and threw it at my feet. I filled it with anything which looked interesting. By the time I had finished, the scribe had disappeared. Sobeck told me he'd thrown off his robe, crawled under the awning of the tent and fled. He would do what many of the enemy would, dispose of anything which marked him as a follower of the usurper and merge with the victorious troops.

I sat for a while, soaked in sweat. The girl had stopped her screaming. She lay at the far end of the pavilion, throat cut, eyes staring sightlessly. Virtually all the furniture and furnishings had disappeared: chests, chairs, stools and weapons. As Sobeck grimly remarked, 'If it was on two legs it was killed, otherwise it was taken.' He dismissed our guard and crouched down beside me.

'Is this what you were after, Mahu?'

'It is my treasure trove.' I pressed the sack to my chest. 'My plunder.'

'And?' Sobeck asked.

Figures danced outside the tent, shouts and yells echoed, a firebrand was thrown in, whilst at the same time the awning around us was put to the torch. We left hastily. The Royal Enclosure had ceased to exist. The palisade had been broken down, the altars overturned, the fortress given over to wholesale devastation. Sobeck and I forced our way through. Our men were now fighting each other, some already drunk, quarrelling and bartering over the spoils of battle. The main gates had also been torched. Two great bonfires flared on either side of the entrance, flames leaping up into the afternoon sky, billows of smoke curling about. From the plain below we could still hear the clatter and clash of battle, the screams of dying men. Sobeck found a wineskin propped against the corpse of a Hittite officer and we went searching for our chariot. One of Nebamun's officers, fearful of fire in the camp, had ordered it, together with the rest, to withdraw to the plain below. Drinking the wine and clutching my precious burden, we forced our way through the press of men down to where Nebamun's men were milling about before the gates leading to the Field of Fire and the House of Darkness.

'What's in there?' Nebamun demanded. His face was smudged with dust and smoke, and splashes of blood spoiled the finery and glitter of his leather mailed jacket and war kilt. 'I daren't go in lest there be a trap, yet the place seems deserted. What's beyond there?'

I recalled the day we took the oath. 'Why, Colonel, a vision of the Underworld. You are right to be prudent. Send across a few archers first.'

Nebamun repeated my request. A group of nimble-footed archers scaled the palisade; we heard their exclamations of surprise. The gates swung open. Nebamun, surrounded by his officers, walked in and stared speechlessly around.

'By all that is in heaven and earth,' he whispered. 'How many, Mahu?'

'Well over a hundred stakes, Colonel. Possibly two hundred. This is only a fraction of those the usurper killed.'

'Shall we remove them?' one of the officers shouted. 'Sir, this is an abomination.'

'No, no.' Nebamun, hand raised, walked towards the grotesque statue of the Destroyer. He paused at the roar from that hideous Mastaba. The ramp leading up to the great door was now unguarded.

'Is it the din of the battle, or did I hear a lion roar?'

Sobeck explained what the Mastaba contained. Nebamun, shaking his head, told us to withdraw.

'We will touch nothing here,' he said, 'until General Horemheb sees it for himself.'

We left that gruesome place and sat down on the grass outside, sharing the wine skin, half listening to the chatter of Nebamun's officers. Now and again the Colonel would go back to convince himself of what he had seen; that he had not suffered a nightmare. Somebody asked him if we should rejoin the battle.

'It's no longer a battle.' The old colonel shook his head. 'It's a massacre. General Horemheb's orders are strict. We led the advance; let others finish it.'

The aftermath of a battle is always haunting, as if you have left life hanging between heaven and earth. All around us men were groaning, pleading for water, only to be dispatched with a swift thrust of a knife. Smoke billowed across the fortress. The late afternoon air was rent with ghastly cries and yells. Soldiers drunk on wine staggered about, arms laden with booty or leading away female captives. Hideous cruelties and brutalities were inflicted upon the dead as well as the dying. The sky blackened with smoke, through which the vultures curled, drawn by the scent of blood. The cacophony of sound eased, and was followed by the onset of a chilling silence, like sweat on your body after you have run a race. The sun began to set. Soldiers drifted back from where the massacre had ended, down near the river. They too were eager to plunder and were busy looting the dead, showing no mercy whatsoever to the enemy.

Horemheb must have called a halt to the killing. Lines of prisoners began to appear; most of them were naked except for their loincloths, arms and hands bound tightly behind their backs. They were forced to kneel. Some of them begged piteously for help for wounds, others cried for water, as their thirst must have been dreadful. They were herded together like frightened sheep under the guard of Nakhtu-aa, and a makeshift fence was formed around them: chariots were unhitched, the carriages used to pen them in whilst the horses were led away. At first there was only a trickle of prisoners, but eventually they came in one long, dusty column. Most were mercenaries, though Horemheb had captured a number of high-ranking Hittite officers. They too were shown no mercy but treated like the rest. Following them came the chariot squadrons, their horses exhausted. Finally, amidst a blare of trumpets and preceded by his fan-bearers and standard-carriers, Horemheb himself arrived, exulting in his moment of glory.

The entire plain outside the fortress now became a vast

barracks housing victor and vanquished alike. The cries of the
wounded faded. Officers moved through the ranks imposing
order, beating the drunks with their sticks, confiscating booty,
ordering the dead to be dragged out, their right hands chopped
off so that Horemheb's scribes could draw up a tally of the slain.
Makeshift hospitals were set up with cloths and coverings
filched from camp awnings. A line of water carriers was organised. Stretcher-bearers began to comb the entire battlefield.
Armed with sharp knives, they finished off the enemy wounded
but tenderly lifted on to pallets the Egyptian injured. Horemheb
ignored us; surrounded by his own staff officers and entourage,
he had solemnly processed around the fiercely burning fortress
to receive the plaudits and salutes of his victorious troops. The
triumphant procession ended in front of us. Horemheb, still
clutching his bloody sword, his right arm splattered with gore
up to his shoulder, stepped off his chariot. Staff officers gathered round clapping their hands, kneeling before him to offer
their congratulations. Standard-bearers came hurrying up to
brief him and provide news of what was happening. Horemheb
listened to them all, now and again turning to the scribe
crouched on the ground beside him. He then climbed back into
his chariot and raised his bloody sword skyward. A gust of
smoke from the fortress came billowing down, carrying black
soot. Horemheb waited until it had passed.

'Gentlemen.' His voice was hoarse. I was standing pressed
against the chariot and noticed how his eyes were red-rimmed,
his lips dry and caked with dust. I offered him a wine skin but
he shook his head. 'Gentlemen,' he repeated, 'a great victory!
Our dead lie only in hundreds, but the enemy are in thousands.
We have taken much plunder and booty. To be fair, all spoils
of war must be gathered together and distributed evenly. No
man shall profit more than another. Here.' He gestured towards
the main gates of the fortress. 'Here I shall set up my altar and
give thanks to Amun-Ra, the Ever Silent but All-Seeing God,
who has provided us with victory.'

I caught Sobeck's eye and grinned. Horemheb was getting the
protocols right. The day of the Aten, of the One, was over. This
was a victory for the old Gods of Egypt, especially Amun-Ra of
Thebes.

149

'Before this altar I shall sacrifice the prisoners, or at least their chiefs and princes. I shall make a tally of the hands, a true count of those Horus had delivered into our power. I give thanks to Horus of Henes.' This was a reference to his birthplace, not far from where the battle had taken place.

On and on Horemheb went, the same message over and over again. How Amun-Ra and Horus had chosen him, their divine son, to shatter the power of Egypt's enemies. As Sobeck drily remarked later, if the Lord Ay wished for any evidence about Horemheb's secret dreams, then this speech provided it. Horemheb saw himself as divinely selected, a man anointed by God himself. Of course, he was carried away with elation and the victory of the moment; only when he caught me staring at him did he begin to falter and bring his bombastic speech to an end.

He climbed off the chariot.

'Now, Lord Mahu, I will take the wine.' His rugged face was wreathed in smiles as he realised he might have said too much and, perhaps, not acknowledged the contribution of others. 'You know how it is,' he declared, wiping the dust from his lips with the back of his hand. 'When the blood is hot, the tongue babbles.'

He paused as a staff officer pushed his way through the throng and whispered in his ear. Horemheb's smile faded.

'My lord General.' I stepped forward. 'I too am a member of the Royal Circle. What has happened?'

Horemheb's eyes, full of fury, glared at me. 'I know who you are Mahu,' he whispered. 'I recognise what you have done, but the usurper and his entourage have escaped!'

Senfiu
(Ancient Egyptian for 'the Gods of Blood')

Chapter 8

Horemheb listened to the reports from his officers.

'At least twenty,' the standard-bearer declared. 'The usurper, his woman, the two priests, Djoser and Khufu, and Prince Aziru, escorted by Hittite officers, left the fortress early. Scouts saw them heading due east.'

'The Horus Road,' I intervened. 'They'll take the Horus Road across the Sinai. They are hoping to flee back to Canaan to plot again.'

'And what do you advise?' Horemheb demanded.

'That we pursue and kill them.' I pointed to a line of horses being taken away. 'Your mounts are exhausted, they need food, water and rest, and so do we.'

Horemheb wiped the sweat from his face. 'They left the battle early?'

'They never struck a blow,' the standard-bearer confirmed. 'One of the Hittite captains is very bitter; he believes they were deserted.'

'I can well understand that,' Horemheb replied. He walked forward, staring out over the plain, oblivious to the groans and moans coming from the lines of prisoners and the war cries and cheers of his own men.

'We trapped them near the river, my lord Mahu,' he called over his shoulder. 'The dead are piled five or six deep there, the waters tinged with blood. Oh! I mustn't forget.' He called across a herald. 'Tell the men to be careful: the crocodiles and other night prowlers will feast well tonight. Now,' he pointed to the entrance of the palisade leading to the Field of Fire, 'show me this.'

We took him in. Horemheb later confessed to me that, despite the blood-spilling, bitter conflict he had just won, never had a place provoked such a sense of horror. He advanced towards the Mastaba, climbed the ramp and listened to the roar of the savage beasts within.

'I am tempted,' he declared, walking back to where his officers and I waited, fearful of those blood-curdling growls, 'to take the Hittite commanders and thrust them through that trap-door.' His harsh face creased into a smile. 'But we never know how fortune may turn: one day Egyptian officers may be taken prisoner.'

Horemheb promptly ordered archers to bring scaling ladders, remove the trap-door and loose arrow after arrow into the darkness. The roars and growling were fearsome; as one archer became exhausted, another took his place. The beasts within, maddened and hungry, flung themselves at the doorway, making easy targets. Darkness was falling when the captain of archers pronounced both beasts dead. Horemheb ordered the door to be broken down. Torches were brought, and those who dared followed their general into the foul-smelling interior.

Although the Mastaba looked large from the outside, it housed only a passageway leading into a grim square chamber. Bones and human remains, globules of fat and flesh, caked floor and walls. The place reeked like a charnel house. Two of Nebamun's officers had to leave to be sick. Horemheb inspected both the chamber and the lions; these were the African kind, huge and powerful black-maned beasts. We could tell from the wounds on their hides that they had been turned into man-eaters, possibly because they had been injured by hunters and found humans easier prey than the fleet-footed gazelles. If anyone ever asks me, 'Have you visited the Halls of the Underworld, the Place of the Scavengers?' I always answer that I have. Now, years later, when I have nightmares, that chamber in the Mastaba comes back to haunt me, with its brooding aura of unspoken horror, of cruel death and torture.

Horemheb ordered the place to be fired. Oil skins were emptied, flooding the floor; brushwood, anything which could burn, was thrown in. The same happened to the Field of Fire. The stakes were knocked down, the entire ground soaked in oil, into which the archers loosed fiery shafts. The night was lit up by roaring flames and clouds of smoke. The fortress too was levelled, its bothies and tents now cleared of all plunder. Once their right hands had been severed, the enemy dead were thrown on to the fire.

A gruesome, fearful night of fire and smoke. All sound was drowned by the roar of the flames. The destruction continued until the early hours. Horemheb seemed to have forgotten those who had fled. He had his great camp chair brought into the pool of light from the fires and held a summary court-martial of the prisoners. I, as a member of the Royal Circle, sat on his right, with Colonel Nebamun on his left. The Hittite officers were brought first. Horemheb asked for their defence. Why had they invaded the land of Egypt? Of course they could only reply that they were mercenaries hired by the usurper.

'In which case,' Horemheb declared, 'you are no better than outlaws and pirates.'

He ordered their execution by decapitation, and the men were hustled away into the darkness. Soon after came the hideous sound of the falling axe as it smote through necks, cutting into the log on which they had to place their heads. Horemheb then dealt with the other prisoners. Any Egyptian was condemned immediately as a traitor and a rebel; they were to be dispatched to Sile, Avaris and the other cities of the Nile to be executed and hung upside down in chains above the city gates. Some of the other nationalities were to be executed; the rest would serve as slaves in the mines and quarries of Egypt.

Horemheb paused now and again for food or wine. My limbs began to ache. I felt cold. I wanted to sleep. Horemheb, however, was not only a general but an expert on military law; he was insistent that justice be done quickly and ruthlessly as a warning to every other rebel. At the same time his officers were busy in the camp enforcing discipline, putting drunkards under arrest, taking the women they had found into the slave pens and demanding, on pain of death, that all booty be handed over. A makeshift altar to Amun-Ra had been set up, surrounded by Horemheb's standards, and through the night the mound of severed hands grew higher. The place reeked of smoke, blood and burning flesh.

Once Horemheb announced himself satisfied, he turned and gestured at the leather bag Sobeck was jealously guarding.

'My lord Mahu, I said all plunder.'

'My lord Horemheb,' I replied. 'If we may have a word in private?'

Groaning and muttering, he pushed himself up from his chair. He wiped his face and washed his hands in natron and water, though he still remained smeared with blood, streaks of sweat marking his dusty face. Horemheb, at peace, was not the most easy of men, but when the blood lust of battle was upon him, he was truculent and dangerous. He had imposed his will on the imperial army, his men regarded him as a God, and the stream of orders he had given as we sat in judgement on the prisoners had been accepted without protest. The mound of plunder was at least two yards high and about five yards across. It comprised chairs, tables, gleaming cabinets, couches and beds, personal jewellery, precious jars, skins full of wine and pots of spices. Horemheb grunted in satisfaction and, gesturing at me, left the place of judgement to stand some distance away from his entourage.

'My lord Mahu, you have difficulty with my orders?'

'My lord Horemheb, do you have difficulty with mine? May I remind you I am a member of the Royal Circle? I am official Protector of the Crown Prince, an imperial envoy.'

'You don't look it!'

'What I look and what I am, General, are two different things. I am your equal, not some junior officer.'

'The leather bag?' Horemheb snarled, pushing his face closer. 'You left the battle to search for it, I understand?'

'I am the Chief of Police of Eastern and Western Thebes, my lord General. My writ runs from the Delta south to beyond the Third Cataract. I too, am a Child of the Kap, a member of the Royal Council, adviser to the Prince. You have won a great victory today in which I too played a part. I discovered the usurper to be just that. I gauged the enemy strength and gave that information to you. I judged Meryre was a traitor and should be confined. If he had continued his journey north, only the

Gods know what would have happened to me, or indeed, to you. Now what I found in the usurper's tent is not my property or your property but that of the Royal Circle. I shall not let it go.'

'I could kill you,' Horemheb whispered through the darkness. 'I could kill you now.' His hand fell to the bronze dagger in its elaborate sheath. 'Or I could put you on trial.'

'Do so, General, and there will be those in Thebes only too quick to point out how you usurped your power. If you kill one of the Royal Circle, my lord,' I stepped closer, 'why not kill the rest? I am sure God's Father Ay and his brother Nakhtimin have been very busy in Thebes. Let me guess! I suspect they have been raising fresh regiments. They can't control yours at Memphis, but God's Father Ay will ensure that within the year there are two armies: one of Upper and one of Lower Egypt. Kill me, General, and it would start a civil war.'

Horemheb stood, hands on hips, staring at the sky, the very pose he used to adopt in the House of Instruction when he was wondering whether to hit someone or not.

'Do you believe I am a traitor, Mahu?'

'Why no, General, of course not. I found none of your letters in the usurper's archives.'

'I am sure you didn't. What did you find, Mahu, you cunning baboon? Trust you in the heat of battle to think of documents.'

'Let me put it this way, General. Those documents are no threat to you. You have your regiments to protect you.'

'And you have your papers.' Horemheb smiled. 'Mahu, we are friends, aren't we?'

'And allies,' I added cheerily.

Horemheb snorted with laughter. 'I heard what you did to Meryre. You should hold on to your leather sack, Mahu. My lord Ay and other members of the Royal Circle are moving up to Memphis. They'll move a little quicker when they hear the news of our great victory; they'll wish to reflect and bask in its glory. You are correct about Lord Ay: he and his brother Nakhtimin, and the rest, are busy raising regiments. There are already two: the Glory of Kush and the Power of Ra. They are building new granaries outside Thebes and every member of the

157

Akhmin gang is being given posts of power in the Houses of Life, the temples.' He waved his hands. 'Or whatever.'

'Huy and Maya?'

'They are with Lord Ay, body and soul.'

'And at Buhen?' I demanded. 'Tutu and the rest?'

'I don't know. There's been some unrest in Kush, but once the news of this victory seeps out, I suspect Meryre and the Atenists will either flee or take poison. You have enough in that leather sack, haven't you, to send them to the slaughter yard?'

'They are traitors,' I replied. 'Do you know how they did it? Meryre was such an eager proselytiser for the cult of Aten, he sent statues of the Sun Disc across Sinai as gifts to the princes of Canaan. He even had the impudence, under the guise of his office, to send similar statues to the Hittite court.'

'And?' Horemheb demanded.

'Oh, let me finish, General. Statues from Egypt's High Priest are sacred; no border guard would interfere with them.'

Horemheb opened his mouth. 'Of course!' He struck the heel of his hand against his forehead. 'Meryre's person is sacred, and the same goes for his gifts.'

'The statues were hollow,' I explained. 'They were made in the temple workshops at the City of the Aten, fashioned to contain a roll of parchment, not necessarily written by Meryre, but by one of his scribes. I have yet to read the entire collection, but he gives information about the disposition of troops, the level of supplies in granaries, the quality of the harvest . . .'

'And the situation in Thebes? Keep your leather sack,' Horemheb growled. He gripped me by the shoulder. 'How the wheel turns, eh, Mahu? Do you remember when we were Children in the Kap and we used to squabble over a piece of bread smeared with honey or a ripe date in sesame oil?'

'The only thing that's changed, General,' I replied, 'is that what we squabble over now are matters of life and death.'

'Will you go tomorrow?' Horemheb asked. 'I am dispatching Nebamun and his squadron after the usurper. Will you accompany them, my lord Mahu, and bring the bastard back? Dead or alive, I don't give a damn.'

I promised I would. I wanted to be away from the place of slaughter. I was also beginning to feel faint and weary from lack of sleep and food. I went back to collect Sobeck and we both retreated, away from the camp and into the palm groves which separated the plain from the small market town. I was too exhausted to answer Sobeck's questions but seized a cloak from someone and, rolling myself up, fell into the deepest sleep.

Sobeck woke me the next morning. He had found a pot of fire and was now cooking a meal: dried strips of meat on a makeshift grill, some overripe vegetables, and bread from the army bakers. We ate hungrily, sharing a jug of beer, staring out at the devastation before us. Horemheb's army occupied the plain. Most of the camp was still asleep; only the occasional fire glowed, pinpricks of light in that half-waking time between night and day. I felt stiff; my knees and ankles groaned in protest. When Nebamun's herald came calling our names, I found it difficult to stagger to my feet. The Colonel was on the other side of the camp, seated on a three-legged stool, a barber shaving his face and head. A short distance away the squadron was preparing to leave. The chariots had been cleaned, the horses groomed, even the harness polished.

Nebamun had dispensed with his armour. He was dressed in a simple white robe, sandals on his feet. He grinned up at us, telling the barber to stop his chatter.

'It will be hot along the Horus Road. I am taking sixty chariots and a change of horses; some of the chariots will carry water and food as well as extra archers. We are leaving within the hour. Oh, by the way, you look dreadful. But,' he squinted at me, 'as Lord Horemheb has reminded me, you are a member of the Royal Circle, Lord Mahu. I am to take my orders from you.'

I was too exhausted to engage in any banter and was relieved when we left the camp, following the broad Horus Road out of the Delta and into the deserts of Sinai. Sobeck drove the chariot, that precious leather bag tied securely to a clasp near his feet. I hung grimly to the rail, watching the broad sandy road beneath us change colour under the strengthening sun. The heat became so intense that each chariot used a parasol or awning against the glare of the sun. They say the demons live in the Sinai; I

159

can well believe it. Nothing but a broad stretch of rock and hillock, all burning under a fiery sun. No breeze, and when one did rise, it brought clouds of dust and sand. We passed the occasional oasis, its palm trees black against the sky. The heat so oppressed the eye that by midday the blinding whiteness played tricks with your sight. The road was deserted. There's nothing like the clash of armies to make merchants and traders decide to shelter wherever they can and hide till the crisis has passed.

We stopped at some lonely oasis to fill our water skins, sitting on the walls the Great Pharaoh, Tuthmosis IV, had built around the precious well. At first I thought Horemheb had made a mistake, until we found evidence of the usurper's flight: discarded boxes, coffers and weapons. Two of their entourage must have been wounded, for their corpses, half eaten by night prowlers, lay in the shade of some rocks. We sheltered from the noonday heat and continued our pursuit. Nebamun reasoned that our horses were fresh and well provisioned. The usurper, however, despite his hours' start, was totally dependent on what he had taken from the battlefield and his fortress. A group of sand-dwellers told us how they had caught sight of Egyptians but had not drawn too close.

We rested that night in an oasis, Nebamun sending out scouts. For the first time since I had found the records in the usurper's tent, I was able to scrutinise the contents of that sack. The more I read, the more my heart glowed. Meryre and his faction were traitors, hand in glove with the usurper, Prince Aziru and his confederates, not to mention the Hittite court. There were other items, which I vowed to keep close to my heart. One of these did fascinate me: a piece of gold, thin and delicate, showing Pharaoh Akenhaten receiving the rays of the sun. Akenhaten, dressed in the Royal regalia, had his face turned towards the sun, hands welcoming the life-giving rays. At first I thought it was a brooch or some form of pendant, though I could find no hole or clasp. I took it closer to the fire. I am an expert on the work of goldsmiths, and in calmer days loved to go down to their workshops in Thebes or the City of the Aten and watch them work. Each craftsman has his own sign, his own way of working, yet the more I studied this piece, the more intrigued I became.

'When would you say this was made?' I handed it to Sobeck, who had been squatting on the other side of the fire, half watching me whilst keeping an eye on Nebamun's men lest anyone approached too close. He took the piece of gold, turning it over and over.

'I'd say it might be Egyptian,' he remarked. 'Have you noticed it's the same on either side? It's not a pendant or brooch. It could be a gift.'

'And?' I asked.

'The carving is singular. The gold is very thin. I am not too sure if it *is* Egyptian. I have seen similar gold work,' he grinned, 'being sold rather secretly in the markets of Eastern Thebes. I'd say it was Canaanite made to look as if it's Egyptian. Canaanite work is thinner, not as elaborate or as thick as the workshops of Thebes or Memphis.'

He handed the gold back. I placed it in the sack, tying its neck securely.

'If something should happen to me . . .'

'You don't trust General Horemheb?' Sobeck demanded.

'If something should happen to me,' I continued, 'keep this leather sack, Sobeck. Share its contents with Djarka. He'll know how to use it, as will you, to protect the Prince.'

I gazed up at the stars and listened to the roars of the hyaenas and the other stalkers of the night, drawn to our camp fire by the smells.

'You found something which interests you?'

'Well, of course, but what really intrigues me,' I tapped the sack, 'is that these documents make constant reference to one member of the Royal Circle I had almost forgotten about. Oh, Horemheb and Rameses are mentioned, naturally; they are soldiers. Nakhtimin and Ay? Well, I'll deal with these later; the same goes for Maya and Huy. However, Meryre makes one constant reference which is picked up by the priests, Khufu and Djoser.'

'About what?' Sobeck asked impatiently.

'Think of the Children of the Kap, Sobeck. You were raised with us. Who keeps in the shadows? Quiet during meetings, away from the hustle and bustle of the court?'

Sobeck stared back in puzzlement.

'Pentju,' I whispered. 'Pentju, Royal Physician to Akenhaten. Friend of the Lady Khiya, Tutankhamun's mother. Guardian of the Prince as a child before he handed him over to me. Pentju was never a politician; the great physician was more concerned with his wealthy patients and his treasure hoard.'

'He is the Quiet One,' Sobeck agreed. 'We know his beloved wife and children all died during the plague or shortly afterwards. In fact, scarcely any member of his family remains. Well, what does Meryre say about him?'

'He says he'd love to have Pentju with him in this embassy. He promised to do his level best to include Pentju in our journey north. Now, that's something I never knew.'

'Does he see him as an ally?' Sobeck asked.

'I have to study the documents more closely,' I replied. 'However, the impression I get is that Pentju is important because of what he knows rather than what he does. Isn't that strange? I wonder what our noble physician knows that is so valuable?'

Two days later we caught up with the fleeing rebels. They had left a trail of corpses, abandoned goods and weapons and soon realised their pursuers were closing on them. The Sinai is a bleak wilderness; leave the Horus Road and the well-beaten tracks and you would die in the desert heat. Of course they resisted. They fortified an outcrop of rocks but they were short of water and weapons. Nebamun's men loosed one shaft after another, distracting the rebels whilst others moved up behind, gaining the higher ground. Our chariot squadron watched and waited below. The rebels survived that afternoon and the following night but the noonday heat forced them to ask for terms. Nebamun was uncompromising: unconditional surrender or he would simply lay siege until, as he put it, their hearts fried and their bodies were reduced to dry skin. They threw their weapons down and came out of the rocks, no longer the power and the glory but a pathetic group of dirty, dishevelled men and women.

'What shall we do?' Nebamun whispered.

'You have your orders,' I replied. 'Carry them out!'

The Hittite officers were promptly executed, as were the

captains of the mercenaries. I immediately seized the impostor and his woman, together with their chaplain Khufu, and Prince Aziru. I went searching for Djoser and found him in a small gully beyond the rocky outcrop, face grey, eyes awaiting death, clutching the arrow wound in his chest.

'Who are you?' His tongue was clasped between dry lips. 'Water?' he begged.

I allowed him to sip from the skin I carried.

'Who *are* you?' he repeated.

'Don't you remember, Djoser? Mahu, Chief of Police in the City of the Aten!'

He coughed, a bloody froth staining his lips.

'Well, well. Once upon a time, Mahu, we all basked in the sun, didn't we? Lords of the earth.'

'Why?' I asked. 'Why did you do it?'

'Why not?' he taunted back. 'Better that than bend the knee to the Akhmin gang, or that burly peasant Horemheb.' He coughed and spluttered.

I made him more comfortable. From below I could hear the screams of the women.

'I am glad I'm dying,' Djoser whispered. 'I don't want to be part of Horemheb's victory parade.' He clutched the water skin again and took another slurp, splashing it over his face.

'Did the Lord Akenhaten die?' I demanded.

'I don't know.' Djoser coughed.

'And his treasure?'

'Meryre knows about that. Some in Egypt, most taken away.'

'Who is behind this?' I asked. 'The cause, the fount and origin?'

'Cause, fount, origin?' Djoser leaned his head back and, pulling himself up, broke the shaft of the arrow and tossed the broken end away. 'It doesn't ease the pain,' he grated, 'but at least it's something to do.'

'Are you all right, sir?' I waved away the soldier who had come up behind me to see if all was well.

'The cause?' I asked.

'Meryre. He had dreams of becoming Pharaoh's First Minister, Grand Vizier or, who knows, Pharaoh himself. He thought you might join him. He certainly wanted Pentju; he prayed for that.'

'But you all supported the usurper?'

Djoser leaned forward. 'Usurper? And what are you supporting, Lord Mahu?' He coughed and gagged on his blood, then the light in his eyes dimmed and he fell back with a sigh.

I left the corpse amongst the rocks and joined the chariot squadron. Nebamun had executed the officers but decided that the rest, nothing more than common foot soldiers and mercenaries, together with their women, should be given water skins. He pointed into the distance, where the heat haze shifted and buckled and the dust devils blew clouds up against the sky.

'Walk!' he ordered. 'And if the Gods are with you, you will live!'

His men drove them off; I turned to the other four prisoners. Aziru had tried to disguise himself, hiding his oily hair and fat body under a coarse striped robe. He, like the rest, was now tied by his hands to my chariot wheel. Sobeck, crouching beside them, drank his water but offered them none.

'I am a prince.' Aziru tried to rise; Sobeck punched him in the ribs. 'I am a prince.' Aziru lowered his head to remove the hair from his eyes. 'I was once Egypt's ally.'

'You are a rebel and a traitor.' I smiled down at him. 'You have fomented trouble and rebellion. You take to mischief as a fish to swimming.'

I looked at the other prisoners. The woman's face was concealed by flaming red hair. Next to her, bereft of all his finery, the usurper looked what he really was, a pathetic pretender with not even a passing resemblance to my great lord. Khufu was blubbering like a child; the lower part of his tunic was wet with urine. I cut his bonds and pulled him up.

'Do you know who I am?' I pushed him towards Nebamun's curious charioteers, who'd been watching the mercenaries trudging off into the distance. Now they hoped I would provide further sport.

'Lord Mahu.' Khufu's soft, round face creased into a suppliant smile. 'My lord Mahu, you remember me? I was a chapel priest in the Great Temple of the Aten. I served in the Holy of Holies.'

'And now you serve a rebel!' I pulled him by his coarse robe. 'Colonel Nebamun, have you found any treasure?' I called over.

'Nothing much,' he replied. 'Trinkets, personal possessions.'

164

'The treasure?' I demanded of Khufu. 'My great lord's treasure, it was pillaged and taken out of the City of the Aten.'

'I truly don't know.' Khufu raised his hands. 'My lord, I did not leave the City of the Aten immediately but joined the rest much later. Undoubtedly,' he gabbled on, 'the treasure was taken. They say it was divided and is now in Canaan.'

'What?' I pushed him out of earshot. 'Do you want to die, Khufu? Do you want me to peg you out like a lion skin on the desert floor?'

This dirty, unshaven, smelly priest began to shake so violently I though he was having a fit. I slapped him on the face and roared at one of Nebamun's men to bring a wine skin. I forced open Khufu's mouth and made him take two or three gulps. His trembling stopped.

'I can tell you more, my lord,' he blinked, 'but not here. I am a priest. If I was given consideration . . .'

'I'll tell you what.' I clicked my fingers and demanded a parasol to protect me from the sun. 'You, Khufu, shall be my prisoner. I'll keep you safe. I'll even arrange for your release. Exile to some pleasant little village.'

Hope flared in those greedy little eyes.

'On one condition: you tell me what I want to know.'

Khufu fell to his knees, clutching at my ankles, head banging against my legs as he promised to be my devoted slave. I kicked him aside and turned to the impostors. The woman was no beauty despite her resplendent hair so reminiscent of Nefertiti, the haunter of my heart: a rather coarse face beneath the paint, with slanted green eyes and full voluptuous lips now cracked and bleeding. Nebamun's men had been poking and prodding her, and she'd screamed back; now she was not so defiant. I crouched down between her and the usurper.

'It is finished,' I whispered. 'You know it is. So you had best tell me who you really are and why you are here.'

The woman, casting hateful glances at Aziru, began to chatter. I told her to shut up and forced back the man's head. He was balding, with high cheekbones and lightly sunken cheeks; his bony, angular body was now stripped of all its finery. I noticed tattoo marks on his arms and chest.

'You're Babylonian?'

The man nodded, his small, dark eyes fearful; he had a slight cast in one. He and his so-called Queen were easy to break, both gabbling together, wanting to please, hoping to be shown some mercy. Now and again Aziru tried to protest, but I slapped him quiet and listened intently to the usurper. Both he and his Queen were Babylonians by birth, wandering musicians and actors who had come to the attention of Prince Aziru. They had been drawn into his plot, given the dress and ornaments of Pharaoh and schooled in the ways of the imperial Egyptian court. After that they had become the standard around which all the rest of the rebels had gathered, being visited by Hittite dignitaries and envoys. I learned that the rebel army had been financed by Aziru's allies in Canaan with gold and silver bullion dispatched by the Hittite court. In truth, the pair were nothing more than puppets, who had revelled in their moment of glory and power. The more they chattered and gabbled, the more I became aware of how Aziru, now bound silently beside them, was the moving spirit behind all that had happened. A man who dreamed of throwing off Egyptian rule and proclaiming himself king in Canaan. He wanted to bind its tribes together with a vision of being one kingdom, Egypt's peer and equal, playing off one great power against another: the Babylonians, the Hittites, the Mitanni, the Egyptians. It also became apparent that, apart from their charades, this precious pair knew very little. I handed them over to Nebamun's men to guard and pushed Aziru into my chariot, binding his wrist to the rails. The squadron re-formed, and leaving the dead to rot under the sun, we made our way back to the camp.

Sobeck rode in the chariot beside me, Khufu crouching at his feet, hands and feet bound. Aziru was different. He showed no fear, and in return for petty courtesies, such as the occasional mouthful of wine or water, he talked seriously about what had happened. Despite the heat and dust, the numbing sense of weakness and exhaustion from the events of the last two days, I was fascinated by his confession.

'Did you plan the attack on Memphis?' I asked.

Aziru nodded.

'Did Meryre know of it?'

'No, no.' Aziru steadied himself as the chariot lurched. 'That was my decision. We knew you were coming north and would leave the Prince at the City of the Aten. So I sent bargeloads of mercenaries to lie in wait. It was easy enough. The captains were provided with false letters of commission. They were to pretend they were mercenaries journeying to Thebes to reinforce some garrison along the Nile.'

'You know the attack failed?'

Aziru glanced at me and smiled.

'Yes, yes. Our men were told to watch your flotilla carefully and seize their chance. Apparently you did not stop at the City of the Aten but journeyed direct to the outskirts of Memphis. The commander of our flotilla must have thought there was a chance of achieving his task, though if I had been there I would have counselled against it. Memphis is a garrison city, isn't it? Too dangerous, far too dangerous. Ah well!'

'And these letters and proclamations?' I asked. 'You were in possession of Pharaoh Akenhaten's seal, his cartouche?'

'We had the contents of his writing office.' Aziru laughed. 'Some of his scribes, when they fled the City of the Aten, took everything they could lay their hands on. It was they who gave me the idea, one I shared with the Hittite court.' He threw his head back and laughed. 'And now you see the results.'

'Did Meryre tell you that we were coming north?' I asked.

'Meryre? No.' Aziru shook his head. 'Your friend Sobeck informed me of how you had seized our records during the battle. You must know, my lord Mahu, who truly informed us that you were coming.'

'Did that person tell you directly?'

Aziru's smile faded and he shook his head. 'Find out for yourself,' he muttered. 'But at some time or other, my lord Mahu, as well you know, everybody in the city of Thebes dispatched letters north to me. Some were defiant, others, how can I put it, more diplomatic and probing. You wouldn't say they were traitors.' He glanced at me out of the corner of his eye. 'But you could see they were thinking about it.'

'And what was your plan?'

'To hold the Delta and advance south. The only reason we didn't is that we were fearful of the garrison at Memphis. Khufu and Djoser had described Horemheb; that's where we made our mistake.' He added bitterly, 'Do tell the good general, if I had my way we would have assassinated him and his dark shadow, Rameses.'

'You'll expect no mercy?' I asked.

Aziru shrugged. 'I have thrown the dice and I have lost. I'll try to bargain for my life, but there again, I won't beg. I am not like Khufu the priest. I won't wet myself and spoil your chariot.'

'And the treasure?' I asked. 'Rumours abound that Pharaoh Akenhaten's treasure, or at least part of it, disappeared from the City of the Aten.'

'I know nothing of that,' Aziru declared. 'But I'll tell you what I did. I sat in my palace, I watched and listened. I learned how the Great Pharaoh of Egypt was lost in his own religious dreams, how he would not send troops across the Sinai, so I thought I'd pipe a tune for all of us to dance to. It wasn't hard playing one chief off against another, one petty prince being drawn into a blood feud with his neighbour. The Hittites, too, became interested. Like men watching a dog fight, they drew closer and eventually wanted to place wagers. Matters quickened. We heard your Pharaoh was dead, buried in his strange city; how his wife had attempted a coup but failed. I was joined by Khufu and Djoser; others drifted to my court. Meryre in Egypt assured us of his support.' He shrugged. 'And the rest you know. If Fortune had not been so fickle, you would have been in my chariot bound hand and foot, the heads of Horemheb and Nebamun perched on poles. But as for your Pharaoh and his treasure?' He shook his head. 'I know nothing of them.'

He chattered on as if we were old comrades discussing tactics. He laughed when I told him how Sobeck and I had entered his camp as mercenaries and fooled Captain Usurek.

'You were lucky,' he replied. 'If I had known about that, I would have questioned you more closely.'

I was intrigued by Aziru: small and fat, to all intents and appearances an effete Canaan prince, with his curled hair and beard still smelling faintly of perfume and oil, his plump cheeks, small black eyes and woman's mouth. Yet he was tougher than he looked, his heart as sly as any I had met. He was also curious, asking questions about the Prince Tutankhamum and the

Princess Ankhesenamun; these two had created divisions between Aziru and his Egyptian allies.

'What we intended,' he confessed, 'was to humiliate the power of Egypt. To defeat its armies in open battle, sack its cities, plunder its temples.' He smiled thinly. 'Or at least some of them. Teach the land of Egypt a lesson it would never forget. Stir up rebellion in Kush. Draw in the Libyans.'

'And then?' I asked.

'Demand that Egypt withdraw completely from Canaan and recognise our right to determine our own future; to make alliances and treaties with whomever we please. To be free of tribute and taxes, of sending hostages and goods into the ever-full belly of Thebes.'

'And in Egypt itself?' I asked.

'That did not concern us. There was no visible heir except for the young boy. The Hittites hoped for civil war, that Egypt would divide from within.'

I reined in the chariot. 'So you had no ambition about who would wear the Two Crowns?'

'What did it matter to us?' Aziru sneered. 'We'd support the temple dancers as long as they were useful. Meryre nursed a great dream. Isn't it true in the history of your people,' he stared directly at me, 'that a high priest became Pharaoh? Meryre had visions of marrying the Princess Ankhesenamun!'

'And Tutankhamun?' I asked.

Aziru steadied himself with his hands. 'Mahu, cut my bonds! I am not going to jump down.'

I slowed the horses and slashed the coarse ropes which bound his wrists. He thanked me with his eyes, rubbed his arms and picked up the wine skin.

'The Prince Tutankhamun?' I repeated.

'Now that, my lord, is debatable. The likes of Meryre and Khufu had their own plans about what would happen once they had seized power in Egypt. Djoser regarded Tutankhamun as a pretender.' He smiled at my surprise.

'But he was Akenhaten's son.'

'Djoser dismissed him as a by-blow of the Mitanni monkey.'

'The Lady Khiya?' I murmured.

I recalled Djoser's dying words, and quietly vowed that Meryre

169

would pay for his treason. If Aziru was telling the truth, and I suspected he was, Meryre would have shown little mercy to that young boy. I questioned him again, but Aziru had told me all he had learned. He turned to other matters, grudgingly praising Horemheb's speed and military skill.

'I never imagined,' he admitted, 'we'd be attacked so fast. Now, my lord Mahu, what will happen to me? Trial for treason?'

His question was answered as soon as we reached Horemheb's camp. Rameses had now arrived, bringing a whole host of mercenaries with him, as well as units of regiments he had collected on the way. I was pleased to see some of the soldiers I had left at Memphis; they greeted me, toasting me with their cups, hailing me as one of the great heroes. Of course they were drunk, enjoying the spoils of victory. They, like the inhabitants of Sile, were now sightseers to the battlefield, which Horemheb had turned into a plain of desolation, a sea of black ash; all grass, trees and vegetation were burnt. Apart from mounds and cracked masonry, nothing was left of the usurper's camp or that hideous Mastaba where he had tortured his prisoners. The army had pulled back close to the Nile, taking advantage of the greenery and shade. Some troops had already been dispatched south. Other units fanned out across the Delta, searching for any fugitives.

I received an invitation to join Horemheb and Rameses in their pavilion. I told Sobeck to keep the leather sack and Khufu under strict watch, to wait till my men sobered up and then move away from the camp, where both those precious records and my prisoner would be safer.

Horemheb was still basking in his triumph, Rameses lavishing flattery after flattery upon him. They were both in their cups, staggering to their feet to grasp my hand. I told them that Khufu was my prisoner. Rameses made to object, but Horemheb nodded his agreement. They also questioned Aziru. Despite my protest, Rameses punched him in the face and chest, similar indignities being inflicted upon the usurper and his woman. Rameses forced the latter to kneel, pushing his groin into her face before he tired of the game and ordered both to be shackled to the standards outside the General's tent.

'My lord Aziru.' Horemheb clapped the Canaanite on the

170

shoulder and tugged viciously at his beard. 'The Royal Circle have made a decision regarding you.'

'I am to die.' Aziru had conducted himself with dignity throughout Rameses' insults.

'No, no, my lord.' Horemheb, still tugging at his beard, forced him to turn. 'The Lord Ay has made known the judgement of the Royal Circle. It is as I thought. Hittite prisoners and chieftains are to be summarily executed, as are mercenary captains. Their followers are to be sent to the mines, and the usurper is to be loaded with chains. But you, my lord, you may return to Canaan, without your eyes.'

The blinding took place an hour later. Despite all my protests, a glowing red-hot knife was held to Aziru's eyes. Afterward he sat, face all bandaged. He was still fighting back the sobs of pain as he was loaded into a cart with wine, water and provisions, given an escort of his own mercenaries and, to a chorus of catcalls, sent on his way.

Apiabu
(Ancient Egyptian for 'the Counter of Hearts')

Chapter 9

We travelled downstream, harps and lutes in hand,
We are bound for the white walls of Memphis.
I'll say to Ptah, lord of the light,
Grant me my beloved tonight.
The river is as wide,

Ptah is its reed thicket,
The Lady Neith its bouquet.
She is a dew goddess adorned with lotus buds.
The Golden Goddess who rejoices!
The land grows bright with her beauty,
Memphis is a gold bowl of fruits
Set before Ptah of the pleasant face.

The steersman sang the famous song as our barges, festooned with streamers and garlands, nosed their way towards the quayside of Memphis. The White-Walled City's famous docks, wharves and shipyards were known as Nereu Nefer, the Place of the Beautiful Sailing. We had passed the greenery of the city's surrounding fields, with the pyramids in the far distance glowing pink-gold in the sunlight. Trumpets blared, cymbals clashed and the crowds along the shoreline caught the words of the steersmen and sang them back. A rain of flowers descended on our barges and the marshy odour was hidden beneath the smell of frankincense, cassia and incense. On the principal quayside, Ay, Maya, Huy and others of the Royal Circle clustered to greet us under a gold-red fringed canopy. Just before I disembarked I looked back. The host of other war barges, like great fat water beetles, were taking up their positions ready to move in.

As I climbed the steps behind the rest, I glimpsed Pentju, rather lonely; he stood at an angle, as if to keep the Prince Tutankhamun in view. The heir of Egypt's glory stood under his own little parasol, his hand held by God's Father, Ay. Tutankhamun was dressed in a snow-white tunic, gold-embossed sandals, silver armlets on his thin arms and a necklace of cornelian, which I thought too heavy, around his neck. Ankhesenamun, in her thick wig, a gold gorget around her throat, gauffered linen robes billowing about her, looked as beautiful as a goddess. She stood on Ay's left, holding her grandfather's hand, the other busy with a red and blue fan. She caught my eye and winked impishly.

Ay hadn't changed. Gold necklaces shimmered at his throat, his dark saturnine face watchful. He gave me the kiss of greeting amidst a gust of perfume, clasping my arms with his beringed fingers. I immediately suspected what was happening. Ay was surrounded by fan-bearers and flunkeys, set apart from the rest of the Royal Circle, emphasising his own power and dignity by holding the hands of the boy and the young woman who were to be Egypt's king and queen. He was reminding everyone that these were his offspring. I looked over Ay's shoulder. Djarka stood at the back of the crowd, fearful of meeting my eyes. I moved on to greet the rest: Huy, then Maya, who almost pushed me aside to grasp Sobeck's hand. Of course, Horemheb was the hero of the day. Ay greeted him formally, bestowing upon him the gold collar of bravery and the silver bees of valour. The rest of the Royal Circle gathered around to offer their own personal congratulations whilst the ceremonial chariots were prepared. Once they were ready, we solemnly processed through the city to the Temple of Hathor of the Southern Sycamore, through the *ankh-tay*, the holy district, past the Temples of the King, the Pool of Pedjest-she, then round to visit the Temple of the Lady Neith of the White Walls and down to the central Temple of Ptah.

The entire city had turned out to throw flowers and greenery, lift bowls of smoking incense and intone the paean of praise.

They gathered along the avenues before racing across the green fields of wheat and barley and through the palm groves to greet the victorious general yet again. We passed granaries full of barley and corn, open so each citizen could receive a free cup, whilst tables had been set up to offer cheap wine and beer to slake the throats of the excited citizens. Ay had done well. He wanted to show one of the greatest cities of Egypt that Ma'at had returned. Peace had been established. Harmony reigned.

Ay rode in the first chariot, pulled by jet-black Syrian mares. Horemheb processed slightly to his right. These were followed by chariots bearing other of Horemheb's high-ranking officers, as well as members of the Royal Circle. After them came line after line of prisoners. The usurper and his woman had been virtually stripped naked, smeared with dung and placed on a farmer's cart pulled by oxen. Around their necks were placards proclaiming their crimes. As they passed, the mob's cheers turned to howls of protest: rocks, rotting fruit, anything the crowd could lay their hands on were thrown at them. Both prisoners sat in a huddle whilst behind them tramped line after line of captives, necks yoked, hands and feet manacled. We processed past the great blue enamelled doors of the Holy Places, their copper-plated gates being opened to the sound of gongs and cymbals.

At the Temple of Ptah, Horemheb, amidst a sea of scented petals and puffs of incense, smashed the skull of the woman who had pretended to be Nefertiti, and a number of enemy captains selected for that occasion. The rest of the prisoners, the usurper included, were forced to kneel and watch whilst heralds proclaimed that similar executions would be carried out at Thebes and other cities. The corpses were dragged away by their heels, to be hung from the walls by chains. Horemheb and Ay sacrificed to Ptah, Amun-Ra and the other great gods of Egypt before receiving the final acclamations of the crowd and retiring to the domain of Ankheperkere, the old rambling palace of Pharaoh Tuthmosis III, its towered walls ornamented with carved lions, some black with red manes, others red with black manes. I shivered as I recalled those man-eating beasts in the House of Darkness near the usurper's camp.

When we had passed through the lofty gates, the formal

celebrations came to an end. I immediately went to greet the young Prince, who seemed delighted at my return. Forgetting all dignity, he leapt into my arms and clasped my face in his little hands, squeezing my cheeks and kissing the end of my nose. He asked if I had brought him a present. Of course I hadn't, but I said I had and winked quickly at Sobeck to find something appropriate. Ankhesenamun was all flirtatious, gently mocking me with sarcastic comments about the returning hero and did I want her to leap into my arms? Ay broke off from his discussions with Horemheb and gestured at me to approach. I ignored him, shouting for Djarka to take care of the young Prince and keep him out of the sun. Djarka, still looking rather dejected, forced his way through the throng, but Ay and Nakhtimin came between him and the Prince.

'I do not think so, my lord.' Ay opened his silver filigree fan, shaking it vigorously before his face.

'My lord,' I retorted, 'I am the Prince's protector and guardian. I have now returned to his sacred presence. His safety and security, as you know, are my concern.'

Ay sighed and stepped closer. 'There have been changes whilst you have been gone, my lord Mahu; perhaps it's best if we discuss them away from here.'

I was going to object, but there again, the courtyard was full of Nakhtimin's men, foot soldiers in their leather armour and red and white striped head-dresses. They weren't Neferu, raw recruits, but grizzled veterans whom Nakhtimin must have bribed to leave their fields and return to the ranks.

'Things have certainly changed, God's Father Ay.' I smiled. 'Djarka, follow the Prince wherever he is taken whilst God's Father Ay has a word with me.'

That mongoose of a man, that cobra in human flesh, took me through a side door of the palace, along the corridors, the walls on either side decorated from top to bottom with lurid scenes extolling the exploits of Tuthmosis I.

'Very war-like,' Ay drawled over his shoulder. 'A great boaster.'

'The way of all flesh,' I replied.

Ay walked deeper into the palace. Sometimes I must give the impression that Mahu, the Baboon of the South, is sly and cunning in all things. I am an old man now and I reflect. I have made foolish mistakes, and I did that morning. The ancient palace was full of Ay's and Nakhtimin's soldiers. They thronged the courtyards, guarded every entrance and lined the passageways. Ay was preparing to arrest me. By the time we reached the small writing chamber I must have passed at least three hundred well-armed soldiers. Once inside the chamber, Ay was all courteous and hospitable, gesturing that I sit on a camp stool whilst he offered sliced fruits from a silver bowl and filled the goblets of wine himself. He didn't sit down, but stood over me, staring down rather sadly.

'A great victory, Mahu,' he murmured. 'The usurper's woman has been sacrificed! Her corpse and that of others, dangling over walls or above gates, will send a powerful message to those who wish to plot against the Royal Circle.'

'Will Meryre join her?' I toasted him with the wine.

'Unfortunately, no.' Ay ran a finger round the rim of the goblet. 'About four days after I arrived here,' he continued, 'Meryre and his entourage escaped from Colonel Nebamun's house, seized a barge and disappeared.'

'Are you organising a manhunt?'

'I tried to, but . . .' Ay smiled apologetically. 'We have other things to do than chase will-o-the-wisps across the desert.'

'And I suppose Lord Tutu and the other Atenists,' I asked, 'have also disappeared from the fortress of Buhen?'

'Very clever, my lord Mahu. How on earth did you guess that? Yes, they fled, but they are no real danger. They are exposed as traitors, their armies defeated, their allies in Canaan nothing more than broken reeds.'

'Or a blinded one.'

'Oh yes.' Ay's face grew sadder. 'My lord Aziru has been sent back to Canaan as a warning to other princes. Rebels against Egypt will be crushed. He can sit in his tawdry palace like a blind beggar at the gates. He can dream and plot, but he'll never be a danger again.'

'These changes?' I asked. 'Carried out during my absence, when I was working for the good of all?'

'We all do that, my lord Mahu. But I have discussed this with the rest.' He continued briskly, 'The Royal Circle is too large.

We need to be more businesslike, more united, with a clear chain of command.'

'And so you are going to ask me to retire? You will take the Prince under your protection?'

Ay placed his wine cup down on the table, steepling his fingers together. 'You look leaner, Mahu, more sharp-faced. Your foray north has made you more sensitive. Yes, you are correct. Perhaps it's time, my lord Mahu, that you retired. An opulent mansion? Fertile estates?' He leaned down. 'Perhaps you will take a young wife, have a family? Forget the affairs of state?' Ay lifted the wine cup.

'And Huy and Maya agree with this?'

'They see what has to be done in Egypt.'

'And has the matter been raised with Lord Horemheb?'

'In time, in time.'

'Isn't it rather dangerous?' I asked. 'I am being asked to retire, resign. Who will it be next year? Huy? Or why not Pentju? He's only a physician.'

Ay gazed dreamily at me.

'And if I don't,' I continued, 'what will happen then, my lord Ay? Will I be placed under house arrest? Or perhaps there will be an accident? I'll eat or drink something disagreeable to me.'

Ay shook his head, tutting under his breath.

'The Royal Circle is not united!' I snarled back, getting to my feet. 'It's dividing into two: Horemheb and the northern army; Lord Ay and the army of the south under his ghost-like brother General Nakhtimin, ably supported by the lords Huy and Maya. Two scales equally balanced, but if Mahu goes into the dark and you have custody of the young Prince Tutankhamun, then the balance tilts very heavily in your favour. Of course,' I mimicked Ay's gestures, 'I will not be retiring, resigning, abdicating, farming or anything else. I will leave this chamber and I shall take the Prince into my care.'

Ay made to protest, moving towards the door.

'I wouldn't call the captain of your guard, my lord. I was prepared to sacrifice my life for the safety of our Prince and the well-being of the Two Lands. I entered the enemy camp. Both Sobeck and I gathered information which was of great use to Lord Horemheb.'

'And we are grateful for that,' Ay purred. 'Truly we are.'

'I also discovered the usurper's archives. Or should I say those of Prince Aziru?'

That faint smile disappeared from Ay's face. He now leaned against the door, arms behind him, head tilted back. In some ways he reminded me of Nefertiti, his daughter: watchful, careful.

'In the course of a battle,' I continued, 'such records could easily be destroyed, but I found them. They are still in my possession. Ah, my lord Ay, General Horemheb hasn't told you that, has he? But that's because he doesn't really know what this leather sack contains. I discovered a letter from you to the usurper. It carries your seal. How does it go? You say that you are writing on behalf of the Royal Circle, that you are sending envoys to meet with him, that I will be leaving Thebes by barge and that the messenger who took this letter will provide other necessary details. You close with the sentence, yes, that's how it goes: "The message is important but the messenger isn't." Whom did you send, my lord Ay? Some hapless scribe, some luckless merchant? Or was it one of your mercenaries, armed with a pass and carrying a secret letter which was also his death warrant?'

'I wrote on behalf of the Royal Circle!' he snapped.

'By whose authority?' I retorted. 'We'll gather the rest and ask when you were given such powers!'

'But the letter was innocuous. It simply declared what was going to happen.'

'I don't think so, my lord Ay. Your messenger also took details about our journey up the Nile, how we were taking the Prince Tutankhamun to the City of the Aten. Perhaps because of your letter, that attack was launched.'

'I didn't tell them that. I didn't want that. I wouldn't hand my grandson over to a usurper.'

'No, I don't think you would, but you were, how can I put it, showing the usurper and his chief adviser Prince Aziru where your sympathies lay. Your envoy also carried verbal messages which would sound meaningless to him but very meaningful to Prince Aziru and those advising the usurper. Perhaps an indication that, at a given time, after certain events, you might shift

181

your allegiance. That's why the messenger was executed: what he carried was more important than his person.'

Ay lowered his head, staring at me intently.

'That is fanciful nonsense,' he murmured. 'No one will believe you.'

'They will certainly listen,' I replied. 'I'll raise the question of why Prince Aziru was blinded and dispatched back to Canaan immediately. You didn't want him here, did you? You couldn't have him blabbing before the Royal Circle or trying to barter for his life and security in return for information. Finally, we come to Meryre. Did you organise his escape? And the same for Lord Tutu at Buhen? You wanted them out of the way. You wanted the whole incident conveniently forgotten.' I sat back on the stool and picked up my wine cup. 'I also have a prisoner, the priest Khufu. He may yet prove to be a source of interesting information. This is the way my accusations will go. My lord Ay presided over the Royal Circle. One faction, Meryre and the Atenists, posed a serious threat. You know, I know, and Meryre knows how the Shabtis of Akenhaten were merely a façade so that Meryre could act the victim, screaming about how his followers were being assassinated by some secret society loyal to the old order. You didn't know which way to jump. You fear Horemheb and you don't really trust Huy and Maya, so you cultivated Meryre, you allowed him to paw your granddaughter and nourish his secret ambitions. You quietly supported them but were not party to them. The usurper appeared in the Delta. Meryre wanted to join him, so he used the excuse of being an envoy from the Royal Circle to travel north. He had already been communicating with the enemy, you know how, sending hidden messages in statues and carvings of the Aten Disc. He demanded my presence, hoping I would take the Prince with me; you supported this, unaware of this daring raid planned to kidnap him. At the same time, you did not oppose Meryre's demands that the fortress of Buhen be handed over to Lord Tutu's supporters. You also communicated secretly with Prince Aziru; an ambiguous message, but Aziru would probably be sharp enough to read between the lines. You sat back and waited. If the usurper was defeated you'd soon get rid of Meryre and his faction so as to deal with the new problem, General Horemheb and his victorious regiments. You and Nakhtimin have already begun that, haven't you? Raising troops and quartering them outside Thebes. Of course, the only fly in the ointment was the possibility that someone might talk, but there again, you can take care of that. Did I say one fly?' I smiled. 'I meant two. I am the second. You want custody of the Prince, so it's time Mahu retired. You daren't have me murdered; that might raise suspicions, and as you know, I am a hard man to kill. Nor do you want to invoke a blood feud with Sobeck and Djarka or incite the curiosity of General Horemheb.' I sipped at my wine.

Ay walked over to me and placed a hand gently on my shoulder. When I glanced up, he was grinning down at me.

'Do you have anything else to say, Mahu?'

'Yes, my lord. You are not thinking clearly. Horemheb and Rameses will only trust you as long as I have custody of the Prince. I am the balance between your two factions. They will have noticed what happened in the courtyard.' I pointed to the gold collar of office around Ay's neck. 'I would wager every piece of jewellery you are wearing that General Horemheb is already discussing matters with General Rameses. How prominent you were in the victory parade. How you insisted on keeping the Prince close to you. How you seemed intent on usurping the agreement of the Royal Circle that I am the Prince's protector.'

Ay sat down on a chair, resting his elbow on its arms, fingers before his face.

'What will you do?' I whispered. 'Arrest me? Kill me? Force me to retire? Do you think Horemheb is going to accept that?'

'Will you be with me, Mahu?'

'If it's for the good of the Prince, I'll sleep with the hyaenas in the desert.'

Ay threw back his head and laughed.

'Do you know, Mahu, I have always enjoyed our little chats. I am so glad I talked to you first. I do appreciate what you have done, and . . .' he laughed softly, 'and what you know.'

'That's our little secret,' I replied. 'A bond between us. Now,' I got to my feet, 'what I propose, my lord Ay,' I crooked my arm, 'is that we leave here arm-in-arm, the best of friends, the closest of allies.'

Ay stretched out his hand.

'Welcome back, Baboon of the South. I agree with what you say. Let's walk arm-in-arm, smiling to the world. Let's celebrate our friendship and be ready to meet the Royal Circle.'

Ay was a rogue, a charlatan, a viper beneath the rock, a cobra basking in the sun. He had a heart as black as night and a wit as sharp as any dagger. He also had a charming insolence, a ready laugh; he was a man who would slip one mask off and another mask on. He was like a gambler, but not the sort who'd throw the knucklebones and weep because he had lost. Win or lose, Ay always smiled as he walked away from the gambling pit, and that time was no different. We strolled out into the passageway. He made me stop to examine a glowing wall painting in brilliant blue, gold and dark blood-red depicting Pharaoh's victories against a host of vile Asiatics. The horses pranced, their plumes stiff in the breeze, as the chariots charged over hundreds of fallen enemy. So dramatic that the more you looked, the more certain you became that the standards held aloft were now swaying and that you could hear the thrilling blast of the trumpets.

'We are friends, Mahu,' Ay whispered. 'Look at this painting and the hieroglyphs beneath. Spell them out for me.'

'*User Maa Traa. Sete Eera* – the justice of Ra is powerful,' I translated. 'He is chosen by Ra.'

'And this?'

He went through the rest of the hieroglyphs: Kemet for the Black Lands; Deshet for the Red Lands; Tashemau for Upper Egypt; Tahu for Lower Egypt. He was like a teacher taking me around the painting, oblivious to the guards who thronged the corridor. He pointed to the *isu*, the joint of meat offered in sacrifice after ritual; to the creatures and plants of Egypt, such as Mut the vulture, Ashear the lizard, Awadj the papyrus plant, Nkhd the rush plant.

'What is all this, Mahu?' He gestured with his hand. 'The victorious Pharaoh, the plants of Egypt, the Black Land of the Nile and the scorching sands of the desert? It's all the kingdom of Egypt, that land beloved by the gods, blessed by the sun, washed by the Nile.' He beat his hand passionately against the wall. 'To this is my allegiance; this is my soul, my Ka, my dream. I would sacrifice myself, you, my daughter, the Prince and all of the Royal Circle for the sake of Egypt.'

All cynicism had drained from Ay's face. His eyes were hard, his lips a thin line. Yet even then, I didn't trust him.

'You look doubtful, Mahu?'

'There is one flaw to your argument, my lord.'

'Which is?'

'Who will decide what is best for Egypt?'

I was sure he was going to reply, 'I am Egypt', just from the way he opened his mouth and leaned closer; then he thought different. He relaxed, smiled, patted me on the shoulder and led me out.

The courtyard was now empty. Horemheb and Rameses had left with their entourage. Grooms and stable boys were putting away the chariots. A few officers, courtiers and priests lounged by the fountain, dipping their hands into the cool water, splashing their arms and faces. The glory of the occasion was passing, like incense growing faint in the air. I made my farewells to Ay.

'Mahu!' He shouted me back. 'You are not staying at the palace?'

'No, my lord. I feel safer with Colonel Nebamun. I would ask for the Prince to be sent back there. Where the Lady Ankhesenamun goes is a matter for you to decide.'

Ay agreed, and walked away. Nakhtimin stepped out of the shadows and, surrounded by his staff officers, escorted Ay from the temple courtyard. I found Sobeck and Djarka in one of the small gardens overlooking a canal dug in from the Nile. They were throwing pebbles at the lotus blossom floating on its surface.

'An interesting meeting?' Sobeck asked.

'Meeting my lord Ay is always interesting.' I smiled. 'Djarka, how on earth did he get his hands on the Prince?'

'I had no choice.' My manservant's dark face looked rather pinched, his cheeks unshaven. His black hair, usually combed straight and carefully oiled, was unwashed, his eyes red-rimmed from dust or lack of sleep. 'Ay swept into Memphis like a storm wind, soldiers everywhere. All I had was a mercenary corps. Horemheb and Rameses were absent; he soon became cock of the dunghill.'

A hoopoe bird swooped low over the canal in a flash of colour. In a thicket beside us a hare suddenly coursed out, making me start.

'That's Horemheb's idea,' Sobeck murmured. 'He likes hares; the bloody palace now teems with them. Apparently his dwarfs have to chase them. I have been listening to the gossip: Horemheb keeps his wife under lock and key.'

I recalled Mutnojnet, Nefertiti's unlikely sister, a quiet, comely-faced woman who seemed to worship the ground Horemheb stood on.

'And?'

'Well, not so much under lock and key,' Sobeck retorted. 'That's unfair to the good general, but they are preparing for themselves the most exquisite tombs out in Sakkara. You must go and see them.'

'Why are they interesting?'

'Horemheb regards himself as if he was Pharaoh or his heir.' Sobeck's eyes were watchful. 'According to the paintings ordered for his tomb and the inscriptions carved on the walls, you'd think he had spent most of his life saving Egypt from a myriad of enemies. What I am saying, Mahu, is that it gives you some insight into the man.'

'The rest are no different,' Djarka intervened. 'Look at the tombs abandoned in the City of the Aten. What was it Maya wrote on his? "When I began I was very good, when I finished I was brilliant." He's still a young man. They will be trouble, won't they?'

'They'll be trouble,' I agreed, 'but not yet. Everyone is watching everyone else, strengthening their position. Now Meryre and his gang have gone, the lines will be clearer. There will be no more talk about the Aten or returning to its city, or,' I added drily, 'the Shabtis of Akenhaten. How did Meryre escape?'

'One day he was here,' Djarka replied, 'the next day he was gone. He was confined in Lord Nebamun's house, close to the river. The guards were few. About three days after Lord Ay's arrival here, Meryre and his retinue disappeared.'

'Any news from Buhen?'

'The same,' Djarka replied. 'It was becoming a gathering place

186

for every refugee from the City of the Aten. Tutu was lording it over the garrison commander. The news of the great victory at Sile seeped out; Tutu and his entourage left, and haven't been seen since.'

'Where will they go?' Sobeck asked.

'Where can they go?' I replied. 'They are traitors, and priests or not, the Royal Circle will post rewards on their heads, dead or alive. The Red Lands will be scoured. They'll be safest in Canaan or the Hittite territories, but we'll see.'

Sobeck threw his last pebble into the canal and stretched out his hand. 'I have done what I can; now I must go. I have business in Thebes, Mahu.' He gave his crooked smile. 'I am sure there will be those who think, out of sight out of mind.'

'Sobeck, I haven't thanked you . . .'

He clapped me on the shoulder. 'Oh, don't worry, Mahu, you will. I'll make my farewells of Maya and leave.'

I felt sad as I watched him go, my comrade-in-arms. We had gone through the dangers in the Delta and Sobeck had played his part; now he wanted to return to the slums of Eastern Thebes and what he called his own private kingdom! Djarka and I returned to Colonel Nebamun's house. The old soldier was delighted that we were his guests. I asked him to organise the mercenaries, receive the Prince and keep a close watch until I returned.

'Where are you going?'

'I want to look for my old friend Pentju.'

After some searching, I discovered the physician had decided to go to the Red Chapel at the Temple of Ptah to make an offering. I was intrigued. Pentju was like myself: he didn't disbelieve in the Gods, he just didn't bother them and hoped that they wouldn't bother him. I collected a dagger from the House of War, together with a stout cudgel, and made my way up to the temple. For a while I became lost in the wretched slums, cobbled lanes nothing better than dark tunnels, which squeezed themselves past buildings. The squalor and dirt were a sharp contrast to the luxury and opulence of the palace. Flocks of crows and kites and packs of yellow pi-dogs scrabbled raucously, fighting with beak and claw over the heaps of filth where flies swarmed in dark clouds. I passed rickety doors, half opened to reveal stinking passageways, a place as dangerous as any war camp. I was glad to reach the basalt avenue leading down to the Temple of Ptah. I went through the monumental gates set between orange walls over which majestic lions of blue, yellow and red enamel mounted guard. A dense crowd clustered here: peasants in their short tunics, and elegant noblemen with their wives in perfumed robes. In the central courtyard a group of priests gathered before the soaring statute of Ptah, chanting their hymns and offering incense:

Lord, the countenance of the sky.
Thy shape is the god . . .

Once into the temple proper, moving through the smoky torchlight, I found a temple guard and introduced myself. He agreed to take me to the Scribe of Offerings, the priest who made a faithful record of all who visited the temple to pay their devotions. He led me across the precincts and through the court-yard where the executions and sacrifices had been made earlier in the day. The place still seethed with excitement; clouds of dust blowing like gold still hung heavy after the victory cele-brations. We passed workshops, schools and granaries, and the house of the God's handmaids. I was truly intrigued at why Pentju should come here. He had no devotion to Ptah and there were temples enough in Thebes to make offerings. At last we reached the Red Chapel, set amidst fertile lawns and fringed by palm groves. The Scribe of Offerings, bathing in the Pool of Purity, acknowledged Pentju had been there.

'I remember him only too well.' He climbed out of the pool, a servant hurrying forward to fold a robe about him. 'Lord Pentju was most generous: a hundred ounos of silver for one of our mortuary priests.'

'A priest of the dead?' I queried. 'For whom were the sacri-fices to be made?'

'For his wife and family slain in the City of the Aten.'

'Slain?'

'No, no.' The old priest's face crinkled up. 'That was my mistake. No, died.' He wiped beads of water from his face. 'Ah, was it? Come with me.'

We entered the Red Chapel, an elegant building of quartzite stone, which glowed as if containing hidden fire, and into a tiled antechamber tastefully decorated with couches. An acacia-wood table stood in the centre, holding a gold-topped coffer. The priest opened this and took out the Book of Life for temple offerings. Pentju's entry was the last. I noticed that the word *khai-I*, or slain, had been hurriedly crossed out and replaced with 'died'. The entry also stipulated that the priest issue an execration text against a Child of Evil: 'The Ur-sht, the Chief Slaughterer from the Aatiu, the slaughter house.'

'Why should he do that?' I asked.

The priest, who was only interested in profits, just sniffed.

'Lord Pentju arrived here,' he squeaked, 'just before I bathed. I do so nine times every day. Well,' he hurried on, glimpsing my impatience, 'I brought him in here; he made the offering, but he seemed nervous, agitated. He explained how his wife and family had died of the pestilence in the Great Heretic's city.' The priest abruptly became fearful; fingers went to his lips. 'My lord Mahu, I didn't mean . . .'

'I don't care what you mean,' I replied. 'What did Lord Pentju say?'

'I shouldn't really be telling you this.'

I let my hand fall to the dagger beneath my robe and grasped my cudgel more tightly.

'But you are a friend, my lord Mahu. There's no real mystery. Lord Pentju asked for a priest to sing hymns and say prayers and curse the evil spirit who brought sickness to his family.'

'And where did he go afterwards?'

'He said he wanted to go to the House of Life. Our school of medicine is famous.'

I took directions from the priest and found Pentju in the Chamber of Salts and Potions at the temple House of Life. He was sitting behind the other scholars, listening to the physician describe how ripe almonds mixed with wormwood and sweet beer evacuate the belly. Most of his audience were dozing. Pentju didn't notice me. I stood and watched for a while. As a young man, Meryre's friend and companion, Pentju had been arrogant, full of smug righteousness. The years had changed him: a long, lined face, furrows of anxiety around his eyes and mouth, ears slightly protuberant, his sharp eyes lost in some constant reverie, shoulders faintly hunched. He moved constantly as if in discomfort, clutching his belly or scratching his face. A nervous, agitated man, whose heart seemed to be grieving over something. I had seen the type before, or at least the mood. Men and women who live in a dream world as if constantly distracted by something they can't share with anyone else. I had always considered Pentju eager to amass a fortune as well as win the reputation as a great physician. The City of the Aten had changed all that. He had lost his wife, family and kin. He had not been with them during the pestilence but had been protected in his own private mansion, having direct custody of Tutankhamun during his infant years. Why should Djoser babble about him before he died? Or Meryre make reference to him in his letters? During my journey down to Memphis I had studied every document, every sheet of papyrus and clay tablet seized in the usurper's camp. Meryre often cited Pentju with the hope that the physician would join their cause, but despite all entreaties he had proved indifferent. While others, including Maya and Huy, had expressed an interest in rejecting the Aten cult but developing the City of the Aten as a place of importance along the Nile, Pentju's reaction had been one of bored indifference.

The old lector priest giving the talk on diet and the effects of certain herbs on the belly and bowels finally drew his talk to an end. Pentju got to his feet and walked straight across to me.

'Mahu, are you following me? I saw you arrive.' His tired face eased into a smile. 'But I thought the talk would do you more good than me.'

'Why did you come to the Temple of Ptah?' I asked.

'Because their House of Life is famous. On reflection, its importance is much exaggerated.' He rubbed his hands together. 'I passed the execution wall. They clothed the red-haired woman in sheepskin cloth and hung her by her heels in chains. She did have,' he added wistfully, 'beautiful hair. It hangs down like a veil about her face. I stood there. I half closed my eyes, Mahu, and thought it was Nefertiti.'

'You hated her that much?'

'No.'

'She hated you then?'

Pentju led me out of the chamber and into a high-walled courtyard with a small tile-edged, ornamental pool. A rather lonely place. I can recall the sunlight, the first coolness of the evening. Baskets of lupins stood around the pool. We sat down on a marble bench.

'I always wondered, Mahu, when you'd come. You are a baboon, you know. You sit on your rock and watch.'

'Nefertiti?' I persisted.

'Akenhaten's wife.' Pentju smiled. 'His great Queen, Nefertiti!'

'She hated you?' I asked.

'She hated me because of the Lady Khiya. You know how it happened, Mahu.'

'Tell me again,' I insisted.

'Akenhaten built his city.' Pentju sighed. 'He was lost in his worship of Aten, the One. He suffered from delusions, believed he was the only one who could communicate directly with the All-Mighty, All-Seeing God, and then he moved a step higher. He believed that he was God's son incarnate, and it's only a small journey from there to believing that he was god himself. Nefertiti did not help. She offered her husband wine and drugs, the juice of the poppy, which disturbed his humours and forced him to live in a dream world. Some call him the Great Heretic, others a madman. He was just an idealist who became lost in drugged dreams. He was not the Chosen. He began to resent Nefertiti, the way she insisted on being his equal, and, of course, she never produced a son.' Pentju leaned down and tapped one of the lupins with a finger. 'Lady Khiya, Tutankhamun's mother, was different.' He kept his face hidden from me, but I caught the sob in his voice. 'She was soft as a little mouse and would chatter to me. I discovered the red-haired bitch was feeding her potions and powders so she'd never conceive. I wanted to help the Lady Khiya.'

'And have your revenge on Nefertiti, who had humiliated you?'

'Yes, yes. She had.' Pentju straightened up. 'But it was Khiya I wanted to help. Akenhaten used to visit her; often about

191

now, as the breeze cools, they'd go walking in the garden.' He smiled. 'Khiya became pregnant. At first Akenhaten was fearful of Nefertiti's rage. For a short while, Mahu,' Pentju stared at me, his eyes welling up, 'Akenhaten was young again. You know the way he was. Like a young boy who's stumbled on a clever idea. He was truly frightened that Nefertiti would damage either the Lady Khiya or the baby. He entrusted both of them to me and left secret instructions that if I should die,' Pentju nudged me playfully, 'you were to take responsibility.' He shrugged. 'Khiya died in childbirth. I looked after the boy walled up in that mansion, protected by mercenaries, then the plague struck, ravaging the City of the Aten as it did the rest of Egypt.'

'Your wife and children died?' I asked.

Pentju drew himself up, tightening his lips as if hiding some secret pain. 'My wife, my boys, my girl, my brother and two other kinsmen all died in the last few days of the plague. By then Nefertiti had wormed her way back into Akenhaten's affections, proclaiming herself joint ruler.' Pentju scratched a spot on his hand. 'Akenhaten came to visit me. He seemed fearful, suspicious. He told me that if anything happened to him he had left documents proclaiming you as the official custodian of his heir. The rest you know.'

'The rest I don't know, Pentju,' I retorted. 'A short while ago a battle was fought in the Delta which could have cost us all our lives. A usurper proclaimed himself Pharaoh because no one knows what did happen to Akenhaten.'

'But neither do I. Oh, I have heard the stories that he may have been poisoned by Nefertiti, or even by his daughter, Meritaten; that his corpse lies hidden somewhere in the City of the Aten. I asked Meryre once when he invited me to dinner. Oh, he never talked treason but he hinted at it. One thing I did learn: Djoser and Khufu, the two priests? They did not leave with Akenhaten but afterwards; they may have taken his treasure. Did you find any trace of that?'

'No, we didn't.' I edged closer. 'But I found something more interesting. The False Pharaoh's archives. They were very interesting, Pentju. Djoser, as he died, babbled about you knowing something.'

'The mutterings of a traitor.' Pentju became agitated. 'But I did nothing wrong. I kept well away from Meryre's scheming.'

'I know you did,' I soothed.

'Well, they are all dead.'

'Except Khufu,' I murmured.

Pentju turned, face stricken, mouth slack. 'Khufu!' he whispered, then put his head in his hands and began to sob quietly.

Ari-Mehiu
(Ancient Egyptian for 'the Keeper of the Drowned')

Chapter 10

For a while Pentju could not control his agitation.

'What is it?' I asked. 'Why are you so concerned that Khufu has survived?'

'I couldn't care if he burns in the Underworld, in the Pit of Eternal Fire.' Pentju lifted his head. 'I want this all brought to an end, Mahu. Egypt has its Prince.'

'Why did you come to the Temple of Ptah?' I asked.

Pentju wiped the tears with the back of his hand. 'Am I under arrest, Mahu? Will I be summoned to the Court of Amun or be made to answer to the Royal Circle?' Has the Lord Ay gathered his policemen?'

'No.' I stretched out my legs and forced myself to relax. 'I am here because I am Mahu, Child of the Kap, and so are you.'

'When did you care for anyone, Mahu, apart from your hunting, your poetry and that servant of yours, Djarka?' Pentju leaned over, plucked a flower and sniffed at it before tossing it into the pool. 'And that's wrong too,' he apologised. 'You do care for the Prince; that's why I'll answer your questions, or try to.'

'Let me help you, Pentju. You came to the Temple of Ptah to make offerings to pay a mortuary priest, because it is far away from Thebes and the inquisitive eyes of the Lord Ay and his gang.'

Pentju didn't protest.

'What I want to know is why you described your family as slain. Why you paid for an execration text for a Child of Evil to be cursed.'

'I regard my family as murdered, Mahu. I should have looked after them. I was the physician. I should have done something, but I was guarding the Prince. I brought them to the City of the Aten: that's the Child of Evil; that's also what I called the plague.'

His answers were too easy, bland, the words came tripping off his tongue, so I knew it would be futile to press the matter further. He got to his feet.

'So, you have Khufu?' He stretched out his hand and grasped mine. 'He may be interesting. You should keep him safe.'

Pentju left. I returned to the emptying streets. The celebrations were now finished. In the squares some temple girls still lingered, watching a conjuror breathe fire from his mouth whilst two dwarfs performed lacklustre somersaults. Beggars clustered like locusts, eager to test the generosity of those going to and from the wine shops and temple booths. Market police, cudgels in hand, kept a wary eye on the throng of soldiers and mercenaries drifting into the town as their officers relaxed discipline at the barracks. A balmy evening, one I will always remember after the stench of the Delta; the homely smells of cooking shops, cheap perfume, as well as the smoke from burning tamarind seed and incense, came as a welcome relief. I passed the slaughter house near the Wall of Death and glimpsed the cadavers of the red-haired woman and the mercenary captains who had supported her, bound in sheepskin, hanging by their heels in chains.

I kept away from the slums. The hour was too late, and even my club and dagger might not be protection enough. I walked up the main avenue, dominated on either side by its line of copper-headed bulls. People of every nation streamed by, chattering in various tongues: striped-robed sand-dwellers, Libyan shepherds, merchants from Punt and Kush. Whenever an army assembles, the traders always follow. Heralds armed with conch horns were still proclaiming Horemheb's great victory in the Delta. Already the storytellers were busy for custom, offering to provide their audience with graphic and truthful accounts of 'the hideous struggle against the usurper'. Some enterprising trader claimed he had red hair plucked from the false Pharaoh's Queen, and offered to sell it as a memento to any interested

You say the Veiled One sent you, but I tell you, the Veiled One is dead. Akenhaten is no more.'

'Did the sun rise this morning?' the warlock replied. 'Will he not set tonight? Will he not sustain the light in the darkness? Does he not show his magnificence to everyone? So, how can you say he dies? No man dies, Mahu. The Aten is the God of the living, not the dead. In the eyes of the Aten, no man dies.'

'Is Akenhaten dead?' I edged closer. 'Did he truly send you?'

'Is Akenhaten dead?' the warlock whispered back. He stretched out swiftly and touched my chest before I could flinch. 'Has he died here, Mahu? Here, in your heart?'

'Whoever has sent you,' I replied, as the warlock edged away, 'tell him that in my heart, no one dies. But why trouble us now? Why leave us in the first place?'

'A soul has to be purified,' the warlock replied. 'Look around at the glory of Memphis, Mahu, and weep, for one day it will be no more. Keep your promise. Keep your promise to your master.'

'About the Prince?' I pleaded.

'Keep your promise,' the warlock repeated, nodding his head.

He scurried away as swift as a monkey. I called out, but he became lost in the crowd. I rose to my feet and stared up at the sky. In a few heartbeats all my past seemed to come rushing back along that busy avenue: ghosts and memories were never far from the caverns of my soul, ever ready to haunt my heart. The Veiled One! I had given Akenhaten that name when I had first met him when he was a prince, kept hidden from public view by his father, who regarded him as a misshapen grotesque, an abomination in the eyes of men. I had met him out in the woods of the Malkata Palace, worshipping the rising sun . . .

I was acting so strangely, a kind peasant woman seized my hand, her direct eyes red-rimmed from the dust.

'Are you well, sir?'

I fumbled for my purse and handed over the last piece of silver I carried, muttering that it was nothing. I went across to a narrow beer house erected in the shade of a date palm tree. I shouted at the owner that I was Lord Mahu and the palace would pay. The poor man, frightened out of his wits, handed me a cracked earthenware jug and provided a tawdry stool for me to sit on. I crouched and waited for the shock to pass. It was like the clash of battle, arrows winging out of the curling dust. Akenhaten! Years ago, when we had first met, he had given me a similar amulet as a token of favour, a gesture he had often repeated in the early days of our friendship. My heart calmed. I turned the amulet over and over as all the possibilities came rushing in. Had it been sent by Akenhaten? Was he truly alive? Had he slipped back into the city to see justice done to the usurper? What did the warlock mean by a soul being purified? There were so many explanations. Had Akenhaten been poisoned by his wife and family? Or by Meryre? Had he slipped into madness and gone out into the Red Lands to die? Had he been killed there? Or had he found a certain form of peace, escaping into the darkness to live out his years? He had only reached his mid-thirties when his reign ended after seventeen years. Had Akenhaten drunk too deeply of the cup and sickened of what he had seen? Yet how could he desert his throne? Give up the two crowns? Forget the vision? Ignore his son? And why had he sent this amulet to me? And the warlock?

I put the beer jug down and rubbed the amulet in my hand. Perhaps it wasn't a question of power. Perhaps Akenhaten had recalled the intimacy of our youth when he and I had been close friends, two lonely boys bereft of their parents, he being rejected by his father whilst I was happy that I had escaped the malign influence of that witch woman, my Aunt Isithia. So, had he come back for one more glance and glimpsed me in the chariot? I picked up the beer jug. It held very sweet date wine. I sipped carefully. Or was it all part of some subtle plan? A devious ploy by Ay, Meryre or some other hyaena in the pack?

'My lord Mahu?'

I glanced up. Three figures stood black against the sky; I caught a glimpse of gold, the flash of light from beringed fingers.

'My lord Mahu.' Nakhtimin raised his hand and snapped his fingers for the beer shop owner to bring a stool. He sat down, and the two colonels from his regiment stood slightly back. I hadn't met them before, yet I recognised the menace in the way they stood, far enough away not to hear but close enough to intervene.

'My lord Mahu?'

far west as Libya and as far north as the land of the barbarians. He will be seen on board ship, on the Great Green, driving a chariot across the Horus Road or parading in glory through some city of Canaan. He'll come back to haunt us.'

'This is different.' Nakhtimin shook his head. 'He was seen by no less a person than Colonel Nebamun. He had taken a squadron beyond the Purple Gate on the road leading north. Do you remember those mercenaries who attacked his mansion? Well, some of them fled. After the victory parade Nebamun heard that they were hiding out in a village on the borders of the western Red Lands. Now, Nebamun regarded the attack on his house as a personal affront. Whilst you were all busy in the Delta, he had this city searched for any fugitives. General Horemheb had to almost shake him by the neck to make him think about something else. If Nebamun hadn't been pursuing his own feud, those regiments would have moved a day earlier.

'And?' I asked

'Anyway, after the victory parade, Nebamun continued the hunt. He and his squadron stopped to rest the horses and take on some water. A group of pilgrims passed by, travelling north, on their way to Bubastis. They were carrying a sacred statue of a cat. You know how these pilgrims are dedicated to their own cult: singing hymns and chanting songs. They stopped by the well to draw water. They were excited by what they had seen in Memphis and were discussing it amongst themselves. Nebamun drifted over to inspect the statue of the Goddess Bastet, which was accompanied by two priests, one short, the other very tall. Each had a mask of a cat concealing his face. Nebamun ignored them and the procession moved on.'

'So, he didn't see their faces?'

'Ah, but he did. One of the pilgrims offered the priests water. They removed their masks to drink. Nebamun glimpsed a face, a strange chest and wide hips, but thought nothing of it. Only when the pilgrims had passed did he reflect on what he had seen, and the more he remembered, the more certain he became that the man he had glimpsed was Akenhaten, former Pharaoh of Egypt.'

'Did he set off in pursuit?'

'Of course he did. But you see, he had left the road, stopping

205

at the village to conduct his own search, and when he caught up with the pilgrims he found the priest in question had disappeared. He was informed that the priest had forgotten something precious and returned to Memphis. Nebamun was convinced that this priest, our former Pharaoh, suspected he had been recognised and decided to slip away.'

'So the city has been searched?' I declared.

'Whatever we can do without raising too much of a fuss.' Nakhtimin got to his feet. 'Lord Ay asked me to search you out and give you the news.' He waved away the sweaty beer stall owner holding a cup of date wine and tossed him a deben of copper. 'I don't want it now. Give it to my friend.'

Nakhtimin bowed and strode away, leaving me to my wine.

I stared across at the bustling square and smiled to myself. I have had years to reflect about Akenhaten. How he began worshipping the Aten, the one omnipotent, invisible God, because of secret teaching by his mother, the Great Queen Tiye, whose ancestors had wandered down from Canaan, driving their flocks before them to feast on the riches of Egypt. Others argued how the worship of the Aten was already in place during the reign of his father, that it was a political move to counter the growing power of the Temple of Amun-Ra at Karnak and that of Luxor in Thebes. Still others maintained it was a mixture of the two, but the older I grew and the more I listened, the more clearly I saw a young man obsessed with an idea, rejected and insulted by his father, who, if he had had his way, would have had him murdered at birth. I thought of the humiliation Akenhaten had suffered at the hands of the priests of Amun-Ra. How he'd been banished from the Mansions of a Million Years and not allowed to mix with the others in the Great House. Was Akenhaten's devotion to the Aten simply revenge? A reason to stir the pool just to see the dirt rise? On that evening in Memphis I wondered. Akenhaten's shadow still hung over everything; his personality and his policies still dominated the land of Egypt. Was that what he wanted? For people to recognise that once he had walked this earth, that he was not to be ignored?

'Great of mischief,' one priest had described him. 'Great of mischief and great of lies.' I have no son, but if I had, I would teach him the one true lesson I have learned in life: what we are as children, so shall we be as adults; how we are treated as children, so shall we treat others as adults. Oh, we don our wigs and put the chains of office around our necks. We garb ourselves in gauffered robes with gold, silver and precious jewels so we shimmer like dazzling images. Yet in the end, the heart cannot be adorned. It doesn't change, it simply reflects everything it has learnt.

On that evening, sitting under a dusty palm tree sipping cheap date wine, I recognised that what was true of Akenhaten was also true of me; that was the bond between the two of us. In my early days, as a Child of the Kap, I had been ridiculed and taunted by the Pharaoh's Chief Minister, the great Hotep, that I was not truly my father's son. Perhaps this explains why Father hardly bothered with me but left me to the sinister care of Aunt Isithia, a woman with a heart steeped in darkness. A woman who, if reports were true, drove my own mother to her grave and liked nothing better than to bait me, a child, with all forms of subtle cruelty. As a man, I paid her back coin for coin. I told Sobeck she was responsible for the betrayal of him and the Royal Concubine whom he'd secretly seduced. Isithia suffered an accident, stumbling off the roof of her house. I ordered flies to be buried with her, something in life that she could not stand. I also told her embalmers to burn her heart so she'd wander for ever the Halls of the Underworld.

I reflected on how Ay had tried to drive me from the Royal Circle and I knew why I had resisted. First, my loyalty to the Prince, the living clasp between myself and what had gone before. Secondly – yes, there was another reason, one I've told my own interrogators, so simple, so lucid, almost childlike. True, I had nowhere to go and nothing else to do, but that was not all. The true reason was that I was curious. I was like a man who wanders into a marketplace and watches the most dramatic quarrel take place. Insults fly, secrets are revealed, grudges surface, and although it has nothing to do with you, you are still caught up in the drama; you want to stay and see what happens.

I finished my palm wine and, clutching my cudgel, walked out of the city through the great gateway dominated by carved figures of Ptah, arms crossed, his unseeing eyes staring out over the Black Lands. Many of the peasants were leaving now the markets were closed. They were sleepy after their wine and beer, hearts full of wonderment at the doings of the Great Ones of the land. I listened to their chatter, the rumours that Akenhaten had returned. The Great Heretic would not leave them alone! They talked of him as if he were some evil spirit out of the west, a sombre ghost. I smiled to myself. The legends and stories were already being born, the truth slowly being twisted.

I approached Nebamun's country mansion, that elegant house perched on the banks of the Nile yet shielded from it by long grass, bushes and clumps of trees. Now it lay all serene, but I recalled the frenzied attack by the usurper's mercenaries, how close they had come to victory. Nebamun certainly had not forgotten it. Members of his regiment camped amongst the trees, as did my mercenaries round their camp fires, still celebrating the day's events. Their captain rose to greet me, aggrieved that I had wandered into the city alone, remonstrating that it wasn't safe. I agreed with him. He pointed to the two great pillars leading into the courtyard. At the base of each Nebamun had placed a skull, a grisly reminder of what had happened. I told the man to keep close watch and wandered into the courtyard, where more of my men sprawled in the shade. The captain came running after me, saying how members of Ay's retinue had brought the Prince back. I found him and Djarka in their old quarters. Colonel Nebamun was still absent at the victory banquet and his chamberlain fussed about me till I snapped at him to leave me alone. Tutankhamun came to greet me, dancing from foot to foot, little arms held high. Djarka still looked downcast and apologetic. I told him that the matter was finished.

'You could not have opposed the Lord Ay,' I reassured him. 'Perhaps I should not have left you, but there again, I had no choice. Now come, something to eat and drink?'

Djarka went down to the kitchens and brought back food and wine, with apple juice for the Prince. I sat and listened to Tutankhamun's chatter, his constant stream of questions. How many had I killed in the Great Battle? Was I a Great Warrior? Could I show him how the battle went?

I arranged his toy soldiers and chariots and gave him the most vivid description, whilst he sat round-eyed, sipping at the juice and nibbling at sesame cake. I took Djarka aside and asked him if there had been recurrences of that trance-like state when the Prince seemed not to recognise anything or anyone. Djarka shook his head. I asked him to bring up the box of *shets*, the small tortoises which fascinated both me and Tutankhamun, I had brought these from Thebes. The boy loved them. I had painted their shells different colours. We shared a secret. Each tortoise was named after a member of the Royal Circle: Horemheb, Rameses, Meryre, Tutu, Huy and Maya. The last was the fattest. Tutankhamun thought this was amusing, and often giggled behind his fingers. I watched the little things crawl over the floor.

'My lord?'

'Yes, Uncle Mahu?'

'Where are Meryre and Tutu? You have two missing.'

'I drowned them.' Tutankhamun stood, hands hanging by his sides. He must have caught my look, for his lower lip came out and began to quiver. 'They were traitors,' he declared. 'They were no longer members of the Royal Circle, so I drowned them in a pool and buried them in the garden.'

I glanced sharply at Djarka, who just shook his head.

'Did I do wrong, Uncle Mahu?'

I was going to say yes, when I thought of all the men I had killed in battle or executed silently and swiftly in the darkness of the night. I stretched out my arms. He ran towards me.

'They were only tortoises,' I whispered.

'They were traitors,' he declared fiercely. 'They would have killed you, Uncle Mahu.'

Whilst the tortoises crawled about, I arranged the board and pieces for a game of Senet and played until the Prince's eyes grew heavy. Djarka scooped him up and took him to bed, and I went along to the other side of the house. Nebamun's chamberlain assured me that Khufu's room was closely guarded. The prisoner hadn't been troubled, but had been given food and drink, which the chamberlain had tasted first. I opened the door and peered in. Khufu lay on his bed, snoring like a pig.

*   *   *

Nebamun returned slightly drunk, a floral collar about his neck, a lotus behind his ear, whilst the cone of perfume bestowed on every banquet guest had melted so he reeked like a temple girl. He was assisted by two of his staff officers, who helped him into the hall where, perched drunkenly on a stool, he bawled for a jug of light beer. He opened the small casket he was holding.

'Look, Mahu.' The old soldier swayed dangerously. 'Look what they have given me.'

It was a gold-bejewelled collar of bravery, which proclaimed Nebamun as 'Great of Valour'. He put this back into the cask and demanded that I join him in a drink. Once again he recounted his version of the battle, the glories of Horemheb's victory, and my, as he put it, major part in it. Nebamun was a true soldier, a veritable treasure house of funny stories which mocked both himself and his superiors. He chattered about the banquet too: I gathered the rest were still feasting.

'But,' Nebamun tapped the side of his nose, 'they are not as drunk as they pretend. They want you to join them tomorrow, just before dawn, for a hunting party. Now why should they want to go hunting?'

'Because that's what we always do, that's what we have always done, the Children of the Kap, the Royal Circle: we go out in the desert where there are no ears, no eyes, no scribes.'

'I thought as much,' Nebamun drunkenly agreed. 'They want to discuss the *saati*, the usurper.'

'They say you saw the True Pharaoh?'

'I didn't call him the True Pharaoh.' Nebamun sobered up. 'He was not *my* True Pharaoh. I glimpsed Akenhaten and I spoke with true voice.' He waved his finger at me and recounted the same story Nakhtimin had told me.

'But are you sure?'

'A mere chance,' he slurred. 'You know how it is, Mahu. You see something, at first you don't recognise or don't realise what's happening. It was only afterwards.' He shook his head. 'I hadn't been drinking. I know what I saw. Tall he was, angular, chest sticking out, his belly like a pouch, the wide hips, but above all those spindly fingers, those eyes, the line of his face, the long jaw. He was fingering a circle of turquoise beads. I once stood near him in Thebes.' He smiled. 'Or rather I nosed the ground before him. I took my opportunity to study the man who was busy turning everything on its head. I remember faces. I would remember his. I wish I had captured him, but . . .' He shrugged.

'You could have been mistaken?'

Nebamun smiled. 'No, no, my lord. Ay has already been busy searching for the truth. The usurper and his accomplices, including some of the mercenary captains, have been taken to the Kheb-t and put to the torture.'

'My lord Ay is impatient.'

'He brought his own torturer with him,' Nebamun replied. 'The Usernu.'

I recognised the title for the Chief Torturer from the Temple of Osiris. He was one of Ay's minions, who governed the hideous dungeons and chambers beneath the House of Secrets.

'I thought you'd know,' Nebamun drawled. 'Isn't the House of Secrets in your care?'

'It's supposed to be,' I agreed. 'A minor bone of contention between myself and Lord Ay, but we have reached a pact. I don't interfere with him and he certainly doesn't interfere with me. So, what have these torturers learnt?'

Nebamun held up a forefinger and thumb, as if measuring something small. 'Tiny nuggets,' he murmured. 'But one thing is certain. According to everything Ay has learnt – and he's already telling this to the Royal Circle, making no secret of it – Akenhaten has been seen in Canaan. They believe he is still there. Now, what do you think of that?'

'It could be true,' I agreed. 'But if Meryre can play with impostors, so can Lord Ay.'

The old colonel drew his brows together.

'I trust you, Colonel.'

He leaned over and patted me affectionately on the knee.

'And you are not a bad fellow either, Mahu, for a policeman.'

'What if,' I continued, 'Ay has decided to play the same game? To spread rumours that Akenhaten is still alive. It will bind the Royal Circle together to face a common enemy.'

Nebamun scratched his head. 'I am only a soldier, Mahu. No, that's just an excuse. I see your point. If Egypt is strong, united, the likes of myself will kill its enemies.'

'After I left here,' I asked, changing the subject, 'how was Meryre?'

'Very quiet.' Nebamun blinked. 'Yes, very quiet, rather subdued. I made sure his armed retainers were kept well away, though I allowed him to meet with his gaggle of priests. He was . . .' Nebamun blew his lips out, 'you'd think he was waiting or listening for something. He asked my permission to look at the *per-met cha*.'

'You have a library?' I asked.

'Just a small one. Documents, books, items I have picked up. I like to read, Lord Mahu. I understand you are a poet.'

'And what did Meryre want?'

'He said he was interested in the Amnett, the Land of the Dead. I asked him again. He replied the same. He wanted to see the Land of the Dead.'

'Do you know what he meant?'

Nebamun shrugged. 'You know these priests. They babble on about this and that. I saw no harm in it. The library is a small chamber at the back of the house. It's dark and dry, suitable for manuscripts. The only ones to go in are myself and the cat; it lives there to keep the mice down.'

'And Meryre's escape?'

Nebamun pulled a face. 'You know how it is, my lord Mahu. God's Father Ay arrived, all-important, but by then I had left. We had received our orders to march and I was ready to go. One night Meryre and his companions were here, the next they were gone.'

'Do you think Lord Ay arranged their escape?'

'The thought has occurred to me, as well as to Lord Horemheb.' Nebamun grinned. 'Perhaps Lord Ay did not wish Meryre to be put to torture? After all . . .' Nebamun got to his feet, dropping his beer jug, which I caught and put on the table. 'Thank you. After all,' he walked to the door, 'it would be highly embarrassing to execute members of the Royal Circle, not to mention a high priest of the Aten cult. Anyway, I am to bed.'

I waited for a while, then went down across the house to the small chamber on the second floor which served as Nebamun's library. I asked the chamberlain to bring oil lamps. I lit these. The cat, sleeping in a corner, sprang to its feet and padded silently around its kingdom. It was a typical soldier's room, everything neatly filed and ordered. Scrolls were kept in baskets of thick stiffened reeds. The puffs of dust when I lifted the lid showed these had not been disturbed for weeks. I crossed to the shelves where other papyrus rolls had been placed in their niches, each carefully labelled. Again the polished sycamore wood was covered with a fine layer of dust. Carrying a lamp, I checked every ledge until I found where the dust had been disturbed. I pulled out the document. It had been rolled up in a rather haphazard way; this was the document Meryre had looked at. I laid it out on the table and was rather disappointed, for it was only a map. The hieroglyphs across the top proclaimed it to be the property of the Aauaaul-Shet Aiu, the Gods of the Secret Doors and Ways, a rather pompous label for nothing more than a crude map of Egypt, Sinai and Canaan. The Nile was clearly delineated, as were the various cities, the Great Green to the north, the lands of the Hittites and Mitanni, the Sinai peninsula and the Horus Road. Moving an oil lamp, I realised Meryre had marked where the City of the Aten stood.

'Why did he do that?' I whispered.

I searched the library again, but could find nothing else. I went down to the kitchen and told the sleepy-eyed cooks to bring a light meal of beef grilled over charcoal and sprinkled with herbs, fresh bread and a jug of wine to the eating hall. I went and kicked Khufu awake. He was drowsy, rather slurred, but I told him to wash and meet me for something to eat. A short while later we dined in the light of oil lamps. Khufu was ravenous, eating quickly, drinking the wine so deeply I told him to be careful. He stopped, his mouth full of juice.

'You will keep your word, Lord Mahu?'

'Your life, limb and security are guaranteed,' I replied. 'I swear that by earth and sky. You will be given money, provisions and turned out to make your own way in the world. Now, tell me, Khufu, when that happens, where will you go?'

He swallowed hard.

'Or let me be more blunt. If you wished to follow Meryre, where would you go?'

He stared at the wine cup. 'If,' he slurred, 'if I had to go, I'd travel to one of the villages in the Eastern Desert.'

213

I recalled the map Meryre had been studying.

'And then you'd travel north?'

Khufu nodded his agreement. 'Go east, then north to avoid the Medjay, across the desert and into Canaan; that's the safest place for the likes of us. We'd still find refuge at the Hittite court but it would be perilous. There are bound to be rewards posted, whilst Prince Aziru is a broken reed. However, I will not join them.' He gazed bleakly at me. 'When you release me, Lord Mahu, I shall journey south to Kush. Find some small temple town and end my days in peace.'

'What would Meryre mean by the Land of the Dead? He wasn't talking about the Far Horizon?'

'I heard him talk about the Sea of the Dead, a passing reference, a great inland lake in northern Canaan. The water is so salted it contains no life and lies surrounded by harsh deserts. Local wanderers claim that two great cities, Sodom and Gomorrah, once stood there before they were destroyed by fire from heaven which scorched the land and turned the water to poison.'

'Anything else?'

Khufu shook his head.

'And these rumours about Akenhaten being seen in Canaan?'

'As you say, my lord Mahu, they were rumours. A search was made . . .'

I leaned across the table, my knife held only inches from his eyes.

'My lord Mahu, I tell the truth. Why should I lie? Prince Aziru searched but could find nothing; that's why the impostor emerged.' He drew a deep breath. 'I was excluded from the War Council, as was Djoser. I suspect they hoped that if they were successful the real Akenhaten would emerge later. My task was to proclaim that the usurper was the True Pharaoh, nothing more, nothing less.'

'Tell me.' I withdrew the knife. 'Djoser was killed out along the Horus Road, but before he died, he babbled about the physician Pentju, how Meryre was very keen to draw this physician into his plotting. Now Pentju is a very powerful man, a great physician, but why would the conspirators be so interested in him?'

'He was another member of the Royal Circle?' Khufu stammered. 'He had been guardian of the Prince Tutankhamun, a friend of his mother?'

I caught it, the shift of fear in his eyes. My only regret is that I never forced him then.

'I want you to tell me.' I put down the knife and pointed across the chamber to where I'd placed a writing palette with papyrus pens and inkpot. 'I want you to go over there and write down everything you know, from the moment the City of the Aten began to crumble.' I seized his wrists. 'I want to know everything. You have slept well. Your hunger has been satisfied and your belly has taken enough wine. I shall wait.'

Khufu rose to his feet and scampered across.

I have the document still. I have kept it close: let Khufu tell his own story.

heri-sesh
(Ancient Egyptian for 'chief scribe')

Chapter 11

Khufu's Tale

I have taken a great oath upon my life to tell the truth, or what I can, about the Pharaoh Akenhaten, He-who-is-pleasing-to-the-Aten. I am Khufu, son of Iputy, a priest of Isis in the city of Thebes. I studied at the House of Life and later moved to a small temple of Aten in the Malkata Palace, where I was noted for my industry and my skill, my dedication to letters and my submission to the will of the Divine One. I am a priest who has studied the sacred writings of Thoth but one who came to recognise his error that all such Gods are shadows, phantasms of men's imaginations. They are the darkness which comes before the dawn and the rising of the Aten, the Sun Disc, above the horizon. I revered the symbol of the All-Seeing, All-Knowing Invisible God, who has commanded us not to make an image of Him but has chosen to reveal Himself in our hearts through His son Akenhaten. I renounced my errors in the presence of the Divine One and his Great Queen Nefertiti, the beautiful woman, She-who-is-pleasing-to-the-Aten. I confessed the mistakes of my life and dedicated myself to the adoration and service of the All-Seeing God.

My zeal was soon noticed by Lord Meryre, High Priest of the Aten and Chief of Ceremonies in the principal temple at the City of the Aten. I was eaten up by zeal whilst the love of the Lord's House filled my days. One hour there was worth a thousand years elsewhere. I was most obedient and listened

219

attentively to the teaching of the Divine One. This teaching was eventually frustrated by Nefertiti, who wished to assume the status and title of a God and whose interference cast a shadow across the sunlight of the new revelation.

I also acknowledge that I have wandered from the path of righteousness in my zeal to serve my master. I have sat at the camp fire of Egypt's enemies and taken part in their evil deliberations. I have sinned, and my sin shall always be before me. I am grateful to the Lord Mahu for the great pardon and mercy he has shown me. I have sworn to tell the truth and to do reparation. I shall leave this place and go into obscurity. I shall end my days far away from the great stirrings of Egypt.

Lord Mahu has asked when did it begin? What were the seeds of this great mystery? Now, he knows the history of the City of the Aten, though the events which led to its downfall are hidden in the murk and swirl of the strife. So when *did* it begin? I shall answer bluntly. A rift occurred between the Divine One, Akenhaten, and his Queen Nefertiti over the birth of the Divine One's son by the lesser queen and wife Khiya, Princess of the Mitanni. It was common gossip that Nefertiti had tolerated Khiya on the understanding that she would never conceive. When she heard that the Princess of the Foreigners, as she termed her, had not only conceived but died giving birth to a living son, her fury knew no bounds. A woman of deep pride and soaring ambition, Nefertiti believed that she could rage and vent her anger in public. The Divine One refused to tolerate this and banished her from his presence. After this breach, the Palace of the Aten was plunged into gloom and despair, the glory of the court dimmed. The splendour of its temples was cloaked in darkness, their lanterns and lights extinguished by a sense of creeping despondency. Akenhaten was alone, Khiya dead, Nefertiti exiled to her quarters in the northern part of the city.

The Divine One, by the fifteenth year of his reign, allowed his head to be turned and his heart spoiled by strong wine and the juice of the poppy. His soul became unquiet, wearing out his body as an over-sharp sword wears out its sheath. Anxious and agitated, Akenhaten would prowl the palace corridors. Sometimes he would cry for his God; other times for Nefertiti, his baby son or his comrades from years past. He was a man who forsook the sacrifice, the morning and evening prayer, living in the sombre caverns of his past. He would act as if attacked by an evil spirit out of the west, as if his soul was possessed by demons. He cursed his father, Amenhotep the Magnificent, and bewailed the tragic death of his elder brother Tuthmosis.

Often Akenhaten would treat me as if I was his ear priest, ready to listen to his confession. He would recount how his elder brother Tuthmosis had been hideously poisoned in the Temple of Amun-Ra at Kransk; how he could have prevented it but failed to do so. He would describe his other sins, his lust and his pride. He would seek relief from his obsession, playing and relaxing with his two daughters whom he now proclaimed as his queens. Both became pregnant, but even then, his seed was cursed, the children of both unions dying in childbirth. Ankhesenamun remained strong, but Meritaten, weak from the start, became terrified of her father's sullen isolation, his fits of dejection and despair broken by mad bouts of fury. He insisted on sitting in lonely glory in his throne room or prowling round it like a panther in its cage. On other occasions, particularly as the shadows grew longer and the sun began to set, he would become obsessed with unspeakable terrors and demand the company of the Lord Meryre, my humble self and Djoser. We would crouch for hours and listen to his plaints.

'Oppression, agony and fear haunt me,' he'd shout. 'The demons have frustrated my desires. I have sinned. I am sick, my sins are many and my faults are grave.'

He would sit staring down the throne room, lips moving as if talking to beings we could not see. He'd then recover and start screaming, 'What have I done? What have I done?'

At times we became frightened that he was possessed or that his true soul had left his body. The plague came, sweeping into the city like the Angel of Death, dealing out retribution and suffering on every side. The Divine One saw this as a curse, and his dejection deepened. He would kneel and pray, screaming for us priests to gather around him

He fell into the darkness and we thought he would either remain so or do himself an injury. He'd later recover and crouch

221

on his throne, nibbling his fingers like a frightened child. Weeks passed into months. Sometimes he would neglect to wash or shave, driving away his servants with blows and curses.

Later in the sowing season of that same year, we became aware of others in the palace, at first nothing more than dark shapes and shadows, men out of the desert. The Imperial Guard were dismissed and these newcomers took up positions. This lasted for at least a month before they too disappeared. The Imperial Guard were ordered to return and we were allowed into the Divine One's presence so he could show us his face. We found him calm upon his throne. He issued a proclamation, which startled us all: Nefertiti was to be restored. My lord Meryre, summoning up his courage, asked if others of the Royal Circle would be assembled, but Akenhaten rejected this. God's Father, the Lord Ay, he replied quietly, would deal with them.

His Great Queen Nefertiti was brought to him. She arrived gowned, beautifully adorned, and knelt as a suppliant at his feet. On that day, and for the following days, she stayed alone with him. When we were summoned once again to his presence, Akenhaten was calmer. Nefertiti now shared his bed and throne, his lamentations grew less, and he took to sifting a set of amber turquoise beads. As time passed Nefertiti's power became more apparent. She was declared regent. Cold and imperious, she took to shaving her head and dressing herself in the garb of Pharaoh. Whilst her status and glory increased, Akenhaten's diminished. He drew apart from his Queen and from us, as if his former madness was a filthy robe he had shrugged off. He grew concerned with maps, charts and stars. He would also pray, not in the Temple of the Aten but alone in his own private chamber. If he sacrificed, it was not the blood of lambs or bulls, but grains of incense sprinkled over a brazier of fire. The Divine One also resumed hunting trips, often going out into the Red Lands alone.

One day, just after the New Year, when the Dog Star could be clearly seen high in the heavens and the white ibis had returned to the banks of the Nile to show the inundation was imminent, Akenhaten returned from a hunting trip. He was accompanied by what we thought were mere sand-dwellers, desert wanderers, in their striped robes with bushy hair and beards. My lord Meryre's spies reported that these were the same who had often visited the Divine One as a boy and whose presence in the Palace had been noticed earlier. They came with no proclamation or trumpets, no pomp or ceremony, but soft as the wind, slipping down the tracks and paths of the eastern limestone cliffs into the City of the Aten. Lord Ay and officers of the Imperial Guard were under strict instruction: these visitors were the Pharaoh's friends; they were to be welcomed and allowed into his presence without fear or trouble. Their leader was Yakoub, a tall, fierce-looking warrior, though he was friendly enough.

As the year progressed, the Divine One allowed these visitors to mingle freely with his priests. Yakoub was a great storyteller, a man who knew the deserts like the palm of his hand. He told me how he and his kin were of the tribe of Israar, a sect of the Apiru who, many years ago, had come from the western hill country of Canaan, travelling south into Egypt. Some of their tribe had settled in the Delta area, where they had become skilled stonemasons. Others had remained tending their flocks, moving along that lonely part of Egypt between the Black Lands and the Red Lands of the desert. He claimed how the Great Queen Tiye, wife of Amenhotep the Magnificent and mother of Akenhaten, was the descendant of their tribe. He boasted how others in the service of the Divine One, such as Djarka, servant of my lord Mahu, Chief of Police and Overseer of the House of Secrets, was also of them. Yakoub would share wine and break bread with us. He'd talk of his mysterious God whose name cannot be uttered, about how a Temu or Aput, a Messenger God or Messiah, was prophesied to come from his tribe.

During this time, the Divine One's recovery improved. Serene and calm, he took to washing and purifying himself, whilst the business of the palace and the city was left to Nefertiti and others of the Royal Circle. However, one thing did alarm the Lord Meryre. Yakoub and his people were being paid direct from the Divine One's *per hatch*, the household treasury. At first Lord Meryre thought these were bribes; he later became convinced that the Divine One's companions were actually moving royal treasure out into the Red Lands. The High Priest, virtually excluded from Akenhaten's presence and no longer consulted over rites and liturgy, became alarmed at the secretiveness of our divine master. Meryre often gathered myself, Djoser and the other priests for secret counsel. He made us swear an oath of loyalty to him declaring how others of the Royal Circle could no longer be trusted, that something was about to happen and we should prepare ourselves against the evil day. Eventually, one morning, when Akenhaten was in the Window of Appearances greeting the rising sun, Meryre demanded an audience. We were ushered into the imperial presence, but Akenhaten remained kneeling, keeping his back to us as if he didn't care if we came, went or stayed. Lord Meryre, deeply insulted, was about to withdraw.

'Why do you leave, my lord Meryre?' Akenhaten's voice was strong and clear.

When we turned in the doorway, Pharaoh no longer had his back to us but was squatting cross-legged. He was dressed only in a loincloth, with a thin linen shawl about his shoulders. His head and face were shaved and oiled, and the lines of worry about his eyes and mouth had disappeared.

'You may, if you wish,' he smiled and gestured, 'come and speak to me.'

'Perhaps,' Meryre retorted, 'we should be joined by your Great Queen and God's Father Ay?'

The smile disappeared from Akenhaten's face.

'You must have wondered what happened to me, my lord Meryre. Come, be seated and I shall tell you. For my time with you is short.'

Alarmed and intrigued, Meryre, Djoser and I knelt before him.

'Do not mention to me,' Akenhaten's head went down, his voice strong and echoing, 'the Batiui, those red-haired devils of Akhmin, those fiends, those creatures of abomination who do not speak, and have not spoken, with true voice.'

The Divine One's eyes rolled back in his head. He stretched out his hands. I thought he was having a fit.

'My lord, what is the matter?' Meryre demanded.

'When you mentioned their names,' Akenhaten's eyes were now closed, 'blood-stained phantoms surrounded me. I hear rushing and roaring like that of a powerful wind.'

'But my lord,' Meryre whispered, 'the palace is silent. The morning sky is darkening over.'

'It is my heart which speaks.' Akenhaten kept his eyes closed. 'I leave the things of the evil one and my heart travels. The rushing and roaring must be the wind blowing through the tops of lofty cedars.'

'But my lord,' Meryre insisted, 'there are no cedars in the City of the Aten.'

'I am here,' Akenhaten sighed, 'but my heart is in a place where cedars grow. I tire of this place. I have had visions of a city and the glory of Egypt as nothing more than lumpish grey mounds of clay cracked by the sun, scored by the rains. This city as a dark smudge on a wasteland of sand.'

'Your Majesty,' Meryre asked, 'has Your Majesty been given a vision of the future?'

'I have lived in visions in the darkness of the night. I have seen the shadows shift. I have been in the *tertrati iati*, the landscape of the night. I have had a taste of things to come: a dream about the power of the One and the future of Egypt.' He put his hands over his face, then opened them, keeping them by the sides of his face like a veil. 'Open are the double doors of the Far Horizon,' he intoned. 'Unlocked are its bolts. The divine cause is clear, though storms darken the sky. The stars rain down, the bones of beasts tremble. The demons are silent. I shall not die on this earth.'

'Your Majesty,' Meryre insisted, 'if you have seen visions of the future, you must share them with us, leave your wisdom to your own son! Can we not,' he hurried on, 'take down your writings, convey your teachings to others?'

'I would speak but they would not listen. I would tell but they would not understand. I would write but they would not learn. I would sing but they would turn away.' Akenhaten's shoulders slumped. 'And as for my son,' his eyes brimmed with tears, 'or he who has been proclaimed my son . . . I have left my wisdom in the custody of the Watchers.'

'Who are the Watchers?' Meryre demanded.

'When I go to my place,' Akenhaten replied, 'and if it be the will of God, my son will receive my wisdom. Until then . . .'

'Your Majesty, what will happen to us?'

225

'Each man follows his path, but where I go, you cannot come. When I am gone you shall long for me and search for me but you will not find me in my new place, in the mansion of my own making.'

'And where is this?' Meryre questioned.

Akenhaten opened his eyes, staring at us; his gaze was as fierce as a lion. 'I wish to go, I am already in the land of no return.'

'Why should you go there, my lord?'

'Because I have striven after evil. I have transgressed the bounds of righteousness.'

Oh, my lord Mahu, I speak the truth. In that chamber I felt a sudden dread, the chill of fear. The sky was darkening with storm clouds. Djoser, to ease the tension, made some reference to this.

'I am glad the clouds have come.' Akenhaten smiled. 'They will bring the rain, they will wash away the demons of the south-western winds.'

'Who are these demons?' Meryre asked.

Akenhaten gazed at a point above our heads.

'They are seven in all. Yes, in the hollows of the great abyss lurk the seven, that's what I have been told. They are neither male nor female. They take no wives, they beget no children. These demons of the seven know neither pity nor kindness. They do not listen to prayer or supplication; they are the messengers of death and the servants of the Devourer. If they meet a man like me, with whom God is angry, they fall on him like a lion takes a gazelle. They fill both his soul and body with poison. They bind his hands, they tie his feet and claw his sides.'

'Have you seen these demons?' Meryre asked.

'They are skeletons who gather around my throne and bed. Red hair sprouts from their skulls; black wings conceal their hideousness; great flat hands stretch at the end of long arms. They take my body and claw my flesh.' He gripped his stomach. 'Like eagles' talons, they grasp my heart and grind it like meal.'

'And how do you combat them?' Meryre was genuinely interested. He had often confided how he wished he possessed the power of an exorcist, the skill to drive out demons.

'I called the priests of Apiru,' Akenhaten confessed. 'They

sacrificed a lamb and daubed my body with its blood. They gave me powders to eat, to plunge my heart into a deep sleep. In my dreams I saw the demons, a howling, hideous throng who pay court to the Fetcher of Death.' Akenhaten smiled. 'When I woke, the demons had gone. My heart was purified. So do not threaten me, my lord Meryre, with bringing the red-haired ones here. I do not wish their presence.'

The High Priest was much dismayed and sought an immediate audience with the Lord Ay and the Great Queen Nefertiti. I was present at that interview. Lord Ay, anxious-faced, discussed the many possibilities, including that Akenhaten might be planning his own death. The Great Queen remained pale-faced and tight-lipped with fury. Although Nefertiti had been restored to favour, she, the Lord Ay and others of the Royal Circle were now banned from the imperial presence. At the end of the meeting Lord Ay concluded that I should be sent back to discuss certain possibilities with the Divine One.

I did so, expecting to be turned away, but Akenhaten graciously allowed me into his presence. He was now robed, an embroidered sash around his waist, a simple collar of gold about his neck. He was seated before a table. I remember the smell of cooking, of roast duck highly spiced. He offered to share this with me but I was too dry-tongued and frightened to eat.

'Are you timid?' Akenhaten asked. 'Shall I tell you something, Khufu? My Great Queen and her wily father, for the first time in their lives, are truly frightened of me. They thought I was clay in their hands and that they could mould me. They cannot. They have failed in their true mission. It was they who led me from the path of righteousness.'

'My lord,' I dared to whisper, 'you talk as if you are about to leave us. What about your baby son?'

'I am always leaving you, Khufu, and as for my son, I shall share with you a great secret. For every secret must have a witness. Do you know why I banned the Great Queen from my presence? Because she dared to threaten my infant son! And do you know why she has been restored?' He didn't wait for an answer. 'Because she had taken a blood oath by earth and sky that neither she, nor any of hers, shall lift a hand against him.'

'My lord, are you to leave us?'

'I wish to go to the Seshent.' He smiled. 'The Place of Purification.'

'And your son?' I insisted.

'The Stegout.' Akenhaten referred to the Watchers of the Gods. 'They hold the secrets my son wishes to know.'

He was speaking in riddles, deliberately teasing me. He flicked his fingers, a gesture that the audience was over, so I withdrew. I reported faithfully what had happened. God's Father Ay and Meryre were deeply discomforted, and perplexed at what to do.

On my oath, Lord Mahu, as I hope to live, that was the last time I or any others saw Akenhaten, the Divine One. The next morning Lord Meryre, who had summoned up enough courage, demanded an audience, but the guards turned him away, saying Pharaoh had gone out in the eastern Red Lands to hunt. The High Priest accepted this, and when he approached the next day, the same excuse was given, though the captain of the guard looked both troubled and intrigued. Two more days passed before a careful search was made. The Divine One had left the city. Chariots and horses had been taken from the royal stables but no huntsmen, whippers-in or hounds had followed. No one had seen him leave. No one knew when he had gone or when he would return. God's Father Ay sent out a chariot squadron; they scoured up to a distance of ten miles but could find no trace or trail. Lord Ay believed that Akenhaten may have left for a period of solitude, but after two weeks had passed he reached the conclusion that something else had happened. He and Queen Nefertiti decided to send out an expedition into the eastern Red Lands; they were confident, from the reports of spies and guards, that Akenhaten had not crossed the Nile into the western desert.

My lord Tutu intervened. He laid before us letters about the situation in Canaan and argued the Divine One might have gone there. Queen Nefertiti questioned why her husband should go into the hill country of the Canaanites. I suspect she knew the answer before he replied. 'Your Majesty,' Tutu reasoned, 'is it not from such hill country that your people come?'

'My people,' Nefertiti snapped. 'My people are those of Egypt!' And would not discuss the matter again.

Meryre, however, did not trust her or God's Father Ay. He began to cast about to discover what had happened. An expedition was prepared. Then, one night whilst I was serving sacrifice in a small sun temple, I heard the most hideous scream, like that of a soul in anguish, caught by the hellhounds, trapped in the *ketet*, the darkness of the Underworld. The scream was short but full of agony, like that of a man in a death trap. At first I thought I was dreaming. I hurried to investigate, as did the Lord Ay, who had been in a chamber nearby, but the Queen's mercenaries had sealed the corridors and would not let us pass. I made a careful enquiry the next day. I reasoned that if a man had been killed, sent to the slaughter, his corpse would be thrown into some pit or crocodile pool. Others in the palace had heard the scream, and so the story began, the suspicion that the Divine One had been murdered, possibly assassinated by his own wife. Yet there was no proof and it became one story amongst many. One thing I did learn from an acquaintance was that the chief embalmer in the House of Life at the Temple of the Aten had also disappeared. He was Queen Nefertiti's creature, a thin-faced, one-eyed fellow who rejoiced in the name of Keket, the Stammerer. During these days of mystery Keket vanished for a while, and when he rejoined his colleagues, he kept his own counsel. Nevertheless, for a man who had served in the embalming house of Thebes, Keket now appeared to enjoy great favour and considerable wealth, the source of which remained a mystery.

In the end, Lord Meryre had his way. An expedition was dispatched under General Rahmose into the eastern Red Lands, even as far as Canaan, to discover the whereabouts, if possible, of the Lord Akenhaten.

Lord Meryre was insistent that Djoser and I were part of this expedition. Meryre had now openly broken with Queen Nefertiti and refused to submit to the Lord Ay. We had no choice but to undergo that harrowing experience! We crossed the burning desert, stopping at the Oasis of Sweetness before eventually entering the Sinai and on into Canaan. A strange country, with its reddish sandy soil, twisted oaks, deep woods and muddy rivers infested with crocodiles. We continued north into the meadow plains, avoiding the squalid towns, journeying slowly along roads infested by outlaws and bandits. The inhabitants treated us with suspicion. Each valley is occupied by a separate tribe, so no force was strong enough to oppose us. Eventually we reached the territories of Prince Aziru and were taken under his protection. Rahmose explained the secret purpose of our expedition. Aziru solemnly agreed to help us. He had profited and prospered because Akenhaten had ignored the affairs of Canaan. Even when we reached the court, we found Hittite envoys being entertained as guests of honour.

Aziru made careful search for Akenhaten. At first he considered our expedition was a pretext for some other mystery but his spies also whispered strange tales about a group who had come out of Egypt, a caravan fiercely protected by sand-dwellers which had moved north into the hills around the Dead Sea. Aziru's greed sharpened at the stories that this caravan contained not only an important person but also a fabulous treasure. It was there that the great lie was born. Armed with letters, General Rahmose was sent back into Egypt, whilst Djoser and myself remained at Aziru's court. As the months passed, Hittite visits to the court became more frequent. At last Aziru took us into his counsel. He was now openly supported by the Hittite king, who sent nobles, military advisers and treasure south. Aziru reasoned that if the true fate of Akenhaten was unknown, then why not put forward a usurper and interfere in the affairs of Egypt? He opened secret correspondence with Meryre, who responded that such a scheme had his full support, whilst Djoser and I would act as his envoys. Meryre used the pretext of sending statues, symbols of Aten, as gifts; they secretly contained his treasonable correspondence. On the plains outside Aziru's city, an army began to assemble: Hittite troops, mercenaries, as well as those princelings and chieftains of Canaan eager to support Aziru in mischief.

I speak the truth: I was not as fervent in my support of this mischief as my companion Djoser. When I first met the usurper and his woman, I openly derided their appearance and character. They were no more the great King Akenhaten and his Queen than desert sand is the finest gold. Nevertheless, Aziru was determined. Stories came from Egypt how Nefertiti had attempted to rule as sole Pharaoh, only to be overthrown; how a regency council governed the kingdom in the name of Akenhaten's son. The change in his name from Tutankhaten to Tutankhamun symbolised the way things were going in Egypt.

Meryre's rage was unbounded. In secret correspondence he informed us that the City of the Aten had been abandoned. How the Royal Circle had returned to Thebes, determined on the restoration of the old ways. Nevertheless, this Royal Circle was divided, so the decision was reached to invade the Delta and draw the power of Horemheb north. In the meantime, Aziru persisted in his search for the real Akenhaten and his treasure but was unable to discover anything new.

In the second year of my stay in Canaan, during the third month of the harvest season, we moved from Canaan down across Sinai and into the Delta. The rest, my lord Mahu knows. I have spoken the truth, and can say no more . . .

I questioned Khufu closely about everything he had written, but he was tired, he had drunk deeply and he was still frightened. His answers were often slurred and rambling, so I dismissed him to bed. I preserved his account, a manuscript I have kept close by me over the years. I pored over it that night, going through every line. Some of it I recognised. The confusion in the City of the Aten following Nefertiti's disgrace had cloaked everything in secrecy. Akenhaten's depression, his bizarre behaviour and lonely prowling of the palace precincts were well known. Khufu's story did shed some light. Akenhaten had suffered some form of madness; whether this was divinely inspired or not I could not say. He claimed to have had visions of the future and left some secret wisdom in the custody of these mysterious Watchers, but who were they? Were they the same people who had helped him? Ever since he was a boy, Akenhaten had received assistance from the wandering tribes of the Apiru. Khufu had named the clan or sect directly responsible: Israar. According to Khufu, they had brought in their own priests and exorcists to purify Akenhaten's mind. He had discovered a new serenity and peace and resolved to leave the City of the Aten.

This might appear ridiculous to some. Why should anyone abandon wealth and power? Yet, as I have said, the child begets the man. Akenhaten's early days had been spent in lonely

231

obscurity. He had experienced the austerity of a poor priest. When he became Pharaoh, although he exulted in the pomp and grandeur, he saw this only as a means to the worship of his God. So had he abandoned his city? Or was he murdered? The breach between Nefertiti and himself, whatever the pretence peddled to the rest of the court, had been irrevocable and final. Apparently, according to Khufu, the main reason for Nefertiti's restoration was that she had taken a solemn oath not to harm the Prince Tutankhamun, which meant that even during her exile she had probably tried to injure the infant. The second reason for her restoration was so that Akenhaten could conjure up the illusion of normalcy, of harmony. He ceded the affairs of state to his ambitious, arrogant wife whilst he secretly prepared to abandon his family, his court and his empire.

Akenhaten had reached that calmness often found in a man who has experienced an agonising struggle and come through it to confront his own death. He had been determined to leave and was undoubtedly helped by Apiru, the men of Israar. They had removed treasure, gold, silver and precious stones, as preparation for Akenhaten's secret life. Moreover, these were men who knew the desert, its secret paths, its hidden wells and oases. They would have experienced no problem in crossing the burning sands into Sinai and then north into Canaan. And who would take notice of them there? A country riven by petty blood feuds and tribal jealousies?

Grasping Khufu's manuscript, I went and sat on a small balcony, staring out into the night. If Akenhaten had truly left, if he wished to remain hidden, pursuing his own vision, then what had Khufu heard? According to the evidence, someone had been murdered in the imperial apartments, but instead of a corpse bring thrown into a pit or a crocodile pool, this creature of Nefertiti, the chief embalmer, had been summoned into her quarters and lavishly rewarded for some secret task. The embalming of a corpse? The tombs in the eastern cliffs of the City of the Aten were full of unmarked sarcophagi, coffins and corpses. What had Nefertiti plotted to do? Only a few months after this, she had attempted to assume supreme power in Egypt and been brought down by a pack of hyaenas, of which I was one.

I should have felt tired, but sleep escaped me. Had Akenhaten truly fled? Was Khufu's story about a man being slain mere distraction? Ankhesenamun had whispered how her sister Meritaten had claimed to know about the poisoning of her own father-husband. Meritaten's heart had been disturbed, nothing more than a weak girl terrified of her sombre father. Was her boast more a result of wishful thinking than the truth? Or was it all the work of Ankhesenamun's fertile imaginings? Had Akenhaten travelled into Canaan determined on a life of seclusion only to be forced out by the rise of the usurper and the hideous events in the Delta? Had he come south once more to see justice done? To visit his son and communicate quietly to me that he was still alive? Nebamun undoubtedly spoke the truth. He claimed to have seen a man disguised as a priest with more than a passing resemblance to Akenhaten, fingering turquoise amber beads. Khufu had mentioned the same in his confession.

I recalled the golden emblem found in the usurper's tent, and the map I had consulted in Nebamun's library. I went and fetched both. I searched out the location of the City of the Aten and placed the emblem with the sun on it, noticing that its rays pointed to an area in south Canaan. Aziru, using a different map, must have done the same in his searches. I looked at the area and tried to recall the stories I had heard, of valleys and plains, thick woods, turbulent rivers and stretches of blistering desert where not even a blade of grass or the sturdiest bush could grow. I put the map away and went to the antechamber; Djarka lay asleep on a cot bed. I shook him awake. He staggered from his bed, threw water over his face and peered through the window.

'My lord Mahu, it must be the third decan of the night? Can you not sleep?'

'Tell me about your people,' I demanded.

Djarka, rubbing his eyes, sat down on the floor, his back to the wall. I lit some more oil lamps.

'Could this not have waited until the morning?' he moaned.

'Tell me about your people!'

'You know it,' he protested. 'I am of the Apiru, who come from Canaan. Some remained with their flocks, others settled

233

in the Delta, whilst the rest colonised Akhmin, becoming more,' he laughed abruptly, 'more Egyptian than the Egyptians. I belong to the latter. You know that. I served Great Queen Tiye, that's how I came into your service. The loyal archer, the manservant, the Protector of the Prince.'

I ignored the sarcasm in his voice.

'And do you know the men of the Israar?'

I made two mistakes that night. First, I should have questioned Khufu more closely. Secondly, I allowed Djarka to remain hidden in the darkness, even though at the time I sensed something was wrong.

'The men of Israar,' I repeated. 'What do you know of them?'

'They are the heart of our people.' He sighed. 'They have more priests than the rest. They have not been tainted by Egypt, by its glorious splendour, its luxury, its opulence. They tend their herds, moving backwards and forwards, sometimes in Canaan, sometimes along the rich Black Lands of Egypt.'

'Have you heard rumours,' I asked, 'that they were involved in the abduction or escape of Akenhaten?'

'Master, if I had heard,' the answer came too easily, 'I would have told you. When the Divine One,' he sighed again, 'left or was killed, I, like you, was banned from his presence. You were weak due to the plague. I had still not recovered from her death . . .' He let his words hang in the air, a memorial of his deep love for the woman whom I'd discovered to be an assassin. Then he clambered to his feet, 'I know nothing of Akenhaten. I know nothing at all,' and went back to his bed.

I returned to my chamber. Once again I went through Khufu's story but could learn nothing else. Nevertheless, I was convinced my old master was alive, that he had revisited Egypt and would now return to his secret place in Canaan. I also went through the documents taken from the Delta. In the main they were interesting: letters between Aziru and his allies in both Canaan and the kingdom of the Hittites. I cleared the documents away, so intent on what I was doing that I started at the soft touch on my arm. Tutankhamun was standing dressed in his night shift, his eyes filled with tears. He held a small wooden box; he silently offered this to me. I took the casket and lifted the lid. Inside were the two mummified corpses of the tortoises he had drowned.

'I did not intend to do wrong, Uncle Mahu. I just thought I should punish them.'

I closed the lid and crouched down. He put his arms round my neck and stood trembling. I took him across to the table, removed the cover cloth and gave him a sweetmeat and a sip of wine.

'Forget the tortoises, my lord,' I whispered. 'They were good tortoises and have now travelled across the Far Horizon.'

'Will there be tortoises there?' Tutankhamun asked.

'If you want, my lord, there will be tortoises, gazelles, cats and dogs.'

'When will I go to the Far Horizon?'

'Only when you are very old,' I replied. 'And the father of many children and the grandfather of countless others.'

Tutankhamun giggled, licking his fingers and staring at me like the little owl he was.

'Is it true, Uncle Mahu, that my father is still alive? I heard the servants talking. If he is alive, why doesn't he visit me? Why did he leave me?'

'Your father had to leave you, my lord, for his safety and yours.'

'When I become a man,' Tutankhamun declared, 'I shall be a warrior. I shall sweep north like Ahmose did, carrying fire and sword against the People of the Nine Bows.'

I prised the wine cup from his hands and placed it back on the table. 'My lord, how old are you now?'

'Uncle Mahu, you know how old I am. Since you left, my day of birth has come and gone. I am now midway between my seventh and eighth year.'

'Can you remember,' I asked crouching down, 'your father ever visiting you?'

The young Prince shook his head.

'Did he ever send you a gift?'

'Many gifts, toy soldiers, a chariot, a hippopotamus . . .'

'Did he,' I intervened, 'or possibly Lord Pentju ever mention the Watchers? Think, my lord.'

Tutankhamun squeezed his eyes shut and opened them quickly.

'Never, Uncle Mahu. Who are the Watchers?'

'Finally, my lord,' I scooped him up in my arms, 'how often have I told you never to leave your bedchamber in the dead of night?'

Joking and laughing, I took him back, placed him in his bed and sat down to wait until he had fallen fast asleep.

hui
(Ancient Egyptian for 'to shoot venom')

Chapter 12

Our hunting party left Memphis early the next morning, ostensibly to enjoy a day's relaxation, but as Maya wryly observed, our true quarry would be more elusive. We were accompanied by a host of chariots, a swarm of retainers, huntsmen and a pack of yelping hounds trained to the horn, whip and whistle. The guest of honour was Horemheb, still very much the Themum, the Hero of the Hour. Rameses and Huy were still drunk from the previous night. Maya was distraught at Sobeck's departure. Pentju seemed the most alert of us all, although sombre-faced and withdrawn. Lord Ay was in his usual fine form.

'It's good,' he announced from his glorious chariot as we assembled outside Nebamun's mansion, 'to be free of the heretics and traitors.'

No one dared mention how he had been foremost in that heresy, as his unfinished tomb at the City of the Aten bore witness, its walls inscribed with fulsome praise of both Akenhaten and his God. Ah well, there again, politicians have all the memory of a butterfly – when it suits them. Watching him grasp the reins, talking and joking with his companions, I wondered how much the Lord Cobra really knew about those sombre last days of Akenhaten. However, for Ay, that door was closed, bolted and sealed. He'd never tell the truth even if the Goddess Ma'at came over the Far Horizon and ordered him to do so.

We had chosen a fine morning, a glorious dawn promising a

warm day. We moved through the grass and trees heading into the west, the sun behind us, its light catching and illuminating the wild flowers. Our dogs, yapping and snarling, were eager for the hunt. Now and again a hare would start from the grass or a flock of webbed quail burst up in a flash of colour, wings beating the air, their cries of alarm carrying out to the flocks of gazelles and wild goats, who would gallop away in clouds of hazy dust. Wild grey asses kicked up their hoofs, whinnied and threatened our dogs before cantering away. We scattered a line of game before us, our chariots fanning out in the morning light, huntsmen calling in the dogs.

We reached the end of the grasslands and came upon our real prey, a formidable herd of wild bulls, hefty and muscular, with pointed horns and mad, fiery eyes, a clever disguise for their speed and cunning. They always reminded me of Horemheb, the same bulk, ferocity, bravery, cunning, and above all, surprising speed. Our great hero, the noble general, was intent on a kill, eager to make his offering to his patron God, Horus of Henes. The dogs were released and streamed like a flight of arrows towards the herd. The huntsmen followed after. Immediately the bulls broke up, but one of their leaders, an old scarred beast, angry and agitated, turned, swinging its head, lowering its horn, snorting in fury and pawing the ground. The danger with wild bulls is you never know until the last moment whether they are going to flee or charge. This one charged, a sudden burst of speed, heading straight for our pack of dogs. I loosed shaft after shaft. The other chariots ringed the bull as, confused, it turned to face the new danger. Arrows whistled through the air. The bull went down, losing the power of its hindquarters as barb after barb scored its flanks and withers, cutting muscle and sinew. At last it lay quiet, flanks quivering, eyes glowing, blood pumping out of its nostrils and mouth. Horemheb climbed down from his chariot and stood astride its thick muscular neck. He raised his hands towards the sky, the knife in his right hand dazzling in the sun as the great general recited a hymn to Horus. We all joined in the chorus, then Horemheb sliced the animal's throat and cut off a tuft of hair between the horns. He took us over to the fire a huntsman had quickly built and sprinkled the hairs, followed by a handful of

240

incense. The scented smoke rose against the blue sky. Horemheb stood, eyes tightly closed, quietly communicating with his God.

'Who,' Maya hissed spitefully, 'Horemheb truly believed guided his every action at the great victory in the Delta.'

Once the sacrifice was finished, the huntsmen closed in. They slit the belly, drained the blood and quartered and pickled the various joints. The air turned sour with the smell of tumbling intestines and gushing blood. The hunting party moved on, reaching the edge of the grassland, where the soil became sparse and the only water lay in stagnant pools ringed by coarse, dirty weeds. We moved cautiously through the thickets of brambles and robe-rending gorse. We were on the edge of the desert, where the night prowlers lurked. We surprised an old lion, a tawny beast with a jet-black mane. Disturbed and alarmed, it turned on our dogs, savaging two, till it was dispatched with arrows and a lance in the mouth by Horemheb. The sun rose higher in the heavens, the heat draining the strength of man, dog and horse.

We reached the Oasis of Sweet Grass and pitched our camp, unhitching the chariots and establishing horse lines. Cooking fires were built; food and wine baskets unloaded and brought out. The stinking quarry we'd killed was taken downwind and piled in carts, sprinkled with salt and covered with a leather awning. At last everything was ready. Horemheb, very much the soldier, insisted that we were not out of danger yet, and that even on a hunting trip we should act as if we were on the march. Huy and Maya raised their eyes heavenwards. On reflection, we were the fiercest beasts in the desert: the hunters, the hyaenas of the Royal Court. The real business of the day was about to begin. We washed and cleaned in the oasis pool, gratefully accepting the chilled wine offered by servants. Once they had withdrawn, we sat on our cushions and Lord Ay, tapping his long nails against his goblet, brought us to order with a stark question.

'Is he still alive?'

All eyes turned to me.

'You do have the prisoner Khufu?' Ay cheekily remarked. 'As well as the records of the Usurper? Indeed, my lord Mahu, we are surprised that you have not handed both over to the Royal Circle!'

'We should not be surprised,' I retorted. 'You know, my Lord Ay, I was considering retiring from the Royal Circle. If that had been the case I would have paraded the truth before you and provided you with a copy of everything I had found.'

Ay smiled dreamily back at me. Huy and Maya lowered their heads. Rameses hid his smile behind his cup.

'If you had resigned, Lord Mahu,' Ay murmured, 'we would all have been distraught. Your support and your strength, particularly in this crisis, are deeply appreciated. I know you will speak with true voice!'

'How would you know what a true voice is?' I jibed.

'The truth,' Ay demanded. 'My lord Mahu, you are Chief of Police, Overseer of the House of Secrets.'

'And you have brought your torturer with you,' I declared. 'The usurper and the other captives have been put to the question.'

'Nothing but babbling,' Rameses declared. 'Nothing much at all. Vague rumours, fanciful stories.'

'I believe he is alive.' I cut across Rameses' voice. 'I think he fled from the City of the Aten.' I narrowed my eyes, peering at the heat haze across the desert. 'He was given help and sheltered in southern Canaan. I think we know as much as Meryre did: the rest he concocted to help the Hittites and Prince Aziru.'

'Then Colonel Nebamun is wrong?' Horemheb asked.

'No, I believe he spoke the truth. I trust the Colonel implicitly. One of the few men I do.'

Horemheb allowed himself a smile.

'Akenhaten may be living in south Canaan, but you have seen the roads, the boats and barges on the river. Sooner or later all the world comes to Egypt. Akenhaten may have returned one last time, perhaps for a glimpse of his son, as well as to see justice done. What we have here is, perhaps, something none of us are acquainted with. On this matter we must not put our trust in Pharaoh,' I quoted the proverb, 'or place our confidence in the war chariots of Egypt.'

'What do you mean?' Rameses demanded.

'We deal in power,' I replied. 'We are the lords, the masters; my lord Horemheb raises his hands and chariot squadrons, whole hosts of men, march to his command. I send out a writ

242

to my subordinates, the mayors of Eastern and Western Thebes,' I added, 'and unless my lord Ay interferes, my orders will be carried out. But this is not about power. Akenhaten drank deep of power and it made him sick. In the City of the Aten he vomited, he purged himself. Now he wants to be at peace. It is about ideals, about conversion.'

'So what do we do?' Rameses asked.

'For the glory of Egypt,' Horemheb retorted, 'kill him.'

'I agree.' Ay spoke up. 'For the sake of Egypt, for the protection of his son, in order that we can establish true Ma'at, harmony throughout the kingdom of the Two Lands, we must kill him.'

'What happens if there is no need?' I declared. 'What happens if Akenhaten does not pose a problem to us or to Egypt? Why not let the problem wither on the branch? The present troubles are not caused by him, but by the usurper.'

'He could be used by others,' Horemheb declared.

'I don't think he'd allow that.'

'Why did he take his treasure?' Maya asked. 'If he had found true peace and harmony, what does he need his treasure for?'

'He doesn't,' I smiled, 'not for himself, but it can buy silence, the co-operation and connivance of others.'

'And this correspondence?' Huy asked. 'The documents found in the usurper's tent?'

I smiled at Ay. 'Nothing more than sand in the wind, Lord Huy.'

'And Khufu?'

'A mere babbler.'

Horemheb straightened up. Ay gestured for silence as servants carried platters of woven reed heaped high with meat and vegetables, laying out napkins and refilling goblets.

'Don't worry.' Ay toasted me with his cup. 'I have had General Nakhtimin,' he gestured to where his sinister brother stood with the other officers, watching intently what was happening, 'make sure that our food is, how can I put it, free of any potions or powders.'

'And I put my trust in Colonel Nebamun,' Rameses simpered. 'I asked him to keep an eye on everything. Well,' he smiled, 'we shall eat and drink safely.'

I gazed around. The hyaena pack was still unified, but the tensions were there: Horemheb and Rameses confronting Ay, with Huy, Maya, Pentju and myself in between.

'Has Meryre been found?' Rameses asked, his mouth full of food. 'Surely a fat priest and his followers, not to mention Lord Tutu and the group from Buhen, would be clear targets in the desert? I mean, from what I gather, they not only fled but took their wives, servants and children with them.'

'One thing at a time,' Ay countered. 'A search will be made. If they have become lost in the desert, then that's one problem solved in the best possible way. On our return to Thebes we will redouble our efforts, carry out a proper investigation, release the hunters.'

'He should be captured.' Horemheb slurped from his cup. 'Meryre and the rest should be put to the question.'

'My lord Pentju,' Ay toasted the physician with his cup, 'you remain silent. You have become nothing but a watcher of our activities. Is it true,' Ay glanced quickly at me, 'that Lord Meryre approached you? Those we tortured say the High Priest was most eager for you to join his company.'

'Meryre can ask the stars to fall,' Pentju quipped, 'but that doesn't mean they will. As for my silence, Lord Ay, that is my own business. I was appointed by Pharaoh Akenhaten to this Royal Circle. I was chosen to guard his infant son. He is still my concern.'

'He's *our* concern,' Ay soothed. 'I propose that if Generals Horemheb and Rameses stay in Memphis to keep an eye on affairs in the north, the Prince and my granddaughter should return to the Malkata Palace in Thebes.'

'No.' Horemheb put his platter down.

All the bonhomie of our meal and the hunt disappeared.

'My lord General,' Ay whispered. 'Is there a problem with what I proposed?'

'Yes.' Rameses answered for him. 'Why can't the Prince stay in Memphis with his official protector, Lord Mahu, and, perhaps, Lord Pentju?'

'He is my grandson.' Ay's face assumed that stubborn, pugnacious look. 'He is heir to the throne. He is to be crowned. Thebes is Pharaoh's city.'

244

'Memphis it should be,' Horemheb retorted.

I gazed across at Huy; he stared blankly back. Maya was the same. This was the point of power. Whoever controlled the Prince would eventually control Egypt. I recalled Khufu's story; the City of the Aten with its honeycomb of tombs.

'My lords,' I intervened, 'may I propose a solution? A compromise? The city of Memphis is in the north; Thebes is in the south. In between lies the City of the Aten, in many ways still a thriving community. What I propose is that I, the Lord Pentju and his Highness the Prince, together with the Princess Ankhesenamun, return to the City of the Aten. No. No!' I raised my hand to still the objections. 'The city is well guarded by my mercenaries. They have taken an oath of personal loyalty to myself as well as to the Prince. It can also be easily guarded: it is built on a cove surrounded virtually on three sides by cliffs and on the fourth by the Nile. Perhaps it will be best if the land routes, the clifftops, were patrolled by Colonel Nebamun's chariot squadrons, the river by soldiers and marines sent north under General Nakhtimin, whilst the city itself can be policed by my mercenaries. It will be good for the Prince to be away from Thebes whilst matters are harmonised and the restoration of the old ways continues apace. Once this has been done, the Prince can be returned to Thebes, where he will be crowned in the Temple of the Amun-Ra, and, of course, like his predecessors, process annually between Thebes and Memphis displaying his crown and power.'

Rameses made to object, but Horemheb tapped him on the shoulder. Ay clicked his tongue, a favourite gesture whenever he was thinking deeply.

'Of course,' I added, 'the City of the Aten will be an ideal place for the Royal Circle to meet every so often to discuss matters. All members of the Royal Circle will have equal access to the Prince. No major decision will be made without us all agreeing.'

'I would accept that,' Horemheb snapped.

Huy and Maya immediately voiced their support.

'There is another problem.' I waited for a servant to bring a fresh wine jug. 'Outside the City of the Aten lie the Royal Tombs. Some of the dead were casualties of the plague. They include members of the Royal Family, Lord Ay, your own daughter, Queen Nefertiti, your sister, Great Queen Tiye, the Princess Ankhesenamun's sister and others of the Royal Court.' I was pleased to see everyone nodding. 'It is obvious,' I continued, 'that the City of the Aten will one day die, return to the desert. However, we have a duty to the Gods, as well as the dead, to ensure that these graves are not violated, their treasures plundered.'

'What do you propose?' Ay demanded.

'That every coffin and sarcophagus be removed by river to new tombs in the Valley of the Nobles or the Valley of the Kings, and that this be done sooner rather than later.'

'That will be major work,' Maya remarked, 'requiring much silver. Caves have to be excavated. It should be done secretly,' he added. 'If the grave robbers around the City of the Dead learn of what can only be termed a rash of royal burials taking place in the Valley of the Kings, their curiosity, not to mention their greed, would be roused. These tombs,' he declared solemnly, 'should be excavated and prepared in secret, the coffins brought by night and sealed away.'

'And how should we do that?' Rameses asked.

'Use General Horemheb's great victory.' Ay joined his hands together. 'We have a horde of prisoners of war. They can dig and they can excavate. They can be given as much food and water as they need. Afterwards, what the eye has seen, the ear heard and the mouth spoken can remain a secret.'

'You will massacre the slaves?' I asked.

'They will be taken out to the Red Lands,' Ay agreed, 'once their task is finished.'

'And who will be responsible for emptying the tombs in the City of the Aten?' Pentju demanded.

'Why, my lord Mahu!' Ay smiled. 'Assisted and helped by the Chief Court Physician, Lord Pentju. We will send barges and escorts north when you are ready. It is an excellent proposal.' He plucked up a date and popped it into his mouth. 'At the same time, we'll begin stripping the palaces in the City of the Aten of all their furniture, gold and silver.' He licked his fingers. 'I am so glad we are reaching agreement on so many things.'

'Akenhaten!' Horemheb's voice cut like a lash. 'We should send troops into Canaan.'

'We are going to send an army into Kush,' Maya countered. 'The treasury is exhausted. My lord Horemheb, to invade Canaan we would need an army prepared and provisioned for at least a six-month campaign. The House of Silver cannot afford it. Until the present crisis passes we need every soldier this side of the Horus Road.'

A murmur of agreement greeted his words.

'We could send assassins.' Rameses glared at me. 'My lord Mahu?'

'Nonsense,' I countered. 'It was dangerous enough in the Delta. It will be like looking for a pearl hidden in the sand. That will have to wait. Now, other matters . . .'

So there, in the Oasis of Sweet Grass, the power of Egypt was settled, the lines drawn, the agenda set. Akenhaten would have to wait. The old ways needed to be published and proclamations posted about what was to happen. It was agreed that stelae would be set up in every major city of Egypt proclaiming that the crisis was over and Egypt once again returning to its former glory. So we passed to other matters: the listing of enemies, of those to be arrested, fined or exiled. The number of executions would be kept to a minimum. Each of us argued for friends. Maya, in particular, demanded a general amnesty and pardon to be issued to Sobeck, that he should be restored to royal favour and given some high-ranking post in the city of Thebes. This was agreed. We moved on to the granaries, the prospect of a good harvest, the need for fresh taxation, the problem of the rebels in Kush. We argued and debated, but beneath the surface, the truth emerged. There were to be three sources of power in Egypt: the first, Horemheb and Rameses and the northern garrisons based at Memphis; the second in Thebes under the thumb of Lord Ay, General Nakhtimin and others of the Akhmin gang; whilst the third would be the Prince and the Keepers of the City of the Aten. For the time being that was the way things would be. Nevertheless, as we finished and prepared to return to Memphis, I wondered what would happen if Tutankhamun died, which of these powerful factions would gain ascendancy.

★　　★　　★

The sun had set, the desert wind turning chilly as I left the rest of the Royal Circle and returned with Colonel Nebamun to his house on the outskirts of Thebes. A runner, drenched in sweat, greeted us. He threw himself before Nebamun's chariot, babbling out his message. The Colonel, still slightly drunk from the previous evening as well as the deep cups he had drunk at the Oasis of Sweet Grass, staggered down from his chariot, pulling the man to his feet. He made him repeat the message, whilst I stood in my chariot next to Pentju.

'The prisoner Khufu, late this afternoon, they had to force his door. He's hanged himself.'

We hastened back to Nebamun's house. All was confusion and chaos. My mercenaries, swords drawn, were already gathered in the courtyard. Djarka, locking the young Prince in his room, came to greet me and took me up to Khufu's quarters. The door lay resting against the splintered lintel and inside, swinging on a rope from a beam, a stool lying on its side beneath, hung the body of Khufu. The thick rope was tied tightly about his neck, his face had turned purple, his eyes were bulging, his swollen tongue caught between his lips. He'd lost control of his bladder in his death throes. A tragic, pathetic corpse swaying slightly on the creaking rope.

'I came up,' Djarka explained. 'A servant had brought him food but he wouldn't answer the door!'

I ordered Djarka to cut Khufu's body down whilst I examined the chamber. A square, comfortable room with limewashed walls, a cot bed, a stool, two small tables, chests, and a small divan in the corner piled high with cushions. The door, undoubtedly, had been locked; its stout wooden bolts drawn across the top, bottom and centre. These were now broken, as were the heavy hinges. I noticed the scuff marks on the floor, probably due to the door being forced. The window was square, a thick trellis framework which could be slipped in and out, but only from the inside; the stone lintel on the outside was edged by a rocky rim as protection against robbers. By the dust on the ledge I gathered this wooden framework had not been removed. I gazed through the slats. The chamber overlooked an overgrown part of the garden where the grass sprouted long, thick and high, as if eager to reach the overhanging branches of the sycamore trees. I turned back as Djarka laid the corpse on the floor. I inspected the wrists and fingernails, the ankles, neck and shaven head, but could see no other mark or injury, no bruise or contusion, nothing to suggest that this heretic priest had been the victim of murder. The rope was thick and oiled.

'Where did he get it from?' I asked.

'He was allowed to wander around,' Nebamun's chamberlain replied, wringing his hands and looking dolefully at me as if I had lost a close friend rather than a valuable source of information. 'He wandered the house and out into the garden. My lord,' he swallowed hard, 'you told me yourself that Khufu had no desire to escape, that he was safe here.'

I nodded in agreement. When I had left Khufu the previous evening, he had been calm and reassured. He himself had admitted, his final words to me, that he felt safer in Colonel Nebamun's mansion than any other place in Egypt. At the time I thought it was quite a perceptive remark. Khufu had the wit to realise that other members of the Royal Circle, particularly Lord Ay, might not show him such favour.

'So what happened today?'

The chamberlain spread his hands. 'The house was quiet. Apart,' he added spitefully, 'from the songs and shouts of your mercenaries. The Prince kept to his chamber with your man Djarka. Khufu wandered down to the kitchens for his food.' The chamberlain pulled a face. 'And then, late today, a kitchen boy came up to tell him that food had been served. He knocked and knocked at his door. There was no answer, so I sent for Djarka.'

'And you forced the door?' I asked.

Djarka, sitting on the divan in the corner, nodded. I gazed down at Khufu's face: ugly, contorted in death. According to all the evidence he had committed suicide, taken a rope from the storerooms and returned to his chamber. He had used that stout hook in the ceiling beam, fashioned a noose, stood on the stool and kicked it away. A suicide, the death of a man with no hope. Yet even then, such an explanation didn't ring true. What had Khufu to fear? I had promised him life, security, exile in some obscure town, but his fate had been far better than others who had been paraded through Memphis in chains. So who would want him dead? The other hyaenas of the Royal

249

Circle? But they had been out with me, hunting in the western desert.

'Did any strangers call at the house?'

Nebamun's chamberlain shook his head.

'I was quite explicit on that.' Colonel Nebamun spoke up. 'I gave orders that no one, unless they carried the authority of the Royal Circle, was to be admitted to the upper courtyard.'

Pentju knelt beside the corpse, loosening the rope around the neck, allowing the air to escape from the belly. The dead man's legs jerked, a macabre scene, as if his Ka was trying to revive the heart. Nebamun cursed quietly under his breath. I asked Pentju to check the corpse carefully. He too looked for injuries, feeling the back of the head and neck, turning the corpse over, pulling up the robe to scrutinise arms and wrists, carefully examining the fingernails for hairs from the rope.

'Was he drugged?' I asked.

Pentju smelled the man's mouth and shook his head.

'He had drunk some wine but only enough to make him comfortable, hence in his death throes his bladder relaxed.'

'How long did he take to die?'

Pentju felt the man's neck and throat. 'Not long really. He wouldn't fight against the rope, perhaps a little in his death throes. The life force would be cut off. He would fall into a swoon and death would follow immediately.'

'And how long has he been dead?'

'Perhaps three to four hours. His flesh is growing clammy and cold, the muscles hardening.'

A knock on the door, and Nebamun's chapel priest entered, a small, wizened man. He knelt by the corpse and began to intone the sacred text recited for a man who'd taken his own life: 'Go back now, you fiery friends from the pit. Go back now, you shadows deeper than the rest. Go back to the Devourer, Fire-eater, Scavenger of Souls . . .'

I waited for the priest to finish his babbling, and once he had left, asked Nebamun to provide a cart.

'Have it taken down to the House of Embalming at the Temple of Ptah,' I ordered. 'Tell the priest to send all bills, whatever the cost, to the Lord Maya.'

'Why not throw him into a crocodile pool?' the old colonel

barked. 'Or better still, I'll have my men take his body out to the scavengers in the Red Lands.'

'I promised him life and limb,' I replied. 'As a suicide he should fall into the power of the God of the Fiery Hands. So, let his body be embalmed, the chapel priest pray, the hymns be sung, the incense burnt. Find him a tomb in the Necropolis. If you do that, Colonel Nebamun, I have discharged my debt.'

'He was a traitor.' Djarka spoke up, using the old Egyptian word, *ut-en*, to describe a violent man.

'He was a suicide,' Nebamun's chamberlain added. 'Perhaps his heart should be removed and burnt.'

I gazed at all their faces and realised my mistake. I had forgotten that here in this house, Khufu had been surrounded by his enemies. Good men had been killed in the Delta, members of Nebamun's squadron, not to mention others.

'What's the matter, my lord?' Djarka asked.

I bit back my reply. I would have to wait. However, standing in that chamber, that gruesome corpse sprawled on the floor, I was as certain as I was that I had two hands and feet that Khufu had been murdered, though by whom, how and why remained a mystery.

I asked Djarka to return to the Prince. Nebamun and his people left. Servants came up with linen sheets to wrap Khufu's corpse and take it away. Once they had gone I conducted a thorough search. The coffers and chests were empty. Khufu had been dependent upon me for the robes and sandals he wore; all his other property had been declared the spoils of war. I went and stood by the window, staring through the small gaps. The sole way into this chamber was through that trellis, but it could only be removed from the inside. Khufu had been suspicious and wary; he would not allow anyone into his chamber. I went outside and examined the ground beneath the window. It was damp, and looking up, I realised that someone in the chamber above had emptied out a pot of dirty water. There was no sign of anyone standing here; the ground was slightly disturbed, but that could be due to anything.

I returned to the chamber, pulling the bed aside, taking off the sheets. It was then that I found it, a piece of coarse parchment, crumpled and thrown away. I unrolled it; it was in Khufu's

251

hand. In the centre of this scrap of parchment he had printed the Prince's name, in its Aten version: 'Tutankhaten'. Above that, 'Akenhaten, Nefertiti, Pentju', and beneath it *Budge net ut – Net er ai – en – Hotep*'.

'What did you mean by that?' I whispered. I racked my memory: Hotep was the son of the God Ptah, the third member of the Memphis triad.

I folded the parchment, put it in my purse and left the chamber. I walked round the house, out across the courtyards and into the musty storerooms. I caught sight of the coils of rope and paused. Surely, I reflected, if Khufu had removed the rope and taken it to his chamber, someone must have seen it? Or had he taken a sheet from his bed and bundled up the rope in that, as if he was carrying a load of dirty linen? I picked up a coil of rope. It was thick and rough, but easy to carry. I sat down on a battered chest and ruefully conceded that I had made a mistake. According to all the evidence, Khufu had committed suicide. It was understandable enough. He might have mistrusted my promises and guarantees for the future. Yet I knew he had been murdered, and this made me admit to a second mistake. Khufu had known more than he had told me. Perhaps he was biding his time before making a full confession about other mysteries, such as why Meryre and his fellow conspirators placed so much importance on Pentju. Did that learned physician also know more than he had ever told us? About what? The Prince's health? I got to my feet. Was that it? Did Pentju know something as a doctor? After all, I had seen Tutankhamun experience that eerie trance when he seemed unable to hear, see or be aware of anyone around him. How old was the Prince now? Between seven and eight? Akenhaten had been disturbed in both body and mind, and although Princess Khiya, Tutankhamun's mother, had been a friend, I knew nothing about her ailments.

I left the storeroom and, absorbed in my thoughts, returned to my own chamber, where I washed and changed, turning the problem over and over in my mind like a piece of meat on a spit. I oiled and perfumed my face and hands and went along to the Prince's chamber. He had the small tortoises out, laughing at how slowly they walked, urging Djarka to join him, but his

Protector just sat on a stool, lost in his own thoughts. Tutankhamun jumped to his feet and threw himself at me, burrowing his face in my robe. I crouched down.

'Your Highness, you look well.'

'He slept very late,' Djarka replied. 'He heard you leave for the hunt and then went back to bed.'

I held the Prince's face between my hands, beautiful, oval-shaped, those great lustrous dark eyes watching me intently, trying to anticipate my mood. Sometimes he had a look of Akenhaten, a stare full of innocence yet, as with his father, that could be a pretence, a mask concealing the emotions seething within. Of course Khiya was the same. When she first came to Akenhaten's court she would sit at my feet and stare adoringly up as a disciple would at his master.

'Uncle Mahu, what is wrong?'

'Are you well, Your Highness?'

'I am always well, Uncle Mahu. Is it true what Colonel Nebamun said? Did you kill a bull today?'

'With my own hands, Your Highness.' I got to my feet, spreading out my arms. 'I chased after him in my chariot, the Lord Pentju driving it as fast as a storm cloud. We drew alongside. I leapt from the chariot on to the bull's back, seized its horns and twisted its neck.'

Tutankhamun stared at me open-mouthed.

'I wrestled it to the ground,' I continued, watching him intently, fear pricking at my heart. Was the Prince a simpleton? Or just so full of hero-worship he truly believed my ridiculous story? 'The bull crashed beneath me,' I continued. 'I drew my dagger and slit its throat, then another one charged me.'

Tutankhamun broke from his reverie; he threw his head back and laughed, a beautiful, soul-catching sound.

'You lie, Uncle Mahu, you are telling me stories.'

'How did you know?' I picked him up, hugging him close. 'How did you know that I was telling a story? Are you saying,' I kept my face stern, 'that I am not strong enough to wrestle a bull to the ground? That I am not fleet of foot, strong of arm, cunning of mind?' I pressed my face close to him. 'You are my prisoner,' I continued, squeezing him. 'I'll hold you fast till you answer.'

253

Tutankhamun loved the game, squealing with delight.

'I'll confess. I'll confess.'

I placed him on the floor.

'You couldn't do that,' he said. 'Not because *you* can't, but the Lord Pentju cannot control horses. Djarka has told me. An ox can pull a cart faster.'

I beamed at the little fellow.

'How is his schooling going?'

Djarka gestured at the writing tray, stacks of parchment and clay tablets scattered on a nearby table.

'He can write and count.'

'He can write and count,' Tutankhamun abruptly mimicked. I caught his stare, the first time I had ever seen it; his quick glance at Djarka was full of imperiousness, or was it resentment? When he looked back at me, that dazzling smile had returned. 'Next time you hunt, Uncle Mahu, can I come with you?'

I promised him he could, kissed him absent-mindedly on the forehead and left. I went up on the roof to catch the cool evening breeze. Nebamun's chamberlain brought me some fruit and a jug of chilled beer. He was still full of regret at Khufu's death. I asked if he had seen anything untoward.

'If I had, my lord, I would have told you.' And mumbling under his breath, he left me to my own thoughts.

Ankhesenamun, together with Amedeta and other members of the Princess' retinue, arrived just after dark. She was garbed in perfume, eyes kohl-ringed, all flirtatious, seizing my hands, kissing me on either cheek, allowing me to smell her beautiful fragrance.

'The great hero,' she teased. 'You will, Uncle Mahu,' she mimicked Tutankhamun's favourite name for me, 'tell me about your exploits. After the battle, did you seize the maidens of the usurper and take them roughly,' her eyelids fluttered, 'amidst the corpses of their menfolk?'

'You should have been a storyteller, my lady.'

Still grasping her hand, I led her deeper into the house.

'A storyteller, Uncle Mahu?'

I looked over my shoulder. Amedeta and the other maids were now being greeted by Colonel Nebamun, Pentju and the rest. I pulled her into the shadows.

'My lord!' The smile disappeared from her face.

'That story you told me,' I hissed. 'One lie amongst many! You claimed that your sister Meritaten said your father was poisoned.'

'That's what she said to me, but you know Meritaten.' Ankhesenamun's beautiful eyes sparkled with life. 'She was a greater storyteller than I.'

'Did your mother,' I asked, 'ever tell you what happened?'

'Why should she? Mother disliked me. She saw me as a usurper. The same for Meritaten. If she had survived, I doubt I would have.' She withdrew her hand. 'I do not know what happened to my father. I do not know what thoughts filled my mother's heart. Now they are gone, yet I remain. Think about that, Lord Mahu. Our little Prince grows. One day I shall introduce him to the pleasures of the bed. I shall be Egypt's Great Queen.' She brushed by me, walking stately down to join the rest, lovely robes billowing about her.

Pentju must have noticed our altercation, because he came hurrying up. Now I thought, for even in the poor light Pentju was obviously agitated, here's a man who hides something in his heart.

'My lord, there is something wrong? You look troubled.' Pentju took me by the elbow and led me away. 'I grew up with you, I was a Child of the Kap. I know you.'

'Do you, my lord?' I replied frostily. 'Then you are a better man than I.'

Pentju led me into a small courtyard.

'What is this, Mahu? We are friends.'

'Are we?'

Pentju made a gesture of annoyance, walked away but came back. 'What are you so suspicious about, Mahu? You don't believe Khufu committed suicide, do you?'

'No, I think he was murdered.'

'But by whom? Why?'

'I asked the same question myself. I also wonder why my lord Meryre was so eager for you to join him.' I took out my purse and drew out the scrap of parchment, unfolded it and held it before Pentju's eyes. 'Why should Khufu write that?'

Pentju went to take the scrap but I held it tight. 'Why does

255

he mention you, Akenhaten and Nefertiti in the same line, then make these references to Hotep the son of Ptah and other members of the Memphis trinity. What do you know, Pentju, about Tutankhamun? Are there further secrets?'

Although he tried to hide it, the physician's agitation quickened so much he had to turn away, rubbing his hand up and down his chest as if trying to soothe some pain. I grasped him by the shoulder.

'Come, my lord, you've confronted me. I am the Prince's Protector, his guardian. We can discuss this here or in the presence of the rest.'

Pentju turned round. I was shocked by the change in his face. He seemed to have aged.

'What is it?' I insisted.

'You've seen the Prince,' he replied slowly. 'I know from Djarka that you once found him in a trance, acting like a blind-deaf mute.'

'And?' I asked.

'We physicians know nothing of the heart, of the soul. If a snake bites you we know how the poison will race through your body and stop your heart. But madness, insanity, the strange workings of the soul?' He shook his head. 'We know nothing.'

I sat down on a small wall seat.

'I am concerned.' Pentju chose his words carefully. 'As you know, my lord Mahu,' he lapsed into formal phraseology without realising it, 'I was appointed physician to the Royal Household. Great Queen Tiye took me into her confidence. She told me that her blood was marred by a streak of madness. These trances the young Prince suffers from,' Pentju licked his lips, 'Akenhaten, when he was a young boy, suffered the same.'

Even then, yes, I will admit, I sensed that Pentju was not telling me the full truth. Yet at the time, the implication of what he was saying was sufficient to chill my heart.

'I do worry.' Pentju came and sat beside me. 'Mahu, we have all walked down a long, dangerous road, only to find ourselves not at the end of the journey but at the beginning of an equally terrifying one. My dreams are full of that. What happens if Tutankhamun is his father come again? Has Akenhaten's son inherited the same vision, the same absorption? Will he, too, turn Egypt on its head?'

'That's for the future,' I rasped. 'These attacks? Are they dangerous?'

'I have studied every medical text.' Pentju sighed. 'That's one of the reasons I was in Memphis. I visited its House of Life. These trances cannot be explained. I don't know what causes them or how to treat them, except to keep the patient warm and comfortable.'

'What brings them on?' I asked. 'Will they pass?'

Pentju edged closer. 'As you say, Mahu, that's for the future. What terrifies me is the likes of Horemheb discovering what you know and arguing that our Prince is not fit to govern the Kingdom of the Two Lands.'

seshetat
(Ancient Egyptian for 'a true mystery')

Chapter 13

My love, my lover,
My heart is yearning,
All my dreams sing of you,
Your face like a ghost haunts my heart.
Your perfume comes like an inviting cloud
Taking me back . . .

I remember this poem. I composed it that evening as I tried to quieten my heart. Pentju's words had quickened my own agitation, my deep concerns for the future of the Prince. I felt soiled, dirty, polluted by the past, the way it would give no release and allow us to continue. In a way Akenhaten still ruled Egypt. He certainly ruled my heart. I thought as much when I bathed again in the Pool of Purity, then oiled and perfumed my body, putting on my chain of office and sparkling rings in preparation for the small banquet Nebamun's cooks were preparing. I asked Djarka to play the double flute and, for a while, listened to Tutankhamun sing. He had a good, carrying voice and his singing always thrilled me. When he had finished, I let my soul go back into the past, to meet her, the Beautiful Woman. No, not Nefertiti the murderess during those last gloomy days in the City of the Aten, but the red-haired, blue-eyed young woman who had captivated my heart when I had first met her. I wrote those lines that night but, after a while, gave up to stare through the window, half listening to the sounds of the servants as they prepared the tables.

Colonel Nebamun was most gracious. He allowed us to sit and eat, as I jokingly put it, 'as a family household again'. Ankhesenamun simply glowered at me, but Tutankhamun clapped his hands and thought it was a splendid treat. We sat before the small tables, cushions piled around us. Alabaster cups, brimming with wine and beer, were served first to whet our appetites and appease our thirst. We began with dried and salted roe, grey mullet and small fishcakes. The main dish was roast goose, served in a spiced sauce in which we could dip the soft white bread fresh from the house bakeries. Djarka and Pentju were there. Khufu's death soul hung like a shadow around us, though the conversation grew livelier when I announced that we were to return to the City of the Aten.

Ankhesenamun was furious. 'The City of the Dead,' she snapped. 'Everybody is leaving! Thebes is the place to be. How can we go to the markets? What about clothes and perfumes? No one goes to the place of the Aten.'

Tutankhamun, however, was pleased at the news. Thebes had frightened him, with its busy streets and soaring temples. I explained patiently how it would be best if, for a while, the Royal Family stayed in the shadows.

'Egypt is not at peace,' Pentju confirmed. 'The City of the Aten is much safer. Colonel Nebamun will be our guard, we shall be protected.' He smiled at Tutankhamun. 'Whilst its gardens are truly beautiful.'

'Do you want to go there, Uncle Mahu?' Tutankhamun chewed nosily on a piece of bread. 'And what about Sobeck?' The Prince had taken a great liking to my companion, who had regaled him with frightening tales of life in the slums and ghost stories about the Necropolis.

'I think it's best, Your Highness, if we do. You and the Princess Ankhesenamun will one day marry and then be crowned Pharaoh and Queen of Egypt.'

'I am going to ride in the state chariot,' Tutankhamun declared. 'Uncle Mahu, you will be my charioteer. I shall wage war on the vile Asiatics and the Kushites; they shall tremble before my name.'

We all began to tease him; I let the conversation drift for a while.

'There's something you want to say, isn't there, Uncle Mahu?' Ankhesenamun asked spitefully. She and Amedeta sat close together. They looked like twins, two beautiful spoiled women with an eye for mischief. Both of them had spent most of the meal flirting outrageously with Djarka. At first he had been dour, but as he had drunk more deeply, he had responded wittily to their barbed remarks.

'Yes, Uncle Mahu.' Djarka now joined in the teasing.

I glanced warningly at them and nodded towards Tutankhamun, now rattling an ivory-handled knife against his alabaster cup.

'Do you know who the Watchers are? Has anyone ever made reference to them?'

Pentju shook his head. Djarka cracked a joke about Horemheb and Rameses. Ankhesenamun wondered aloud if I was referring to spies, so I let the matter drop.

The next morning we slept late, and when I rose, I immediately became involved in the preparations for the return to the City of the Aten. Colonel Nebamun was pleased that he had received a commission, loudly declaring that he would rather be patrolling the Red Lands than confined to barracks.

A week later we left Memphis. The other members of the Royal Circle came down to the quayside to make a solemn farewell, their shouts and good wishes carrying across the water. Horemheb and Rameses were eager to return to the Delta to reinforce law and order, whilst Nakhtimin, Maya and Huy were full of the preparations for their return to Thebes. I gathered from Nebamun that prisoners were still being tortured, but if fresh information was dragged from them, Ay kept it a secret.

Our journey back to the City of the Aten was full of pomp, a colourful flotilla led by two great barges, *The Glory of Amun* and *The Power of Ra*, bedecked with standards and streamers, gilded prows and sterns dazzling in the sun. All around us clustered war barges full of soldiers with their armour, chariots and horses. For a short while a boatload of musicians, together with the temple choirs, made sweet music, their songs and hymns echoing across the water. After a while they left us and we continued our journey with as much speed as I could urge. Ay

263

had made sure that Tutankhamun would want for nothing. Big-bellied barges full of provisions accompanied us, as well as a host of flunkeys and court retainers to serve in the Prince's household. Some of these officials were from Thebes, others handpicked at Memphis. Djarka and I had already decided that once we reached the City of the Aten, we would interrogate them ourselves and try to discover which were the Lord Ay's spies, not to mention those whom Horemheb, Rameses, Maya and Huy would also place with the Prince to watch and whisper and keep them informed about what was happening.

'We'll have more spies here than we do in the House of Secrets,' I murmured to Djarka as we stood in the stern, staring at the flotilla of boats around us.

'Each of the Great Ones,' he agreed, 'have nominated people, flunkeys or musicians, stable boys or kitchen cooks. How dangerous are they?'

'To the life of the Prince,' I replied, 'no danger whatsoever. It's in everyone's interests that our young boy reaches maturity, becomes Pharaoh and begets an heir. It's as simple as that. Tutankhamun will keep the peace in Egypt.'

'And what about Meryre?'

'You heard my lord Ay. He will be hunted down. That is,' I smiled thinly, 'if he isn't dead already.'

Indeed, the whereabouts of Meryre and the other members of the Aten cult still concerned me. Despite my diffident observations about him, Meryre was a Child of the Kap, a cunning, astute man who had come within a hair's-breadth of bringing about a revolution in Egypt. A man full of his own ambition and vision of the way things should be, rather than what they were. But while the Royal Circle had been busy issuing proclamations and decrees against him, one serious problem had been virtually ignored. Canaan was still gripped by unrest, and every report we received pointed to the growing power of the Hittites. Nebamun had voiced this concern. Would the Hittites break out of their mountain fastness and sweep south, over-running the Canaanite princelings, not stopping till they reached Sinai? What if, I wondered, Meryre and his followers fled to the Hittites for protection, or even tried to set up a government in exile? Or worse still, discovered the true whereabouts of Akenhaten?

I decided to let matters rest, though they were lurking night-mares. All I could do was look after the Prince and take what-ever measures were necessary for his safety.

Five days after leaving Memphis, our barges swung left towards the City of the Aten and its waiting quaysides. Go there now and it is nothing but a burning, desolate sea of sand, a warren of ruins in a vast amphitheatre ringed by limestone cliffs. However, on our return, the city dazzled in the sun, the fertile strip beside the Nile was still being cultivated and the quay-sides were busy. The vineyards and gardens were flowering and the temples of pink and white limestone eye-catching in their beauty. It was a city of sun temples and pleasure parks, of well-laid-out paradises with fruit trees and orchards planted in the black soil of Canaan. Artificial lakes, stocked with golden fish, shimmered in the sun; the blue and white lotus buds floating on top exuded a powerful, cloying perfume. The great avenue was kept in good repair and lined with colonnaded walks, their pillars and columns of different colours. The City of the Aten still glowed like a jewel.

The Royal Palace towered over all, an elegant building with its bricks of glazed blue faience, its lintels, doorways and entrances of dazzling white limestone surmounted by silver masts from which red, blue and green streamers fluttered in the breeze. Inside the palace lay splendid chambers with glazed tiled floors, walls decorated with vivid, eye-catching paintings. At first sight, it had all the splendour and majesty of the Malkata, except for one aspect which Djarka shrewdly commented on as we left the quayside and made our way up to the great central palace of the Aten. The city was quiet, lacking the frenetic clamour, the constant noise of Memphis or Thebes. The market squares had their booths and stalls, and yet the crowds did not surge there; it was more of a mausoleum than a great city of Egypt. Some of the population had stayed, especially the craftsmen and the merchants, because the City of the Aten was well placed on the Nile, halfway between Memphis and Thebes, an important trading post for those who made it their business to sell and buy along the river. Of course, Lord Ay had been busy, issuing orders and proclamations for the palaces, temples and other royal buildings to be prepared for our return. Yet in reality, the City of the Aten was no better than a summerhouse, a place of retreat for quiet and calm. No decrees, edicts or proclamations had been issued against it. The Royal Circle did not want to kill the city or destroy its buildings; simply leave it to its own devices. If it survived then it would be just another city; if it lingered and died, it would be quietly and quickly forgotten.

We took up quarters at the heart of the palace, in rooms which looked over a central courtyard where the passageways and entrance could be easily guarded. The next few weeks were busy with the unloading of cabinets, beds, chairs and chests. Flowers had to be gathered for bouquets, the kitchen organised. Djarka and I interrogated all the servants, sifting out those who might be spies, though, of course, Ankhesenamun was the principal source of information for the Lord Ay. My mercenaries I trusted, men of the Medjay, Kushites and a few Libyans, braggarts, drinkers, but good fighting men. I paid them well and made sure they were comfortable in defensive rings around our quarters. They were under strict orders: people were only to be allowed to pass if they carried warrants or letters bearing my seal. Anyone else was to be treated as hostile. Colonel Nebamun's chariot squadron arrived, organised on a rota basis; they set up permanent camp along the clifftops with regular forays out into the eastern desert, whilst General Nakhtimin's guards supervised all river traffic.

The news of the Prince's return soon became well known. The city became an attraction for the merchants and traders eager to sell their goods and produce to the court. The weeks slipped into months as we settled down, establishing a harmonious if boring routine. I was determined on that. Naturally, I listened to the news from Thebes. If Ay and the rest had their spies in the City of the Aten, I still controlled a legion of whisperers and tale-tellers in Thebes organised by Sobeck, who was always eager to pass on the chatter and gossip of the city drinking-booths and eating-houses. Lord Ay was quick to move, establishing his power as First Minister in practice if not in name. Justice was ruthlessly and speedily dispensed. The usurper and all his companions were paraded in chains through

Thebes for the mockery of the mob. Ay himself carried out public executions in the incense-filled courtyards of Karnak, crushing the skulls of his enemies and hanging his victims in chains from the Wall of Death. Huy and Maya were equally busy. New taxes were raised, the House of Silver replenished, granaries filled, whilst envoys were sent across Sinai and beyond the Third Cataract to inform our allies that the new power of Egypt was not to be taken lightly. Ay also kept his word about the dead. Slave gangs were moved into the Valley of the Kings, where caves were dug, tombs constructed, the Mansions of Eternity prepared for those whose corpses mouldered above the City of the Aten.

Late in the season of Shemsu, the second year of Tutankhamun's reign, Ay dispatched a letter asking that the tombs in the eastern cliffs of the City of the Aten be emptied and the coffins and sarcophagi be transported by night along the Nile to Thebes. I personally supervised this. I had made my preparations well. The tombs in the limestone cliffs above the City of the Aten, about thirty in all, were arranged in two patterns, some in the northern cliffs, others in the south, whilst Akenhaten had chosen a sepulchre in the centre of these mountains, in line with the rising sun. Of course, Ankhesenamun, and even Tutankhamun, wished to be present. The tombs themselves were ringed by high protective walls, entered by a double-barred gate, which was guarded by my mercenaries. Some of the tombs contained nothing, empty caverns with little more than wall paintings; others were full. I began the grisly task of bringing out the dead. The tombs were treasure troves, full of costly possessions and beautifully gilded coffins and caskets. My scribes made a precise inventory. Each item was tagged and carefully noted before being lifted on to a waiting cart and transported down to the quayside. I had commandeered certain warehouses where these relics could be stored till the barges arrived. It was an eerie experience to walk amongst the dead, to stand in a burial chamber, the oil lamps and torches flickering, the air thick and cloying with the smell of natron, perfume and the rich odours of the embalming oils.

In some cases the task was easy. The coffins and caskets were all carefully prepared, but I also witnessed the devastating effects of the hideous plague which had swept through the City of the Aten. The embalmers had been too busy, their ranks depleted by the ravages of the pestilence. Bodies had been hastily prepared, often doused in baths of pure natron, which dried the flesh and turned the bones brittle, before being hastily lifted into makeshift chests and boxes and lodged in the burial chambers with little ceremony. Many of these had rotted and crumbled, the remains inside nothing more than a heap of bones and dust. I did my best, with the help of the priests and scribes, to observe the rites, to honour the dead, yet it was a thankless task. I did not believe in the afterlife. When a man dies, his soul dies with him. Standing in those gloomy chambers where dried-out corpses half protruded from arrow chests or wooden boxes, it was difficult to conceive of the Land of the Blessed, of the fertile fields of Yalou where the green-skinned God Osiris ruled. We worked, our mouths and nostrils covered with strips of linen dipped in perfume. Occasionally we had to stop, to be free of the dust, to go out and catch the soothing air, or simply to sit in the sunlight so as to drive the shadows away.

The news spread through the city. Crowds of sightseers surged up the cliff paths. There were few protests. The tombs had been the preserve of members of Akenhaten's family and court, the coffins of the workers and traders being buried elsewhere. Every day the macabre work continued. After sunset, a sombre torch-lit procession escorted the creaking carts, pulled by lowing oxen, down from the clifftops. The treasures, of course, were carefully hidden under cloths and closely guarded. We began in the north and then moved to those in the south. Pentju was present when his family tomb was opened. He cried quietly as the coffins of his wife, children and kinsmen were taken out into the sunlight, the treasure buried with them stacked about. The coffins were sealed and secured. I would have loved to have examined their contents, but that would have provoked a major confrontation. I hid my curiosity, putting more trust in the letter I had sent to Sobeck in Thebes.

On my return to the City of the Aten, I had made careful examination about the chief embalmer Nefertiti had used, the one Khufu described as 'the Stammerer'. At first no one knew of his whereabouts; a few claimed he had died. However, a well-to-do trader who did business with the fishing fleets sold me the information that the Stammerer, together with his wealth, had boarded a barge shortly after Queen Nefertiti's death and secretly returned to Thebes. I decided to wait on developments.

At last all the tombs were empty. I let matters rest for a while and then, accompanied by my mercenary captain, entered the courtyard which led to Akenhaten's tomb, the royal burial place in the centre of the limestone cliffs. The courtyard in front of it was empty of all statues, the flower baskets had long rotted to nothing but dark dried masses in the corner. The workmen I had brought were most reluctant to start, but I paid a chapel priest to gabble a few solemn prayers. I informed the workmen that their task was blessed by the Gods and would be the source of great profit for themselves and their families. The wall leading into the entrance of the tomb was shattered, the plaster and brickwork beyond pulled away to reveal a long passageway. The tomb followed the pattern of others except that its tunnels and chambers were most majestic, a truly sombre underworld. The torchlight illuminated the paintings on the walls. The tomb had been planned as a place of glory, though its artwork had never been finished, due to the plague as well as the crisis caused by the rift between Akenhaten and Nefertiti. I walked into the royal burial chamber, which housed the coffins of Akenhaten's five daughters and the blue and gold casket of his Queen, the Glorious Nefertiti. I stood for a while staring down at this, recalling how after her death the Lord Ay had given his daughter's corpse over to the embalmers. The seventy-day funeral period had not been observed. Haste had been the order of the day. Nevertheless, she had been given a coffin worthy of a queen, though probably not the one she had intended.

I went back to the entrance and led the workmen in. The coffins were taken out whilst I continued my search of the underground passageways and chambers. It was like walking the empty cellars of a house. Here and there frescoes caught my eye, yet there was nothing else. A gloomy place, manifesting the glory and majesty of Akenhaten's court. I reached the end of the tunnel and walked back. Ahead of me I could hear the cries of the workmen as they manoeuvred the coffins up the steps. I had to walk carefully; the floor was still strewn with rubble, and in many places the walls of the tunnel were of rough, undressed stone. When I reached a part of the tunnel where the wall was smooth, I stopped and peered closer, raising my torch to make out the outline of a small square neatly plastered over. I shouted at the workmen, and their supervisor came hurrying down. He too examined the plaster carefully, tapping at it, pressing his ear against it.

'My lord, there is another chamber beyond. A secret one. This is not a door, but a window leading into it.'

I stood back. The square was about two yards high, the same across.

'Break it down,' I ordered.

'My lord, be careful.' The overseer's dusty face was full of fear.

'Why, man, what's the matter?'

He wiped his mouth on the back of his hand.

'It's a hidden chamber.' The overseer pointed to the marks around the plaster, ones that I hadn't noticed. I lifted the torch and peered at the magical symbols cursing anyone who broke through this wall. The usual nonsense: the eye of Horus, the striking Cobra . . .

'The Gods are far too busy,' I replied, 'to care about a hole in the wall.'

'It's not the Gods,' the overseer replied, 'but what might lie beyond.'

I told him to break the plaster down, and stepped back as he and his companions swung their mallets and picks. The plaster was thick, but eventually they cleared a space no bigger than a window. I peered through the darkness and glimpsed pinpoints of light, as if there had been holes drilled in the rocks above. I tossed the torch inside. It extinguished as it fell, but in its final flare, I glimpsed the outline of a red quartzite sarcophagus at the far end of a low-ceilinged chamber. The workmen stood back, chattering amongst themselves. I returned to look at the hieroglyphs and could make out the faint words Shesha Shemet, the Arrows of Sekhmet. It was a common curse, threatening an intruder with the fury of the Destroyer, but it only whetted my curiosity. I reasoned that this was the Royal Tomb, and that

270

the only people who had had control over it were Akenhaten and Nefertiti. Akenhaten had given up all hope of realising his vision about the City of the Aten, so this secret chamber and its concealed entrance must be the work of his estranged wife.

Once the dust had cleared, I poked my head through. The faint streaks of light came from small holes or vents piercing the rock above. The overseer was now jabbering with his comrades. An argument broke out. I was about to intervene when a young man pushed his way through, boasting that he was not frightened, openly deriding his companions' fears.

'My lord, I will go in.'

'Are you sure?' The workman was free-born, not a slave or servant.

'My lord, I am not afraid.'

He jumped on to the crumbling sill and stepped down. He had hardly taken a step forward when, with a hideous crash, he disappeared in a cloud of dust. The entire cavern was riven by his shrill cry, followed by the most hideous screams. I seized a torch and looked over. The floor beneath the opening had concealed a trap: a simple plaster covering concealing a pit with sharpened stakes. The young man lay gruesomely impaled, eyes bright with agony, blood-smattered mouth gasping in horror. The stakes were long and sharp as spears and had pierced his body in a number of places. He screamed, trying to raise his hands, then sagged, head falling to one side. There was nothing we could do for him. Planks were brought and lowered over. The ground beyond the pit seemed firm and hard. Another workman, bribed by the overseer, gingerly climbed on to the plank and clambered down. The light of the torch he carried revealed more of the chamber. It was roughly cut, the walls unplastered, and contained nothing but the blood-red quartzite sarcophagus. The workman reached the end of the plank and probed the ground before him with a stick.

'It stands firm,' he called out. He stepped off the plank, moving towards the sarcophagus, but tripped face down. He rolled in agony, screaming and yelling, then pulled himself up, still clutching the torch. He lifted his head: a nightmare sight. His face and chest were streaked with blood. He staggered back, dancing in pain, and scrambled towards the plank across the

271

pit, but screamed, lost his balance and tipped on to the stakes below.

The workmen would have fled, but by now the mercenaries at the entrance, alarmed by the noise, had come hurrying down and forced them back. I ordered skins of oil to be brought, cut and thrown, one after the other, into that hellish chamber. Flaming arrows were loosed in a volley of fire. The arrows caught the oil and the fire leapt up. In its glare the true horror of the chamber was revealed. I glimpsed the trip cord pulled across the floor and the razor-sharp glass, copper and bronze blades embedded in the ground, but the real danger were the black curling shapes, rock vipers, coiled skins gleaming in the light.

'A common trick, my lord,' the overseer whispered hoarsely. He pointed to the gaps in the roof. 'They were placed here and allowed to nest.'

In the flames I could see how the far wall of the chamber jutted out like a ramp. The snakes could leave, squirming out into the daylight whenever they wished, and return the same way.

Nefertiti had planned well. A concealed pit, a trip line, razor-sharp points embedded in the floor and baskets of vipers to turn the chamber into their own nest. I ordered more fire to be brought so that every inch of the floor of that concealed chamber was purified. Whilst the flames roared, we withdrew to the entrance, the smoke billowing out behind us. The news of our terrifying find had quickly spread. Pentju and others came hurrying up the cliff paths to discover what was happening. Once the flames had died down, we returned to the gap; part of the roof, deliberately weakened, had also come crashing down.

'*Kheb*, *kheb*,' Pentju breathed. 'A trap within a trap. Why, Mahu? What does the sarcophagus contain?'

'I don't know,' I smiled grimly, 'but I am determined to find out.'

Once the fire was out and the chamber cooled, I climbed over, stout marching boots on my feet. Armed with a sword, a club thrust in the sash round my robe, I clambered down on to the freshly placed plank, moving cautiously, ignoring the chatter of the others behind me. I edged across the floor until I reached the sarcophagus, and grasped it, my hands protected by the thick

272

leather gauntlets the overseer had warned me to wear. I felt tentatively beneath its rim. Here, too, razor-sharp pieces of copper and bronze had been embedded. I carefully walked round the sarcophagus. It was at least a yard and a half high and about two yards across. I crouched down and ran my hands across the surface. I made out the hieroglyphs cut into the quartzite: an owl, a human hand and arm, a pool of water above a mouth sign, a lion at rest, a quail chick under the night sky, a broken sceptre, a loop of cord over a water ripple. The inscription contained a dire curse: anyone who tampered with this sarcophagus would be cursed by the Gods from morning till evening and know no peace for his soul. I was already cursed, so I didn't care.

The others now joined me, Pentju included. The workmen brought mallets and crowbars and, after a great deal of exertion, broke free the lid. We pushed it to one side and it crashed to the ground, splitting as it bounced against the nearby wall. The coffin inside was a work of art, its blue-gold dazzling in the torchlight. The death mask was that of a Pharaoh, with brilliant dark blue faience serving as the eyes. The sarcophagus contained no traps, but nothing to indicate what it actually held.

It took us two days to remove the coffin from its concealed chamber and take it out to a waiting cart. I realised the casket would contain others within it, so I ordered it to be taken into the palace and kept in a small garden temple carefully guarded by my mercenaries. I decided not to investigate immediately. On that same day, a flotilla of barges arrived from Thebes to take the other coffers and treasure back along the river to the Necropolis in the Valley of the Kings. It took most of the day and late into the evening to load the barges, the coffins being received by officials wearing the black and gold jackal masks of Anubis. An eerie sight, as darkness fell: priests and guards in their hideous masks, torches lit, the evening air full of the smell of incense and the mournful song of the funeral march. The crowds were kept away. Only Pentju and our mercenary officers were on the quayside to watch that sombre procession leave, boat after boat, each carrying coffins, caskets and hoards of treasure.

The chief mortuary priest had informed me how the new tombs had been prepared in the Valley of the Nobles and the Valley of the Kings, but that would not be enough. Other royal graves had been opened, so coffins could be placed there as a temporary measure. At the time I did not care what the Lord Ay had arranged. I was more concerned with my own discovery, which I kept secret from Lord Ay's spies. The next morning I began the grim task of opening the coffins. The first was quite easy; it contained a second within, again a work of art, its gesso overlaid with gold leaf and blue faience studded with precious jewels. The mask was that of a Pharaoh with features similar to those of Akenhaten's elder brother Tuthmosis. I realised that whoever had supervised this burial had plundered the royal store-rooms for the coffins and funeral paraphernalia. I was assisted by my overseer and two of his workmen, who were both sworn and bribed to secrecy, whilst Pentju, as a physician, was also ready to help. He had already pointed out that neither the funeral chamber nor the sarcophagus contained any treasure. More importantly, the four canopic jars were missing: the sacred vessels, their lids carved in the shape of the head of a God, which were supposed to hold the preserved entrails of the dead person.

The second coffin was much more difficult to prise open. So much embalming resin had been used that the lid stuck and we had to use crowbars, hammers and chisels to break it free. It revealed a corpse bound in funeral cloths held in place by tight cords. The cloth and cords had turned black due to the embalming resin which had been poured in. The corpse itself was shrunken and shrivelled, the heart plucked out, the skin stone dry, the bones so brittle they crumbled in our hands. The eyes had also been removed but no jewels or precious stones placed there.

'Whoever did this,' Pentju observed, 'did not wish this man well.'

At first I had been fearful that these were the remains of Akenhaten. The corpse was that of a tall, broad-shouldered man. However, the face and head, completely shaven, betrayed none of the tell-tale features of a man I had served since childhood, and there were no inscriptions, no marks, nothing to indicate who this dead person had been.

274

'He certainly wasn't loved by those who buried him,' Pentju repeated. He tapped the desiccated stomach and pointed to the embalmer's long incisions on the left side. 'The belly was opened and the entrails removed, but they weren't buried with him in canopic jars; they were probably burned. The heart has been removed, the eyes not replaced, so he will not be able to find his way through the Underworld.'

'Who?' I asked. 'Who could it be?'

Pentju inspected the corpse noting the high cheekbones in the long skull, and the thigh and feet bones.

'He was not a courtier,' he declared, 'but someone who walked a great deal over rough terrain so the soles of his feet became coarsened.'

'Why is the corpse so dry?' I asked.

'Because he was buried in haste,' Pentju replied. 'The usual period for embalmment is seventy days; that's how long it takes to dry out a corpse. However, if you place the cadaver into a bath of natron, specially strengthened, the process is quickened. This is the result. Skin dry as a dead leaf, bones as brittle as stale bread.'

I now became aware of the rather vile odour seeping from the grisly remains: a mixture of natron, embalming perfume and that foul stench of corruption which Pentju claimed was the result of the corpse not being properly cleaned before being sealed into its coffin. We inspected both the corpse and the two coffins, but could find no clue. I ordered the remains to be gathered together, the second coffin placed back inside the first, which was to be resealed, whilst the small temple was to be fumigated and doused in perfume.

'What will you do?' Pentju asked as we left.

I told the captain of the guard to maintain a close watch and led my physician friend across to the Pool of Purity, where we stripped and bathed. Pentju repeated his question as we clambered out, drying ourselves with the towels servants brought, together with fresh robes I had ordered from the palace.

'What shall we do, Pentju? We shall reflect. That secret chamber was definitely built by Nefertiti, the sarcophagus probably intended for her husband. The coffins and the death masks are from the royal storerooms. I suspect Nefertiti intended to proclaim herself as Pharaoh and to use that corpse, claiming it to be her husband. If she had established her rule, if the coup had not taken place, Nefertiti would have arranged a state funeral, a mockery of a public ceremony, to quell all rumours about her husband still being alive. I don't think she intended to bury him here but arrange some solemn flotilla which would have taken his coffin back to join those of his ancestors in the city of Thebes. Don't forget, Pentju, in the early years of his reign Akenhaten did order a tomb for himself in the Valley of the Kings.'

At first Pentju disagreed, but reluctantly he conceded that my theory might be correct.

'I just wonder,' he added wryly, 'how much of this the Lord Ay knew.'

'More important,' I replied, 'whom did she kill? When Khufu confessed, he declared he'd heard a hideous scream from the imperial quarters, as if someone was being murdered. I suspect we have found Nefertiti's victim.'

Three days later, whilst I was still wondering what to do with the corpse and its coffins, Sobeck arrived in the City of the Aten, accompanied by what he called his 'retinue', a gang of the most ruthless ruffians from the slums of Thebes. He came to the palace and demanded an audience. When we met, he clasped my hand and embraced me warmly, kissing me on each cheek.

'You should be careful, Mahu,' he whispered, his lips next to my ear. 'The Lord Ay's power grows. He's making himself a king in Thebes.'

'And you?' I asked, stepping back.

He spread his hands. 'I have been pardoned. I have now been proclaimed "Great Friend of the Royal Circle". My sins, although scarlet, are washed away. I have been appointed Overseer of the Imperial Granaries in Eastern and Western Thebes. I have also been given a mansion standing in its own fertile grounds near the Great Mooring Place only a mile from the Temple of Luxor.' He let his hands drop. 'The mansion once belonged to one of Meryre's supporters; Maya tells me he won't be needing it any more.'

He then related the rest of the gossip of the city. Now and

again he'd turn to look back down the garden to where his retinue rested in the shade of fruit trees, filling their stomachs, quenching their thirst and teasing the maids.

'Why did you tell me to be careful of Ay?'

'Because, Mahu, Prince Tutankhamun gets older by the day. Soon he will be of age to marry, be crowned Pharaoh. He will no longer need a guardian or a protector.'

I leaned back to catch the shade of the alcove we were sitting in.

'He will still need a friend, Sobeck.'

'Ah yes, but our lord Ay will also decide that. Is the Lady Ankhesenamun well?'

'Flirtatious as ever.'

'Do you see the letters she sends her grandfather?'

'Yes, and his replies. My scribes are very good at removing sealing wax and reimposing it so no one can notice. She gives him the chatter of this city. He provides her with the gossip of Thebes. I know, and they know that I know. Yet,' I grinned, 'they are also communicating in a secret code, one I can't break. I suspect the messages she sends are all about the Prince and whatever mischief Ay might be stirring up in this dying city.'

'Is it dying?' Sobeck asked. 'The streets seemed to be lively with trade. The quaysides are busy.'

'For a while,' I replied. 'But when the Prince leaves, the heart of this city will stop beating. Within five years it will be a ruin.'

'I have heard all about the removal of the coffins.' Sobeck tapped the nail of his thumb against his teeth. 'Ay tried to keep it a secret, but such a funeral flotilla cannot be missed. Anyway,' he grinned, 'did you discover anything of interest?'

I told him about the secret chamber, the traps it contained and the mysterious corpse concealed in its splendid coffins.

'And I have brought you some help.' Sobeck stood up. 'I always read your letters intently.'

'What do you mean?'

'You don't think I came just to see your ugly face?' He winked at me. 'I have brought you a gift. The embalmer, the one they call the Stammerer.'

277

Akesi
(Ancient Egyptian for 'a region unknown even to the Gods')

Chapter 14

'My lord, my lord Mahu?'

The chamberlain of the Palace of the Aten, a pompous little man, came waddling up the path, clutching his robes lest they be caught by the bushes on either side.

'My lord,' he repeated, 'that overseer, the one with the dust all over him.' I sprang to my feet. 'He's at the palace gate. He demands to see you. He's most insistent.'

I gestured at Sobeck to follow. The overseer was in the porter's lodge, breathing hard in his agitation.

'My lord,' he gasped, 'we were working in the gallery of the Royal Tomb. You've got to come.'

We hurriedly left the palace along the great eastern road, past the temples, through the market squares, up the dusty chariot paths and into the enclosure before the Royal Tomb. Mercenaries and workers milled about the entrance. They stood aside as the overseer led us through, down the steps and along the passageway. The secret chamber was on our right, but the overseer led us a further twenty paces and stopped where he'd placed a pole against the wall.

He grasped a flaring cresset torch and held it up, exposing a smooth expanse of plaster, carefully done to blend in with the wall. Once again it was surrounded with minute magical inscriptions. I immediately ordered the plaster to be broken. The workmen set to with mallets and hammers, the plaster cracked and fell away. I thrust the torch through the gap and gasped in amazement. This was no empty chamber but a storeroom of treasures. In the light of the dancing flame I glimpsed chariots, weapons, caskets of jewellery, their lids thrown back, beds, stools and tables.

I stilled the workmen's cries. Sobeck grabbed a torch, and before I could intervene had clambered through. I shouted at him to be careful, but Sobeck was absorbed with what we had found, exclaiming in disbelief at the precious goods which filled the chamber from floor to ceiling.

'A treasure house,' he shouted. 'Akenhaten's House of Silver.' I climbed through after him. 'Nefertiti's preparations,' Sobeck whispered, staring round-eyed in amazement. 'This is what she would have used for the Royal Burial.' He picked up a beautiful gold-embossed fan and wafted his face. 'Look at it, Mahu. Chairs and thrones, chariots and harnesses. We must keep this a secret,' he chattered on. 'We must prepare against the evil day.'

'What evil day, Sobeck?'

'When we fall from power.'

'Then we fall from life!'

'No, no.' Sobeck pushed me deeper into this treasure house. 'Mahu, one day the Prince will be a man. You and I will not be needed. What should we do in our old age, eh? Sit on a stool in our doorway, chomping on our gums?' Sobeck gestured at the treasure hoard. 'I am different from you, Mahu. I have fallen from power. I have spent months out in the prison oasis in the Red Lands. I've prowled the streets and alleyways of Thebes. I have sat with poverty and smelt its horrible stink. Why give this to the Lord Ay?'

I didn't answer, but pushed my way through the various items. Crouching down, I opened a casket piled high with precious stones; beside it was a pair of gold-embossed sandals displaying scenes of a Pharaoh smiting vile Asiatics.

'At least we know where Akenhaten's treasure is,' I declared. 'Or at least some of it. Have you noticed, Sobeck, how much of this is heavy and couldn't be carried away?'

'You mean there's more?' Sobeck asked.

'I know there's more,' I replied. 'Akenhaten took some of the gold and silver bars, the precious stones, and left this. Nefertiti would have used it, melted it down and sold it, to finance her plans.' I got to my feet. 'We'll leave this for the while. We'll make a decision about it later.'

We left the secret treasure house. I gave orders for a wooden hatch to be placed over the gap. Sobeck was equally insistent, grasping the overseer by his tunic and threatening him and the workmen with the most dire punishment if they revealed the secret. Caught up in greed, Sobeck even distrusted me, demanding that some of his mercenaries join mine to guard the entrance.

'Sobeck, friend.' I tried to reason. 'What is this?'

I had taken him further down the gallery away from the rest. Even then Sobeck was agitated, wiping the sweat from his face, staring back at the entrance to the treasure house as if fearful that robbers would break in.

'It's not yours,' I whispered.

'It is now,' he retorted. 'I went into the Delta with you out of comradeship; my loyalty deserves reward. If we had been captured, we'd now be rotting at the end of some pole. I've returned to Thebes and what do I see? The Lord Ay, Maya and Huy, swaggering rich and powerful. Horemheb and Rameses are no different, generals of the army showing off their collars of gold and silver bees of valour. That treasure's mine, Mahu.'

'No, Sobeck,' I smiled, 'it's ours.' The anger drained from his face. 'But we'll talk about that later. I wish to see the Stammerer.'

We returned to the palace and my own House of Chains, a small prison in the cellars beneath. I called two of my mercenaries and told them to prepare a room.

'Just a bench and a stool,' I declared. 'And both of you go further along to another cell. You'll hear the prisoner arrive. When you think it is appropriate, I want you to give the most chilling screams.'

Both men, Kushite archers, eagerly agreed.

'And remember,' I shouted out to them, 'make it convincing.'

I waited for Sobeck to bring the Stammerer from the quayside. He arrived shouting and protesting at being pushed along by Sobeck's retainers. He was a one-eyed, rat-faced man with lank hair and pitted skin. The robe he was dressed in was of fine quality, though it was stained and marked after his journey along the river. He was one of those petty palace officials, full of their own importance and always ready to take a bribe. He was all nervous, or pretended to be, as Sobeck thrust him down on the stool.

'I wish to object,' he declared. 'I have been kidnapped, manhandled from my home. I have been given little food or drink and forced aboard ship to live with the filthy riff-raff of Thebes.'

Sobeck smacked him across the face.

'That's no way to speak about my cousins, my own kin.'

The Stammerer nursed his left cheek.

'Why do they call you the Stammerer?' I asked. 'You chatter like a monkey.'

'I used to stammer,' the man declared, 'but now it's cured.' He turned his head, peering at me with his good eye. 'I have been told you are the Lord Mahu, Overseer of the House of Secrets. I wish to know why I have been brought here. By what right? Whose warrant? I am a citizen of Thebes. If I have done wrong, I should answer to the mayor.'

Sobeck smacked him again. The Stammerer would have jumped to his feet, but Sobeck pushed him back down. He was about to protest again when a hideous scream echoed along the passageway, a long-drawn-out cry of pain, followed by another. Even Sobeck started, whilst those on guard outside hurried along to see what was happening.

'You are in the House of Chains.' I spoke up. 'And you are beginning to sweat with fear. You are not a reputable citizen. I think you are a murderer.'

'I am an embalmer,' the Stammerer yelped. 'My services are well known in the House of Life.'

'You have also got a reputation in Thebes.' Sobeck leaned down. 'I have heard the stories,' he hissed, 'about what you embalmers do with the corpses of comely women.'

'That's all lies,' the man declared, wincing as Sobeck hit him again. 'Stories put about by my enemies.'

'We could put you on trial for that.' I winked at Sobeck. 'What's the sentence for interfering with the dead? Impalement? Perhaps we could stage it on the riverbank as a warning to everyone else. After you die, which will take hours, we could arrange for your corpse to be hung from the Wall of Death.'

'What is it that you want? What do you want me for?'

'You've forgotten to mention,' I declared, but paused as another blood-curdling scream made the Stammerer quiver. 'You've forgotten to inform us,' I continued, 'that you are no stranger to the City of the Aten, nor this palace. You once worked as an embalmer here didn't you?'

The Stammerer stared longingly at the door.

'Doesn't that scream provoke memories?' I asked. 'One night three to four years ago, wasn't it? In the imperial quarters of this palace. You were brought here to serve the great Queen Nefertiti!'

'A treasonable bitch! She now—'

I hit him in the mouth.

'My mistress,' I said softly, 'fair of form and fair of heart. A woman steeped in blood, but still my mistress, my Queen. Now answer my questions. You had a man murdered, didn't you, and later embalmed his corpse. You shaved the hair and face and sent this miserable creature into the eternal night, having burned his heart.'

'She murdered four men,' the Stammerer blurted, wiping the stream of blood from the corner of his mouth.

'Four?' Sobeck asked. 'Come, come.'

The Stammerer put his face in his hands and for a short while rocked himself backwards and forwards. 'I promised,' he murmured. 'I took a great oath never to reveal what happened.'

I forced his face up. 'Did you have a hand in these murders?'

The Stammerer nodded.

'Years ago,' he breathed out, 'my family and I were fishermen. We hailed from the town of Akhmin.'

'Ah,' I sighed, 'the same city as the Lord Ay. Now, would the likes of him have anything to do with fishermen?'

'We were fishermen during the day, but at night we . . .'

'You were pirates.' I finished the sentence. 'River killers. Men who lurked amongst the reeds, waiting for some hapless merchant; a swift arrow, and whatever he was carrying becomes yours.'

'One night we were captured,' the Stammerer continued. 'We'd attacked a powerful merchant a few nights previously.

He escaped and returned to set a trap. During the fight I lost my eye. We were taken before the courts and found guilty. We were sentenced to death, three others and me. The Lord Ay came down. He said he had certain tasks for us. We were taken to the nearby House of Life. He enrolled us in the Guild of Embalmers; at first we couldn't believe our luck. We praised his charity and generosity.'

'Go on,' I urged. 'And then the corpses began to arrive, the remains of those whom the Lord Ay wished to dispose of.'

'Yes.' The Stammerer swallowed hard, then moaned quietly as another hideous scream echoed along the corridor.

I nodded at Sobeck. 'Do tell the guards to leave that prisoner alone. Give him some time to think. Perhaps he will agree to answer our questions.'

A short while later Sobeck was back. The Stammerer must have thought his smile was symptomatic of his sadistic mood, for he promptly fell to his knees.

'My lord Mahu, pardon, mercy! The Lord Ay used us to embalm the corpses of his victims and sometimes we carried out other tasks for him.'

'Get back on your stool.' I prodded him on the shoulder. 'You smell. I don't like you too close.'

The Stammerer scrambled back.

'Is that what cured your stammer?' I asked. 'The shock of being caught, the prospect of being impaled?'

The Stammerer nodded.

'And of course when the Lord Ay moved to Thebes, you came with him?'

Again the Stammerer nodded.

'You and your companions were given posts in the Necropolis. When Akenhaten and his court moved here you were given the usual licence and warrants to follow? What happened when Nefertiti used you?'

'Four men had been caught, 'the Stammerer gabbled. 'They were not Egyptians but Apiru. They were often seen in this palace, allowed to come and go carrying documents bearing the cartouche of Akenhaten. No one dared stop them. This was during the time of the Great Mystery.'

'The what?' I interrupted.

'The Great Mystery: that's what the Great Queen Nefertiti called it when Pharaoh, her husband, was seen no more.'

'So did she not know what had happened?'

The Stammerer shook his head. 'She knew that these Apiru had been visiting her husband. When he had been missing for three to four days, they were discovered near the King's own treasure house. When the guards accosted them they showed their royal warrants, but,' the Stammerer shrugged, 'everyone realised something serious had happened. The officers became suspicious and brought the men before Queen Nefertiti. She had them imprisoned in a nearby chamber and asked me and my companions for our assistance.'

'You tortured them?' I asked.

'They were brave men,' the Stammerer replied. 'Especially their leader, Yakoub; he was the last to die. The Great Queen asked where her husband was. What had become of him. She threatened them with public trial and execution, but Yakoub scoffed at her and asked how could they be accused of any crime.'

'Who was present at this interrogation?'

'Nefertiti's mercenary captain, and others, two or three, men she trusted.'

'Was Lord Ay there?'

The Stammerer shook his head again. 'She asked them why they were in the palace so near to the treasure house. Yakoub replied that they had one more task to carry out for their master.'

'Their master?' I interrupted. 'So that was when Nefertiti learned that her husband had left the palace but was still alive.'

'That's what I believe.'

'Take him out.' I turned to Sobeck. 'Tell the guards to keep him in a nearby chamber.'

Sobeck pushed and shoved the man out of the cell, returning immediately.

'So you now have proof that Akenhaten didn't die here, but escaped?'

'It's not that,' I whispered. 'Why did he send a man like Yakoub and three of his followers into the Palace of the Aten?'

'To take some treasure?'

'No, I don't think that was it.'

287

'Then why were these Apiru found near the treasure house?'

I couldn't answer Sobeck's question. Instead I asked for the prisoner to be brought back. I thrust him down on the stool.

'What happened to the Divine One,' I whispered, 'is neither here nor there.'

'But I thought you wanted to know that?'

'I'll tell you what I want to know. Tell me again what Yakoub said.'

The Stammerer closed his one good eye, screwing up his face. 'We were torturing him; being embalmers, we know a lot about the human body, where to inflict the greatest pain. By then the other three had died. Yakoub was beginning to fail. He spent a great deal of time cursing Nefertiti in his own tongue. She was seated in a chair behind us. She was dressed in the full regalia, as if she was at the Window of Appearances ready to give audience.'

'Why was she there?' I demanded. 'What did she want from him?'

'She asked why Yakoub had returned to the palace. He replied, "As I've said, to finish a task."'

'And?'

'That's all he would say. A day later, he died. Now the corpses of the other three were taken down to the river and thrown into a crocodile pool. However, Nefertiti ordered us to embalm Yakoub's corpse, but not in the proper way. We were to take out his heart and place his corpse in a heavy bath of natron. We did what she asked. She had coffins brought from the Royal Treasury. We placed Yakoub's corpse inside, soaking it in resin, and took it up to the Royal Tomb. There was a hidden chamber: its opening had not been sealed. We pushed the coffin through the gap. At the far side of the chamber stood a quartzite sarcophagus, I remember that.'

'And the traps?' I asked.

'Nefertiti's work. She told us what she wanted: the shaft holes for the snakes, the copper and brass embedded in the floor. We deliberately weakened the ceiling. We dug the pit, placed the stakes and covered that up. Nefertiti had the gap plastered over and ordered us to put the magical formula around it.'

'Did you ask her why?'

288

'She was terrifying,' the Stammerer whispered. 'My lord, she was truly frightening, face tight with anger, eyes blazing with fury. She reminded me of a panther. She walked so softly. I . . . I was terrified. She made me swear the blood oath.' He shrugged. 'The rest, my lord Mahu, you know. Nefertiti ended her days. I and the rest were only too pleased to flee back to Thebes.'

'She rewarded you well?'

'A basket full of treasure, my lord, from the House of Silver. She said if we ever breathed a word . . .' He left the sentence unfinished.

'Go on,' I urged. 'You're released from your oath. I have found the coffin and Yakoub's corpse.'

'She said she knew our crimes, that no one was beyond her reach as Lord Pentju—' The Stammerer stopped, fingers going to his lips. I leaned across and dug my fingernails beneath his good eye.

'Do continue. What do you know about the Lord Pentju?'

Sobeck got up and went and stood behind him.

'The Lord Pentju?' I repeated

'She had his family murdered. At the time the plague was raging. The physician was locked in his own house; a small mansion where he looked after the baby Prince . . .'

'I know all that.'

'She had them poisoned,' the Stammerer declared. 'She claimed that people thought they were victims of the plague. She sent them wine and other delicacies as a gift.'

'By all that is Holy,' Sobeck breathed. 'She killed Pentju's wife and children!'

'And the others in the house,' the Stammerer whined. 'They were sheltering there. They all ate and drank. The poison was quick-acting.'

'You know more, don't you?'

'We were sent in.' The Stammerer spread his hands. 'What could we do?' he wailed. 'One of my companions delivered the food and wine. We visited the house, pretending to be scavengers coming to remove the corpses of plague victims.'

'And was Lord Pentju informed?' I pressed my nails harder.

'Lord Pentju was informed. I was the Queen's messenger. I

told him that his wife and family had died in the plague but that the Queen, recognising his duties, realised he could not leave the Prince. She claimed she would see to the funeral rites.'

'And Lord Pentju?' I asked.

The Stammerer hung his head. 'He listened to my message and walked away.'

'He walked away?' Sobeck asked.

'Yes,' the Stammerer agreed. 'He walked back to the gates of his mansion; the mercenaries closed them in my face. I remember the bar being lowered, the bolts being drawn. I went back to the Queen and told her what had happened.'

'And?'

'She gave that terrifying smile, not looking at me direct as I knelt before her, but at some point beyond me.'

'Why do you think Pentju's family were murdered?'

'I don't know,' the Stammerer gabbled. 'My lord Mahu, you know how it is.'

'No I don't,' I interrupted.

'You deal with murderers?' he whined.

'Yes I do. But not ones who kill women and children.'

'Nefertiti cursed Pentju and the baby Prince. She dismissed him as illegitimate.'

'Illegitimate?' Sobeck queried.

'She meant he wasn't of her blood line.'

'And Yakoub?' I asked. 'Why was Nefertiti so cruel towards him?'

'She was convinced he had come back for something, that he knew the truth about her husband. She suspected Pentju was involved in this with others of Yakoub's blood. She mentioned a man called Djarka.'

Sobeck glanced quickly at me. I gestured at him to keep quiet.

'My lord, we did what she asked, her rage was formidable.' He fell to his knees again. 'Lord Mahu, I beg forgiveness. I know nothing else.'

We left the cell.

'Well?' Sobeck asked. 'What do you do now?' He gestured back at the door. 'Shall I have his throat cut?'

'Take him back to the river,' I snarled. 'Where you put him is up to you!'

290

I wanted to hide my own rage. I ran from the House of Chains, across the courtyards into the deepest part of the garden, sheltering under the shade of the date palm trees. At first I was so distracted I could not keep still. I reflected on what Khufu had said, and that priest's strange death. Everything else I had learned was also sifted as I tried to impose some order on the chaos agitating my heart. I must have stayed there for at least two hours, alternating between bouts of depression and anger at being fooled. Sobeck discovered where I was.

'I am taking the Stammerer back to Thebes,' he announced. 'I think I can use him before I have his throat cut.' Sobeck stood tapping his foot.

'You haven't come about the Stammerer,' I accused. 'It's the treasure, isn't it? You are not taking it, Sobeck!'

'I didn't say I was. I just want my share. When you return to Thebes the treasure will come with you. I want your promise that I'll have half.'

'Agreed.' I clasped his hand.

'And what about Yakoub's corpse?'

'I'll take it back to its tomb.'

'What are you plotting?' Sobeck demanded.

'Sobeck, take your Stammerer and any of the treasure you can safely conceal; the rest leave to me.'

He left. A servant came to tell me that one of Nebamun's squadrons had brought in some desert wanderers with a girl they had kidnapped and tried to sell.

'Fine them and whip them,' I shouted.

'The girl is Egyptian and highborn.'

'She'll have to wait. She'll have to wait.' I dismissed him, still restless and uneasy. I wanted to lash out. To distract myself I went to look at some acrobats training in a courtyard; one of the chamberlains had hired them for a feast he was planning. I watched their sweaty, oil-drenched bodies twist and turn, followed by the jugglers and the fire-eaters. I grew bored and began to mentally compose a poem about a hyaena, wounded and alone in the Red Lands: a ridiculous effort! I felt imprisoned by my obsession. Why not leave the court and my duties, I wondered, and take Lord Ay's offer of a country mansion? I thought of the hyaena. You can lecture it, imprison it, but once free, it still hunts.

I went back to the garden. Amedeta came looking for me, ostensibly carrying a message from Ankhesenamun. A servant directed her to where I sat under a tree, almost hidden by the long grass. She flounced up shredding a lotus flower, her lovely face framed by a perfumed wig with silver fillets. She was all perfume-drenched, her dark sloe eyes, ringed with green kohl paint, bright with passion, lips full and red, breasts thrusting against her thin linen robe, bangles and anklets clattering and jangling. I was aware of her high-heeled sandals, the soft gold flesh of her legs, the golden gorget round her throat and the cornelian pectoral displaying Nekhbet, the Vulture Goddess, glinting against her chest. I took her as she intended to be taken, had plotted to be taken, soft arms around my neck, thighs either side of mine, eyes closed, mouth open in cries of pleasure. I took her and took her again, my nails digging into her back, lips pressed against hers. Afterwards she rose, smiled at me, throwing the last of the lotus petals down on to my stomach, and left, her hips swaying, singing softly under her breath.

I stayed for a while then returned to the palace. I invited Djarka and Pentju to dinner out on the terrace. The darkness was lit by beautiful coloured oil lamps. The cooks served us a choice of dishes: strips of beef, aubergine salad, rice with broad beans and coriander, whilst the alabaster chalices were kept brimmed with the rarest wines. Djarka sang a song as a hymn of thanks. I dismissed the servants, explaining that I would serve my guests. For a while we ate in silence. Djarka and Pentju were watchful, now and again moving to wipe the perfumed sweat from their cheeks.

'My lord,' Djarka began, 'why are we here?'

'Because you are my friends.'

'What is it you want to ask?' Djarka was wary.

'Why you murdered Khufu.'

Djarka swallowed what he was eating. Pentju lifted his cup, gazing at me across the rim.

'You did murder Khufu,' I declared. 'You were both involved.'

'Impossible!'

'Djarka.' I leaned across the table and pressed a finger against his lips. 'You are my friend, as dear to me as any son. Now don't,' I raised my voice, 'sit at table with me and lie when confronted with the truth. The only comfort I can take,' I added bitterly, 'is that you lie and deceive me to keep some great secret hidden. You murdered Khufu. You went to that window and enticed him to remove the wooden grill. Perhaps you said you had messages from me, or you wanted to help. Khufu followed you into the garden. You shared a wine jug, but you made sure his contained some powder which sent him into a deep sleep.'

'But I examined the corpse.'

'Shut up, Pentju! When Khufu was drugged you took him back to his chamber, going back through the window. You already had the rope ready, and what you did is what I found. You removed the door bolts as if they had been wrenched off and pulled the door shut. A wooden wedge was placed under the bottom to make it seem locked and bolted. You also replaced the wooden window grille from inside. When the alarm was raised the door was forced. I noticed the scuff mark on the floor. To those breaking in, however, it looked as if the bolts had been snapped. They found Khufu hanging by his neck, a pool of urine beneath his feet, the stool knocked over. When I examined the window it looked as if the wooden frame hadn't been removed. Djarka, you've worked with me often enough to know what I'd search for. It's easy to strew dust on a sill as if nothing's been disturbed. You also prepared the ground outside, making sure there was no trace of what had happened; a full jug of water from the window of Khufu's chamber would also help disguise any marks on the grass. To all appearances Khufu, frightened out of his wits, had hanged himself. In truth, he was murdered by you, Djarka, on the advice of the Lord Pentju. He wanted Khufu silenced because of what he knew.' I paused. 'Do you remember that scrap of papyrus I found in his chamber? I showed it you, Pentju. It listed Akenhaten, Nefertiti and Pentju, followed by a reference to Hotep the Son of Ptah, one of the Memphis triad, associating him with Tutankhaten. I also recalled the other references Djoser and Meryre had made: how they wanted you, Pentju, to be a member of their circle. When the Lord Akenhaten left his city, he must have told you, Pentju, guardian of his son, about his departure. I was ill at the time, or recovering still from the plague. Those who assisted Akenhaten

293

must have taken him out to the Red Lands to the members of a clan called Israar of the Apiru tribe. Are you of Israar, Djarka?'

'Of course, my lord.'

'Did you help the Divine One to leave the city?'

'I knew it was about to happen. You were very ill at the time. I often brought Yakoub and his companions into the city. The night they were captured by Nefertiti's guard, I was waiting here in the palace grounds. When they never appeared, I knew what had happened.'

'Why were you waiting?'

'They had a message for me which I was to give to the Lord Pentju.'

'What about?'

'My lord, I don't know. The prisoner you interrogated today, the one Lord Sobeck brought up to the quayside, I am sure he told you the reason why Yakoub and his companions failed to deliver it.'

'What was Yakoub doing in the city?' I insisted.

'My lord, all I know is that he and his companions were to take something from the treasury and give it to me to hand on to Lord Pentju. I repeat, I don't know what it was.'

I glanced at the physician. 'Do you, Pentju?'

He shook his head and drank deeply from his wine cup.

'Why,' I asked him, 'did Nefertiti murder your family?'

'As an act of revenge.'

'Or a warning,' I added. 'She really wanted to get her hands on you,' I insisted. 'And you know the reason why, Pentju? She had heard rumours, as had Meryre and others, that Akenhaten might not be Tutankhamun's father, but that you were. You confided such a secret to Djarka but not to me, true?' I paused. 'Most of what I now say is a matter of logic. This scandal is something Khufu never confessed but only hinted at. Ptah is the third God of the Memphis trinity. Hotep is his son. On Khufu's scrap of paper, you, Pentju, become Ptah; Tutankhamun is Hotep: in other words, father and son.'

Pentju closed his eyes. 'The truth, Mahu, is this. I loved my wife and children but I also fell in love with the Lady Khiya. Nefertiti, as you may recall, humiliated me at a banquet when I joked about her not producing a son. I plotted my revenge. I advised the Lady Khiya to take no more of the potions and powders sent by Nefertiti. I also gave her medicines to improve the fertility of her womb.'

'Did you sleep with her?'

'Yes, yes, I did. If the Divine One had discovered that, both I and the Lady Khiya would have suffered death and disgrace.'

'But he never did. Is the Prince truly your son?'

'Others would like to say so, but no: he is Akenhaten's. Of course, when I stare at his face I sometimes like to think he is mine, yet I must not say that.' Pentju shook his head. 'Tutankhamun is of the imperial bloodline, True Pharaoh in nature and name. Nefertiti started those rumours. In time she would have tried to poison Akenhaten's mind. Meryre and his fellow conspirators also found such stories useful.'

'Of course.' I breathed. 'If they had been successful, they could have swept Tutankhamun aside as the illegitimate by-blow of some court physician; that's why the dying Djoser referred to him as the true usurper.'

'Khufu was the last of such conspirators.' Djarka spoke up. 'My lord, we trusted you but you promised Khufu life and limb. He was a snake in the grass. Whatever you promised, would the rest of the hyaenas keep faith? Wouldn't Lord Ay's spies have searched him out? Brought him back to Thebes for questioning?'

I filled both their cups. 'So,' I stared into the night, 'everything makes sense. Khufu's death, the whisperings of Meryre and Nefertiti's plot. She must have realised her husband wished to abdicate. If she'd managed to retain power, she would have staged a mock public funeral for him using Yakoub's corpse and encouraged those stories about Tutankhamun being illegitimate.'

'Do you think the Lord Ay knows?' Djarka asked. 'Nefertiti was his daughter.'

'Lord Ay may know,' I replied, 'but it is not in his interest to publicise such scurrilous rumours.' I held my hand up, fingers curled. 'Tutankhamun is the clasp which holds everybody and everything together. What we have discussed here should go no further.'

Djarka and Pentju glanced at each other and nodded in agreement.

'Tell me,' I sipped from my cup. 'According to Khufu, Akenhaten, in one of his mad speeches, talked about the Watchers holding a secret. I don't think he was referring to rumours regarding his son's legitimacy. He didn't know about them, and even if he suspected, he would have kept such a matter quiet: no man wishes to publicise that he has been cuckolded. So, what was he referring to?'

'I don't know,' Djarka retorted.

'But you had conversations with Yakoub?'

'Yakoub brought physicians and doctors to purge Akenhaten's body and soul, to purify his flesh from the drugs of madness which had turned his head and blinded his heart. They talked to him about the true nature of the One, the Hidden God. They may well have talked about the future.'

'And?' I asked.

'My people come from the western hills of Canaan. The Apiru are a tribe of herdsmen, of farmers and shepherds. Many years ago they wandered into Egypt; some, like Great Queen Tiye, became more Egyptian than the Egyptians, assuming high office, deserting their own beliefs. Queen Tiye paid service to the Fertility God Min, though in her case it was pretence. She returned to the old ways and taught them to her son Akenhaten.'

'What is this teaching?' I asked.

'That there is only One God, an invisible being who creates all things and sees all things.'

'There's more?' I insisted.

'Yes, my lord, there's more: stories that the Apiru, particularly my tribe of Israar, have been chosen by this Invisible God, whose name cannot be mentioned, to produce a great Messiah whose rule will stretch from the great river to the far islands, who will bring all kingdoms under his way . . .'

'And Queen Tiye believed her son Akenhaten was this Messiah?'

Djarka nodded. 'Queen Tiye's theories became known to the priests of Egypt. They also knew of prophecies about the Gods of Egypt being overthrown, of a Messiah coming, of a great nation being formed. Most of it is superstitious nonsense: that's why,' Djarka held his hands up, 'on the one hand Tiye and

Akenhaten pursued their vision, and on the other the priests of Egypt opposed it.'

'Akenhaten truly thought he was the Messiah,' Pentju commented. 'In his madness he really believed he would found a new city and a new empire, that all men would come under his sway. The dream died and Akenhaten became absorbed with wine and the juice of the poppy.'

'And Yakoub?' I asked.

'Yakoub told the truth,' Djarka replied. 'Akenhaten was not the One but only a precursor. There would be other precursors, heralds, prophets. A nation would be formed out of Egypt, but he must withdraw to allow this to happen.'

'How true is this story?' I felt as if a cold breeze had tingled the sweat on my back. 'Is it nonsense? The babble of priests?'

'It's dangerous nonsense,' Djarka declared. 'My lord, for twenty years Akenhaten turned everything on its head: the Gods, the temples, the rituals of death, life and the hereafter. He brought Egypt to its knees. Many in Thebes think the nightmare is over. Akenhaten has gone and this city will be allowed to die. However, if they suspected, the likes of Horemheb and Rameses and the other powerful ones of Thebes, that only the plant had been cut but the roots still survived . . .'

I held my hand up for silence. 'I follow what you say. First we have Akenhaten and his madness. He disappears, but Meryre picks up the standard and brings foreign troops into the Delta to threaten Egypt . . .'

'So far,' Djarka leaned across the table, 'people think Akenhaten's madness has died with Meryre. If they knew the full truth, they would lash out at my people.' He spread his hands. 'Now you understand why I'm so reluctant to speak, or to trust even you, Lord Mahu.'

I felt a chill of danger, yet secretly marvelled at Lord Ay's cunning. Horemheb and the rest had to be assured, comforted that Akenhaten's vision had died, but if they began to suspect that those same ideas were still flourishing . . . Tutankhamun was Akenhaten's son; Lord Ay and others of the Akhmin gang were of Apiru descent.

'There could be a blood bath.' Djarka broke my reverie. 'Horemheb and Rameses would demand that anyone of Apiru blood be removed from high office either in the council or in the temples. The Apiru, like the Hyksos of old, would be declared to be the enemy within, to be ruthlessly crushed or driven beyond Egypt's frontier. My people would pay a heavy price, as would those who have any ties with us.'

'Tell me more about these rumours,' I urged. 'About the Messiah.'

'What I say,' Djarka replied, 'is the chatter round our camp fires, but they talk of an albino, a man with hair and skin as white as snow, of strange eyes. He will lead our people out of Egypt into a Promised Land.'

'What Promised Land?' I asked, though I suspected the answer.

'Canaan, a land flowing with milk and honey. Can't you see, my lord Mahu, the new dangers? If Horemheb and Rameses, and those who support them, suspected what we are discussing now, they would regard it as treason! Stories about how a tribe Egypt has housed and sheltered would one day bring chaos to the Gods of Egypt before marching across its frontiers to occupy a land which Egypt regards as its own . . .' Djarka shook his head. 'They would offer only one solution: the total destruction of every single member of our tribe.'

'How much do you know of this?' I turned to Pentju.

'Djarka has told me what he has told you,' Pentju admitted ruefully. 'But there is one difference, my lord Mahu. I believe what he says: one day the prophecy will be fulfilled. After all,' he smiled bitterly, 'Akenhaten did overturn the Gods of Egypt. What happened once can happen again.'

I picked up my wine cup. How long, I wondered, would it take for Horemheb to reflect on what had happened? He and the other officers of the Imperial Army would regard the dreams of the Apiru as a serious threat to Egypt's very existence. Egypt depended on Canaan for wood, wines and the rich produce of its river valleys.

'Perhaps it will never happen?' I whispered.

Djarka held my gaze.

'Then pray that it doesn't happen,' I snapped.

'It will happen, or so my people think. They talk of it constantly. How long before others realise that the blood of Akenhaten is Apiru? Tutankhamun is of the same, so it may all happen again.'

I put my wine cup down and rose unsteadily to my feet. I walked to the balustrade and stared down at the gardens. Here and there a pinprick of light glowed from the guard posts. I turned quickly and caught the stricken look in Pentju's eyes; he had not told me everything.

'You are right, Djarka,' I murmured. 'It's not finished! It's not finished at all.'

tcgar
(Ancient Egyptian for 'enemy, rebel')

Chapter 15

The next morning I felt tired, my mouth still bitter-sweet with the taste of stale wine. I rose and checked on the Prince, already busy with his studies. He was kneeling before his table practising the writings of hieroglyphs. He smiled shyly at me, waving his hand. I returned to my own quarters and stayed there for most of the morning, busy with the scribes. I was disturbed by my captain of mercenaries but I yelled at him to go away. As usual, before noon, I rejoined the Prince. We often ate out on the balcony above the pleasure gardens. Djarka had been busy in emptying some of the treasures from the tombs: chairs and stools, tables and couches had been brought to decorate the young Prince's chamber. I was particularly intrigued by two guardian statues standing on their pedestals. They were both carved from wood; the flesh part of each statue, a young man glaring fiercely, had been painted directly on to the wood with shiny black resin, the head cloths, broad collars, kilts and other details overlaid with gold on a linen base. The forepart of a bronze Uraeus had been attached to each statue's brows; the lifelike eyes were created by carbuncle jewels inlaid with limestone and set in frames of gilded bronze. The statues were standing, one foot forward on their pedestals, almost identical except for their headgear. Djarka was busy directing workmen to inscribe on the front of the triangular kilt of each figure Tutankhamun's name as proof of ownership.

'I thought they were appropriate.' Djarka smiled up at me. He pointed to the doorway. 'They can stand on either side of that: they will protect the Prince as well as remind him of his father.'

The statues had the faces of young men, sloe-eyed, round-cheeked, works of superb craftsmanship. I walked around them. They stood about six foot three inches high; the inlaid precious metal caught the light and created an aura of gold around their faces.

'Do you like them, Your Highness?' I crouched down before Tutankhamun, who was gazing open-mouthed at these lifelike statues from that mysterious treasure hoard.

'Do you like them, Your Highness?' I repeated.

'Of course he does,' Djarka interjected. 'Look at their faces. Don't you see a likeness between the carvings and His Highness?'

I did: the same youthful chubbiness, the wide-eyed stare. 'Pentju,' Djarka added, 'and the craftsmen here, believe Pharaoh had these statues made as gifts for his son, to act as guardians. It's a common enough practice.'

Tutankhamun kept walking around the statues, staring beneath their kilts, touching their legs. On one occasion he pressed his little face against one of their arms.

'I like them,' he declared proudly. 'My father had them made to protect me. Djarka is right. Where I go, they shall follow. When I enter the House of Eternity, they shall guard me. They shall be Shabtis in my tomb outside Thebes . . .'

'May that not happen for a million years!' the craftsman quickly intoned, head down, bowing towards the Prince.

'When shall we go to Thebes, Uncle Mahu? Ankhesenamun says . . .'

'What does Ankhesenamun say?'

I whirled round. The Princess, dressed in gauffered robes, stood in the doorway, fanning herself lightly. In the shadows behind her was Amedeta, eyes bright with mischief.

'Well?' Ankhesenamun approached me, hiding her face behind the fan.

'We are talking about returning to Thebes, Your Highness, but I am sure,' I smiled, 'you and your grandfather will decide on the best time.'

'What our grandfather decides,' Ankhesenamun grasped

Tutankhamun's hand, 'is what Grandfather decides. But come, little Prince.' She crouched down. 'I want to show you the carp, and some new frogs have appeared.'

They left in a patter of feet and gusts of perfume.

Amedeta, as she passed Djarka, flirtingly trailed her fingers along his arm.

'When will we return to Thebes?' Djarka walked over, indicating that we move out of earshot of the craftsmen.

'Why the hurry?' I asked. 'We have Colonel Nebamun's brave squadrons guarding us on the clifftops. The Prince is safer here than in Thebes.'

'It's this city,' Djarka whispered. He pulled a face. 'Murmurs of discontent. People are beginning to ask about Meryre's whereabouts. They know he escaped from Memphis.'

'What you are implying,' I retorted, 'is that Meryre's followers here in the City of the Aten have not heard from their master.'

'They must be concerned,' Djarka agreed, 'as well as about what might happen in the future. They have seen the coffins and treasure leave on the barges.'

'In which case, Djarka, we all have a great deal in common, and—'

'My lord?' I turned. My captain of mercenaries, lower lip jutting out, stood in the doorway glaring at me. 'My lord, the prisoners?'

'What prisoners?' I shouted. I recalled the report the previous day, and his attempts to see me earlier that morning. I walked to the great window and stared down. Tutankhamun was standing next to the pool; he was beginning to favour his left side, as if his right leg or ankle gave him discomfort. On either side of him were the two women, Amedeta standing, Ankhesenamun crouching. They were sniffing the lotus blossoms, allowing the Prince to see what they were pointing out. Tutankhamun stamped with excitement, his hand resting on Ankhesenamun's shoulder. I decided that Pentju and the other physicians must examine the young Prince again. Amedeta looked directly at me over her shoulder, as if she had known all the time I was staring at her.

'Amedeta seems very fond of you, Djarka.'

'She flirts with everyone, my lord.' Djarka's voice was devoid of any humour. 'My lord, I think the captain of your guard,' he forced a smile, 'has business to do.'

'Ah yes.' I rubbed my hand. 'You captured some sand-wanderers. Now why should they concern you or me? Are they smugglers, outlaws?'

'I think you should see for yourself. It is not so much them, my lord, but what we found with them.'

I followed him down to the great courtyard. The sand-wanderers were chained in one corner, squatting in the shade against the fierce sun. The smell from them was like that of a jackal den. In another corner crouched a young woman, olive-skinned, hair black as a raven's wing falling over her face. She sat with her arms across her chest, knees up, as if to protect her modesty from the sand-wanderers and those who guarded them. I went across, knelt before her and picked up a wooden bowl.

'Do you want a drink?' I asked.

Delicate fingers moved the black hair. She lifted her head, and even though her face was bruised and dirty, I was astonished by her beauty. That was the first time I met Mert; no wonder she was called 'Lovely of Face'. She was tall and elegant, her features perfectly formed, full-lipped, smooth-cheeked, but most surprising was the colour of her sloe-shaped eyes, blue as a rain-washed sky. Her skin looked like it had been dusted with gold, and even though her nails were dirty and her lips chapped and cut, I could see why my captain of mercenaries had been intrigued. I took her hand and felt the soft skin of her palm.

'She is not a sand-wanderer,' Djarka harshly intervened. 'Her skin is too fair.'

'And her eyes are blue, just like yours, Djarka. Is she a member of your people?'

Djarka was glaring at the captain of the mercenaries, angry that he had not been informed immediately.

'She could well be,' he murmured.

'What is your name?' I turned back to the girl; she must have been about fifteen or sixteen summers old. 'What is your name?'

She opened her mouth. 'Aataru!' She spat the word out. The name for the blood-drinking serpent. 'Aataru,' she repeated, pointing at the sand-dwellers.

'That's all she'll say, my lord.' My captain squatted down next to me. 'We were out with some of Colonel Nebamun's squadron, hunting fresh meat. The eastern deserts are empty and we came across these.' He gestured towards the sand-dwellers. 'Four in all, with two pack ponies. We decided to investigate as they were taking the path away from the city. They claimed to be acrobats, dancers, *tchapqa*.' The Kushite stumbled over the term. 'Their guild name is "The Drowning Men", that's what they call themselves. We would have let them pass; they smelled like a midden heap. We thought she was one of their women. We were about to turn away when she started screaming, the same word, "*Aataru*." The sand-dwellers tried to silence her. One of them drew a dagger, so I drew mine. Now the Drowning Men are three, not four. We brought them in here. I thought you'd be interested in their story.'

I thrust the water bowl into the girl's hand and walked across to the sand-dwellers, who crouched together, staring fearfully up at me. They were bedraggled, dirty hair reeking of cheap oil, faces darkened by the sun. I pinched my nostrils and crouched before them.

'So you are the Drowning Men.' I smiled.

'Your Supreme Excellency.' Their leader, a middle-aged man, tugged at his beard. 'Your Excellency has it correct. I praise your wisdom. My lord,' he whined, 'we are simple actors, mummers, we dance.'

'What are you doing out in the desert?'

'We had been entertaining the villagers, the caravans, the merchants who pass. We earn a little for a crust and some wine.'

'Show me,' I demanded.

The sand-dwellers got to their feet and picked up some moth-eaten lion skins, the fly-bitten heads serving as masks. Two of them put these on, whilst the third, searching amongst his bundle, brought out a reed flute. The two actors pretended to be lions. At first their shambling gait provoked laughter from the mercenaries, but the reed player began to tell a story about two lions called the Devourers who lived out in the desert and hunted human kind. As he talked, his voice rising and falling, his two companions acted out their parts. Now and again the

307

storyteller would return to his reedy music. The mercenaries stopped their laughter; the sand-dwellers were good. We forgot these were two men in shabby skins; against the background of their companion's voice and the haunting reedy music, they became savage predators, provoking memories of that hideous Mastaba in the Delta.

'Very good, very good.' I interrupted the performance. The Drowning Men took off their masks, smiling from ear to ear. 'I accept your story, you are entertainers.'

'Aataru! Aataru!' The young woman jumped to her feet, coming out of the corner, gesturing at the sand-dwellers.

'We are not blood-drinkers,' the leader whined, wiping the sweat from his face. 'Once we were four, now we are three.' He glared at my captain, then gestured at the girl. 'She has brought us nothing but ill luck. She's a witch!'

I grabbed the man by the beard. 'What were you doing with her?'

'We bought her,' the man yelped, straining to break free. 'We bought her from other desert wanderers. We were going to sell her as a slave. She's comely enough for a pleasure house.'

'Have you had your pleasure?' I demanded. 'She's Egyptian. You know the law. She cannot be a slave.' I tugged his beard again. 'Now, tell me the truth, or where there were four there will now be two. You didn't buy the girl, did you?'

The sand-dweller shook his head, tears of pain in his eyes. I released my grip.

'We became lost in the eastern desert,' he gabbled. 'We wandered far and reached an oasis, the Place of Dry Water. Well, that's what they call it. We found her there, sheltering under the trees. She had survived on dates and whatever water the oasis could produce. She wouldn't tell us what had happened or how she came to be there, but kept pointing further east. One of my companions,' he went on, 'the one who was killed, tried to pleasure her but she fought like a wild cat and kept pointing further east. We thought she might be the survivor of some massacre but we wondered what caravan, what merchants would be travelling so deep in the desert. We told her to take us back there. On the way we picked up a local guide, a nomad, who told us a fearful story about a massacre which had taken place further east. Eventually, after two days' travelling, we reached what's called the Valley of the Grey Dawn. At the mouth of the valley stands an oasis, an island of green with a sweet-water spring.'

'What was there?' I demanded

'My lord, you should see for yourself. They call it the Valley of the Grey Dawn; I'd say it's the Valley of Bones. Skeletons of men, women and children whitening under the sun, picked clean of all flesh. Here or there, a bracelet or a ring.'

'Massacred?' I asked.

'We found arrow shafts, broken javelins, but nothing else.'

'How many people?'

'My lord, we counted at least four score, but darkness was falling and the night prowlers, huge hyaena packs, haunt the valley. We searched for any treasure, anything that might tell us what happened, but we could find nothing. The young woman was screaming, gesturing with her hands, so we left, putting as much distance between ourselves and that evil place as possible.'

I watched his two companions as he spoke. They were nodding in agreement, whispering to each other. I walked back across the courtyard. The girl still stood defiantly.

'Aataru,' she repeated.

'What is your name?' I asked. 'Where are you from?'

She looked, puzzled, at me.

'Your name? My name is Mahu.'

She shook her head.

'Mahu,' I repeated. 'What is your name?'

'Mert,' she replied.

'Ah, lovely of face.' I smiled.

I returned to the sand-dwellers. 'This place of slaughter? What did you find?'

'A horrifying dark place,' the leader replied, 'full of howling hyeanas. The air was always noisy with the rustle of wings, vultures black against the sky. A fearful place, my lord, that haunting, long valley where the wind whistles and the dust devils blow. The oasis lies at the mouth. Our guide said it was sacred.'

I listened to the man even as I watched Djarka's face. He was ignoring the sand-dweller, but his face had become pale and sweaty as if he had been too long in the sun.

'Do you know this place, Djarka?'

He refused to answer. I turned back to the sand-dweller. 'You will be our prisoners. No, no.' I lifted my hand in the sign of peace. 'You will also be highly rewarded, compensated for the death of your companion, provided you tell us the truth and, if necessary, lead us back to this place.'

In answer the man knelt down and searched amongst his tawdry possessions. He brought out a ring, a dark red ruby, the silver clasp engraved with the sign of the Aten. Then he handed us a scarab, a dark blue sunstone showing the sun rising between the Sacred Peaks.

'We found those, my lord.' He glanced fearfully at me. 'Some of the skeletons of the women still had their hair, even though scorched by the sun and wind.' He let his words hang in the air.

'People of the court?' I whispered.

The man nodded. 'People unused to the desert, master. They had either been journeying there or had gone to meet someone. Every one of them was massacred.'

Behind me, Mert began to sob. I stared at that pathetic scarab and the ring, once the property of some noblewoman.

'That is all, master.'

'The remains?' I asked. 'The skeletons?'

'Most of them are grouped round the oasis,' the man replied. 'But others were found closer to the valley mouth, as if they had fled only to be hunted down. We were fearful of going in.'

'What else did you find?' Djarka asked sharply, pushing his way forward. His hand went to grasp the sand-dweller's beard, but I knocked it away.

'We found nothing, master,' the man wailed. 'By the Leopard God and all that is holy.'

'Any clothing, tattered remains of clothes?'

'Nothing else. There may be more further up the valley.'

I grasped Djarka by the shoulder and pulled him away, then told the captain of my mercenaries to take Mert to the women's quarters and hand her over to Ankhesenamun. The sand-dwellers were to be treated as guests, allowed to wash and change, and to be fed until their bellies were full. With their shouts of praise ringing in my ears, I left the courtyard and went immediately to my *kah*, or muniment room, where I pulled down maps of the eastern desert. I unrolled the best of these, placing copper weight on the corners whilst telling Djarka to stand close.

'You know this place, don't you? Don't lie, Djarka, I can tell by your face. What is it, the Valley of the Grey Dawn?' I glanced up. 'Now, I know the nearside of the eastern desert well. Only a march away are the alabaster, turquoise and diamond mines, but further east, towards the Great Green . . .' I shook my head.

'This place is sacred to our people,' Djarka replied. He pointed his finger along the map. 'When we first came into Egypt, we did not follow the accepted routes but crossed the Sinai, keeping away from the fertile lands of the Delta.' He traced the line with his finger. 'We came south before striking west. The Valley of the Grey Dawn and its oasis was a good place to rest and replenish water supplies. I understand we buried our dead there, those who had perished on the journey. They also held,' he moved closer, 'the Gerh en Sheta Aru – the Night of the Secret Ceremonies.'

'What were those?'

He shook his head. 'I have only heard stories. My people talk of the Gerh en Sheta Kheb Ta, the Night of the Ploughing up of the Earth, after it has been soaked in blood.'

'Your sacrifices?' I asked.

'We sacrifice animals, just as the sun sets.'

'Have you ever been there?'

Djarka shook his head. 'I have heard the stories. It lies directly east. Draw a line from the City of the Aten towards the Great Green, follow that line and you'll reach this place of slaughter.'

'A place of slaughter,' I repeated. 'You know, Djarka, and so do I, that that's where Meryre and his people died, those who fled Memphis and Thebes as well as the great fortress at Buhen.'

'I agree.' Djarka tapped the map. 'I suspect Tutu and Meryre, probably helped by their own people, the Apiru, went north to the oasis near the Valley of the Grey Dawn. They may have been given an escort, which turned on them, or a force was already waiting for them.'

311

'Horemheb?' I asked.

Djarka sucked on his lips, wiping the sweat from his forehead with the back of his forearms. 'Mert is one of my people,
probably a daughter of one of the guides. Whoever is responsible for the massacre committed treachery. They wouldn't trust
Horemheb or Rameses. The killers posed as friends and allies.'

'Ay,' I breathed. 'He's the only one who could do that. He
could command his brother Nakhtimin.' I beat a tattoo on the
map with my finger. 'What I think happened is that Ay allowed
Meryre to escape from Memphis, at the same time giving Tutu
safe conduct to the Valley of the Grey Dawn. Once there, they
were massacred. Ay demands Akenhaten's memory be forgotten.
He doesn't want the Atenists fleeing into Canaan and stirring
up more trouble, so he decided to wipe them out, root and branch.
That's my theory. Your people still consider Ay one of them?'

'My lord Ay.' Djarka smiled sourly. 'My Lord Ay is whatever
he wishes to be. Of Apiru descent, certainly of the tribe of Israar,
but more Egyptian than the Egyptians. He is not interested in
legends, or Gods, only in power.'

I returned to studying the map.

'But Ay's a politician,' I continued. 'If you know the legends
and stories of your people, so does he.'

'Before Ay left Ahkmin,' Djarka gestured round the muniment room, 'he had all the records of our people destroyed. I
suspect that he had the same done in the libraries, record offices
and archives of Thebes.'

I rolled the map up and sat on a stool, staring at the floor.
Ay would cover his tracks carefully. He had to assure Horemheb,
the priests and generals of Thebes that the days of Akenhaten
were finished, that a new Pharaoh would rule Egypt. Horemheb
would accept that. I recalled Rameses' cold, cruel face, his
shrewd eyes. If I was following this path about the true source
of Akenhaten's Great Heresy, then it was only a matter of time
before Rameses stumbled upon it himself.

'When I questioned Khufu, yes,' I beat the map against the
floor, 'when I questioned Khufu, he talked of Akenhaten's
prophecies. How Pharaoh wrote down his visions, and entrusted
them to the mysterious Watchers. So there are records left. But
where, Djarka?'

My lieutenant remained stony-faced and cold-eyed.

'Do you know anything?' I snapped.

'Master, if I did,' Djarka replied, 'I assure you, you'd be the first to know.'

I caught the sarcasm in his voice, and standing up, thrust the map back into his hands.

'You, Djarka, represent the danger. Rameses would regard you as as much of a threat to the power of Egypt as Akenhaten. You only tell me what you have to. What do you think will really happen, Djarka?' I stepped closer. 'Tell me now, in this room, dark and empty; our only witnesses are the oil lamps and the mice which scurry about. Tell me now, not as my servant or my lieutenant but as my friend. I ask you to speak with true voice.'

Djarka opened his mouth to reply.

'The truth.' I caught him by the wrist. 'Tell me the truth, Djarka. Be the good archer you are, hit the mark full in the centre. You have not told me everything, have you?'

'My lord, I have told you what I can.'

'My name is Mahu. I am not your lord. I am asking you as one friend to another.'

Djarka gave a great sigh and slumped down on the stool I had vacated.

'What I believe is that one day the prophecies will come true. My people will become a great power in Egypt. One day we will leave the banks of the Nile for the lands promised in Canaan. But when and where? The times and seasons? Only our nameless god knows that.' He shook his head. 'More than this I cannot, will not say.'

I left Djarka in the muniment room and wandered the palace. Undoubtedly, Meryre and all his people had died in a hideous massacre. Ay was attempting to close the door on the past, lock and seal it, but the likes of Djarka proved the roots were still there. It was only a matter of time before fresh shoots appeared. I became so agitated I decided to go into the city, carried on a litter, its curtains half-drawn. I would visit one of the pleasure houses. As I journeyed, I listened to the sounds of the city, glimpsing the passing scenes through a gap in the curtains. I tried to calm my mind, half watching the greenery, the sycamore and acacia as they jutted above whitewashed walls which gleamed in the sunlight. The heat of the day was gone. The avenue had been washed by slaves carrying large goatskins of water from the canal, strewn with rose petals. Settling back on the cushions, soothed by the rhythm of my bearers, I recalled the story of the sand-dwellers. How many men, women and children had died in that massacre? I could imagine them grouped round the oasis as Nakhtimin's war chariots, supported by foot soldiers and archers, swept in at dawn, or dusk, to wreak bloody havoc. In such a desolate place very few would have escaped. Some would have tried to flee up the valley, but Ay had chosen his place well. I wondered about Mert. She must have hidden and, shocked by what she had seen and heard, lost her wits. Mert disturbed me. Something about her reminded me of Nefertiti. I pulled close the litter curtains and returned to a question nagging at my heart. Should I go out to the Valley of the Grey Dawn and see what had happened? Yet that would mean leaving the Prince.

I was still turning the matter over in my mind when we arrived at the pleasure house, with its shaded gardens and flower-filled courtyard, its doors decorated with gold and silver and encrusted with lapis lazuli. The Place of Soothing, as the beautiful handmaids who worked there called it. It was not just a pleasure of the flesh which took me there. Its chambers of delight were an oasis of calm, where small boys wafted ostrich plumes soaked in the most precious of perfumes. Wine as sweet as honey was served in silver-chased goblets. I was always a welcome guest. Even as I stepped out of my litter, the beautiful, gold-skinned handmaids were waiting, dressed only in their white-fringed kilts, soft golden flesh glittering with jewellery, heavy curled wigs drenched in khiphye shading their lovely faces, sloe-eyes ringed with green kohl sparkling with excitement. Cool fingers, their nails hennaed a deep purple, stretched out to touch me. Lips, as red as the ripest cherries, were eager to kiss. I had promised myself an evening of indolence. Nevertheless, that pleasure house was also a place of business where I could listen to the rumours and gossip of the city, the chatter of the marketplace, the grumbles of the merchants who flocked there after the labours of the day. The handmaids, chattering like beautiful birds, would, as they served me silver platters of date cakes or dishes of the ripest grapes, tell me about this and that. On that particular evening I caught a refrain I had heard before in reports received from my spies. News about the emptying of the tombs had spread; people were openly wondering what future, if any, lay in store for this most splendid city.

Of course, if the handmaids spied for me, they also spied for others, so my reply was always the same: the City of the Aten would last for a thousand years. Yet even as I spoke, I realised that I was lying, and the handmaids themselves sensed that.

On that particular evening I left the pleasure house late. Darkness had fallen, the stars were bright in a black sky. I was slightly drunk as I climbed into my litter. Around me I heard the chatter of my mercenary escort, the overseer of the bearers rapping out orders. I lay back on the cushions. We crossed the cobbled courtyard and debouched out into the street, bathed in the light of torches burning fiercely on long poles driven into the ground. The litter stopped. Raucous shouting shattered the night. I pulled back the curtains. A peasant's cart had overturned, blocking the route we were to take down towards the main avenue of the city. I was careless. I ordered my bearers to place the litter down and clambered out. A crowd had gathered, eager to join in the argument or just watch one of the Great Ones being inconvenienced. My mercenary escort was shouting for the driver of the cart. The donkey had been unhitched, and glancing round, I couldn't see its owner, only the cart lying on its side, heavy wooden wheels still spinning. My mercenaries were attempting to move it, offering to pay onlookers if they would help. The wine fumes were still heavy. My wits were slow. Only the creaking wheel of that overturned cart alerted me. No peasant ever unhitched his donkey and left his cart, whatever it contained.

My bearers were standing helplessly. I moved back into the litter, hand going beneath the cushion looking for my knife, even as I heard the strident yell. One of my bearers went down, a dagger thrust through his neck. He had fallen blocking the path of the other assassins, dark-bearded men, faces and bodies hidden by cloaks and cowls. I sprang from the litter. One of the

315

assassins, knocking a bearer aside, came lunging, knife hand back. I ducked, thrusting in my own dagger, aware of an attacker closing in from my right. My mercenaries were now alerted. One of them threw his own sword and, more out of luck than skill, caught the assassin in the leg, bringing him crashing down. I gazed around. The onlookers were scattering. One mercenary was still struggling with an attacker; a second assailant was screaming in pain, clutching at the knife even as he choked on his own blood. A third was trying to crawl away. A mercenary ran up, sword ready to finish him off, but I shouted at him to stop. The cart now forgotten, the mercenaries formed a protective half-ring. Were there any more assassins?

The streets emptied, dark shapes flitting up the alleyways into the night. I glimpsed one face, changed from the last time I had seen him, darkened by the sun, black hair straggling down to his shoulders with a thick moustache and beard. I recognised those eyes, that hateful glance. Atenists may have died out in the Valley of the Grey Dawn; High Priest Meryre had not. For a moment, the measure of a few heartbeats, my gaze met his, but before I could speak he was gone.

The assassin who had taken my knife in his throat now lay silent, blood gushing from the gaping wound, as well as seeping out of his mouth and nostrils. The one struggling with the bearers had been dragged away, arms pinioned behind his back. The other was still screaming at the deep sword cut to his leg. The blade had severed the tendon behind the knee. I stood over him, prodding his shoulder with my walking cane taken from the litter. The man's eyes were already glazing over, his lips were blood-smattered and his death rattle had begun. I sliced his throat. I had my prisoner, and that was enough.

By the time I returned to the palace, entering through a side gate, I was sober enough, though shaken at how close the assassin had come. I cursed my own ineptitude and carelessness. I had always thought the danger was in Thebes. I asked for another bowl of wine, summoned my captain of the mercenaries and had the prisoner taken to the House of Chains. He was spread-eagled on the floor, ankles and wrists manacled. I knelt down, grasped his hair and pulled his head back.

'Speak! Speak!'

The man spat at me. I drove my knee into his face, crushing his nose.

'Speak!' I repeated.

Again the man tried to spit, but this time his lips only spluttered blood. I withdrew. My mercenary captain began to skin him alive, beginning with his arms. The man shook and screamed. I returned and stood over him.

'Speak,' I urged, 'and death will come swiftly. Stay silent or lie and each day my captain will strip part of your skin.'

Another hour passed before the man broke. Gabbling and stuttering, he could tell me very little. Once he had been a soldier, a veteran in the regiment of the Aten, and later body servant to the Lord Meryre. He had not gone to Buhen and was surprised by the reappearance of Meryre and others of his circle who had crept back in disguise into the City of the Aten. They brought a hideous tale. A bloody massacre had occurred out in the eastern desert: Lord Tutu and hundreds of their followers had been killed on the orders of Lord Ay, who had sent chariot squadrons and troops of mercenaries allegedly to provide protection and safe passage through the desert and across Sinai. According to our prisoner, Meryre and about a dozen soldiers had escaped by fleeing across the desert away from the oasis. Using what wealth remained, they had travelled back into the Delta before moving to the City of the Aten, sheltering in the slums south of the city.

I immediately ordered my police and mercenaries to search there, but they returned empty-handed; they had found nothing except deserted hovels, whilst those who lived nearby had heard and seen nothing at all. The prisoner was only a soldier, paid by the Atenists to carry out my assassination.

'Why me?' I asked. 'Why did Lord Meryre return here? I had no hand in the massacre.'

'He holds you responsible,' the assassin replied. 'He thought it would be easier here. He has a blood feud with you, blood for blood.'

For two days I questioned that prisoner. I didn't even allow Djarka to approach him. I alerted Nebamun and his chariot squadrons on the clifftops. Meryre, however, proved too cunning and slipped away.

Eventually I was satisfied. I ordered my captain to cut the prisoner's throat to give him speedy release and immediately made the decision. Urgent letters were drawn up and dispatched to the Lord Ay in Thebes. My chief messengers were entrusted with the task. Ay should be warned that his massacre was now well known. I closed one letter reminding him that he might well reap what he had sown. I also decided to go out to the eastern desert to visit the Valley of the Grey Dawn for myself. Colonel Nebamun objected, as did Djarka, but I was insistent. The Prince would be moved into the care of Pentju, whose residence would be ringed by every available soldier. They would guard the Prince and Ankhesenamun whilst Djarka, myself and Mert, together with the sand-dwellers, would visit the Valley of the Grey Dawn. I demanded twenty of Nebamun's chariots and the best guides and scouts he could provide to accompany half my mercenary corps. Nebamun reluctantly accepted my orders, though Djarka was full of protests.

'If you leave this city,' he objected, 'something might happen. These rumours,' he protested, 'about the City of the Aten being deserted. They have turned ugly.'

'Do you think they are connected with Meryre's return?' I asked.

'Of course! We should forget the Valley of the Grey Dawn.' Djarka stepped closer. 'We should forget this city. It is time, my lord, you returned to Thebes.'

I shook my head. 'Time enough,' I whispered. 'I must visit that valley.'

'Why?' Djarka insisted.

'I don't really know.' I smiled. 'But when I do,' I clapped him on the shoulder, 'you will be the first to know.'

an-cc-kek
(Ancient Egyptian for 'dark valley')

Chapter 16

Preparations for our expedition dominated the next few weeks. We would have to face the savage heat in an arduous journey across arid sands, where wells and springs were scarce and jealously guarded by fierce tribes of desert wanderers. Laden with bribes, envoys were sent out to treat with these. Safe passage was assured, expert scouts hired, sturdy donkeys bought, water skins and provisions carefully assembled.

Only veterans used to the searing heat and desert warfare were selected. Colonel Nebamun promised to supervise everything whilst I concentrated on the reports coming in from my spies in the city, who all chanted the same hymn, of a growing disquiet, a grumbling malice against the palace as well as the Royal Circle in Thebes. Powerful merchants and nobles were hiring retinues, whilst our patrols along the river often discovered arms being brought in, yet for every dagger found, five remained untraced. None of my scribes could discover the source of this growing unrest. Meryre's agents had spread fear, moving like shadows in the dead of night. They had sown their crop and left us to reap the harvest. The news of the hideous massacre somewhere out in the eastern desert was openly discussed in the beer shops and marketplace. Ugly rumour drifted like curls of black smoke, yet there was little I could do to prevent it. Chariot squadrons were brought into the city. The palace was fortified. Masons and builders strengthened its walls and gateways. Watchtowers were set up. All roads leading to the palace, as well as its inner precincts and courtyards, were heavily patrolled, both day and night. No one was admitted unless they carried a document sealed with my own cartouche and knew the password for that particular watch.

Nebamun, Djarka and I pored over maps of the city, organising how, if necessary, the palace could be evacuated, and the Royal Household safely escorted down to the war barges; their captains were already under orders to leave at a moment's notice. Nebamun wanted to send messengers to Memphis and Thebes asking for reinforcements, even permission to withdraw. I told him I would take responsibility, leaving the grizzled veteran to glower angrily back. Journeys into the city were no longer pleasant excursions. The Royal Household was confined to the palace gardens and courtyards. If I, or any of my officials, left the palace, we were always accompanied by a military escort. The Prince seemed unperturbed by these preparations; I would invite him for a game of Senet or, early in the morning, take him down to the courtyard to practise archery.

Tutankhamun was playful and vigorous enough, though he constantly favoured his left side; at times he complained about aches in his legs and arms. Occasionally, he would sit as if drugged, a dreamy look in those doe-like eyes, a smile on his half-open lips, as if he were savouring some secret joke or could see something I couldn't. My suspicions that he was simple, of vacuous wit, would re-emerge, only to be rudely shattered by an abrupt change in mood. Like a scribe learning the law, Tutankhamun would crouch before me and closely question me about his father, the city we lived in, and above all, the worship of the Aten. He was aware of the Apiru and the stories of the people of Israar, and I began to regret Djarka's influence over him. Tutankhamun also became sensitive to my moods. If he believed he was annoying me, he would swiftly change the topic. I found him quick-witted, with a ready humour. I called him Asht-Heru, Many-Face, because he proved to be such an able mimic. I would roar with laughter as Tutankhamun imitated Colonel Nebamun and strode up the room, shoulders back, chin tucked into his chest, glaring at me from under his eyebrows, shouting in a deep voice. Abruptly he'd change, becoming a lady of the court. Only once did such mimicry cause a ripple of fear. Tutankhamun seemed to have little love for the priests, the

Rem-Prieta, or Men of God. He could mimic their pious looks, their sanctimonious walk, their love of being seen to pray publicly, and the way they sang, more like a whine through their nose. On this occasion he must have caught my sad glance because he came running up.

'Uncle Mahu! Uncle Mahu! You are not laughing?'

'Oh, you are funny enough!' I clasped his hands. 'It's just that I have thought of something.' I didn't tell him how, as a young man, Akenhaten had loathed and mocked the priests of Amun. Tutankhamun was intelligent enough to realise this mimicry did not please me, and quickly reverted to imitations of Nakhtimin and Djarka.

I used that time of preparation to study the Prince more closely. I dismissed my secret doubts that he was Pentju's son. The more I watched him, the more I could see Akenhaten. Like his father, Tutankhamun was dedicated to a physical purity. If he spilt beer on his robes, he immediately changed, and during the day would often demand perfumed water to wash his hands. He loved to be anointed with oil and perfume. I put this down to Ankhesenamun's influence; she now seemed to dominate his days.

In the main, Tutankhamun was kind and gentle. He often expressed regret at the two tortoises he had killed, yet that streak of angry malice could still surface. I'd catch occasional glimpses of this: an irritation with a servant, or shoving aside a piece of duck not cooked to his taste. The more serious incident occurred a week before we left. I was in the garden, dictating to my scribes. The laughter of Tutankhamun and the ladies of the court was abruptly replaced by loud screams. I hurried out of the pavilion across to the small palm grove where Ankhesenamun, Amedeta and Mert were resting in the shade. Tutankhamun, a thin cane in his hand, stood over a cowering servant. He was berating him, then he brought the rod down, lashing the unfortunate's head and shoulders. Other servants stood by, watching helplessly. As I approached, Ankhesenamun stopped laughing and called out to Tutankhamun to stop, but the boy, dancing with rage, brought the cane down time and time again, drawing blood from the man's cheek and lips. I hurried over and grasped the cane. Tutankhamun would not let go. His face was no longer serene but blotched with rage, eyes glaring, lips twisted, a slight froth staining the corner of his mouth.

'My lord,' I urged, 'let go.'

'Uncle Mahu! Be gone! This *smett*,' he spat out the word for slave, 'I caught in the act of *ta-ta*.' He glared at the miscreant. 'He was fondling himself to bring his own seed. I caught him there behind the bush. He has polluted himself. He has defiled his body in my presence.'

I pulled the cane from Tutankhamun's hand.

'How dare you?' Tutankhamun yelled back. 'You, too, are a *smett*, Baboon of the South! You are defiled.' He stood, hands clenched, quivering with rage. I glanced up. Amedeta and Mert, together with the servants, had fled. Ankhesenamun was staring coolly at me, her beautiful face slightly turned, clearly enjoying the confrontation. Tutankhamun seized the opportunity to run at me, fists flailing. I grasped his arms, even as I recalled his father's hideous rages.

'My lord, you are unwell!' I snapped.

'I am the Leopard God,' Tutankhamun hissed. 'I am Horus in the South, Horus in the Ground, Horus in the Spirit Soul, Horus of the Red Eyes.' He tried to break free, as if to pursue the servant, who had crawled away on his hands and knees. 'I am Lord of the Two Lands.' He turned back to me. 'I live in the truth.'

I shook him, slapped him gently on the cheek. In the twinkling of an eye the rage disappeared, and both face and body sagged. I let go, and he ran across to Ankhesenamun, crouching for shelter in the crook of her arm, thumb to his mouth.

'He polluted himself,' he whispered. 'Only a Prince can bring forth his own seed.'

Ankhesenamun's hand hung down just above the young boy's crotch. I wondered what teaching she had provided.

'Does this happen often?' I asked.

'Ask your spy Djarka.'

'I do. He's not a spy. He protects the boy.'

'For how long, Uncle Mahu?' Ankhesenamun's eyes rounded in mock innocence. 'How long will you guard us? Weeks slide into months, and months into years. My husband to be,' eyes still watching me, she turned and lightly kissed Tutankhamun's forehead, 'will one day have to emerge and walk in the light of the sun. He cannot stay hidden for ever.'

'When the time comes.'

'The time is already here,' she retorted, leaning forward. 'I have heard the rumours. The city is unsafe. Why do you go out into the desert, Uncle Mahu?'

'You know why, my lady. I am sure your grandfather has written to you, whilst you must have spies amongst my scribes. The Atenists were massacred out in the eastern desert. Lord Meryre escaped and attempted to take my life.'

Ankhesenamun smiled thinly. 'Grandfather always said Meryre was a fool.'

'A dangerous one,' I added.

'Why can't we return to Thebes?'

'Because I have direct custody of the Prince. We shall go when it is right.' I rose, bowed and walked away.

'Uncle Mahu! Uncle Mahu!'

I turned. Tutankhamun came hurrying across the grass, arms out. I crouched and he flung himself at me. I could feel his hands on the back of my neck, his hot cheek pressed against mine.

'I am sorry, Uncle Mahu.'

I pulled him away. 'Why did you do that?' I asked.

'I don't know.' His eyes had that dreamy gaze. 'I don't know, Uncle Mahu. I feel as if the blood bubbles within me. I remember who I am.'

'Does Ankhesenamun . . .' I gazed across at the beautiful cobra still curled beneath the tree, smiling serenely across. 'Does Ankhesenamun tell you who you are?'

'She tells me everything,' Tutankhamun whispered. 'She says we will be a great king and queen. I shall be Horus in the South. My name and power shall reach the ends of the earth. She lies beside me in bed, strokes my body and whispers all sorts of sweet things to me.'

'I am sure she does.' I disengaged his arms. 'Remember, my lord, you are a prince. You are like a soldier in training. That servant, you should not have beaten him!'

'But he was dirty.' The anger reappeared. 'He was defiled. He cannot commit such acts in our presence.'

'How old are you, my lord?'

'Soon I shall be eight.'

'Soon you will be eight.' I went to cup his face in my hands, but Tutankhamun stepped back, gave a cursory bow and returned to his sister.

By now Pentju had moved back into the palace. I wanted him there as guardian when I left for the eastern desert. I asked him to examine the Prince carefully. Pentju had been accustomed to do this, but increasingly, Ankhesenamun had begun to interfere with glib excuses or protest that the time was not right. On this occasion, however, I had the Prince brought to my quarters. For an entire afternoon the physician talked to him, making him run and jump, touching his body, asking him questions. He asked me to be absent, as Tutankhamun did not like to be examined by anyone in the presence of others, the only exception being Ankhesenamun. In the evening Pentju dined alone with me on duck and goose, delicately roasted and grilled, a favourite dish ever since our time as Children of the Kap. On that evening, I noticed how he had aged: he was more flabby, the veins in his cheeks and nose quite marked. I clinked my goblet against his.

'Physician, heal thyself. You are drinking too much.'

'I do heal myself!' he quipped back. 'The wine makes me forget the past, Mahu. It drives away the ghosts which cluster in the corners. My wife, my children, my kinsmen, Princess Khiya.' He bit his lip.

'And the Prince?' I asked.

Pentju stared back into the chamber. We were sitting on a balcony, a place I loved to dine; it was closely guarded against eavesdroppers.

'Is the Prince sick?' I asked.

'No more so than his father.' Pentju sipped at his wine. 'His limbs ache and he has inherited his father's condition. As he matures,' Pentju gestured with his hands, 'his shoulders will grow broader, but so will his hips. He'll have a protuberant belly and the same chest as his father; his hands, fingers and toes will be longer than the average man's.'

326

'Like his father?' I interrupted.

'Like his father,' Pentju agreed, 'but not as pronounced or marked.'

'And his moods?'

Pentju laughed quietly. 'Mahu, I can tell you, as I've said before, how the heart beats, what causes a worm in the intestine or the symptoms of some disease. But a man's soul? Even harder, a child's! He is the son of Khiya; he has inherited her gentleness. He's also Akenhaten's son.' He picked up a piece of firm cheese made from pressed, salted curds and sniffed at it. 'Very tasty,' he mused. He cut a slice.

'He is his father's son?' I insisted.

'Ever the policeman . . .' Pentju sighed. 'Always the question. Yes, he is Akenhaten's son. He suffers what my learned colleagues would call rushes of blood, and changes of mood, when he can become violent. As he grows older he may even suffer from fits, the falling sickness.'

'Could he beget an heir?'

'The boy is only eight.' Pentju grimaced. 'His penis, his manhood are a matter for the future. I don't see why he shouldn't.'

'Could he ever,' I demanded, 'be like his father?'

'No one else could be like Akenhaten.' Pentju laughed softly. 'A great deal depends on the next few years. It is time he returned to Thebes; he must forget everything there is about the Aten.'

'And Ankhesenamun?' I asked.

'Ah, there's a game you've lost, Mahu.' The physician leaned across the table, cleaning his teeth with his tongue. 'As the boy grows older, her influence will grow. There's nothing you can do about that, except, perhaps, kill Ankhesenamun!'

I often wonder now: should I have listened more carefully to Pentju's diagnosis? What would have happened if Ankhesenamun had died and Tutankhamun married another? Yet she was protected by the brooding shadow of her grandfather and others of the Akhmin gang. Ankhesenamun was certainly mischievous enough for anything. She'd taken Mert under her wing, and that young woman had emerged as an exquisite beauty. Ankhesenamun and Amedeta, being the sly bitches they were, soon realised Djarka's interest in this beautiful young

327

woman. They refused her nothing, often braiding her black hair in a net of multi-coloured glasswork bordered by half-circles of pearls. Gold anklets and bracelets shimmered on Mert's legs and wrists; a gorgeous gorget of cornelian emphasised her neck; her beautiful body was adorned in the purest linen robes; a purple-fringed shawl hung about her shoulders and silver-thonged sandals were on her feet. They taught her how to paint her face, using green kohl to accentuate her eyes, and gave her presents of the costliest perfumes. They would often invite us to supper, where those two minxes would sit and watch as Djarka and I competed for Mert's attention. In the end the contest was unequal. Mert remained silent but she could talk with her eyes. Djarka was the chosen one. In the weeks leading up to the military expeditions they grew closer. Djarka coaxed her to speak. I often found them chatting in their own tongue, though never once would she describe what had happened in the Valley of the Grey Dawn. Instead she would simply fall silent, shaking her head, withdrawing into her own private nightmares.

'Is there nothing else she can tell us?' I asked.

Djarka swore solemnly that she could not. 'She remembers her life before the massacre, and what happened afterwards, but if I question her,' he shrugged, 'she knows nothing; her eyes go vacant. She remembers her father and her brothers going out to the valley. They took her with them; they were to act as guides and be heavily rewarded.'

'Guides to where?' I asked.

'I don't know,' Djarka confessed. 'She remembers her journey out; after that, what she calls the blackness falls.'

In the end I had to let such matters rest.

On the day before we left, Nebamun and Djarka made one final attempt to change my mind. I refused. I did not inform them about my most recent letter from the Lord Ay. I kept that to myself. Ay had couched his request in courteous terms, yet he made it very clear that he disapproved of my expedition. Moreover, he added, if I thought the situation dangerous, I should immediately withdraw the Royal Household to Thebes. I dispatched a courier back saying the crisis had passed and I would consider his request.

On the morning of the eighth day in the second month of Peret, our expedition left the City of the Aten: forty chariots, a train of carts and a corps of three hundred mercenaries. Djarka and Mert were also included, as were the three sand-dwellers, now confident that they basked in high favour. They were well fed, and plump after their long stay as guests in the palace. The journey proved to be a nightmare. The further east we travelled, the more desolate and arid the Red Lands became. The heat turned oppressive. Sand storms blasted us during the day; freezing blackness cloaked us at night. Bands of marauders hung on our flanks ready to exploit any weakness. At times we had to hunt for fresh meat, and on one occasion we clashed with these fierce nomads. During the day we moved like a military convoy; at night we formed the carts and chariots into a protective ring. I had thought the journey would take three weeks in all, following a circuitous route which led from one oasis to another. In the end it took a month. I knew we were approaching the valley when the undulating desert began to peter out; through the shifting heat haze I glimpsed gorse, dry trees and rocky outcrops. The shrubs and trees led towards the oasis at the entrance to the Valley of the Grey Dawn. An eerie place, its rocks and cliffs seemed to sprout from the desert floor, shifting in colour, a dull grey at dawn, a fiery red in the full heat of the day, becoming paler as the day wore on.

We approached the oasis lying just within the valley mouth as the sun, that fiery burst of colour, the tormentor of our days, slipped beneath the far horizon. The darkness spread its wings to be greeted by the raucous cries of the night prowlers. The Red Lands had always oppressed me; that fearsome valley was a nightmare: its rocky cliffs rose out of the sands, whirling clouds of dust covered desiccated bushes, gorse and dried-out trees, casting them black against the sky. The ground grew hard underfoot, easier for our carts and chariots. The tree-fringed oasis was a pleasant contrast, shimmering green with its long grass, fresh bushes and groves of sturdy palm trees. The source of all this freshness was an underground spring. The smell of fresh water and wild flowers was as welcome to us as the most fragrant perfume.

We camped for the night. Carts and chariots were pulled into a ring, horse lines protected by rows of small fires to drive back the predators which circled the oasis from dusk till dawn. Even as we arrived and set up our tents and pavilions, we discovered fearsome signs of the massacre: bones, skulls, entire skeletons, arrowheads, javelin points, a broken dagger and small pieces of chewed leather. Everywhere we looked, beneath bushes, in the shade of the trees or the rocky outcrop around the pools, such remains reminded us we were in a place of ghosts where spirits burned and the dead flamed in a darkness beyond ours. Mert was subdued. She clung to Djarka, muttering under her breath. Beyond the perimeters of our camp echoed the ugly coughing roars of lions and the heart-chilling growl of hyaenas.

The captain of the guard interrupted my evening meal, asking me to join him at the makeshift gate in our line of carts and chariots. He was a Nubian, a foot soldier who had cursed every wheeled vehicle throughout the entire expedition; now he tapped the wheels of a chariot and loudly thanked the Gods for such defence. He shouted at the archers on the top of the wagons to loose fire arrows. 'I'll show you why, my lord. You must see this before you retire.'

The fire arrows were loosed, the archers concentrating on one spot. Those eerie growls from the darkness increased. In the light of the falling arrows I glimpsed the prowlers: monstrous hyaenas with great heavy heads, long snouts and powerful jaws; glaring red eyes, their ruffed manes like collars of darkness around their necks.

'They recognise this as a place of slaughter,' the mercenary whispered. 'My lord, they are more dangerous than the lions if they attack in a pack.'

'Why should they?'

'They have been brought here by the corpses,' he muttered. 'We also ring the only source of fresh water for miles. They have smelled our food from the camp fires as well as the fresh flesh of our horses and donkeys, my lord Mahu.' His face twisted in anxiety. 'We should not stay here too long.'

I stayed at the gate, staring out into the darkness, the sweat chilling on the nape of my neck. I had heard about these hyaenas, striped and powerful, and more dangerous than their cousins who prowled the edge of town or slunk into the City of the

Dead in search of some morsel. These creatures were ruthless hunters, as well as scavengers. I recalled stories told by desert scouts: how once these beasts smelt blood they'd track an injured man for days, whilst camp fires and weapons, palisades and fences sometimes proved no deterrent. I ordered the horses and pack ponies to be brought closer into the camp and redoubled the guard. I offered rewards to any man who could devise a better way of defending the camp. The only suggestions were to increase the lines of small fires and issue strict instructions how the perimeter was not to be crossed at night. People were to sleep in groups, whilst, even during the day, no patrols should be fewer than three men, one of whom must be a bowman.

The next morning we began the grisly task of collecting the remains. I sent scouts and carts far into the valley, and they returned carrying baskets piled high with bones and skulls as well as scraps of clothing, leather and weaponry. We burned them as an act of purification as well as reverence. We began work before dawn, resting during the midday heat and continuing until darkness fell. The valley was long and steep-sided; caves lay on each side, concealed behind clumps of gorse and bush, each containing the remains of survivors, men, women and children, as well as the bones of their animals. It was a hideous, heart-searing task. One scout brought in a basket of skulls, all belonging to children, as well as the pathetic remains of their toys. The funeral fires were kept burning not just to purify that place of abomination; the flames and smoke also kept back the hyaenas, who, during the day, would watch from afar. Now and again they'd close in, heads down, almost nosing the ground, loping along before bursting into a full, stretched run, only to be driven back by a hail of arrows or burning cloths soaked in oil. At night they became bolder, drawing closer; on the third night they attacked one of the carts, snatching off a guard, dragging him screaming into the darkness. There was nothing we could do to help but stand and listen to his horrific screams, the yelping of the prowlers, and the sound of their powerful jaws tearing him apart. We lit fires on the far side of the carts; archers were instructed to fire the occasional volley of flaring arrows into the night.

My men became restless. The valley was a haunting, sombre

331

place, a hall of prowling demons and restless spirits. By late afternoon the rocks were fiery to the touch, and above us, an ominous warning of what might happen, great feathery winged vultures circled. On the fourth day the hyaenas attacked early in the morning. One patrol became detached from the rest. Three men struggling with baskets were ambushed just within the valley by a group of hyaenas who attacked so savagely, so swiftly, there was little we could do to help. The men grew mutinous. They hated the brooding, ominous silence and feared these powerful creatures audacious enough to attack during the day. At the end of the week I gave the orders for preparations to leave. I had discovered nothing startling, but had collected sufficient evidence to understand what had happened.

'In all, about four hundred souls,' I dictated to Djarka, sitting like a scribe, a papyrus scroll across his lap, 'died here: men, women and children, soldiers, scribes and officials. They included the refugees from Buhen and Thebes, as well as Meryre's retinue from Memphis. There were soldiers, possibly mercenaries, amongst their company, all fervent Atenists. They gathered here carts, chariots and pack animals, dependent on Apiru guides. They intended to slip north across Sinai into Canaan, protected by a force dispatched from Thebes which consisted of at least an entire chariot squadron, archers and veteran foot soldiers.'

'How do you know that?' Djarka asked.

'We found the wheel of one of their chariots, probably broken off as they were pursuing survivors. General Nakhtimin supervised this massacre on the orders of Lord Ay. Most of the arrowheads found belong to Kushite bowmen, who support the various chariot squadrons. We also found the head cloth of a member of an imperial regiment. General Nakhtimin didn't have it all his own way; the Atenists fought back. The attack began near the oasis. Some fled into the desert, where they died or were killed by their pursuers or sand-dwellers. The rest took refuge in the valley, hiding in its caves. Nakhtimin's force must have stayed here for days, hunting down fugitives; scouts have found evidence of their camp fires and latrine pits.'

'And Meryre?'

'I suspect Meryre and a group of soldiers, probably mercenaries and scribes, fled at the beginning of the massacre. They must have hidden before making their way via a more circuitous route back to the river.'

I was interrupted by a loud scream, more like the keening of a mourning woman, a shrill cry of anguish from the heart which echoed across the camp. I whirled round. Mert was kneeling on the ground, clawing at her hair and beating her breast. She had silently approached us, knelt and listened to what I had said. If Djarka had seen her, he hadn't commented, now used to her constant presence. She had been touched by Ma'at; the truth about what I had said had stirred her memory. Djarka put his writing tray aside and hurried to comfort her, crouching down, arms about her shoulders. She must have knelt for at least an hour, rocking backwards and forwards, eyes closed, cheeks wet with tears. Servants and guards, alarmed by her screams, came hurrying up. I drove them away, ordering one of them to bring a cup of wine with a tincture of our precious opium. Djarka fed her this, and between sobs, she gave her own account.

She and her father and two brothers had been part of the Apiru scouts. They had accepted the task without demur, being promised lavish rewards, reinforced by the bonds of friendship between themselves and many of the Atenists. According to Mert, Lord Tutu had led his people out of the fortress of Buhen and been joined by others from Thebes. They had gathered at an oasis miles to the north-east of Thebes, where the Apiru had met them. She talked of at least four hundred people, a horde of pack animals and carts well provisioned and guarded by mercenaries. They had arrived at the Valley of the Grey Dawn and been joined by Meryre and other stragglers from their company. They were in good spirits, determined to leave Egypt, cross Sinai and enter Canaan. Lord Tutu was of Canaanite birth; he believed that in the new territories they would be able to worship their God under the protection of the Hittite king, as well as those princes of Canaan hostile to Egypt.

The atmosphere in the camp had been festive. The Atenists truly believed they were escaping persecution. Many of them cherished the hope that in Canaan their leader, Akenhaten, would once again manifest himself. This was the constant chatter about the camp fires. They also put great trust in the

333

promises of Lord Ay. Their only fear was of troops from Memphis under Horemheb, as well as those Egyptian patrols which guarded the mines of Sinai. Lord Ay, however, had promised a military escort. After five days of waiting this had eventually arrived: chariot squadrons, a corps of Nubian archers and Menfyt foot soldiers from one of the imperial regiments outside Thebes. General Nakhtimin had solemnly vowed that his presence and the sight of his standard would be surety enough for a safe departure from Egypt. He had been cordial, talking to Meryre and Lord Tutu as if they were close friends and allies. Late on the day they had arrived, the massacre began. The camp was being prepared for the evening meal. After a hail of arrows, the chariots came racing in, followed by the foot soldiers. Some of the Atenists had stood and fought; Lord Tutu and a group of priests had fled deeper into the valley.

'And Meryre?' I asked. 'The High Priest?'

'He wasn't there that evening.' Mert wiped her eyes. 'That's right: we, the Apiru scouts, stayed on the edge of the oasis. Lord Meryre's entourage always left just before sundown to go into the desert.'

'To perform sacrifice,' Djarka observed.

'So that's how they escaped,' I whispered. 'They would leave armed with provisions.'

'How did *you* escape?' Djarka asked.

'I hid in the oasis. Now I remember. I was beneath a bush, my face pressed against the earth. I pretended to be dead. Nakhtimin's men came through. They began to plunder and strip corpses. I escaped unnoticed. I lay there all night. By the morning Nakhtimin had moved into the valley, which he had sealed off. I found a water skin, a linen cloth full of bread and strips of dried meat. I wandered into the desert. The sand-dwellers found me, and the rest you know. I never saw much of the killing, but,' she closed her eyes, 'I'll never forget the screams: men, women and children, my own kin. Some were sleeping. Others were gathering near the cooking pots. Most were unarmed.'

'And the mercenaries?' I asked.

'They were the ones who fought, the only ones to fight.' She put her face in her hands and continued sobbing.

Djarka took her back to our pavilion. He made her comfortable before joining me at the gate to our makeshift defences.

'Have we discovered what you came for?' he asked, coming behind me. 'Was it worth it, my lord, to collect bones and burn them?'

I stared up at that valley, more hideous in the dimming light.

'What did you find here,' Djarka persisted, 'that you didn't know already? Lord Ay simply wished to destroy the last of the Atenists, so he gave them safe conduct here and had them massacred. Will you go back to Thebes, Lord Mahu, and confront him? Who will care? Horemheb and Rameses would have paid to have been part of this.'

'Rameses, perhaps,' I replied. 'Horemheb, no. Rameses is a killer through and through, but Horemheb has some honour, and so do I.' I turned around. 'I am searching for something else, Djarka. This valley is sacred to the Apiru, that's why they met here. I feel it here.' I beat my chest. 'There's something else. Something Ay fears.'

'He fears Akenhaten will return at the head of Hittite troops and Canaanite mercenaries.'

'No, no.' I shook my head. 'Why did he send Nakhtimin here?'

Djarka couldn't answer, but just before darkness, a group of my hardiest scouts returned. I had promised debens of silver to any scout who brought in something remarkable. They returned empty-handed, but their sweaty, grimy-faced leader grinned from ear to ear as he knelt before me.

'My lord, we have found it. Deep in the valley, high up in the cliffs, along a hidden trackway, the mouth of a cave concealed by bushes.'

I pulled the man to his feet.

'And inside?'

'Like a temple, my lord. A great cave, a cavern of the dead.'

'More corpses?' I asked.

The man fought to regain his breath. 'Coffins,' he declared.

'Coffins?'

'Burial places,' the man explained. 'Dug into the wall of the cave are ledges on which bodies, wrapped in linen and fastened with cord, have been placed. I touched one; it crumbled to dust. There are paintings and, we believe, three corpses from the

335

massacre. I suspect these men were not killed, but were wounded and dragged themselves there to die. One of them wore this.'

He handed over the ring. He had already polished it clean. I recognised the hieroglyphs of Lord Tutu beneath the sign of the rising Aten. If it hadn't been for the darkness and the danger I would have gone immediately to that cave. I had already given the order that we were to withdraw the following morning. When I declared that we would stay at least another day, a chorus of protests greeted my words. Nevertheless, I was beside myself with excitement. I had to search this cave and see what it held. Djarka was most vociferous in his opposition, until I tired of his hypocrisy. I grasped him by the arm and pulled him away from the camp fire.

'You knew about that cave all along, didn't you?'

'I knew of it, but not its whereabouts. This valley is sacred to my ancestors. They use it as a burial place for their leaders. It's a holy place, not to be violated . . .'

'By the impure,' I finished for him. 'I mean no disrespect, Djarka, but I must see inside that cave. I believe Lord Ay was searching for the same; it is one of the reasons General Nakhtimin came here.'

Just after dawn I entered the valley with a powerful escort. We moved slowly, following the winding path, alarmed even by the grains of shale tumbling down the rocky sides. The valley seemed to catch the sun. Dust rose in clouds to clog our noses and mouths and sting our eyes. Above us the vultures circled and in the rocky inclines we caught a glimpse of the sleeping hyaenas. There were caves high in the valley sides but the one the scouts had found was hidden by some clever trick of the eye. You had to turn and look back down towards the valley, studying the rock face carefully before you saw the man-made path. It led up to where a cluster of hardy bush and bramble sprouted in the shade of a jutting ledge.

I told the guards to make camp and remain vigilant. Djarka and I clambered up to the ledge. The gorse was fierce, scoring our flesh as we pushed our way through, and the yawning cave entrance came almost as a surprise. I stepped inside. The impression of being in a dream was heightened by the warm darkness, such a glaring contrast to the sunlight beyond. Djarka had brought a fire bowl. We lit the cresset torches fixed in their wall niches, and the cavern came alight. On one side a series of ledges stretched up to the ceiling and disappeared into the darkness beyond. On each ledge lay shrouded corpses. Some, by the texture of the shroud and the cord binding them, were relatively new; others had crumbled to nothing more than piles of dust and shards of bone. Tutu's skeleton and those of his acolytes lay deeper in the cave. I examined each carefully. Untouched by the scavengers, their flesh had simply rotted, but some of this still remained clinging to the bones. They were a grisly sight, particularly Tutu, who in his day had been a man of glory, a Lord of Light in the City of the Aten. One of the skeletons had a hole in the skull, possibly the work of some arrow. Savage cuts to Tutu's left ribs proved he must have known of this cave, been wounded and slunk here with his acolytes to hide and die.

'Shall we bury them?' Djarka asked, his voice sounding hollow. He was kneeling in the light of the torches; I wondered if he was praying in what he considered to be a holy place.

'As the tree falls, so let it lie.' I quoted the proverb. 'Tutu wished to die here; let him remain so.'

I was about to move away when my foot brushed a leather sack concealed in a cleft between the floor of the cave and the wall. I pulled this out and gently emptied its contents: a long bronze cylinder, the type to be found in a temple chancery or writing office. I undid the stopper and shook out the documents inside. The first was a map of the valley itself, showing the location of the cave in which we now stood. The second was a detailed chart showing paths and wells in the eastern desert. It marked routes across the Sinai, far away from the Horus Road, as well as the Egyptian garrisons which guarded the mines. The third comprised simple jottings. In the light of the torch I recognised Tutu's own hand; I had seen enough documents from him. It revealed nothing new, except a list of towns in southern Canaan. The fourth, however, was truly puzzling. Tutu had been an expert scribe, whose command of writing had first brought him to the attention of Akenhaten, yet this piece of smoothed papyrus bore nothing more than a picture of an old man surrounded by leaves. I stared in astonishment. At first I thought my eyes betrayed me. I passed it to Djarka.

'Why,' I asked, 'should the picture of an old man surrounded by leaves be so important to the Lord Tutu? It's scrawled in his own hand.'

Djarka studied it, then lifted his head, staring at something beyond me. When I looked, I glimpsed the paintings, and the terrible secrets they held, on the wall behind me.

Unemui Bain
(Ancient Egyptian for 'the Eaters of Souls')

Chapter 17

I rearranged the torches and studied the wall friezes. They were the work of a professional artist, who had first plastered the rock face before telling his story. The first tableau showed a Pharaoh preceded by his standard-bearers and other officers in war chariots. They were pursuing a sheepskin-clad enemy who had advanced to meet Pharaoh but who now, routed and overthrown, was seeking the protection of a large hill fort on the banks of a river. The citadel was defended by soaring walls and towers with square windows. In front of it some of the enemy who had been captured were in the process of being impaled. Others were stretched out on the ground, wrists and ankles manacled in bronze clamps, waiting to be skinned alive. This grisly ceremony was being watched by the occupants of the fort. Men pierced by arrows fell from the walls whilst Pharaoh's foot soldiers advanced under the cover of tall shields.

In the second tableau, Pharaoh, attended by his parasol-bearer, was questioning prisoners whilst a tally was made of the enemy slain by counting the severed heads heaped in front of Pharaoh's chariot. In the third, the background had changed, and was dominated by hills, some steep, others shallow. The sheepskin-clad enemy, pursued by Pharaoh's soldiers, had arrived before a fortress; its gates had been set alight, and bright red flames were licking hungrily upwards. In other minor paintings, warriors, naked except for loincloths, carried round shields and long spears against Pharaoh's troops. They were led by a warrior who looked as if he had stag horns on his head. In the last tableau,

341

the citadels had been taken; the ground was covered with corpses, heads impaled on poles. Pharaoh and his charioteers were leaving; behind them trundled carts filled with booty and slaves carrying baskets of the severed heads of his enemy.

I examined the paintings most carefully, Djarka standing quietly behind me.

'These were not painted by an Egyptian,' I remarked. 'He is not celebrating an Egyptian victory but the defeat of his own people.'

I looked at the enemy again.

'They are Hyksos,' I whispered. 'These paintings describe the Season of the Hyaena, when Pharaoh Ahmose drove the Hyksos out of Egypt. You know the story, don't you, Djarka? How the Hyksos were a violent and vicious enemy, a motley collection of peoples, an army of mercenaries made up of various tribes, many of them from Canaan.'

I gestured around this makeshift sepulchre and grasped Djarka tightly by the shoulder.

'You should have told me about this!'

He didn't try to break free, but simply wiped a bead of sweat running down his nose.

'Do you know what these paintings say, Djarka? Amongst the Hyksos were shepherd kings from Canaan, aggressive and warlike. These paintings show how they were driven out. Your people were the shepherd kings! They returned to Canaan, where successive Pharaohs pursued them. When warfare failed, your people, these shepherd kings, the Apiru, amongst whom is the tribe of Israar, gave up their weapons of battle and returned to Egypt as travellers and herdsmen. This time they won the favour of Pharaoh. Years had passed, so memories had dimmed. They had brought their God or Gods with them.' I let go of his shoulder. 'This is not in the paintings, but one such group settled at Akhmin. They became more Egyptian than the Egyptians. Rich and powerful, they gained high office. One of them, Lady Tiye, caught the eye and undying affection of the great Pharaoh Amenhotep III. Now your people had their opportunity. Queen Tiye, with her ideas of one, omnipotent, invisible God, began to teach her husband the secret knowledge of her people. By then, everything described here was history, dim folk memory.

342

Amenhotep the Magnificent never realised the connection between his lovely young wife and the shepherd kings who once terrorised Egypt. He didn't care if she worshipped the One God under the guise of the Aten, nor did he really care if she made this the staff of life for his younger son, the one he had rejected, the boy I met, the Veiled One, who later became Akenhaten.'

I went and sat on a rocky plinth, gazing up at Djarka.

'I wonder, Djarka, what Generals Horemheb and Rameses would make of these paintings. They'd quickly realise that the Apiru are the descendants of the shepherd kings, the allies of the cursed Hyksos. That they present a great danger to Egypt, with their notions of One God, of a Messiah, of being a chosen people. They'd declare war on the Apiru. They'd exterminate them as well as launch the most ferocious campaigns in Canaan to wipe out your people root and branch. Did you know of this?'

Djarka went across and picked up his quiver of arrows and his powerful composite bow.

'What are you going to do, Djarka? Kill me? Are you frightened I'll send a message to General Horemheb in Memphis or the priests of Amun in Thebes? About this sacred place, where your people used to stop as they crossed Sinai into Egypt? A place where they could recall the deeds of the past and bury their dead? That's why Meryre and Lord Tutu came here! I don't know whether they are of your tribe; if not, they are still prime examples of how the ideas of you people can suborn the souls of even the most educated Egyptians. This is what Lord Ay sent Nakhtimin to discover. What do you want to do with it, Djarka?'

Djarka plucked the string of his bow. 'What will you do, my lord?' He stepped back so his face remained hidden in the shadows.

'I am going to lose my temper if I think my friend, a man I regard as a son, is thinking of killing me.'

'I don't threaten you,' Djarka stepped into the pool of light, 'but I beg you by all that's sacred . . .'

'To destroy it? Of course I will. This valley is now polluted. It is only a matter of time before one of my merry boys amongst the mercenaries babbles about these caves, and how the Lord Mahu and Djarka took a great interest in one of them. Sooner or later General Rameses will send his own troops here, and they'll comb the valleys till they find it. So, Djarka, put down that bow and bring as many oil skins as we can spare.'

We worked hurriedly. By early evening we had soaked that cave and all it contained: the mummies, the corpses of Tutu and his companions, and above all, those paintings. We threw in torches and the valley side burst into flame, the fire leaping out, burning the gorse and bushes around. Black columns of smoke curled across the valley before rising up against the dark blue sky. I never stayed to see how effective that fire was; I was eager to return to the camp and prepare for the next morning's march. The troops were restive, desperate to be gone, tired, as one of them shouted, of the dead and the hideous night prowlers.

I redoubled the watch. My guards had reported sightings of a huge hyaena pack led by a fearsome brute; the men had nick-named it Seth, as it showed little fear of fire or our weapons. The presence of so much flesh, the sweet smell of the cooking and the lure of fresh water had stirred them into a killing frenzy. During the third watch of the night the entire hyaena pack attacked the camp. If I were superstitious, I would have thought the beasts were possessed by some evil demon: they struck skil-fully and cunningly. They decided the gate was the weak point, and exploited the gaps between the carts. In their first assault they concentrated on two guards, leaping on to the carts, tearing them down almost before the alarm could be raised. The gap they created allowed the others to penetrate the camp. I was woken by screams, by the braying of conch horns, men shouting and yelling. I burst out of my tent, Djarka behind me, and glimpsed the hideous shapes. They didn't so much attack us as try and force their way through to the horse lines, which provided easier prey. The sounds and sights were horrendous. Horses maddened by fear broke their traces, some pounding through the camp, others finding a gap out into the desert where others of the pack were waiting. It was a night of searing screams and hot spurting blood. The hyaenas were cunning. They would attack any man by himself but kept well clear of those sensible enough to organise themselves into a circle or square bristling with lances, shields and the sharp barbed points of our archers.

We lost six men that night and about twenty horses. Six more animals had to be destroyed later, and it took us about an hour to clear the camp. We killed at least eight of the pack, including the leader, but they'd got what they came for. I decided to break camp immediately and flee that place. By dawn we were already on the march, leaving the hyaenas the victors of the field, hoping their kills of the previous night would distract them for a while. We abandoned many of our chariots and only stopped to distribute water when the noonday heat became too intense. We marched by day with a short rest at night; the only way to calm the men and impose any sort of order was to put as much distance between ourselves and the Valley of the Grey Dawn as possible.

After four days of forced marching the men were grey with exhaustion, and our beasts began to flounder, but even the most anxious amongst the standard-bearers conceded that the danger was behind us.

We rested at an oasis where a huge stela of Tuthmosis II boasted how this place was in the power of Egypt and its water belonged to Pharaoh. We were so thirsty, hot and tired, we couldn't have cared if the Devourers from the Underworld had owned it. We took our rest and counted our losses: at least two dozen men over all and about thirty of our beasts. We continued our march in some semblance of order, alarmed by the growing interest of desert wanderers, who had learned that something had happened and realised our strength was considerably weakened. I ordered the men to wear battle harnesses and to advance as if expecting attack. The desert wanderers took notice of this and disappeared. Now and again they would reappear to dog our flanks, looking for any weaknesses or stragglers.

Five weeks after leaving the Valley of the Grey Dawn, we reached the rocky, barren expanse leading to the eastern cliffs and down to the City of the Aten. We entered the city at dawn, and even then I knew something was wrong. The streets were busy enough, the markets preparing for the day, but dark glances and mutterings showed our presence was not appreciated. The palace was heavily fortified and defended. Nebamun was more interested in informing us about what had occurred in the city than asking what had happened out in the Red Lands. I immediately demanded to see the Prince. Once I had satisfied myself about his health and safety, I met with Nebamun and his officers out in the garden. We sat in a circle under the shade of a sycamore tree. Both Djarka and I had bathed and shaved, washing away the dirt and dust. I felt so tired, my limbs ached.

'I have talked to my men,' the old colonel began. 'They have described your expedition to that place of slaughter.'

'My lord Ay and the Royal Circle,' I replied, 'will be informed soon enough.'

Nebamun half smiled at the snub, though his staff officers glowered at me. One of them spoke up.

'We lost good men and horses.'

'Horses die!' I snapped. 'Whilst it is the duty of the Pharaoh's soldiers to lay down their lives if necessary.'

'What did you find?' Nebamun persisted. 'Were such deaths necessary? They talked about a hyaena pack possessed by demons, of skeletons, of a hideous slaughter? How you set fire to a cave high up on the side of the valley.'

'As I have said,' I bit into a sweet grape, 'I shall inform Lord Ay.'

'He has already sent dispatches.'

'I have seen them,' I said. 'My scribes had them ready. More of the same: don't do this, don't do that. What I want to know, Colonel, is how safe is this city?'

'Lord Ay and his Royal Circle,' Nebamun turned aggressive, 'disapproved of your expedition, as did Generals Horemheb and Rameses. They could not see the point; the Prince and the Royal Household were left vulnerable.'

'In which case, Colonel,' I retorted, 'I have more confidence in you than they do. Now, enough of bandying words. The city?'

'The city seethes with unrest,' Nebamun replied. 'There have been attacks on officials and some of our soldiers. I have cancelled all leave to go into the beer shops or marketplace; gangs gather outside the palace gates.'

'What do they want?'

'Assurances that the city will be safe, that you, my lord, and, of course, His Highness, do not desert them. They talk about their livelihood, about their loyalty to Egypt. They have not moved here to live in a city which is going to be left to die.'

'But they are right. You know, Colonel, as I do, for it is common knowledge, that once Lord Ay has settled Thebes, the

346

Prince will return to marry the Princess Ankhesenamun and be crowned Lord of the Two Lands.'

'How dangerous is this unrest?' Djarka asked.

Nebamun spread his hands. 'The occasional attack, noisy encounters, rocks hurled. We are finding it more and more difficult to bring produce into the markets. They would have attacked you if it was not for your military escort. My lord Mahu, we should abandon the city, leave as soon as possible.'

I thought of the treasures, my own possessions, the chest of secret documents buried in my private garden.

'I propose we abandon everything,' Nebamun insisted. 'The war barges are ready. We could be gone within the day, let the city rot.'

'So, Colonel, you have also received messages from General Horemheb. How is he?'

'He wants the city to die and the memory of Aten to be forgotten,' one of Nebamun's officers declared cheekily.

'I will think about what you say.'

Djarka and I returned to our quarters. The Prince was sleeping. Ankhesenamun and Amedeta walked languorously into the room. They must have been testing certain perfumes, for their fragrance hung about like incense. They looked resplendent in shimmering jewellery. Ankhesenamun's speech was slightly slurred; both had been drinking deeply.

'Uncle Mahu,' she lisped, 'welcome back. We did miss you, didn't we, Amedeta?'

The lady-in-waiting smiled at me with her eyes. Ankhesenamun tiptoed towards me and touched my lips.

'They are dry and cracked and not for kissing, are they, Amedeta? You should really take more care.' She simpered at me like a cat, then walked away, glancing over her shoulder, an impudent, insolent smile on her face. 'You should take more care, Uncle Mahu, and do what Grandfather asks.'

'What is she implying?' Djarka whispered, as he kicked the door shut behind her. Usually he would have been impatient to be away. During the last days of the expedition Mert had become ill with a slight fever, which had made her drowsy. As soon as we arrived in the palace, Djarka had asked for Pentju's help; the physician had examined her and said it was nothing

347

that two days' rest and cups of pure water wouldn't cure. 'My lord,' Djarka insisted, 'the Lady Ankhesenamun was sending you warnings.'

I broke from my reverie. 'Yes, yes, she was! Stay there!'

I went out into my garden and into the cypress grove. One tree I'd carefully marked. I pushed away the boulder and clawed at the earth. The chest was there, but the lock was broken. Inside, nothing. I knelt and cursed. All the documents I had found in the usurper's camp had gone. I tossed the chest away and tried to control the surge of fear. Ankhesenamun and Amedeta must have found and destroyed them.

'Are they gone?'

I whirled round. Djarka stood at the edge of the grove.

'Of course they are! Which means Lord Ay must be plotting.'

'What?'

'My removal, even my death. The Royal Circle is shrinking. Meryre, Tutu, General Rahmose and the Atenists have gone. Horemheb and Rameses are busy playing soldiers in Memphis. Maya and Huy? Well, they can be bought. Sobeck is busy about his own affairs, so you and I are the next to go. Ay has one ambition, to have Tutankhamun crowned whilst he himself becomes the real power in Egypt. He wants this city to be abandoned, the Atenists destroyed. He wants to forget the past and concentrate on the future.' I got to my feet. 'He would have had me arrested earlier but he wasn't strong enough, whilst I had the proof of his treason. Now that's gone.'

'Horemheb and Rameses would protect you.'

'They can be bought, as can the rest. Lord Ay will be very clever. A new day dawns for Egypt. Mahu is part of the past, so let's forget him.'

'My lord Mahu, my lord Mahu.' A servant came hurrying up. 'Colonel Nebamun demands to see you.'

Nebamun was waiting in one of the small courtyards. His men had brought in a prisoner, one of those wandering holy men, a gaunt creature with stick-like arms and legs, his skin blackened by the sun, his lean face pitted with scars and holes. Slightly demented, he showed no fear of the soldiers.

'We found him outside the palace,' Nebamun declared. 'We have been wanting to take him for days. A self-declared prophet.'

'A voice from the east,' the man shouted. 'A voice from the west. A voice from the north and the south.'

'Whose voice?' I yelled back.

The man drew himself up, hitching the dirty kirtle around his waist. He grasped the staff he was leaning on. One of Nebamun's men kicked it from his hand, but the self-proclaimed prophet chose to ignore this. Instead he advanced on me, one bony finger pointed, the nail coated in dirt.

'The Voice of Devastation!' he declared. 'And listen to this voice. So say the Gods. I abhor this eastern land. I will not enter this place of destruction. The offerings you bring are detestable to me. I will pass through it. I will not stay. Fire followed by dust, the voice proclaims, the city is doomed.'

'And who are you?' I asked.

'I am a swallow. I am a swallow,' he replied. 'A messenger of the Scorpion Goddess. I bring secrets from the Fields of Rushes. I have announced this city to be doomed.'

'Who paid you?' I asked, grasping the man's finger and bending it. The prophet broke off his lamentations. I kept twisting the finger; he screamed with pain and fell to his knees.

'I have not been paid, my lord. I take my staff and sweep the sky. I see visions: this city is doomed.'

I gazed into his mad eyes and smelled the beer heavy on his breath. 'If it is doomed,' I declared, 'then you had best leave. Colonel Nebamun, throw him into the river!'

The uprising occurred that night. I'm not too sure if Meryre's agents were active. The leaders were Marunet and Pera, two merchants who'd made a fortune in the alabaster mines. They'd planned to seize the Prince, hold him hostage and issue their demands to the Royal Circle. The first proof of their intention was slingshots, which sent our guards spinning from the walls, followed by a hail of arrows. A wooden pillar taken from a house and placed in a cart was used to force the gates, but they were beaten off just as the sun rose. I watched from one of the towers as our archers leaned over the parapet and dispatched the attackers. Corpses sprawled in blood, pierced with arrows; the skulls of others were crushed by our slingers. My view from the tower provided

349

little comfort: already smoke and flames could be seen from many quarters of the city.

'The mob intend to lay siege to us; we have no choice but to withdraw,' Nebamun rasped.

I asked for food and wine to be brought. I ate and drank watching the attackers withdraw back into the side streets off the main avenue leading down to the palace. Occasionally, groups of armed men would re-emerge to loose a few shafts before retreating into the shadows. At the ninth hour Marunet and Pera sent a herald in the name of the so-called Council of the City, an impudent fellow who swaggered up to the gate waving his sword as if he was an officer. He demanded entrance. I let him in, but had him arrested.

'Why?' he spluttered.

'Treason!' I replied.

He was not so arrogant when we tortured him. My mercenaries began to skin his legs and arms, so he agreed to confess. He provided the names of the city leaders and let something slip which chilled my heart: the envoy, I forget his name, protested how their actions had the backing of the palace.

'Which palace?' I asked.

'Why, this palace,' the man spat out, his lips covered in blood. Eventually I was convinced that he had told me all he could. I ordered the guard to execute him and toss his head from the walls.

I stormed out of the House of Chains and up to the women's quarters. Ankhesenamun and her fellow demon Amedeta were in the inner chamber, sitting on a double stool. They'd heard about the uprising and the ensuing chaos, yet they were examining one another's fingernails as if they hadn't a care in the world.

'Why, Uncle Mahu.' Ankhesenamun raised her head. 'You look troubled. Are you worried? I did tell you we should leave here.' I could have slapped her face. Amedeta sat cross-legged next to her, cat eyes smiling.

'My documents?'

'Uncle Mahu, what are you talking about?'

'You know what I am talking about.'

I raised my hand and stood back, shouting for my guards.

They burst into the chamber, swords drawn. The two minxes sprang to their feet. Ankhesenamun protested at such an intrusion.

'Don't worry,' I soothed. 'You are safe.'

I told the mercenaries to search the chamber. Ankhesenamun and her fellow bitch screamed abuse. The outburst brought a servant running; at the sight of my guards' drawn swords, he hastily withdrew. I told the guard to search everywhere. Ankhesenamun and Amedeta sat back on the stool, resigned to what was happening. From outside rose shouts and cries as the rebels renewed their attack. I watched my mercenaries, robbers and plunderers to a man, strip the chamber and beyond. At first I thought Ankhesenamun had been too cunning; in the end she proved to be stupid. I found the documents I was looking for in the false bottom of a large wooden chest: letters from her grandfather containing information and news about what was happening in Thebes, and what she had to do here.

'My dear daughter.' I read the words aloud, pushing Ankhesenamun away. 'You must find what I want and destroy it. In the end Uncle Mahu will be happy that what he held he can hold no longer.'

I pointed at Amedeta.

'You sent her to seduce me. Was she your watcher, your spy?'

'You're getting old, Uncle Mahu,' Ankhesenamun spat back, 'and stupid with it. You are clumsy.'

I told my guards to push her back in the chair. Of course they didn't: the Royal Flesh was sacred. I just wanted that bitch to understand how my patience was exhausted.

The rest of Ay's letters were full of advice, written in code which I now understood. He talked of friends in the City of the Aten. Towards the end of one letter I came across assurances that all would be well and that she and the young Prince would not be harmed. I threw the letters on the floor and gestured at the window.

'You're behind all this, aren't you? You have been feeding these rebels with information, agitating them.'

I would have continued my rage, but Colonel Nebamun came up. Ankhesenamun, the bitch, smiled coyly at him. I could tell from his face that the situation was grave.

351

'We have archers in the palace,' he whispered. 'No, I mean rebel archers, servants who've armed themselves. We must withdraw before dusk. We must take the Prince and the rest and make our way down to the barges. I have checked the kitchen stores: we have enough supplies to last only two to three days here. The rebels are not yet fully organised . . .'

'But soon they will be?'

'By then they will occupy the city between here and the river.'

I went across and studied one of the paintings on the wall, depicting Akenhaten worshipping the sun. Ay knew I was trapped, whilst I realised he was on his way here to play the role of the great saviour. We were in no real danger. If the palace was stormed, the Prince and Ankhesenamun would be held hostage. The rebels would be under strict instruction to keep them safe. I wondered what orders had been given about me.

'I must advise you,' Nebamun insisted, 'unless we evacuate, the palace will fall; there will be a blood bath.'

I wiped the sweat off my face and nodded in agreement. Orders were issued. Many of the servants had already deserted. My mercenaries had also sensed which way the winds were blowing. If the rebels stormed the palace it would be a bitter fight, room to room, courtyard to courtyard; they, too, wanted to go.

As the sun began to set, we gathered in the central courtyard. Nebamun agreed to abandon his chariots. We would fight on foot. The narrow streets and lanes, not to mention the ropes stretched across them, rendered the deployment of chariots as useless. I had every shield brought from the armoury and we formed a defensive wall, six deep on all four sides. The Royal Household was placed in the middle. Nebamun commanded the front; I defended the rear.

We waited until the setting sun dazzled the attackers, then I ordered the gates to be opened and we began our advance along the Avenue of Lions, down to the river. Nebamun had already sent scouts, dressed in the garments of servants, to warn the barges we were coming. It was a bloody fight. We were greeted by a hail of missiles, slingshots, arrows and rocks; we could not stop for our wounded. In the centre, the Prince and Ankhesenamun were protected by royal shield-bearers. My heart went out to the young lad and his sister, who showed no fear as, time and again, the shield wall was attacked, the rebels desperate to break through. The imperial standard was displayed, a sign that the Prince was part of our company; this lessened the ferocity of the attack, the enemy commanders being wary of spilling the Sacred Blood.

It must have been two miles from the palace gates to the river, yet it seemed the longest march. At first we moved quickly, catching the rebels by surprise, but as they realised what was happening they raced along the side streets parallel to the main avenue. Nebamun kept moving to ensure they did not encircle us. I was aware of the houses on either side, statues grimacing down at us, and the air humming with arrows. I stood behind our rear ranks, watching the attackers. Now and again shield-bearers would go down, but there was nothing we could do for them, and the vicious tug-of-war continued. The closer we got to the river, the more desperate the struggle became, but at last we were there. The barges were ready. Nebamun's ranks opened and the Prince and his half-sister, together with their servants, hurried on to the first barge, the archers on board loosing arrows over our heads. Once the Prince was safe, the rest followed. We established a corridor and, as darkness fell, our protective ring began to shrink. Barge after barge closed in and took on board all it could carry before moving away. The rebels had not thought of this. They had no command of the water, while the captains of our war barges were skilled river fighters.

I grew nervous: would the enemy over-run our depleted force? The battle continued by torchlight, men screaming and fighting, every muscle in my body aching. I became aware of the cool breeze from the river, the stench of rotting vegetation, the slap of water. Our rearguard now reached the quayside and broke up, men taking refuge behind carts and bundles. Every so often, a standard-bearer would shout and the next group of men would detach themselves and run down to leap on to the barges. A few missed their footing and tumbled into the water. The cries of the wounded and dying agitated a nearby crocodile pool. Shouts of warning rang from the barges, and oil was thrown into the water and fired with arrows. The screams from the river were heart-rending. Abruptly our attackers retreated.

'What's happening?' I shouted to an officer.

A roar from the river made me whirl round. Our barges were long dark shapes in the water, lit by the occasional torch. To my astonishment, other boats had appeared, clearly war barges, their decorated standards glittering in the light. They displayed the personal banners of the Lord Ay, the Golden Horus, the Falcon of Egypt. The rebels retreated. These new barges landed troops of mercenaries, archers, heavy infantry, who immediately advanced into the city as another force closed in from the eastern cliffs.

'Are you well, Lord Mahu?' I glanced round. Nakhtimin, dressed in the full regalia of a general, collars of bravery around his neck, took off his leather helmet. 'You look rather distraught, Lord Mahu. You must come with me! The Lord Ay requires it.'

I climbed into the waiting punt. We reached the side of a war barge. I went up a rope ladder; oil lamps glowed on deck. I glimpsed the Prince and Ankhesenamun resting on cushions under a blood-red awning, sucking on pieces of fruit as if they hadn't a care in the world. Tutankhamun leapt to his feet, and would have run across to show me the sword Ay had given him, but a figure stepped out of the shadows. I recognised the smiling painted face of the Lord Maya, the treasurer.

'You look as comfortable and prosperous as ever,' I commented.

Huy joined him. Both gazed sadly at me, as they used to when we were Children of the Kap, as if I had done something wrong and was about to be punished.

Nakhtimin pushed me gently on my shoulder. A guard opened the door to the cabin in the centre of the barge and I stepped into the warm, perfumed light. Lord Ay was sitting on a small divan, cushions piled high around him. The small ivory table laid before him was covered in documents and inkpots. Two scribes from the House of Writing squatted either side of the table, carefully taking down Ay's proclamations. The cobra in human flesh ignored me. He picked up a goblet of wine – I remember it was a turquoise colour – and sipped rather than drank before continuing the proclamation he was dictating.

'Anyone found bearing arms will be killed. Anyone found guilty of rape, violence or plunder will be executed. Anyone found resisting authority will suffer the same penalty.' He waved a hand. 'You know the rest. You may go.'

He dismissed the scribes and turned to me, eyes as cunning as ever in that lean face. The robe he wore was of the purest white linen; a chain of office hung around his neck. Rings dazzled on his fingers, and he kept playing with these as he hid part of his face behind his hand.

'My lord Mahu, it's good to see you.' He tossed a few cushions on the floor before him. 'You may sit.'

'I will stand.' I stretched quickly and picked up his goblet. 'I would like to return the compliment, Lord Ay, and say how pleasant it is to meet you.' I sipped the wine. 'From the black soil of Canaan, the Vineyard of Lebanon?' I asked.

'A little further south.' Ay smiled. 'Come, relax. You have blood on your arms and face!'

'I might have more,' I replied, 'if your brother standing behind me does not stop treating me as a prisoner and take his hand from his sword.' I turned my head. 'In fact, I prefer him to go.' I wished I hadn't drunk the wine; it made me feel sick. My arms and legs felt heavy. I wanted so much to sit, kneel or squat. Ay gestured with his head, and the cabin door closed behind me. I sat down on the cushions, still clutching the cup.

'What has been happening here?' Ay murmured.

'Oh don't play cat and mouse with me,' I snapped. 'The rebellion in the city was the work of your agents, or rather your granddaughter. She was under orders to find those secret documents I took from the usurper's camp. She's destroyed them, hasn't she?'

Ay shrugged. 'You would never have used them.'

'The uprising,' I demanded. 'You knew they would not hurt the Prince or Ankhesenamun. You arranged it so as to appear as the saviour who won a victory as great as that of General Horemheb. Does he know about this expedition?'

'He will be told about you running around the eastern desert; your lack of care for the young Prince; your refusal to obey the instructions of the Royal Circle.' Ay paused. 'What did you go into the desert to see, Mahu?'

'What you were looking for, Lord Ay, when you massacred Lord Tutu and the rest. I found the caves; I studied the paintings. I also found Lord Tutu, or what was left of him, as well as certain documents which, I assure you, I keep in a secret place.'

355

'The paintings?' Ay's face was bright with excitement.

'I suspect you know.'

Ay chewed the corner of his lip.

'Why did you massacre them?'

'They were rebels and traitors,' he replied.

'Did you do it on the orders of the Royal Circle?'

'Some day, Mahu,' Lord Ay smiled, 'someone will tell me what you found out there.'

'No, my lord, one day I will tell General Horemheb what I discovered.'

Ay beat a tattoo on the edge of the table as he studied some documents. He lifted his head. 'It's back to Thebes, Mahu. The City of the Aten is finished; not one stone will be left upon another. Now you must sleep, the dream is over.'

We returned to Thebes seven days later. Ay depicted himself as a victorious general, home from the wars. We advanced in glory around the city, along the Avenues of the Rams and Sphinxes, trumpets blowing, standards raised. Young girls threw rose petals, priests offered prayers amidst clouds of incense, whilst temple choirs sang hymns of triumph.

How glorious are you, Horus in the South!
You have bared your arm and scattered your foe,
You have smashed the might of Egypt's enemy,
You have restored honour to the Kingdom of the Two Lands.

Tutankhamun, along with Ankhesenamun, was borne in an open-sided litter, to be greeted with roars of salutations, though the people were singing the hymn to Lord Ay rather than anyone else. I realised how hard Ay and the others had worked. The temples were open, the pylons repainted, new pinewood flag-poles placed on top from which red and blue streamers fluttered in the wind. Temple gates and doors had been rehung and refurbished with copper and bronze. The makets were busy; trade had returned to Thebes. The gold-capped obelisks dazzled in the sunlight. Akenhaten was forgotten, his dream of One God and a new city no more than dust in the wind.

ger re
(Ancient Egyptian for 'silent mouth')

Chapter 18

For his crowning, Tutankhamun was placed on the Great Gold Throne. Sixteen porters carried it on their shoulders, squads of infantry on every side. The musicians proclaimed their strident sounds: the blast of trumpets, the ominous beat of the long drums, the rattling of the sistra. In front of the throne, the ram-headed Priests of Amun, clad in panther skins, walked backwards, raising silver censers towards the face of their little sovereign, who'd been carefully prepared and instructed on what to do.

We had been in Thebes only a few days when the Royal Circle gathered and the decision was made that Tutankhamun was to be crowned Pharaoh of Egypt. He would hold the flail and rod; his name would go forth from beyond the Third Cataract to the Delta. I had been ignored, invited to meetings of the Royal Circle more as an observer than a participant. People avoided me. I recognised the signs. I was out of favour. Now the day had come. Tutankhamun would wear the Double Crown of Egypt; he would be taken to the Temple of Amun, and invested with the Great Office. I was invited, even given a place of honour, but the silence of the others was ominous. I was a marked man.

Tutankhamun was excited. I participated in, as well as super-vised, the gorgeous ceremony. For the first time in almost twenty years a Royal Coronation would take place. The Royal Circle had also decreed that, after his crowning, Ankhesenamun and Tutankhamun would be solemnly married. A day to remember as the Prince was carried up the wide avenue. All around him wafting fans exuded expensive perfume, whilst clouds of incense threatened to hide him. The procession went along the Avenue of the Sphinxes, past the circled walls of the temple and the shimmering waters of the sacred lakes. The heat grew intense. The crowds swelled, a thick hedge of cheering, applauding people. We approached the gigantic soaring pylons of the Temple of Karnak. This was not only the day when Tutankhamun would be crowned; it was also an occasion to show the people of Egypt that the power of the Amun had returned; Egypt's Gods were to be honoured, the days of the Aten, the One God were over. All around Tutankhamun swarmed priests and prophets, the masters of the ceremony, the courtiers. Of course, pride of place had been given to the Royal Circle, especially Lord Ay in his glorious robes of office.

I, and the rest, followed the Prince through the secret doors of the temple into the icy darkness. We approached the Great Room where the God Amun had his sanctuary. The chapel priest appeared, sprinkling holy water and praying the sacred words: 'I purify you with this. It will give you life, health and strength.' Here the Prince was stripped of his garments and garbed in the traditional vestments of High Priest and Pharaoh: a loose mantle over his shoulders and a short kilt with a jackal's tail hanging from the belt at the bottom. The divine instruments were placed in his hands: the crook, the whip and the sceptre. A false beard of gold was fastened to his little chin. Once he was ready, we entered the vast hall for the Feast of the Royal Diadem, where the coronation ceremony took place. Priests wearing the grim masks of hawks and greyhounds personifying Horus, the God of Lower Egypt, and Seth, the God of Upper Egypt, placed crowns upon the young Pharaoh's head: first the White Crown of Upper Egypt, followed by the Red Crown of Lower, around the crowns the golden band displaying the cobra head of the Uraeus, the defender of Pharaoh and the Protector of Egypt.

'I establish my dignity as King of the North. I establish my dignity as King of the South . . .' Once that vow was taken, Tutankhamun, to establish not only his authority but that of Amun, went deeper into the sanctuary to lie prostrate before the Naos, the Sacred Cupboard. He then broke its sacred seals and opened the doors. I was there to help him, an exception to the rule. Inside stood a small statue of gilded wood encrusted with gems, the God sitting on his throne, wearing a head-dress surmounted by two ostrich feathers. I shall always remember those enamel eyes, slightly revolting in the stupid, horrible mask.

Once the coronation ceremony was over, we left the temple, proceeding in triumph through Thebes so Pharaoh could show his face to his people. It was a glorious scene: marching troops, rattling chariotry, the air thick with incense and perfume.

By late afternoon, the Ceremony of Procession was over and the great feasting began in the Malkata Palace. I was looking for my own place on the royal dais when I felt a hand on my shoulder and turned. General Nakhtimin stood, smiling slyly, ringed by a group of officers.

'My lord Mahu,' he intoned, 'you are under arrest.'

I let them escort me from the hall, down the steps and back to my own quarters, and that, I suppose, was the end of my days as the Prince's guardian. The following morning I was summoned to a meeting of the Royal Circle. I was made to stand as if I was a prisoner of war while Lord Ay, acting as Pharaoh's First Minister, listed the charges against me: my dereliction of duty in the City of the Aten; my endangering the Prince; my foolish escapade (as he put it) in going out into the eastern desert; the uprising; my failure to protect the Princess Ankhesenamun.

The charges were a list of vague, empty words. I looked around for support. Horemheb and Rameses avoided my glance. Huy and Maya squatted on their cushions, heads down. In the end my sentence was house arrest in a stately mansion on a road outside Thebes. Pentju, also included in the charges, was declared officially disgraced. The house three miles north of Thebes, was very similar to the one in which I am now detained, with outhouses and gardens, its high circumference wall closely guarded by Nakhtimin's troops. Pentju accepted his fate with resignation, joking how we would settle down like an old married couple. I was given a few servants and allowed to pick ten of my mercenaries to join me. I asked for volunteers and the lovely lads responded. We were taken to the mansion and given instructions not to leave under sentence of death or banishment.

Pentju and I divided the house, each taking our own quarters. Neither of us complained. In my heart I knew that it was neither the time nor the place. Sometimes Pentju would ask me why it had happened. I would respond with the same question. During the first few months possible answers dominated my thoughts. I eventually reached the simple and stark conclusion that I was no longer needed. My post as Chief of Police was taken over by Sobeck, who often visited me. There was no malice or recriminations. Sobeck had prospered. He'd put on weight; I often teased him about his paunch and rather heavy jowls. We'd sit in my garden under a sycamore tree, sipping at wine and reminiscing about our exploits in the Hittite camp. Sobeck was a good choice as Chief of Police: as a former outlaw, he knew every trick and turn of those he pursued. He would bring me news of Thebes and Egypt. How Horemheb and Rameses were now in charge of all garrisons north of Memphis, busy fortifying Egypt's defences, raising new troops and building up chariot squadrons. Horemheb was planning the great day when Egyptian forces would cross the Sinai and invade Canaan. There was little reference to the City of the Aten; it was allowed to die. After the uprising it was abandoned, its palaces and temples, colonnaded walks, avenues and parks given back to the desert. The wells scaled over, the canals dried up; within two years it became the haunt of beggars and outlaws.

Sobeck often asked me why I accepted my fate with such resignation. But what else could I do? When the Prince was taken from my care I was tired of the struggle, the bloodshed and the violence. I wanted peace, a time to shelter and reflect. My life, like water running down a rock, had abruptly taken a different course. Horemheb and Rameses came visiting. They were intrigued by my adventures and often questioned me about the last days of Akenhaten. As the months passed, their visits became less frequent, but when they did come they would always bring gifts, assurances of friendship, and the conversation would always turn to the people of Aten and the tribes of the Apiru.

Djarka and Mert joined me, declaring that they preferred self-imposed exile to a stay at the court. The mansion had many chambers and a spacious enough garden for at least three households. They married, and within months Mert was pregnant. Djarka returned to his old role of being my councellor. He advised me to tell Horemheb and Rameses as little as possible, whilst warning me against Lord Ay's spies in my household. Sobeck was the most regular visitor. He brought me news of the court, the chatter and gossip, mere chaff in the wind. I would ask about the young Pharaoh, the only person I really cared for. According to Sobeck, Tutankhamun was seen very little and kept in the shadows. Indeed, Lord Ay and his granddaughter Ankhesenamun appeared to be the real rulers of Egypt. I informed Sobeck about my expedition into the Red Lands, that strange cave and its dangerous paintings. I also showed him the documents I had found beside Tutu's pathetic remains. He was particularly interested in Tutu's drawing of the old man surrounded by leaves. He studied this for a long time before bursting into laughter.

'What is it?' I asked crossly.

At first Sobeck wouldn't answer.

'What is it?' I demanded

Sobeck handed back the papyrus.

'Look at it Mahu, what do you see?'

'An old man's head surrounded by leaves,' I replied. 'What else?'

'No, Mahu, look at the centre, keep staring at the centre and you will see another picture emerge. It's a common device used by artists, a joke, a way of conveying a secret message.'

I stared at the drawing, but could see nothing. Sobeck was most insistent. He asked me to place it on the ground and study it very carefully. I did so, and gasped in astonishment as a different drawing emerged. It was of a couple kissing, and it was easy to recognise the sharp features of Ay and the gorgeous face of his daughter Nefertiti, hair piled high upon her head.

'A drawing within a drawing,' I exclaimed. 'But it's scandalous.'

'Is it?' I glanced up: Sobeck was no longer smiling.

'You've heard the rumours, Mahu? That Ay and Nefertiti were lovers?'

'Father and daughter!' I exclaimed.

'Father and daughter,' Sobeck agreed. 'Rumours claim Ankhesenamun is not Akenhaten's daughter, but her grand-father's.'

'Preposterous. . . . !'

'Mahu, I am Chief of Police. I have drawn my own informa-tion from palace servants, who listen through half-opened door-ways, or peer from windows. There is even gossip that Akenhaten's rift with his beautiful Queen first began because of his suspicions about the true relationship between Nefertiti and her father. I can produce a maid, a laundry woman, who babbled about Lord Ay being in bed not only with his grand-daughter but with her lady in waiting. Lord Ay truly believes he's the master of everyone around him.'

'Could he, would he,' I asked, 'harm the young Pharaoh, have him removed; take over the flail and the rod?'

Sobeck shook his head. 'To do that would cause civil war. Ay has the support of Huy and Maya only as First Minister, not as Pharaoh, whilst in the north Horemheb and Rameses keep a very, very close eye on him.'

The more Sobeck talked, the more I reflected on Ay, and the more dangerous he became. Did he want to be Pharaoh, ruler of Egypt, and was simply waiting for his opportunity? Sobeck brought me news of how Nakhtimin was building up his own army, placing it in garrisons up and down the Nile, even beyond the Third Cataract. Ay was certainly flexing his muscles. In the second year of my exile he dispatched Nakhtimin with Lord Huy into Nubia to crush an incipient rebellion and bring that prosperous province firmly under Egypt's heel. The army won an outstanding success. Even from my garden I heard the crowds going along the path beside the river, eager to reach Thebes and welcome the victorious troops. Huy brought back carts and barges laden with booty: ostrich plumes, gold, silver, jewellery, as well as many captives and hostages.

At such times I felt a pang of envy, but I settled down, inter-ested in Djarka's little boy and eager to turn my garden into a paradise. Pentju virtually became a recluse. I enjoyed his dry wit, but as the months passed, he became more interested in the wine flagon and sitting by himself. Sometimes he would not shave or wash. I would remonstrate with him. I could see his health was failing, his mind no longer sharp; I was determined not to follow suit. Instead I became a keen gardener, digging a well, planting vines, laying out herb patches and flowerbeds. I built extensions to the house and a small pavilion for the garden. I was allowed to go fishing on the river; a small punt was provided, but my guards always came with me.

I must have been there about two years, whiling away my time, when, during the second month of the spring season, Sobeck arrived grey-faced. I asked him for news. He mentioned one word: 'Meryre.' According to Sobeck, Meryre had moved back to Thebes to carry out assassinations against those he now regarded as his inveterate enemies. Sobeck pointed at the walls of my house.

'Guard them carefully!'

'But I'm in disgrace,' I replied. 'Meryre—'

'Hold your response,' Sobeck interrupted. 'You, like the rest, have to be punished.'

Sobeck's words were prophetic. Meryre's assassins came one evening three weeks later, flowing like water over the walls of my house. Armed with daggers, they killed two gardeners and attempted to rush a side door, but were cut down. Only one survived, but the deep gash to his throat made it impossible to question him. I had the corpses stripped. They were Egyptians, men I couldn't recognise. From the scars on their bodies I deduced they were veterans, discharged soldiers. Sobeck arrived with his police. He too inspected the corpses and pronounced they were probably professional killers hired for the task. They were tossed into the river. Sobeck arranged for more mercenaries to be hired, whilst the guards around the gates and walls were doubled. He also brought news of other assassination attempts in Thebes. Even Lord Ay had not escaped unscathed. Early one morning, whilst visiting the Temple of Ma'at, he had been attacked by a madman just as he entered the central courtyard of the Karnak complex. Of course, the cobra escaped.

After a few weeks, the assassination attempts stopped and life returned to its peaceful and humdrum pace. Occasionally, Pharaoh Tutankhamun would send me gifts and short letters in which he would always describe his own health and ask after mine. Djarka tried to seek an audience with the Divine One, taking gifts and his baby son to present to Pharaoh. He was always turned away, even before he reached the outer court, by some chamberlain or petty official. Of course, I listened to the stories. Tutankhamun was a recluse. He was glimpsed borne on a litter, surrounded by Ay's men, being taken down to the river, or, screened by official flunkies as well as an army of priests, processing up to the temples to offer incense and make sacrifice. They talked of a young man of medium height with stooped shoulders and a slender body, with a beautiful, serene face and peculiarly shaped eyes. Ankhesenamun, always close by, became a famous beauty, known for her love of the most rare perfumes, costly clothing and exclusive jewels.

In truth, Lord Ay was the true power in the land, high priest and vizier combined. There were no more references to the Aten. I heard how that city, once the glory of Egypt, was being eaten away by the encroaching desert. Desert wanderers, sand-dwellers and Libyan raiders were stripping its fine houses, and Akenhaten's beautiful sun temples lay open to the sky. The mansions of the wealthy lost their cedarwood beams and columns to the the owl and the jackal. This was all done quietly, as Lord Ay and the Royal Circle worked strenuously to make people forget the reign of Akenhaten. The army was strengthened, new regiments raised, fresh chariot squadrons formed, stables restocked and great stud farms built. The House of War imported wood and metals for its armoury. The troops were used not only to impress foreign envoys but also to quell the lawlessness in the cities and the Red Lands and along the river. Fortresses and border posts were reinforced. Punitive expeditions were launched to secure the Horus Road across Sinai as well as the routes to the mines, quarries and oases of the eastern and western deserts. Rebellions in Kush were crushed, whilst the military command, under Horemheb and Rameses, pressed for all-out war to secure Canaan and curb the growing power of the Hittites.

Lord Ay, together with Huy and Maya, resisted such arguments. Egypt needed strengthening before going to war. Maya in the House of Silver was busy as a beetle replenishing Egypt's treasure. Gold, silver, precious stones, lapis lazuli, turquoise, malachite, alabaster and rare timbers poured into Egypt. The temples, too, glowed with power and strength under this great restoration. Their Schools of Life were reopened, granaries restocked, ox pens and sheepfolds filled with the best stock. It became common to see fat priests again, bellies bulging with the produce of sacrifice, their coffers full from the offerings of the faithful. The priesthood of Amun, Horus, Anubis and the rest of the Gods resumed their old arrogance, with one noticeable difference: Lord Ay, that spider at the centre of Egypt's web, kept close watch on the high priests as he did on every official, scribe, chamberlain and standard-bearer; only in Memphis and certain cities of the north was Ay's influence checked by that of Horemheb.

The source of all this gossip was, of course, Sobeck. If he had the measure of Ay, Lord Cobra certainly returned the compliment. My friend would laugh about how his spies spied upon Lord Ay's, as his did on everyone else's. Sobeck was amused by it all. A hideous mistake; he should never have underestimated such a man! Of course, I tried to warn him. One day – it must have been in the fourth month of the summer season during the third year of my exile – when I was entertaining Sobeck, I tried to tell him the story about a snake-charmer I'd arrested. 'He was one of those men,' I began, 'the most charming I've ever caught. He could persuade a chick to come out of its shell; he was so witty I released him unscathed.'

'I think I've heard the story,' Sobeck replied. 'But tell me again.'

'The snake-charmer travelled the villages on the outskirts of western Thebes. He sold a sacred snake oil which, if rubbed on a man's genitals, made the penis stronger and more vibrant. This confidence trickster amassed quite a fortune until he tried to fool a police informer placed among the villagers. The snake-charmer was arrested and brought before me. He confessed that the so-called sacred oil was nothing more than the juice of rat fat. Of course, no one ever protested, so what wrong had he done? He was right. Do you know of any man, Sobeck, who is willing to tell people that he has trouble between his legs, then tries to do something to improve his performance only to be fooled?'

'And the moral of the story?' Sobeck demanded.

'That's how Lord Ay works. He fools you, as he charms you, yet the only person you can blame is yourself.'

'Mahu, can't you say anything good about him?'

'Yes,' I laughed, 'his brother Nakhtimin is much worse!'

Now, Sobeck was a former leader of gangs and thieves, yet he possessed some goodness, a sort of decency which his recent marriage to the plump, vivacious daughter of a high-ranking Thebean merchant brought to the fore. He was contented with the world and at peace with himself. I prayed he was still alert enough to perceive the darkness in the soul of General Nahktimin, a man of hard heart and no kindness, a born killer, a ferocious fighter, devoted to his charismatic elder brother. Nakhtimin was now Chief Scribe, commander-in-chief of Egypt's southern armies, their regiments, chariot squadrons, troops of archers and mercenaries. He used these troops to massacre the scavengers who'd come drifting in from the desert looking for easy pickings, exterminating them as he did any threat to his power. Tomb robbers no longer pillaged the Necropolis or the Valley of the Kings. Nakhtimin caught them and had them impaled along the roads and clifftops.

'The thieves came after the treasure, you see,' Sobeck explained as he sipped his wine. 'The robber gangs know all about the treasures brought from the City of the Aten. I'm just sorry I missed my share.' Sobeck laughed. 'Oh, I see you still have the two statues.'

'Ah, yes,' I replied. 'Pentju received them as a gift from the palace for his care of the young Pharaoh, the only present he was given. He placed them at the entrance to our Hall of Columns. By the way, what did happen to the rest of the treasure?'

'Let me put it this way, you will find no beggars in Thebes, Mahu. Nakhtimin marched them into the Valley of the Kings to do hard labour, quarrying new caves and tombs. Men, women and children, they were all dead in a month.'

'Why new caves and tombs?'

'The Aten treasures were first placed in temporary storage in the tombs and burial temples of former Pharaohs. Now Ay is moving them to places known only to himself, Nakhtimin and others of their gang.'

Sobeck fell silent for a while.

'He has his uses,' he murmured eventually. 'I mean General Nakhtimin. The assassinations have stopped. I hunted high and low without sight or sign of Meryre and his coven – they have disappeared like a puff of smoke on a summer's day.'

'Massacred, wiped out?'

'No.' Sobeck sighed. 'They have fled, but I don't know where, probably out across the Sinai, which brings me to another matter.' Sobeck pointed across the garden: Djarka and Mert sat next to the Pool of Purity, watching their baby son Imhotep crawl like a little beetle. I leaned forward.

'Are they in danger?'

'Not at the moment,' Sobeck replied. 'But they did stay loyal to you. Djarka could have left. I would have found him a post, some office at court or temple. Moreover, let's not forget, both know about the massacre.' Sobeck tapped his goblet with his fingernails. 'I do wonder why they supported you.'

'Haven't you heard of devotion, friendship?'

Sobeck just rubbed his earlobe; a common habit when he was suspicious.

'I think Djarka is here to watch you, Mahu, though I don't know the reason.'

'Why are you concerned about him now?'

'Oh, I'm not concerned about them. However, I'm sure General Rameses would like to question them, and I am going to show you why.'

Four days later Sobeck returned after dark. I was writing my journal, describing the coolness of the evening, the scent of the garden where the light from the coloured oil lamps glowed and danced like fireflies. From the river echoed various sounds, the bellowing of the hippopotami almost drowning the fading calls of the birds and the harsh chorus of the frogs. I was sitting on the roof of the house, staring up at the *akhakha*, as the poets call the stars, the 'flowers of heaven', blossoming brilliantly against the night. Such harmony was disturbed by the news of Sobeck's arrival. I went down to greet him. He slipped through the gate, paused, then whistled into the night. An old man dressed in a thick robe, a tasselled shawl around his shoulders, shuffled through, his papyrus reed sandals slapping on the ground. He was small and bony, his wizened face like a dried-out nut, though he was alert and bright-eyed as any boy.

'This is Seenu.' Sobeck introduced my visitor as we took our seats in what I called my Blue Lotus Pavilion. We sat in silence for a while, until the servants, who, I am sure, included Lord Ay's spies, served us sesame seed cake and chilled white wine. From across the garden, cutting through the noises of the night, came the raucous sound of Pentju bawling out a song we'd all learnt as Children of the Kap. The old man laughed.

'A fitting lullaby,' he whispered.

I did not reply. I just hoped Pentju would get drunk, fall asleep and not make a nuisance of himself. Once the servants had left, I closed the door.

'Who are you?' I asked, sitting back on the cushions.

'Seenu was once a scribe of the execution stake where prisoners are questioned,' Sobeck explained. 'He is proficient in tongues. He later became Chief Scribe of the Anubis shrine.'

'That was a thousand jubilees ago,' Seenu chuckled, 'when the Great House of a Million Years was ruled by the Mighty Bull, Magnificent of Forms, and I wore the jackal-headed collar. Oh yes, many, many Pharaohs ago.' He closed his eyes and rocked backwards and forwards. 'I should be with the sleepers.' His voice was hardly above a whisper. 'I should walk with death.' He opened his eyes. 'I have passed my eightieth year. I owe my own life to the patronage of the Great God Buto. I am old now . . .'

He chattered on. Sobeck warned me with his eyes to keep silent.

'Once my loins were fresh and fertile, my seed came pouring out. I used to sleep the four quarters of the night with slave women on either side.'

Again I made to interrupt, but Sobeck gestured to keep silent.

'I was scribe of the Execution House, the recorder of the Slaughter Yard in the House of Chains. I answered directly to Pharaoh, but even then I was growing old.'

'Which Pharaoh?' I asked.

'Tuthmosis, father of Amenhotep the Magnificent. Now, as you know, Amenhotep fell in love with a beautiful young girl from the city of Akhmin. She was of the Apiru tribe. Oh, I got to know them all well,' he sighed. 'Tiye and her brother Ay. I learned all about the legends of her people: how they came from Canaan; how they look forward to a great leader to take them back; how they were special in the eyes of God. I read their records. I even saw the paintings out in the Valley of the Grey Dawn. I also learned about the Aten, the One God. I visited Canaan. I have studied the Apiru more carefully than any scholar in Egypt.'

'And then what?'

'I reported all to Tuthmosis. He was very alarmed. He tried to warn his son, who then was no more than a boy. Amenhotep met Tiye when they were both Children of the Kap.' The old man held his hand with two fingers wrapped together. 'They were inseparable, one of those love matches which begin even before the loins are excited. Tuthmosis was advised by his priests against the marriage.'

'But Tuthmosis died suddenly,' I interrupted, 'a mysterious death. Wasn't he in his late twenties?' The old man agreed. He stuffed sesame cake in his mouth and slurped wine.

'Did you keep any record?' Sobeck asked. Seenu, his mouth full, shook his head.

Sobeck, poking me in the arm, led me out into the garden, telling our visitor to eat and drink as much as he could.

'Why have you brought him?' I asked. 'I know about these legends, you know that I know.'

I heard a sound behind me and whirled round. Nothing, though I was sure someone was there.

'Seenu tells me nothing new,' I continued.

'He lives in Western Thebes.' Sobeck measured his words carefully. 'A week ago he was overheard boasting in a beer shop how General Rameses wished to see him.' I felt a chill, brought on more by fear than the night breeze.

'I had him arrested,' Sobeck continued.

'Who, Rameses?' I asked.

'Don't joke, Mahu. The old man. I gave him a comfortable chamber in one of my houses. I hired a temple girl to keep him warm at night and made sure his belly remained full. He is greedy and lecherous as an old goat. I wanted to know why Rameses was looking for him. He told me about the Apiru. It

371

took some time to get the whole story. Ten years ago people would have dismissed it as the babblings of an old scribe, only too willing to bore you to death for a drop of ale. I also listened to other reports. Rameses has sent spies into Canaan. He has scribes searching the records. He is looking for Akenhaten. He believes he is still alive. He is also hunting for Meryre and growing more knowledgeable about the origins of Akenhaten and the legends of the Apiru. To put it bluntly . . .' Sobeck paused. 'If Rameses had his way, a savage persecution would be launched. They would not only wipe out any member of the Aten, but anyone who has anything to do with the tribe of Apiru. That includes Djarka, Mert and their child.'

'So what do you propose?'

Sobeck paused, as if listening to a bird fluttering in the tree.

'I intend to kill the old man.' He rubbed his hands together. 'I have no choice. He will die peacefully in his sleep and I will hand his corpse over to be embalmed.'

Sobeck walked back to the pavilion.

'Best be warned.' He raised his voice. 'The hunters are out.'

The months turned into seasons, the seasons into years. Six years passed. I grew a little plumper. Djarka and Mert had another child, a girl they called Miriam, a companion for her elder brother Imhotep. Djarka now led his own life. He came and went as he pleased. We very rarely discussed the glory days when we had plotted, conspired and fought, either on the battlefield or amongst that brood of conspirators at the imperial court. Djarka seemed infatuated with his wife and children. A husband and father first, rather than a soldier. We grew apart, like the gap that divides a father from his son when the latter moves away to be with his own family. I was still deeply attracted to Mert, but she had eyes only for her husband. It was a true love match. Oh, we reminisced and, when the wine flowed like water, became nostalgic. Djarka warned me not to discuss what had happened in the Valley of the Grey Dawn, and when Mert was present, Lord Ay's name was never to be mentioned. Their two children were beautiful and delightful. I made up nicknames for them, 'balls of fluff', or 'pots of sweet honey'. If I became bored with my garden, writing in my journal or Pentju's drunken mutterings, I'd always go looking for them. I did so reluctantly at first, not because I didn't like children, but because I felt unclean in their presence. I had blood on my hands. I had killed and killed again. I felt like a jackal put in charge of baby ducks. When I described my feelings to Djarka, his face broke into a smile and he punched me playfully on the shoulder.

'More like a guard dog,' he replied.

I felt better after that. Perhaps it was the children's innocence which frightened me. Somehow or other they might recognise a soul which reeked of sin. They didn't. They enjoyed my games, especially when I pretended to be a lion. I discovered I had a gift for woodwork and would love to carve a giraffe or antelope or fashion a wooden sword or shield. Imhotep, as he grew older, would often seek me out; even when I was squatting like a scribe, he nestled close to me. He regarded me as a great warrior. I was touched and flattered, for this was how Djarka described me. Ah well, it was better that than being called an assassin.

Sobeck's lovely wife gave birth to twin boys. She too visited our mansion, bringing the children together with an army of wet nurses and servants. I grew to enjoy the long evenings, the feasting and the chatter. Sobeck now heeded my warnings, and did everything he could to pose as Ay's faithful retainer.

'There's nothing like children,' he once remarked, 'to make you prudent and careful.'

He also brought news of how the restoration of Egypt's fortune was growing apace. Nowhere more than Thebes, where new buildings of marble and white granite dazzled the eye. Rivers of treasure flowed in from north, south, east and west. Egypt's enemies, the people of the Nine Bows trembled, frightened of Egypt's powerful regiments and teeming squadrons of war chariots. Imperial war barges patrolled the Nile and the shores of the Delta, high-beaked and powerful, crammed with archers and spearmen. They fought off pirates and invaders from the Great Green. I often glimpsed such barges from my rooftop, patrolling the river, standards displayed, great sails billowing out.

People exclaimed how the marvellous days of Amenhotep the Magnificent had returned. Envoys from other nations, even the long-haired Hittites, hastened to pay lip service at least to the Great House, the Palace of a Million Years.

Such reports never disturbed me. I mellowed and remained patient, like a man lost in a dream. I seduced the maids. When I wished to be alone, I put on a broad-brimmed peasant's hat and tended my gardens. I grew rather bored with flowers and cultivated new types of vegetables and herbs, including an original onion. I became expert in growing capers, not so fleshy but still rich in oil. I wrote a learned paper on this and sent it by way of Sobeck to the House of Life at the Temple of Horus. It was well received. I also specialised in poisons, mixing the juice of ivy with fat berries and other ingredients. My strain was virtually tasteless, or so Pentju told me. He examined it carefully whilst I hopped from foot to foot. Sometimes my physician friend was so drunk, he'd eat or sip anything placed before him.

Pentju showed little interest in Sobeck's visits, except on one matter. At first I thought he was keen to learn news about Canaan when he remained sober and questioned Sobeck carefully. After a while, I realised he was more interested in the doings of the House of Envoys, which controlled Egypt's foreign affairs. The generals' desire for war had been constantly frustrated, even though everybody was becoming alarmed at the growing power of the Hittites. Lord Ay, supported by Maya and Huy, had developed a different policy: they turned to the other great powers, particularly the Mitanni, to check the Hittites. Pentju became more alert than ever over this and questioned Sobeck about Ay's furious attempts to win over Tushratta, King of the Mitanni.

'Ay has done everything in his power,' Sobeck reported on one occasion. 'He sends envoys to the Mitanni with costly gifts: kites of gold and silver to raise mercenaries.'

Once Pentju's questions were answered, he would go back to his drinking. He had grown obese and red-faced, and more often than not he was drunk. He could still be a skilled physician and a witty companion, but he insisted on sleeping the day away and drinking through the night. He confided in me that when darkness fell, the 'demon thieves' sprang out of the darkness and plagued his soul.

'They wait for me,' he whispered, tapping his fleshy nose. 'I see them lurking in the cypress groves with the fires of hell burning all around.'

Djarka lost patience with him and declared he was mad. I believe he was as sane as any of us. Like me, he was plagued by ghosts from the past, and not all such ghosts are easily exorcised.

Shta-i
(Ancient Egyptian for 'the Secret Place')

Chapter 19

In the first week of the month of Thoth, – the eighth year of Tutankhamun, Lord of the Two Lands, Mighty Bull, Most Fitting of Forms, Horus in the South, Horemheb and Rameses visited me. I truly thought I would never see this precious pair again. Yet they came swaggering through the main gates, splendid in their robes, all agleam with their medallions, collars, brooches and rings. Outside the gate their staff officers unhitched their chariots, chattering and laughing as they led them off into the green coolness of a palm grove. Horemheb looked a little plumper, a roll of fat beneath his black button eyes, slightly jowly, though his body was still hard and muscular. Rameses was more wrinkled but lean as ever, eyes full of malice, that smirk on his thin lips; he still reminded me of a vicious greyhound. They were pleasant enough, clasping my hands, ordering a servant forward with gifts, joking with Pentju and Djarka. Rameses mischievously asked whether Sobeck, my 'constant visitor', was present.

I just smiled.

'You haven't come about my health,' I suggested. 'So you have come to plot.'

They did not disagree. We met behind closed doors in the Blue Lotus Pavilion. After a few pleasantries Rameses threw down his whisk. I was highly amused by it. The whisk was sky blue, with a golden lotus on the handle; more suitable for a lady of the court rather than a high-ranking officer of the Imperial Staff.

'Are you enjoying retirement, Mahu?' he sneered.

'You mean my exile?'

'Your exile.' Rameses smirked. 'You must miss the heavy perfume of the court.'

'I miss neither that nor your stench.'

'Mahu, Mahu, you don't miss your friends?'

'I miss the smiles of Pharaoh. May he live a million years and enjoy countless jubilees.'

Rameses and Horemheb hastily agreed.

'The Divine One also misses you.'

'How do you know that? I understand very few people are allowed to see him.'

'We do meet him at the Royal Circle,' Horemheb intervened.

'And how do you find him?'

'Quiet, serene.' Horemheb shrugged. 'The Lord Ay is his mouthpiece.' I sensed the hidden tension, a shift in Horemheb's eyes. Rameses was studying me curiously, head slightly to one side, puckering his lower lip between finger and thumb.

'I understand,' I broke the silence, 'that you, General Rameses, have been very busy in your studies about the history of the Apiru.'

'You know why.' Rameses picked up the flywhisk. 'I'm sure your friend Sobeck has told you everything, so let's be blunt, Mahu.'

'My lord Rameses, that would be a change.'

'Akenhaten may still be alive. Meryre is definitely hiding in Canaan with the other heretics, stirring up trouble.'

'But he's not with Akenhaten?' I asked.

'You mean the madman.'

'We all supported him, General Horemheb.'

'For a while, but that's not why we are here.' Horemheb cleared his throat. 'My lord Mahu, would you like to return to power?'

'Why?' I replied. 'To be your spy?'

'Oh come, come,' Rameses protested.

'Oh come, come, General Rameses. Why else are you visiting me? It's certainly not because of my lovely eyes and generous character.'

'We would like to see you appointed as Overseer of the House of Envoys,' Horemheb murmured. 'To lead a diplomatic mission to the Hittites. You are sly enough to assess their power, cunning enough to judge if they are a real danger to us.'

'And report back to you, as well as Lord Ay?'

'Of course,' Rameses agreed.

'You want me to go to Canaan to spy, but you are hoping that Akenhaten will show himself to me; for some strange reason he had a special liking to me. And if he does, you'll kill him.'

Rameses smiled.

'Do you think,' I continued, 'Lord Ay would embrace me and give me the rings of office? He'd realise you wanted me back as your spy.'

'You're our friend.'

'Since when?'

Horemheb laughed. 'Very good, my lord Mahu. Huy and Maya would welcome you back.'

'For what? To keep a watch on Lord Ay?'

'Let's cut to the marrow of the bone.' Horemheb shifted forward. 'The Divine One himself wishes your return.' He smiled at my surprise. 'Our Pharaoh is almost a young man, of seventeen summers. I find him strange. I don't think his health is good, in either body or soul. You know that, Lord Mahu. You lived with him when he was a child. He is given to outbursts. In the last few months he has increasingly demanded in a pained voice, "Where is Uncle Mahu?"'

'Why now?' I asked.

'Why not?' Rameses retorted. 'Perhaps he has done it before, though in private. He wants you and Pentju to return. Oh, by the way, how is the toper?'

'As always, General, a better companion than you. So,' I drew myself up, 'the Divine One wishes me to return. A wish supported by new-found friends. Well, well!' I leaned back. 'My two lions, you have surprised me! Do you really need me, Horemheb? Don't forget you're married to Mutnedjmet, sister of Nefertiti!'

'My wife is as different from her,' Horemheb snapped, 'as gold is from sand. She has nothing in common with her father, that mongoose of a man, or her scorpion sister. She does not like

381

her father.' He shrugged. 'That was the beginning of our friendship.'

Horemheb plucked at the tassels of his robe.

'I want you back, Mahu. I want you in charge of the House of Envoys; I want to find out what is happening in Canaan. Lord Ay spies on me and I on him. Sobeck must have told you about the presents and the money he has sent to the Mitanni. At first, I thought this was just policy, to keep the Hittites contained, but there's more. He has been searching for the Lady Tahana.'

My heart skipped a beat.

'She was principal lady-in-waiting to Khiya, Tutankhamun's mother. She and her husband mysteriously left the City of the Aten and returned to the Mitanni court around the same time the plague struck.'

'Why should he be searching for her?' I asked.

'We don't know. Earlier this year, during the last month of the Season of the Planting, General Nakhtimin and a squadron of troops sailed up the Nile for a meeting with a Mitanni envoy. We don't know why they met or what was agreed. They returned by night to Thebes.' He paused. 'According to my spies, Nakhtimin brought back a man, his face covered by a jackal face-mask. I also heard reports of the same man being imprisoned in the old House of Residence, where we all trained as Children of the Kap.'

I couldn't hide my consternation. 'Was it Akenhaten?'

'No.' Horemheb shook his head. 'The individual was young, we could tell by his belly and legs. I have tried everything,' Horemheb confessed, 'to discover what happened. Nakhtimin's troops closely guarded that part of the palace. In recent months they have withdrawn, which means the young man has either gone or died. Now,' Horemheb scratched his head, 'I'm afraid, Mahu. What is Ay plotting? Will something happen to Tutankhamun, and would Ay claim the throne? So,' he smiled, 'if the Divine One and the Royal Circle ask you to return, will you agree?'

'I will think on it.'

'And if you return, will you be our ally, not our spy?'

'I will think on it.' I made to rise.

'You don't seem worried about the Divine One.' Horemheb clasped my wrist. 'He was your charge.'

I broke from his grip. 'That was in the past, General. I cannot be held responsible for what I have no power over.'

I recalled Tutankhamun's gentle, almond-shaped eyes, his serene face.

'You do care, don't you?' Horemheb asked.

He felt amongst his robes, drew out a leather pouch and shook out the contents: an exquisite strip of gold depicting Pharaoh wearing the war crown of Egypt, smiting the head of an enemy in the presence of the War God Montu, behind him the Goddess Nepthys.

'Lord Ay hired a goldsmith to fashion this for him; an apprentice in the shop made a fair copy.'

I examined the gold strip carefully. On closer inspection it was cruder than any original. The Pharaoh was Tutankhamun, no more than a boy, but from the hieroglyphs on the band of gold, I realised that Ay was the God Montu and Ankhesenamun the Goddess Nepthys.

'Ay made that for his own personal use.' Horemheb took it from me. 'He is becoming arrogant. He sees himself as a God, the master of the Pharaoh.'

Horemheb was not lying. No Egyptian would ever dream of fashioning such a scene. Pharaoh paid service to no one but the Gods; he was their equal, the living incarnation of their will.

'Now we know there is something wrong with Tutankhamun.' Rameses got to his feet. 'Can you imagine, Mahu, Akenhaten bowing to anyone? Is Ay abusing his position? Are there secret ceremonies at the court where Ay and his granddaughter dress up as gods and make Pharaoh bow before them. Now, you think!'

For the rest of that day, I sat in the pavilion, my mind a whirl. Servants brought me food and drink. Why was Ay hunting for some young man amongst the Mitanni? What was he planning? Darkness fell. The evening breeze was refreshing, and through the half-open door I could see the servants. Djarka came over. Did I want to join him and his family for supper? I declined, and he wandered off. A short while later Pentju arrived, followed by his servants carrying a jug of wine and two goblets.

'I heard about the visit of the mighty warriors.' Pentju sat down on the cushions. 'Did they ask after me? I suppose they didn't.'

'You need a bath,' I retorted. 'And a shave.'

'What I need, Mahu, is a goblet of wine and a young maid. I am going to make a nuisance of myself until you tell me what those two cruel bastards came here for.'

I told Pentju how they wished me to return to court. I mentioned the House of Envoys and, only the Gods know the reason, I told him about Ay, his dealings with the Mitanni and that strange prisoner Nakhtimin had brought back from the Delta. Pentju sat, all colour draining from his face, mouth open, eyes staring, as if he'd been visited by some horror in the night. Perhaps I'd drunk too much myself, for I pressed on with the story. The goblet slipped from Pentju's hand and he began to shake like a man in a fit. I called his name, but he stared as if he couldn't see any more. A strange sound bubbled at the back of his throat. The shock sobered me up. I left the pavilion, shouting for help. When I returned, Pentju was convulsing on the floor, his muscles rigid. He had vomited, and for a moment I thought he was choking. A leech arrived and made sure that Pentju's throat was clear, then placed a leather wedge between his teeth and shouted for blankets.

I sent a messenger to Sobeck to ask him to hire the best physicians of the mouth, heart, stomach and anus. They diagnosed some fit brought on by a fever of the mind. In truth, like all doctors they were useless. They grabbed my silver and informed me that Pentju should have bed rest and no wine. I could have reached the same conclusion, so I sent them packing through the gate. When Sobeck learned what had happened he just shook his head, whistled under his breath and cursed his spies for failing him. He confessed he knew nothing about what Horemheb and Rameses had told me. At the moment there was little I could do with such information. I was too busy nursing Pentju, as well as curious to discover why my words had provoked such a powerful reaction. Some of the physicians believed Pentju's ailments were the work of a *gesnu* – an evil being or demon. I heartily agreed. It was a fitting description for Ay and his Akhmin gang.

The weeks passed. Pentju, deprived of his wine, grew stronger.

I teased him: he was a Child of the Kap, he had been trained as a soldier, so despite his fat, he should be as strong as an ox. He was physician enough to diagnose his own condition. He likened it to the shock of a mother who has received the sudden news that her beloved son has died in battle. He cursed all physicians.

'If you want me to stay healthy,' he bawled at me, 'keep those bastards away.'

I was mystified by his comparison of himself to a mother losing her favourite son; I questioned him. One evening Pentju decided to confess, to escape the *Tcha-t*, the guilt which soured his spirit. We'd finished a meal: strips of roast antelope, tenderised and spiced. He abruptly pushed his food away and started to cry. For a while I let him sob, then he said I must be his chapel priest.

'You do remember,' he began, 'the scurrilous stories that Tutankhamun was my son, not Akenhaten's?'

'Yes, but you assured me he was the Pharaoh's true heir.'

'I spoke with a true voice: he was and is.' Pentju sighed. 'Khiya gave birth to him.'

'You told me that.'

'I truly loved her, Mahu, even though I was married. I purged her beautiful body of the poisons Nefertiti kept giving her.' He paused, sipping at the watered wine. 'You know how it was in the City of the Aten. Nefertiti ruled like Queen Bee of the hive; her sting was nasty. I had managed to persuade Akenhaten to give Khiya her own house. We were in the city for three years before Akenhaten, tired of Nefertiti's arrogance, began to show more than a passing interest in his second wife, the little Mitanni princess. Well.' Pentju blinked. 'I committed treason. I had intercourse with the Lady Khiya. She became pregnant, she was terrified, so was I. How could we explain it away? She pretended to be ill and withdrew to her own chambers. Only I, the Lady Tahana and her husband knew the truth. The child, a boy, came out of the egg prematurely, sometime between the sixth and seventh month. Nevertheless, he was strong. We hired a wet nurse whom we could trust.' He paused. 'Are you surprised?'

'Yes and no,' I confessed.

'It was well known that Khiya and the Lady Tahana were very close. We were terrified. I knew what had happened to Sobeck when he had seduced a concubine, a Royal Ornament, of Amenhotep the Magnificent. He was lucky to be branded and sent to a prison oasis; the concubine was put into a cage and torn to pieces by a wild animal.' Pentju wiped the spittle from the corner of his mouth. 'Khiya was terrified for the child and ourselves. She feared Akenhaten's anger and Nefertiti's murderous rages even more. She made special sacrifices to Hathor the Golden One and any other God or Goddess she could think of. In the end her prayer was answered. The Lady Tahana concocted a plan: she would adopt the child as her own and return to the land of the Mitanni. They were not Egyptian subjects; they would not need Akenhaten's permission. She and her husband left when the child was three months old. Khiya's first pregnancy remained a secret. You know how it was in the City of the Aten. Akenhaten and Nefertiti were bound up with their own affairs. On three occasions whilst Khiya was pregnant, Akenhaten visited her. On the first, her monthly courses had just stopped; that was no problem. On the other two, she feigned sickness, a fever.' Pentju pulled a face. 'Being a physician, I could help with the symptoms.'

'And after the Mitanni took the child away?'

'Khiya and I were relieved. We took a vow it would never happen again. Her first pregnancy made her even more fertile, so when Akenhaten lay with her she conceived again. I often wondered about the first child, but it was too dangerous to enquire.'

'So how did Ay find out?'

'That serpent may have heard something, from a servant, a guide; someone must have talked. It would have been easy for Ay to go through the archives and find out why the Lady Tahana had left so abruptly with a child. At first he was probably too busy because of other crises, but Ay's a mongoose. He would not rest until he knew the truth. He must have bribed the Mitanni to hand the young man over.'

'How old must he be?'

'Somewhere between his eighteenth and nineteenth year. The Mitanni, desperate for Egyptian money and supplies, must have been persuaded. Only the Gods know what story Ay peddled. Perhaps he insinuated that this mysterious individual was his own illegitimate child.'

'And why would Ay want him?'

'You know as well as I do, Mahu: the blood feud. Khiya produced an illegitimate child but also gave Pharaoh a living male heir. Nefertiti failed to do that. Worse, the birth of that male heir led to the fatal rift between Akenhaten and Nefertiti. Ay would want vengeance. Khiya had destroyed his beloved daughter; she was the cause of that great Queen's downfall.'

I sat reflecting on what I'd learned.

'You don't have to tell me, Mahu.' Pentju broke into my reverie. 'Ay has killed him. Oh, he will give some excuse to the Mitanni about a fever, an illness. Ay knows poison as well as you and I.' Pentju's voice broke, and he put his face into his hands. 'He has killed my son,' he sobbed. 'He has murdered the Beloved.'

As Pentju slowly recovered, I could only wonder what to do until the Gods, or the demons, intervened.

During the last few days of the final month of the year, we were summoned to the palace. A royal messenger, carrying his silver wand of office, arrived at our mansion accompanied by six armed Nesu, the bodyguard of Pharaoh. The messenger carried a scroll sealed with the imperial cartouche; he kissed it and broke the seal. The invitation was short and blunt: the Lords Mahu and Pentju were to come before the Tau-Retui, Pharaoh and his Royal Circle, on the sixteenth day of the first month in the season of the sowing. So we did, and it was good to be back in the heart of Thebes, to leave the quayside and move through the suburbs of the poor, past their shabby cottages, avoiding the infected pools and the heaps of reeking rubbish. After the loneliness of exile, even the legions of red-eyed beggars seemed welcoming.

The growing wealth of Thebes had brought in peasants, traders and labourers from outlying villages. They'd built their ramshackle houses on every plot of land. Some were successful, most were not and so drowned their sorrows in cups of cheap brandy. Everyone, however, was busy. Women in soiled smocks squatted at dark doorways, grinding their precious portions of corn between pestle and stone. Along the street their children hunted and fought over the dung of livestock, which they would dry to use as fuel and so turn the air foul with its acrid smell. Further up we passed the traders' stalls, displaying jewellery from Canaan, leatherwork from Libya, oil and embroideries from Babylon. Confectioners were busy driving away the flies, whilst offering preserved dates, syrups, and pastries made of honey and spices. Nearby, their apprentices pounded almonds and nuts in a mortar to make delicious brews. Butchers, their stall flowing with blood, hacked at the quarters of geese and oxen, as little boys and girls, naked as they were born, ran around with flywhisks to drive off the insects. Shoemakers offered everything from delicate slippers to marching boots. Customers with pouches of electrum, gold and silver queued in front of the goldsmiths.

After the silence of my mansion, I revelled in the noise and changing colours of the sea of people milling about. The shouts and screams, the conflicting aromas of fresh blood, cooking meats and drying leather mingling with those of burnt honey, spices and perfumes. Songwriters, storytellers, musicians and dancers of various nationalities touted for custom. Prostitutes plied their trade at the mouth of alleyways, pulling their clients towards them, using the hard brick wall as a mattress or kneeling down before them without a care in the world. Further along, near the gateway to the barracks, women screamed and rolled in the dust as the military scribes from the House of War enrolled their menfolk in the army. I kept drinking in the sights, but Pentju walked slumped, head down like a man sentenced to the stake. The Nubian mercenaries in their leopard kilts, silver chains and nodding white plumes kept us clear of the crowds, their great oval shields displaying the ram's head of Amun creating a wall around us.

Eventually we reached the Avenue of the Golden Falcon, leading down to the Malkata Palace, its white and red stone walls refurbished and gleaming like a beacon. The huge copper-plated gates opened into finely laid-out gardens. I wanted to stop and inspect some of the new plants, but the captain of our escort shook his head and so we passed on. They left us in an antechamber, its walls decorated with silver antelopes leaping against a light green background above fields of gold. On either side of them ran an ochre frieze embellished with silver palms. I tried to interest Pentju in the painting, but he sat gazing at the floor. I had taken his reluctant oath that he would do nothing stupid or dangerous. A chamberlain served us iced fruit drinks, and I insisted that he tested them first. He was surprised and shocked, but agreed.

A short while later he returned and we were taken into the Dolphin Room, the great council chamber where the Royal Circle would meet. On its cobalt-blue walls silver dolphins leaped above golden waves. Its floor of polished stone reflected the mosaic in the ceiling of more dolphins and other beasts of the sea. At the far end of the chamber, on a raised hooded dais, stood three gold-plated thrones: their backs and arms were decorated with gold leaf, their legs studded with gems; the carved feet rested on polished black footstools inlaid with ebony and silver. The smaller thrones lacked the majesty of the imperial one, but their message was clear enough.

'A throne fit for a Pharaoh,' Pentju whispered. 'But still, one for Ay and one for Ankhesenamun.' The thrones were faced by a semi-circle of silver-topped tables and cushioned seats, where members of the Royal Circle would squat. I counted ten in all. Three similar tables stood in the centre for the scribes with their writing palettes, reed pens, papyrus rolls and pots of red and black ink.

We had hardly arrived when trumpets blew, cymbals clashed and the great double doors to the council chamber were flung open. Two stole priests entered, swinging pots of incense, flanked by imperial fan-bearers. These took up their positions as the Royal Bodyguard marched in, victorious warriors who displayed the insignia for taking an enemy's head in battle. The bodyguard formed an avenue for more officials. The council chamber began to fill. More cymbals clashed, trumpets blew, and a herald entered and cried out Pharaoh's names.

'He of the Two Lands, the Dynamic of Laws, the Golden Falcon who wears the regalia. He who pleases the Gods, King of Upper and Lower Egypt. The Lordly Manifestation of Ra. The Living Image of Amun . . .'

We prostrated ourselves, nosing the ground. I stole a glance at Tutankhamun as he entered, garbed in his state costume, his head covered by a pure white head-dress and bound by the golden Uraeus. He wore drawers of pleated linen, ornamented at the back by a jackal's tail and at the front by an overlapping stiffened apron of encrusted gold and enamel. Over all this hung a long sleeveless robe of snow-white linen, open at the throat to reveal a brilliant pectoral displaying Nekhbet, the Vulture Goddess; a dazzling piece of craftsmanship of precious stones. On his feet were silver-chased peak sandals. Tutankhamun walked slowly, rather ungainly, resting on a walking stick, the head of which was carved in the shape of a panther. He had that same innocent, boyish look, almost feminine: pouched cheeks, slightly parted lips, his almond eyes ringed with black kohl. He was smiling, looking over his shoulder at his Queen Ankhesenamun, who was a stunning vision of voluptuous beauty. Oh, she had changed! A thick, richly braided wig framed her sensuous face, her lustrous dark eyes were emphasised by green kohl, her dusted skin made more eye-catching by glittering jewellery at her throat, wrists, fingers and ankles. She wore a sleeveless glittering robe fashioned in layers and bound by a brilliant red sash, and she moved daintily on thick-soled sandals. She carried a sky-blue fan, edged with silver, and used this to hide her face but not her eyes.

Ay followed behind, head shaven, his falcon-like face gleaming with oil. He wore all the regalia of high office and clutched a beautiful pair of red gloves, a sign of Pharaoh's personal favour. The other lords followed: Nakhtimin, Huy, Maya, Horemheb, Rameses, Anen, Chief Priest of Amun; all the great masters of Egypt. Their costly robes, gold-edged walking sticks, gorgeous fans and oiled, perfumed faces exuded power and wealth. Maya looked more like a woman than ever, with his thick glossy black wig, painted face and high-heeled shoes. As he turned his head I glimpsed his pearl earrings, and I wondered again about this brilliant man who so desperately wanted to be a woman. The relationship between him and Sobeck had cooled since the latter's marriage. Rumour had it that Maya now enjoyed a harem of beautiful young men.

Tutankhamun sat down on his throne whilst a stole priest chanted the hymn.

Oh Amun,
Watcher in silence,
Whose wisdom cannot be fathomed . . .

Afterwards, the chamber was cleared of soldiers and officials. Ay and Ankhesenamun took their seats, and the rest followed, whilst the scribes squatted in the middle. Pentju and I remained kneeling until Ay imperiously indicated that we should take our seats at the remaining two tables. Ay had prepared the tablet of business; Pentju and I were at the top of the list.

'Due to the great favour of Pharaoh,' Ay proclaimed, 'the Divine One has decided to reveal his face to them and smile at them. Accordingly . . .'

In a word, Pentju was appointed Royal Physician and I was to become Overseer of the House of Envoys, with responsibility for foreign affairs. All the time I watched Tutankhamun staring beatifically at me. Now and again in his excitement he would turn to Ankhesenamun. She slouched on her throne, one pretty sandalled foot tapping ever so imperiously. I would wink at Tutankhamun or slightly raise my hand. Beside me, Pentju glowered as Ay, the Great Mongoose as we now called him, turned to the other business. Most of it was mundane, the greater part being the situation in Canaan. Its petty princelings still squabbled; the real danger were the Hittites, who were now a major threat to Egypt's allies in the region, the Babylonians and the Mitanni. Horemheb and Rameses sang the same old hymn, the need for military intervention. Ay was not so eager to contradict them, the question being when and how. The lions of the desert seemed satisfied with this and eventually the meeting ended.

Pentju and I were brought before the Royal Throne. Ankhesenamun indulged in her usual flirtations, leaning forward allowing her gold robe to hang loose, exposing her breasts, the nipples of which were painted silver. She had that questioning, innocent look as if wondering where we had been all this time; she was most effusive, caressing my cheek or

391

patting Pentju's balding head. Her touch was cool, her perfume the most expensive Egypt could provide, the juice of the blue lotus. She was most solicitous, anxious about our well-being. We both could tell from her eyes that the royal bitch was laughing at us. Tutankhamun, however, was delightful, so pleased to see us he almost forgot court protocol and couldn't sit still with excitement. He gave each of us a gold collar, and leaned closer so that he could fasten mine round my neck, then he brushed my cheeks with his lips and called me Uncle. Ankhesenamun, meanwhile, sniggered behind her hand.

Ay coughed loudly to remind Tutankhamun of court etiquette. The young Pharaoh recalled himself and tried to keep his face straight, but the effort was useless. He returned to calling me Uncle, saying how much he had missed both me and Pentju, how we must come fishing and fowling with him or, perhaps, take his war chariot out into the eastern desert. He seemed healthy enough, bright-eyed and plump-cheeked, though his body was manifesting some of his father's characteristics: a slightly pointed chest, broad hips, long fingers and toes, legs, thighs and arms rather thin. He was also experiencing some discomfort when he moved.

Once the audience finished, some of the Royal Circle approached to congratulate us: the usual smiles and handshakes, shoulders being clasped, promises made, invitations issued. They lied to me and I lied to them, but that was the nature of the court. I recalled the old proverb: 'Put not your trust in Pharaoh, nor your confidence in the war chariots of Egypt.' I only hoped Pentju would not provoke a confrontation with the Lord Ay.

Later that day there was a great feast in the Silver Hawk Chamber at the other side of the palace. Only members of the Royal Circle were invited. Long tables covered with shimmering Babylonian muslin were placed before each guest, bearing jewel-encrusted goblets and platters of pure silver. Around the room stood great terracotta jars of wine for servants to keep the goblets ever brimmed, whilst others served shellfish sprinkled with spices, fried lotus in a special sauce, and a range of baked meats: antelope, hare, partridge, calf and wild ass. Pyramids of fruits were set before us: grapes, melons, lemons, figs and

pomegranates. In the centre of the chamber a small orchestra
with harps, drums and other instruments played soft music
under the watchful eye of the eunuch who marked time with
a reed. A place had been set for Pharaoh and his wife, who were
expected to appear later in the proceedings, though they never
arrived.

Whilst the rest got drunk, I watched Ay, who seemed
distracted as a stream of servants came and went with messages.
Eventually agitated, he got up from his table and left. A short
while later one of his servants came and whispered to Pentju
and me that we should withdraw. He led us hastily along beautiful galleries and passageways, across fragrant gardens and
courtyards where fountains supplied their own music. At last
we reached the heart of the palace, the Royal Apartments. Ay
was waiting for us in the antechamber. Nakhtimin and some
of his senior staff were also present. From the chamber beyond
I could hear Ankhesenamun weeping loudly.

'You've been given the reason for your return,' Ay declared.
'In truth there were two reasons; now you will see the second.'

He snapped his fingers, the great double doors swung open
and we followed Ay into a long decorated chamber, poorly lit
by oil lamps, with a great open window at the far end. In the
centre of the room, dressed only in a loincloth, squatted
Tutankhamun, a wooden lion in one hand, a toy antelope in
the other. He placed these on the floor, pretending the lion was
chasing the antelope. I brushed by Ay and, followed by Pentju,
hurried across.

'My lord.' I squatted down. 'What is the matter?' I sniffed and
glanced down: the loincloth was soiled; Tutankhamun had wet
himself. 'My lord,' I repeated, 'are you well?'

Tutankhamun lifted the wooden toys and smacked them
together. Pentju cursed quietly. Tutankhamun seemed totally
unaware of our presence.

'Gaga.' He lifted the wooden lion and sucked on it as a baby
in a cot would. Pentju began whispering the words of a prayer.
I stared in disbelief: the Pharaoh of Egypt, the Lord of Two Lands
was not insane, but a helpless baby. I tried to touch him but
he flinched, absorbed by the toys in his hands. Footsteps echoed
behind me.

'How long?' I asked.

'The attacks are not frequent,' Ay replied, 'but when they occur they are intense. High excitement or confrontation seems to cause them. Sometimes he is like this, other times argumentative and very aggressive.'

We waited for an hour before Tutankhamun began to relax and grow heavy-eyed. We let him sleep on the floor, cushions and blankets being brought to make him as comfortable as possible. Ay agreed to meet us in the antechamber. He wanted Nakhtimin to stay but Pentju insisted he leave. I had never seen the physician so cold and so implacable.

I shall never forget that night. The window behind Ay opened on to darkness as deep as that of the Underworld. Not one star, not one blossom of the night could be seen; there was no sound, as if the calls of the birds, the night prowlers and the creatures of the Nile had been silenced. Only three men, seated in a chamber, on the verge of the confrontation both Pentju and I had been praying for.

'My son?' Pentju began.

'The Divine One . . .' Ay intervened.

'He must wait,' Pentju rasped. 'My son, the child of the Lady Khiya, you bribed the Mitanni to hand him over.'

'I don't . . .' flustered Ay.

'You do,' Pentju cut in. 'He's dead, isn't he? Why did you bring him here?'

'I wanted to discover who he really was,' Ay retorted.

'You knew who he was.'

'He looked so much like his half-brother, the Lord Pharaoh.' Ay's voice was kindly, but the look in his eyes was chilling. I realised what he'd intended.

'Did you?' I gasped. 'Yes, you did, didn't you? You seriously considered replacing one for the other, that's why you brought him here. They would look so alike! Very few people see Tutankhamun, and only then from afar.'

Ay stared coolly back.

'You said he *looked*?' Pentju kept his voice steady. 'So he is dead?'

'He was sturdy,' Ay replied. 'A good man, Pentju, intelligent and charming. He died of a fever—'

Pentju lunged forward; I pulled him back.

'He died of a fever.' Ay remained calm. 'You, however, think I murdered him, that I brought him here to be killed, true?' He played with the ring on his finger. 'I am a hyaena,' he confessed. 'I kill because I have to, because I don't want to be killed myself.'

'You hated Khiya,' Pentju yelled.

Ay shook his head. 'I did not hate her.'

'She displaced your daughter.'

'Nefertiti was a fool,' Ay snarled. 'She was arrogant, she really believed she was Pharaoh's equal. We are responsible for our children, but not for their mistakes. As for you, Pentju, I shall never reveal what I really intended with your son, but I am innocent of his blood. I will take a solemn oath.'

Pentju sneered in reply.

'I can produce a physician from the House of Life who will corroborate my story. If I had murdered the boy, his corpse would have been consigned to the crocodile pool, I would have denied meeting him.'

'You have the corpse?' Pentju exclaimed.

'Your son's body was hastily embalmed in the *wabet*, the Pure Place in the Temple of Anubis, and buried according to the rites in the Valley of the Kings.'

'Did he suffer?' Pentju asked. 'Did he talk or ask about me?'

'He was well treated,' Ay whispered. 'I would have taken Nakhtimin's head if he hadn't been. True, his face was hidden by a mask, but that was for his own safety. He was placed in the House of Residence and shown every courtesy.' Ay sighed. 'He truly believed he was the son of a Mitanni nobleman, that his parents had died when he was a boy. He was training,' Ay paused, 'strange, he was training to be a soldier, but he confessed he had a deep interest in medicine.'

'What did you tell the Mitanni?' I asked.

'Quite simple. I told them he might be my son,' Ay smiled, 'and that, either way, he would receive good training in our barracks and the House of Life.'

Pentju, head bowed, was sobbing quietly.

'I made a mistake,' Ay confessed. 'The young man was used to the clean air of the highlands of Canaan. The Nile has its infections and often claims its victims, you know that, Pentju.

395

He fell suddenly ill and slipped into a fever. No one could save him. So, Pentju, I have your son's blood on my hands, I recognise that, as I do that you are my enemy. I realise that if the opportunity ever presents itself, you will kill me.'

'I've always been your enemy,' Pentju answered. He raised his tearful face. 'Lord Ay, one day, if I can, I shall kill you.'

Ay blinked and looked away. He was a mongoose of a man, but I was convinced he was not lying, nor was he alarmed by Pentju's threats.

'I am not frightened,' Ay replied, his face now only a few inches from Pentju's. 'The only difference between you, Pentju, and the rest is that you have been honest.'

'So why not kill us?' I asked. 'Why not now?'

Ay leaned back. 'For the same reason I didn't years ago. You have powerful friends. Meryre, Tutu and the rest deserved their fate, but Horemheb and the others would baulk at murder, at the illegal execution of two old comrades, former Children of the Kap.'

'Secondly?' I insisted. 'There is a second reason?'

'The Divine One himself, when in his right mind, would have objected, and thirdly,' Ay coolly added, 'I need you to protect him, to see if you can do something to bring his mind out of the darkness.'

'Where is my son?' Pentju demanded.

'He is in a cave, isn't he?' I asked. 'One of those secret ones you've quarried in the Valley of the Kings?'

'To house the dead from the City of the Aten,' Ay agreed, 'as well as for eventualities such as this. You will be taken there, I assure you.'

Pentju put his face in his hands.

'And now,' Ay placed his hands together, 'what shall we do with our Pharaoh, who has the body of a young man and, sometimes, the mind of a babbling infant? You must help him, Mahu, as much as possible.'

'Why?'

'To put it bluntly, my granddaughter, Ankhesenamun, must conceive a son by him before it is too late.'

'Is he capable of that?'

'Oh yes.' Ay put a finger round his lips. 'My granddaughter can conceive.'

'Or is she your daughter?' Pentju taunted.

'My granddaughter,' Ay replied evenly.

'And if Tutankhamun doesn't beget an heir?' I asked. 'If he dies childless, where will the Kingdom of the Two Lands go?'

I shall never forget Ay's reply, in that chamber on that darkest night, for it brought to an end a period of my life. At first he didn't reply, but just sat, head bowed.

'So?' I repeated the question. 'To whom would Egypt go?'

'Why, Mahu, Baboon of the South, Egypt will go to the strongest.'

Metut ent Maat
(Ancient Egyptian for 'Words of Truth')

Historical Note

We know a great deal about Mahu from his unoccupied tomb at El-Amarna (the City of the Aten), dug deep into the ground against potential tomb-robbers. The paintings in his tomb are hastily executed but do show Mahu's great achievement, the frustration of a very serious plot against Akenhaten (N. de G. Davies, *The Rock Tombs of El-Amarna: Tombs of Pentju, Mahu and Others*, Egypt Exploration Society, London, 1906). Archaeologists have also found both his house and the police station in what is now known as El-Amarna; even the fact that he kept an armoury close at hand (see Davies, above). The character, opulence and decadence of the period are well documented and accurately described by the historian Joanne Fletcher in her excellent book *Egypt's Sun King: Amenhotep III* (Duncan Baird, London, 2000). The rise of the Akhmin gang is graphically analysed by a number of historians, including Bob Briers and Nicholas Reeves, as well as myself in my book *Tutankhamun* (Constable and Robinson, London, 2002). Queen Tiye's control of Egypt, particularly of foreign affairs, is apparent in what is now known as the 'Amarna Letters'.

The collapse of Akenhaten's reign, apart from the outbreak of a virulent plague, is, however, clouded in mystery. The Museum of Berlin holds the famous statue of Nefertiti which reflects her haunting beauty, but it also holds a statue of her when she was much older, and when that beauty had begun to fade. Most historians argue that a serious breach occurred between Akenhaten and Nefertiti, and the cause, as Mahu says, was possibly the birth of Tutankhaten, Akenhaten's only son by the Mitanni Princess Khiya. Nicholas Reeves, in *Egypt's False Prophet: Akenhaten* (Thames and Hudson, London, 2001), cites other sources, and has developed the theory that Nefertiti regained power, acted as her husband's co-regent and even 're-invented' herself as the mysterious Smenkhkare, only to fall abruptly and inexplicably from power.

My book *Tutankhamun* contains the evidence for a great deal of what Mahu says. Horemheb's tomb at Sakkara, with all its inscriptions, depicts Horemheb as Egypt's great saviour, patronised by Horus of Henes. My book also explains the emptying of the tombs at Amarna and their frantic reburial in different, or hastily dug tombs, in or around the Valley of the Kings. Indeed, the recent discovery of Nefertiti's corpse, reported in the press during the late summer of 2003, attests to the fact that not all these reburials have been discovered or analysed. For the first two years of Tutankhamun's reign, the young prince did live a sheltered life in the City of the Aten whilst the work of recovery took place. One of the Restoration stelae (proclamations carved in stone), which has been found, starkly summarises the parlous state of Egypt at the end of Akenhaten's reign and what had to be done. Two centres of power emerged, at Thebes and Memphis, but the peace was maintained whilst Tutankhamun lived. Ay's supremacy is clearly indicated; that gold strip depicting him as the war God Montu does exist and is analysed in my recent research on Tutankhamun. Ankhesenamun's influence is also verifiable. Many of the paintings from Tutankhamun's tomb show the young Pharoah kneeling or resting, gently tended by his ever-present, beautiful wife. The possibility that Tutankhamun had a half-brother is no mere conjecture but a possible solution to the remains found in Tomb 55 of the Valley of the Kings. The young man buried there was certainly linked by blood to Tutankhamun. As for the mystery of the 'Watchers' and the Apiru? I am sure the final part of Mahu's confession will clear the murky, bloody politics which surround the dramatic conclusion to the magnificent Eighteenth Dynasty of Ancient Egypt.

Finally, readers have asked about the validity of my descriptions of Ancient Egyptian life. I have always had a deep

Tübinger Monographien zur Urgeschichte

Herausgegeben von
Hansjürgen Müller-Beck
Wolfgang Taute
Jan Tomsky
Hans-Peter Uerpmann
Band 5/2
1978